CC

A NOTE ON THE AUTHOR

Michelle Jana Chan is an award-winning journalist and travel editor of *Vanity Fair*. She is also contributing editor at *Condé Nast Traveller*, presenter of the BBC's *Global Guide* and a writer for the *Daily Telegraph*, *The Wall Street Journal* and *Travel & Leisure*. Michelle has been named the Travel Media Awards' Travel Writer of the Year. She was a Morehead-Cain scholar at the University of North Carolina at Chapel Hill.

*With very special thanks to
David Matthews for his support
bringing this book to readers*

SONG

Michelle Jana Chan

Unbound

This edition first published in 2018

Unbound
6th Floor, Mutual House, 70 Conduit Street, London W1S 2GF

www.unbound.com

This novel, *Song*, was the recipient of a grant from Arts Council England.

Text Design by Ellipsis, Glasgow

A CIP record for this book is available from the British Library

ISBN 978-1-78352-547-8 (trade hbk)
ISBN 978-1-78352-544-7 (ebook)
ISBN 978-1-78352-545-4 (limited edition)

Printed in Great Britain by Clays Ltd, St Ives Plc

1 3 5 7 9 8 6 4 2

MIX
Paper from
responsible sources
FSC   FSC® C018179
www.fsc.org

With special thanks to the patrons of *Song*:
Louis Gave
Nicholas Johnston
Ginanne Mitic
Hubert Moineau
Philip Muelder
Maia Sethna
Henry Verey

Dear Reader,

The book you are holding came about in a rather different way to most others. It was funded directly by readers through a new website: Unbound. Unbound is the creation of three writers. We started the company because we believed there had to be a better deal for both writers and readers. On the Unbound website, authors share the ideas for the books they want to write directly with readers. If enough of you support the book by pledging for it in advance, we produce a beautifully bound special subscribers' edition and distribute a regular edition and ebook wherever books are sold, in shops and online.

This new way of publishing is actually a very old idea (Samuel Johnson funded his dictionary this way). We're just using the internet to build each writer a network of patrons. At the back of this book, you'll find the names of all the people who made it happen.

Publishing in this way means readers are no longer just passive consumers of the books they buy, and authors are free to write the books they really want. They get a much fairer return too – half the profits their books generate, rather than a tiny percentage of the cover price.

If you're not yet a subscriber, we hope that you'll want to join our publishing revolution and have your name listed in one of our books in the future. To get you started, here is a £5 discount on your first pledge. Just visit unbound.com, make your pledge and type **song5** in the promo code box when you check out.

Thank you for your support,

Dan, Justin and John
Founders, Unbound

For all the Ms in my life

CHAPTER 1

Lishui village, China, 1878

A t first they were glad the rains came early. They had already finished their planting and the seedlings were beginning to push through. The men and women of Lishui straightened their backs, buckled from years of labouring, led the buffalo away and waited for the fields to turn green. With such early rains there might be three rice harvests if the weather continued to be clement. But they quickly lost hope of that. The sun did not emerge to bronze the crop. Instead the clouds hung heavy. More rain beat down upon an already sodden earth and lakes were born where even the old people said they could not remember seeing standing water.

The Li rose higher and higher. Every morning the men of the village walked to the river to watch the water lap at its banks like flames. Sometimes they stood there for hours, their faces as grey as the flat slate light. Still the rain fell, yet no one cared about their clothes becoming wet or the nagging coughs the chill brought on. Occasionally a man lifted his arm to wipe his face. But mostly they stood still like figures in a painting, staring upstream, watching the water barrel down, bulging under its own mass.

Before the end of the week the Li had spilled over its banks. A few days later the water had covered the footpaths and cart tracks, spreading like a tide across the land and sweeping away all the fine shoots of newly planted rice. Further upstream the river broke up carts, bamboo bridges and outbuildings; it knocked over vats of clean water and seeped beneath the doors of homes. Carried on its swirling currents were splintered planks of wood, rotting food, and shreds of sacking and rattan.

Song awoke to feel the straw mat wet beneath him. He reached out his hand. The water was gently rising and ebbing as if it was breathing. His brother Xiao Bo was crying in his sleep. The little boy had rolled off his mat and was lying curled up in the water. He was hugging his knees as if to stop himself from floating away.

Song's father was not home yet. He and the other men had been working through the night trying to raise walls of mud and rein back the river's strength. But the earthen barriers washed away even as they built them; they could only watch, hunched over their shovels.

The men did not return that day. As the hours passed the women grew anxious. They stopped by each other's homes, asking for news, but nobody had anything to say. Song's mother Zhang Je was short with the children. The little ones whimpered, sensing something was wrong.

Song huddled low with his sisters and brothers around the smoking fire which sizzled and spat but gave off no heat. They had wedged among the firewood an iron bowl but the rice inside was not warming. That was all they had left to eat now. Xiao Wan curled up closer to Song. His little brother followed him every-where nowadays. His sisters Xiao Mei and San San sat opposite him, adding wet wood to the fire and poking at the ash with a stick. His mother stood in the doorway, the silhouette of Xiao Bo strapped to her back and her large rounded stomach tight with child.

The children dipped their hands into the bowl, squeezing grains of rice together, careful not to take more than their share. Song was trying to feed Xiao Wan but he was too weak even to swallow. The little boy closed his eyes and rested his head in Song's lap, wheezing with each breath. Their mother continued to look out towards the fields, waiting, with Xiao Bo's head slumped unnaturally to the side as he slept.

'I don't think they're coming back.'

Song could barely hear what his mother was saying.

'They're too late,' she muttered.

Song wasn't sure if she was talking to him. 'Mama?'

Her voice was more brisk. 'They're not coming back, I said.'

Song didn't reply. He looked across at his sisters, who were continuing to push squashed grains of cold rice into their mouths. Song's breathing quickened, losing its rhythm. He felt his body tighten. Lying across Song's lap, Xiao Wan woke up and started to cry.

That night Song slept on the wet woven matting between his sisters and brothers, and dreamed of a place far away which resembled land but in fact was a gigantic lake whose surface was covered in broken rice shoots. At first it seemed beautiful. But then in Song's mind he saw the bloated bodies floating face up and staring wide-eyed at something beyond the cloudless blue sky.

Song woke with a jolt and tried to shut out the image. He pressed himself closer against the bodies of Xiao Wan and San San. Their skin was cold. Song reached his arm across San San's waist and realised how thin she had become. He could hear Xiao Bo moaning in his sleep.

Song stared up at the underside of the roof above him. In the darkness he could just make out the curves and ridges of the pottery tiles. Another land began to appear in his mind, this time protected by giant roof tiles ten times as big as the ones above him, keeping everyone dry, allowing them all to scramble up to safety.

Song sat upright and shook himself. The night was quiet except for the heavy breathing of his family.

Xiao Mei had a raw cough, but it didn't wake her. Xiao Bo continued to moan rhythmically in his sleep. He was too small to pretend he wasn't hungry. Song had been pretending ever since he could remember. Taking less than his share. Knowing that he, the eldest, at the age of nine, was stronger than his sisters and brothers.

'Song'll make it,' he had once overheard his mother tell his father. 'He came to us in a good year. Not like his sisters and brothers. They were born at the wrong time.'

Song shivered in the cold damp room. It was then that he remembered the words of Zhu Wei, the medicine man who travelled between villages, carrying his chinking bottles of tinctures and pots of sweet-smelling balsam, all the while telling stories of places he had seen.

'This world is sweet, my friend. Go. Take yourself away.'

Song tried to piece together what he had heard.

'Malaya. Heady with spices. India. With its regal princes, elephants dressed up in finery, and the vivid colours. Ah, and then there's Guiana. The sugarcane whispers in a sea breeze so salty you can lick it. Mangoes. Mangoes so full of juice they split on the tree and seep nectar. Like sunshine might taste. Rubber trees bleed without so much as a tap and a full bucket fetches a price so high that you don't have to work for the rest of the month. There's nothing to spend money on anyway, with fruit hanging off every tree: papaya, guava, carambola, sapodilla. No one is ever wanting. And don't start me on the gold. Even babies of the poorest families wear solid gold bangles around their wrists and ankles. Diamonds too.

They say there are whole cities built of gold and precious stones.'

Song screwed up his eyes and tried to believe in the place Zhu Wei had described.

'The Englishmen take you there for nothing – not a penny – on huge wooden boats which use the wind and the stars and their magic to reach these new lands. Hundreds are going every day, boy. You don't want to be left behind. Hail down one of the carts. They're sweeping through the villages collecting up young men with dreams and courage, the ones looking for adventure and who are willing to work. You want to get on your way before these places are full.

'The boats leave from Guangzhou. A terrible place. Don't get waylaid, I warn you, or you won't make it to the end of the month. Keep moving. There's a world beyond what you know. Every boy should travel. Go and see new places. Find work. Get rich. Come back if you want to. But see the world first. Don't die here, boy. You're too young to die here.'

Song pictured himself boarding one of the wooden English boats and arriving among lush plantations of sweet sugarcane bordered by trees bearing plump fruit on bowed branches. He licked his lips around the taste of a mango and felt burning cramps in his stomach. Then he imagined himself returning home laden with sugar and gold and diamonds, and the wide disbelieving shining eyes of his sisters and brothers.

Song shivered again. His mother had propped open the front door and the room was cool. He looked up, trying to imagine his father's silhouette in the doorway, but nobody was there. Not that Song ever particularly noticed his father coming home. He was a man who spoke quietly and was soft of foot. But in his head Song could hear his father's voice telling him how to move through life: 'strangers don't like strangers'; 'trouble only comes to those

5

who stand out'; 'keep your head down'. The memory of his words triggered something inside Song. He felt the sudden weight of his family; now he must not only take care of himself but everyone else, too. Song felt himself fold, sobbing, covering his face with his hands.

The village of Lishui felt their way through the days and weeks ahead in a daze. For the women and children left behind there was too much to do to think about mourning men. They could no longer drink clean water from the wells. There was no dry fire-wood. The babies lay listless, too emaciated to cry. The old people had stopped eating. The rest of the village sifted through the debris carried by the floodwater trying to salvage anything useful: a sack of wet seed, odd rice shoots, rotten wood, a sodden shred of cloth.

Every morning they hoped to wake to see the land steaming dry and to feel the heat of the sun, but instead clouds brooded heavy and low in the sky before bursting like blisters. Rain fell so hard it bounced from the ground, raining up as well as down. The grey air and reflecting water drained the land of colour.

Song knew what he had to do. He thought of the sugar, the gold, the diamonds in far-off lands. But he also remembered the dark stories about the city called Guangzhou and how some men returned broken. 'Stay away from them men,' the women told the children, even when it was their own husbands. And the children listened and stayed away, frightened by the way the men sat all day staring out, as if they were asleep with their eyes open. Song shuddered, but he had made up his mind.

He went to find his mother. She was at the back of the house keeping the fire alight. He watched her as she shifted around a pot of water, trying to catch the heat of a flickering flame before it extinguished with a fizz.

'Mama.'

Zhang Je looked up. There were dark shadows under her glazed eyes, red and streaming from the smoke. Her face was drawn. She did not seem to see Song.

He crouched down and took the pot from his mother. 'Let me.'

She let the stick fall from her hands. Song used it to poke at the charred embers and blew into the fire. A cloud of ash billowed up.

'I'm going to Guangzhou to look for work, Mama.'

They both watched a small flame momentarily light up.

'I'll go with the next cart,' Song said. 'They're looking for boys like me. It doesn't cost anything to go, they say. There's lots of work. I'll bring back money and food for everyone.'

Song looked up at his mother's blank face. She was staring down at the fire. Her cheeks were smeared wet.

'It's just for a time,' Song said. 'Until the rains end.'

She shook her head.

'We need some food for Xiao Bo, don't we?' Song continued. 'And the baby and everyone.'

'Not by sending you away, son. Not at your age. You don't know anything about the world out there. I've heard they'll slit your throat for the shirt on your back, even a grain of rice. Your papa wouldn't have allowed it. I won't let you go.'

Song thought of his papa, and it hurt. He wanted to leave the place where memories of his father were so strong, where he felt his absence everywhere: in the flicker of each shadow, hoping it might be him; hearing the echo of his voice in an empty room; remembering the way they caught each other's eye.

'He would let me go.' Song wanted to believe that his father, from his grave, or wherever he was, would take care of him. 'Mama, listen to me, there's nothing left.'

'Nothing left,' Zhang Je repeated.

7

'I must go. Nobody else can. I'm the eldest now.'

'My eldest is too young.'

'But I'm also too young to die,' Song said.

Zhang Je took a sharp intake of breath. 'Don't talk that way.'

Song looked at the tears like grey rain on his mother's face. He felt alone, as if everybody was already dead. 'You've given up,' he said.

Song felt the slap hard across his cheek, and then his mother pulling him to her. She held him firmly against her hard pregnant stomach, with his head resting by her small soft breasts. Her damp shirt smelled of mould and smoke. She moaned as she stroked the side of his head where she had struck him. He stopped breathing to be even more still.

'Nothing left,' she said again.

Song waited, afraid to speak again.

His mother turned him towards her and held his face between her palms like a prayer. 'Find some life for yourself, son,' she said. 'Go and find some life. Find it for all of us.'

Hearing those words, Song suddenly felt alone.

'We'll wait for you,' his mother continued. 'Don't forget. We'll be here when you come back.'

There had been nothing to pack. Song had only the clothes he was wearing. He waited by the road with his sisters and brothers looking for the cart. Xiao Wan began wailing like a sick dog. Song told him to hush and the little boy stopped instantly. When Song sighted the cart in the distance he called out to his mother, who was still inside the house. She emerged from the doorway and hurried awkwardly towards them, one hand cupping her swollen stomach and the other gripping a swing-basket of rice. She held it up for Song like a trophy. He tried to refuse it but she forced it into his hands. The other children stared on.

'No mother sends off a son empty-handed,' she said. 'You never know how long the journey will be.'

As Song took the gift he felt its weight. He was keenly aware how many days this might feed his family. He held back the tears. The cart halted in front of them. It seemed too crammed to take another but a hand reached out to haul Song up from the ground and pull him on to the back ledge. Song clambered inside and then quickly swung around to look back. The cart had already started to roll away.

'We'll call him Xiao Song,' his mother shouted, pointing at her belly. Her words cut. He didn't want to imagine another Song taking his place.

This was his family. His four sisters and brothers seemed even smaller beside their mother with her gourd-like stomach; they gazed up at him in the high-sided cart, above which he barely reached. They raised their hands to wave, all except Xiao Mei, who stared out blankly, the only one who didn't cry.

'I'll be back soon,' Song called out. 'With sugar and gold and diamonds, I promise. You wait and see.'

Song watched his family diminish on the track, their smudged figures in a row: Xiao Wan with his arm pulled up unnaturally high to grip his mother's hand; Xiao Mei, who didn't speak any more; the hungriest, San San, who never complained but whose tummy groaned and grumbled so loudly the others rested their ear upon it just to hear; and Xiao Bo, too small to understand most things but aware today his eldest brother was leaving them. They continued to wave until Song could no longer make out their faces; he could see only their arms fanning to and fro in big sweeps. He watched them turn away and walk along the elevated muddy pathway between the lake-fields where the rice had once grown.

For three days, the landscape barely changed. They passed beyond the villages Song knew and began to skirt those he might have visited once or twice until everybody he saw was a stranger. He stared backwards into the wake of the cart, choosing a point – a bush, a house, a buffalo – to watch shrink away, like his family had. It made him feel he was getting closer to where he was going.

On the cart it was mostly men but Song noticed a few boys as young as himself. Some were brothers. Not even they talked much to each other but Song was used to that, especially since the flood. Lishui had fallen quiet after the loss of its men, as if the village was too afraid to speak or hear anything more, lest there was further bad news.

Song remembered his father's warning and kept his head down and tried not to catch anyone's eye. In the day he tucked his swing-basket of rice tightly under his arm, waiting until after dark to scoop some grains up to his mouth and feeling around his lap for any morsel he might have dropped.

He slept fitfully. He sometimes stayed awake all night staring up at the stars in the sky and imagining a land as far away as that. As the heat of the day rose up he copied the others, and tied his shirt around the crown of his head and dozed. Sometimes he was woken by rain pelting his skin or by his own shivering. He curled himself up more tightly and tried again to drift off to sleep.

One morning he opened his eyes to see sun crackling off the rice fields. He squinted at the glare. Around him the land had suddenly taken on colour. The rounded hills had turned green. The soil was the rich brown of mushrooms. Buffaloes shone like aubergines, each with a white egret upon its back.

Song noticed the other men in the cart as if he was seeing them for the first time. They had become handsome in the sharp sunlight and their features were more pronounced. Conversations began between each other, as if they were slowly emerging from a cold and colourless hibernation.

The city was also taking shape. There were more carts on the road, more people, more haste. Song thought back to the stories he had heard about the city called Guangzhou, some of hope, many of them harrowing. His own uncle had returned rich, leading a pair of buffaloes into their village, each laden with sacks of dried fish, coloured bottles and sweet plums. 'One of the lucky few,' his father had whispered, out of his brother-in-law's earshot but ensuring his children heard. Yet within days his uncle was stone cold dead. His heart had stopped in his sleep. 'I spoke too soon,' his father said. 'Not even one of the lucky few.'

Most came back poorer and thinner than when they had left. They were often too spent to talk about it. Rumours collected like stagnant water until everyone had caught a whiff, building up fear of this big city, where grown men were whipped like animals until they bled from their eyeballs, and wicked women with magical pipes cast spells which could steal someone's memory and money without provoking a whisper of protest.

Of course there were some who never made it back at all. There was a boy from Lishui, not much older than Song, who followed his brother to the city. Some had heard he was running a string of brothels and opium dens and making more money in one day than any of them were likely to see in a lifetime. Others said he'd had his throat slit, and had been left to rot in some fetid bend of the Pearl River.

The cart slowed as it made its way through the narrow lanes. There were stubborn animals in the road and traders hustling, pulling behind them wagons laden with green cabbages, bales of bamboo shoots and cages of chickens. Song was surprised by how much he liked the town, at least from these first impressions. He could smell salt fish, durian and overripe papaya. There was shouting and laughing and squabbling all muddled up; street-sellers touting sticks of fried squid, bowls of spicy bean curd and steamed dumplings. Song gulped at the air to try to taste the food.

The Pearl River was wide and choppy and crammed with boats; captains jostled for a berth while armies of coolies competed to move the cargo. Rice barges lined up. A rope was thrown, a boat was tethered and a dozen men began to transfer sacks of rice from the dock to the deck. Working in pairs, they launched sack after sack through the air while the sailors on board caught the cargo, breaking its fall and positioning it neatly in rows. Slim dugouts shared the river, steered by men clasping poles who stirred their wake as if it was a pudding, directing the nose of the vessel. Other boats carried a half-dozen boys who took turns to dive into the water and scoop up handfuls of riverbed sludge.

When Song's cart pulled up at the dock he was the first to set his feet down on the jetty. Moored in front of him were two large wooden ships. He craned his neck to look up at the stern of the nearest, which swept upwards and away from him. Higher yet, the masts punctured the sky, fixing a lattice of rigging. He followed the thick swaying ropes down to the bulging hull of the boat; an anchor hung impotently at the bow. It was just as Zhu Wei had described.

Song turned back to his group. In that short time the atmosphere had already changed. There was an unease, like that around hunted animals.

'Line up. In a line, I say.' The Englishman in navy uniform

12

struck out with his leather strap. He hit a man's face and Song saw a welt appear across his cheek. There was a swelling of the crowd away from the Englishman. Song was shoved. He stumbled, but someone caught his wrist and kept him standing. 'Thank you,' Song managed to say.

'Kid like you needs to be caught by someone.' The man was gaunt but strong and with close-set eyes. 'What you doing so young going alone?'

'Just got to,' Song said flatly.

'Too young. What they call you?'

'Song.'

'I'm Wei Ling. You about to grow up, boy.'

The Englishman's voice became louder. There was confusion on the dock. Song hated not knowing what the man was saying, not knowing what he should be doing. But he noticed some of the men started falling into line and Song copied them.

Pails of water appeared, as well as brick-sized bars of caustic soap. The men followed each other's lead and crouched down to wash their bodies and their clothes, soaping and rinsing twice over. One man with scissors and a comb walked along the rows and chopped off everyone's hair close to the skin. Song watched as his own hair fell to the ground, bursting like seed pods as it landed. He reached up to feel his scalp and the tufted patches the haircutter had missed.

'Short is best on a boat,' the haircutter whispered. 'Itches less.'

'What else?' Song asked.

'Stay away from the sick and the short-tempered. Get off as soon as you can.'

'Where? After how many days?'

'Tell you that and you won't get on, boy. Don't count the days. Counting's no good for anyone.'

'Do you know the place where there's sugar and gold?'

The haircutter whistled. 'Guiana. But that place is too far, boy. Nobody ever arrived there alive.'

'How far?'

But the haircutter was already out of earshot. Song put his shirt back on and tried to squeeze the water out of the corners of his sodden clothes. 'Guiana,' he repeated softly to himself. Someone kicked his foot to get his attention.

'Who are you?'

Song looked up. The boy was bigger than Song. Skinny, too, but taller. There were sores on the boy's newly exposed scalp.

'I'm Song from Lishui.'

'I'm Hai,' the boy replied. 'I'm paying my own way.'

Song could not hide his surprise. 'Are you? I thought we didn't have to pay.'

Hai chuckled. 'You don't have to. But it's only fools who take up free passage.'

'I'm the one going for free. Ask anyone here who's the fool.'

'You, my friend,' Hai said, prodding Song hard in the chest. 'You are. Go for free and you're little more than a slave in chains. They say those days are over but it's not true. Pay your way like me and you can choose your own destiny. Freedom. You don't know the price of that until you lose it. I swear it's more than some measly passage on a ship.'

Song shrugged at the boy. He didn't fully understand what he was saying but it was enough to make him feel worried on the inside.

'Of course if you don't have any money then you've got no choice,' Hai continued. 'Die a quick death in this dump or take a gamble on a ship. I'd do what you're doing too, if it makes you feel any better.'

Song didn't feel any better. He wished this boy would shut his big mouth.

'I can get on whatever boat I want, and get off wherever I choose, that's the difference. Singapore, Penang, Madras, Calcutta, Mauritius. Like the sound of those? I can decide on any place I fancy.'

'Guiana,' Song said. 'That's where I'm getting off.'

Hai whistled, like the haircutter had. 'What do you know about Guiana anyway?'

'A lot,' Song said. 'Sugarcane grows there, thick and sweet. Rubber bleeds of its own accord from the bark of trees. Upcountry there are gold mines and diamond mines.'

'That's what they tell you,' Hai said.

'And what do you know about it?' Song said.

'It's a long, long way. Nobody arrives there alive. But I'm not saying it's a bad idea. Crabs. You heard about the crabs? Every May thousands of crabs march in from the sea, crawl up the walls of the houses on to the ceiling and fall down into pots of hot water on the stove.' Hai moved his fingers like crabs sidling up and down imaginary walls. 'You can eat crab all of May, even into June.'

Song's eyes widened. 'I love crab.'

'There you go then,' Hai said with a wink. 'Didn't say it was all bad, did I? But you won't catch me going that far. I'm thinking of Malaya. There's rubber there too, you know. Or tea in India. Or anywhere else I fancy. Guiana's not bad though – if you make it through the voyage.'

CHAPTER 2

Song looked down at the square entrance of the dark hold and for a brief moment thought about changing his mind. But then he turned to climb backwards down the ladder. Down and down he descended. Below deck it was cool and damp and dark. The ceiling was too low to stand upright and Song crouched. A few slender shards of sunlight pierced through ill-fitting planks and he put his hand into the light to feel the warmth on his luminous fingers.

After a few minutes he began to make out the shapes of men, some from the cart and others who he had not seen before. They were arranging blankets and clothes to lie on the floor. Some were tying up hammocks they had brought; others were fixing rope across corners of the hold and hanging up wet clothes.

There were already groups forming. Song was astonished to see there were women too, some with babies and others pregnant like his mother. He wondered then if his own family could have come with him. He looked at the families, huddled close, resting their heads in the pillows of each other's laps, speaking softly and stroking one another's shorn heads. Unconsciously Song reached up to feel his own bristly scalp. He thought of his mother cradling him as he waited to hear her say she would let him go. In his mind he could feel the weight of Xiao Wan lying across his own lap, wheezing as he breathed; long nights of Xiao Mei's chesty cough; the soft crying of Xiao Bo, even hungrier now.

Song settled himself. He took off his wet shirt and draped it over his empty swing-basket. That was all he had. Then he watched as more people clambered down the ladder into the hold. He recognised the gangly figure of Wei Ling. Then there was Hai; Song waved and the bigger boy moved towards him.

'There's space here if you like,' Song said.

'You ain't got a hammock either? Follow me,' Hai said. 'Better to be close to the middle. Less rolling around. You don't have the smell of shit either. Buckets are always in the corners.'

Song was grateful. He picked up his basket and shirt, and followed Hai towards the central axis of the boat.

'Have you been on a boat before then?' Song asked.

'May as well have been,' Hai said. 'All my friends have. But I was earning good money in Guangzhou so I decided to stick around. An Englishman hired me. Taught me English. Paid me a good wage. That's how I can pay my own passage. I know about boats. This one's the *Dartmouth*. Made in England but it's been all over the world.'

'If things were so good, why are you leaving?'

Hai hesitated. 'You can't stay in one place forever. Why are you leaving?'

'My family's sick. There was nothing to eat. I promised I'd find work and come back with food and money.'

Hai snorted. 'Don't you have any idea how far you're going? You're not going to come back. If you did, your family would either already be dead or have found their own way without an ounce of your help. The only help you're giving them is there's one less mouth to feed. Don't kid yourself that you're going to save them by getting on this boat. You're on your own now. You won't see them again.'

17

Song smashed his fist into Hai's face. He was too quick for the bigger boy to duck.

'You damn bastard,' Hai cried out, as his hand went up to his bloodied nose.

'Don't you tell me about me and my family,' Song said. 'You don't know anything about us.' Then he offered his wet shirt to the boy. 'You need to quit talking so much.'

Hai took the shirt and held it to his nose to stem the bleeding. He spoke through the blood and cloth. 'You know I'm right. You won't see them again.'

'You're wrong about that,' Song said. Hai's words frightened him. He changed the subject. 'So you decided yet where you're getting off?'

'Maybe Singapore,' Hai replied, still nursing his injury. 'Not far and good for office work, if you can speak English. I speak English like an Englishman. The English are lazy; they don't want to learn other languages. Speak English and you can bet on double pay.'

'How did you learn it?'

'Like I told you, from a real Englishman. Mine is proper English, not some pidgin. I could teach you for a sum. It's easy. It was easy for me anyway.'

Song shrugged. 'I don't have any money.'

'Half your food rations,' Hai said. 'I'm bigger than you so I need more food.'

Song knew there would not be enough to eat, but he was used to that. He nodded. 'Maybe,' he said.

'You crazy?' A voice in the darkness interrupted them. 'What you thinking agreeing to such nonsense? You'll be dead in a week.'

'What do you know?' Hai retorted sharply. Song was surprised at Hai's boldness; the voice belonged to a man much bigger than him. 'Speaking English is more useful than a few grains of rice.' He

18

turned back to Song. 'You want to speak English like a real Englishman?'

The man snorted. 'You listen to Li Bai, son. He knows what's what. Forget this boy's crazy idea.'

Hai ignored the man. 'It's your last chance,' he pressed Song. 'I could teach you a few words that could save your life. Learn English from me and you'll find your way wherever you go.'

'Is that what they speak in Guiana?' Song asked. He didn't dare look at Li Bai.

'Of course. Everywhere the English go.'

Song remembered the confusion on the dock when the uniformed Englishman was shouting at them and nobody knew what he was saying.

'Starting today?' Song asked.

'Starting tomorrow,' Hai replied. 'When the boat leaves.'

The boat did not move for several days and their quarters became hotter and more cramped. By the time the hatch slammed shut there was not a bare patch of floor. The shaft of light extinguished as quickly as forked lightning and the hold was suddenly quiet. Song heard the shouting of sailors above; footsteps pounding the deck; the squeaking of rubbing ropes. The *Dartmouth* shuddered and seemed to lower as it pulled away.

Song lay down, his back flat against the wooden boards, and allowed himself a smile. He had done what he had promised himself: left home to board a ship that would take him to a far-off land – to find sugar and gold and diamonds. Then he would come back and save his family.

The seas were heavy and the air unmoving. But Song didn't mind about that; it was the darkness that got to him. Not being sure of when day became night, or night became day, with no sense of the passage of time. He was glad of his new friend. Hai punctured the darkness with his fantasies, his ideas, his dreams.

Almost everyone else complained of the motion of the swell of the sea, the rise and fall of the waves, the churning inside. Some were sick, including Hai. He said he didn't feel like teaching. Song didn't feel well enough to do much learning either. Families fanned each other, breaking their rhythm to swipe at a fly. One of the men, Dai Jie, played a flute to pass the day. He sang ballads, folk songs, mournful heartbroken tunes. Song drifted between restless sleep and a semiconscious haze. The days were marked only by meals: a bowl of rice and a cup of water twice a day. After eating the men went to the buckets. When the women followed, the men turned away.

Before the end of the first week the first body had to be cleared. They said he was sick when he came on board. Song remembered his hacking cough but could not picture his face. Besides his name nobody knew anything more about him. One of the women, Ji Liu, shrouded his body in sacking and Li Bai volunteered to take him up the ladder. Everyone watched as Li Bai slowly climbed each rung with the dead man slumped across his strong shoulders. He knocked hard with his fist on the underside of the hatch. It opened and there was an exchange. Li Bai lifted himself out, steadying his load. Song thought he heard a dull splash as the body hit the water. He flinched. Not for the man who he didn't know and couldn't remember, but for all the dead men he had known – his uncle, the men taken by the flood, his own father. So many had left his world. Here was another. Li Bai appeared again in the open hatch, carrying only the torn sacking in his hands.

Clearing the dead became a regular occurrence. They mostly passed away in a fever. One woman died in labour. Her screams were so loud that the crew sent down the ship doctor. He delivered twin boys but both were dead. Then the mother bled to death. Song buried his head in his shirt to try to muffle first the woman's cries, and then the moans of her grieving husband. He thought of his sister Xiao Mei who was born with a twin brother but the boy had died. His mother refused to feed her when she was a baby. A woman in the village had to come to the house to give her milk.

Song wished he had brought his little sister with him. Maybe his mother would have let her go. His knew his father wouldn't have if he had have been alive. Xiao Mei had been his favourite. Song remembered her standing on the track as his own cart rolled away. The only one who did not say goodbye.

By the time the *Dartmouth* docked in Singapore, Song had lost count of the days, just like the haircutter had told him he would. He listened to the bustling activity up on deck: the heavy wooden crates banging down on the boards and the dull thud of thrown sacks. There were long hours of creaking quiet, and then sequences of shouting and swearing.

More than twenty of them left the boat there but nearly double that number joined. The hold became even more crowded and tempers flared. A few sharp words turned into brawls. One man bled to death overnight with a knife between his ribs, either too weak to ask for help or too tired of living.

'I'm going to stay on,' Hai announced.

Song looked surprised. 'Didn't know you were still thinking of getting off.'

'I can get off anytime I like.'

'So you keep telling me,' Song said. But he was secretly relieved. He admired the older boy's confidence and was grateful for his English lessons. Song was learning new sounds, beginning to understand the meaning of words and starting to form sentences.

'Want to know two words that'll get you a long way?' Hai asked.
'Sure.'

'"Yes, sir," simple as that,' Hai said. 'No matter what they say, just keep repeating 'Yes, sir' and you'll be all right.'

'I will,' Song nodded. 'Yes, sir. Yes, sir. Yes, sir.'

He felt like he was making good progress. He didn't care about the halved rations; it was as if he had long ago stopped feeling hungry. Besides, Hai was the only one on board who he could pretend to call a good friend. The rest were nice enough, but too focused on their own survival to be bothered with him. Hai took an interest. Song hoped he'd stay on. He needed him to stay on.

'Why don't you come all the way to Guiana?' Song asked. 'You'll have my extra rations all the way. Remember everything we know about the place?'

Hai paused. 'Might do that,' he said. 'I didn't plan it that way but maybe I will. 'Cause I can.'

'Think about all those crabs,' Song said. 'Thousands marching in from the sea, crawling into cooking pots of their own accord. Imagine the soft sweet flesh.'

'I told *you* about all that,' Hai sneered.

'And with our English, remember we'll get double pay. We can cut cane or pick mangoes or work in some Englishman's house.'

Hai softened. 'Okay, Song. I'll come to Guiana. Let's go and eat crabs all day and all night and all in between.'

Song was glad of the new passengers. It was as if he instantly graduated upon their arrival. They looked no different but had a strange staccato accent – like a knife on a chopping board – in a language that sounded familiar but too distant to be understood. There were some who spoke English with even greater fluency than Hai. Song tested out some of his new phrases.

'Good morning,' he said to one man. 'I can speak English. My name is Song. I work hard. What is your name?'

The man laughed. 'I'm Wang. I like the way you speak.'

Song was pleased at the sound of the new words on his lips. It did not feel like his own voice he was hearing but someone older, someone who had lived longer than him.

They said Singapore brought the fever. Song watched as more and more of the passengers around him fell ill. At first there was only a mild stomach ache, but that quickly deteriorated into severe diarrhoea. The routine of the buckets after meals – men first, women second – was abandoned. People were soiling themselves in their clothes. The stench thickened.

More and more went down with the symptoms. The first casualty was blamed for bringing the sickness on board and nobody mourned his death. He passed his last hours screaming for water, even with a cup held to his lips. His skin was burning hot, before it became cold, lifeless, seemingly waxen.

Song had never doubted he would reach the sugar plantations of Guiana. In fact, he had been feeling increasingly confident of how his life would take shape after he got off the boat. He had Zhu Wei's words in his head; he could now speak some English; he had his friend Hai by his side; he knew a lot more than when he had left home.

But then one night he woke up with searing cramps in his belly. He hoped it might only be hunger pangs, that familiar squeezing sensation which he had learned to push aside and ignore. But within hours he was bent double with the pain. He could hear himself letting out a groan with every breath.

'You've got it,' Hai said. 'You've got it like the rest of them.'

Song felt too weak to respond with any conviction. 'I haven't,' he whispered over and over. 'I haven't.'

'You've got it bad.'

'Shut up.' Song rolled over and brought his knees up to his chest.

He watched Hai collect together his things and move away from him. 'I should have left the boat in Singapore,' he heard his friend mutter.

The words hit Song hard and he was afraid. Afraid of losing Hai at the next port; afraid of how ill he was becoming; afraid of dying. For the first time, he began to think that he might not make it. His mother would never hear from him again, unaware of what had happened. She would have no idea what had become of her eldest son. He thought of his papa, and implored him now to keep him safe.

Song curled up on the floor. He closed his eyes and wanted to leave behind everything he knew. The fever was rising in him. His whole body shook. His groans, his bleating voice became a part of his deranged dreams. He saw a face above him and heard his name. There was a woman singing. He heard himself call out for his mother as he slipped between the darkness of sleep and the darkness of the hold. So this was how it was to face death, he thought. A slipping away with no trace.

Yet someone was trying to part his lips and force him to eat. He tasted soft wet rice in his mouth. With every grain that he managed to swallow he could feel his strength returning. The fever began to wane. He started to think clearly again. To let himself believe he might get better.

Song had no concept of how long he was ill, but slowly days began to take some form again. He discovered it was Ji Liu who had saved him. She had nursed him with her own rations of rice and water. Song was moved by her kindness. Even when he had the strength to sit up on his own, she held him in her arms and gently fed him by hand. 'You're too young to be away from your mother, Song,' she'd whisper. 'I'll take care of you till you get to where you're going. Too young to be on your own. Too young to die.'

Song was heavily weakened by the fever and it took a long while for him to feel well again. He slept in such long stretches that he once overheard Hai comment that he thought Song was dead. He was unsteady on his feet. He found himself crawling to the buckets, unable to raise himself on his two feet.

But in time, he began to feel himself again. He even started to help look after the dying, as a way of saying thank you to Ji Liu. He was no longer afraid of the disease. He had beaten it. He could beat it again if he had to.

About half the boat was sick. Song copied Ji Liu and held cupfuls of water to the lips of the men and women who cried out with thirst. In between he fanned their feverish bodies. There was a new camaraderie on the ship, as if the passengers had begun to realise they could only survive by helping each other. Song was one of the few who had made it. Some hadn't even caught it, like Hai. Nobody knew why some were struck down, and some were spared.

One night the groaning of a man woke Song and he semi-consciously pulled him over, cradling his upper body until they both fell asleep. The next morning the man's skin was cold next to his own.

Song continued to hold the man in his arms; he believed he could still feel a faint pulse in his chest. But when Li Bai came to carry him away Song didn't protest. Nobody wanted the dead around any longer than necessary.

'He is dead, isn't he?' Song asked.

'You tried your best, son.'

'I thought he might come around . . .'

Li Bai shook his head.

Song sighed. 'What's it like up there? On deck?'

'Better than down here,' Li Bai replied.

'Can you see land?'

'I ain't seen no land, but there's not much time to look around.' Li Bai closed his eyes. 'The sea is bright. The air is cool. Even with a dead man on your back it's good to be up there.'

'Can I come up one time?'

Li Bai laughed. 'Think you can lift a dead man?'

'I mean to help you with the sacking,' Song persisted. 'After you throw out the body I can bring the sacking back down to Ji Liu to wrap the next man. I'm quicker than I look. I'd get it back before you know it. Then the next body would be ready before you were down.'

Li Bai smiled at him. 'I'll see what I can do.'

'You awake?' Hai said.

Song opened his eyes. He looked across at his friend, who was on his back staring up at the ceiling.

'I'm getting out in Madras,' Hai said.

Song sat up. 'What?'

'I'm getting out, that's all. Figure Madras is the place.'

Song had dropped his voice to a whisper. 'What about Guiana? We were going together, remember.'

'Like I said before, I can get out whenever I want. That's the difference.'

Song laid his head back down upon his folded shirt. 'I know. You've told me enough damn times.'

'Guiana's too far,' Hai went on. 'I'm not so sure about the place any more. I like the sound of Madras. Heard there were jobs on the railways. Driving trains. Office work. Collecting tickets. Nice clean work.'

'Never said so before,' Song mumbled.

'I just decided, that's why.' Hai's voice was firm. 'I'm done with this wretched boat. Everyone's sick or dying.'

Song had repeatedly imagined them working together in Guiana. He had pictured them cutting cane or climbing mango trees to collect fruit from the highest branches. Or maybe Hai would find work in an Englishman's house and get him a job there, too.

'Might be fever in Madras, too,' Song said. 'You don't know anything about it.'

'You don't know what I know. In fact, I know a lot about Madras. Textiles. That's what they do there. Clothes for rich people. Good work for someone like me. They speak English. Like me. If you'd paid your way you could get off too.'

'You can't be sure of Madras,' Song said. He didn't want his friend to leave. 'But we've heard enough that we can be sure of Guiana.'

It had been several weeks since his conversation with Li Bai and Song had not brought it up again. Instead he watched as the big man pulled himself up the ladder, another limp body slung across his shoulders.

The atmosphere in the hold was sombre. Two more had died of fever overnight, including Ji Liu. Song wouldn't allow himself to cry in front of everyone, but he hurt inside. She had saved him and promised to take care of him until they reached Guiana.

Li Bai lifted her up on his shoulders. 'Gonna come up with me then?' he asked.

Song realised Li Bai was addressing him. He was so surprised he couldn't speak.

'Changed your mind?' Li Bai asked.

Song jumped to his feet.

He followed Li Bai up the ladder. It had been many weeks since Song had descended into the hold and his legs trembled as he climbed.

'You all right?' Li Bai called out, looking down.

'Right behind you,' Song said.

At the opening of the hatch Song crawled out on his stomach, squinting in the light. He couldn't see anything in the strong sunshine.

He heard Li Bai whisper under his breath. 'Don't let me down, boy.'

Song had just begun to make out the blurred shapes of figures when Li Bai gave him an order. 'Take it down. Quick now.'

Song reached out and felt the sacking as it was pushed into his hands. 'Hurry,' Li Bai said. 'Another body needs wrapping.'

Song turned to descend with the shroud as he heard Ji Liu's body hit the water. He remembered her soft voice calling out to him, her hand caressing his forehead. Song gripped the sides of the ladder as he made his way back down. He tried to adjust his eyes again this time to the darkness of the hold. He missed some of the rungs and fell the last few feet landing on his backside. It was Li Bai who pulled him to his feet.

'I'm all right,' Song said. 'I'm ready again.'

'Won't need you this time, Song,' the big man said. 'Only two dead. You stay down here now.'

Song froze. 'Can I come another time, Li Bai? I swear I'll be better.'

Li Bai was already halfway up and did not reply.

Someone spoke from a hammock behind Song. 'Tell us what you saw then.'

Song recognised the resonant voice of Dai Jie from his singing. But he could not recall anything except for the blinding light.

The voice grew irritated. 'Come on. What d'you see?'

Song hadn't noticed the sea, or the sailors on deck, or the billowing sails he had imagined, or the birds, or the colour of the sky. He moved away. 'Nothing,' he muttered.

He threw himself down on the hard floor and closed his eyes. The hatch slammed shut. At the same moment he passed his tongue across his lips and thought he could taste the wind. A sea breeze so salty you could lick it, that was what Zhu Wei had said.

Song knew it was wrong to wish for someone to die, especially those he had grown to know so intimately. But he had come to rely on the ritual of clearing the dead in order to keep up his hope – and for a chance to go up on deck and breathe.

He felt a quiet excitement mixed with shame when he heard of someone's passing. His heartbeat quickened. A second death before the morning and he would be allowed to follow Li Bai up the ladder.

Song learned to stare straight up at the bright light of the open hatch as he climbed the rungs. That way his eyes adjusted more quickly to the daylight on deck. But he was careful to keep his gaze low and only flicked quick glances up at the broad watery-blue sky and the dark expanse of ocean.

The great cream sails tugged at their knots, blowing fully open and rounded like a swollen belly. Loose cloth flapped and beat like a flight of geese while sailors shouted to haul and ease the ropes. Song stole glances at the men moving swiftly around deck dressed in loose white shirts, their brass buttons glinting on the sides of their navy trousers. Their skin shone like polished pomegranates. Thick brown hair covered the lower half of their faces. Sometimes when they spoke to each other Song could understand. He felt glad for Hai's lessons, no matter what Li Bai had said.

'If it goes on like this, there won't be any left,' he heard one of the sailors say. 'No wonder they're dying; I can smell the shit from up here,' said another. 'We'll have to source dozens more in Madras.' Song sensed they must be nearing the port where Hai said he would be leaving. He hoped he could still persuade his friend to stay.

'They've been sick up there, too,' Song told Hai, hoping the lie might make his friend feel better about their lot. 'It's not just us. They're saying it'll soon clear up. And they're all talking about how Guiana's going to make them rich. How they would be prepared to face a voyage twice as long to get there.'

But up on deck, Song overheard the desire to get off the boat. 'I've a good mind to quit,' one sailor said. 'This boat is cursed.' The words turned Song cold. He wasn't going to repeat that.

Still, Song longed for another death. It wasn't for the snatched conversations but for the light, for the wind, for the wet unsalty rain that he could suck off his forearms. On clear days, Song returned to the hold and hours later he could still smell the sun on the back of his hands and feel its heat in his black hair.

'First thing I'm going to do is steal a chicken. I'm going to wring its neck, rip out its feathers, cook it with ginger and eat the whole thing myself.'

Hai had been speaking that way ever since he had made up his mind to leave. He was driving Song mad with his talk of food.

'You steal a chicken and they'll string you up at dawn.'

'You've never seen me steal,' Hai said. 'These feet are so soft that not even the ghosts can hear me.'

'The whole city will be down with fever, just you wait. Even the chickens.'

As hard as Song tried to keep his friend on the boat, Hai did what he said he was going to do and left at Madras. He clambered up the ladder, his silhouette becoming smaller and smaller. Song tried to swallow the hard lump in his throat.

At the hatch Hai swung around. 'Good luck, Song,' he shouted in English. 'Don't forget who taught you how to talk like a real Englishman.'

'You get that office job, Hai,' Song yelled back. 'Then you come on to Guiana, like we said.'

Hai waved back. And he was gone.

Song stood blinking back the tears.

'Forget him,' Li Bai called out from his hammock. 'He'll forget you as soon as his feet have landed on solid ground.'

'He said he might come to Guiana after he's made some money here.'

Li Bai's voice softened. 'Get on with your own life now. You gotta be tough too. Like Hai was tough.'

'He just came across tough.'

'That's all you need to do. I don't want to see you let anyone else go taking half your food. You got to start thinking harder about surviving.'

Anyone who was able left the boat in Madras. With fewer in their quarters the air felt less stifling, even fresh. Yet within several hours, dozens of new passengers boarded. This time many came on board as families: women wearing bright colours of lime and cerise with jewels in their noses and ears; men carrying bales of cloth and packets of powdered spices which smelled good and rich; and so many children, even babies strapped to their mothers' back. Song noticed how the newcomers' skin shone, how their white teeth glinted even in the darkness. Then he looked down at his own body: his wracked thinness, the oozing pustules. He was painfully aware of his aching joints and sore gums. He didn't want to consider how much longer he could go on this way.

The new passengers looked so well, so healthy. They seemed so happy. He studied the way the families stuck together, the way they looked out for each other and chatted in a language he didn't understand, yet he was still able to detect the familiarity between them as they spoke. He watched them tease each other, sometimes laugh together. Song felt pangs in his stomach, like hunger but different, and closed his eyes to see in his mind his sisters and brothers playing in the rice fields, his mother by his side, caressing his head, reaching out a hand just to make sure he was there.

Among the families, Song noticed one other boy alone, like himself. He heard his name, Jinda. He was bony but pigeon-chested and with raised shoulders, which gave the impression he was bulkier than he was. He wheezed when he talked and whistled as he slept. Song was curious, but he kept to himself. He was focusing only on surviving till the end of the journey.

As the boat left the harbour Song thought of Hai exploring the streets of Madras. He wished they were together, out there in the city or on the boat. He missed his friend's big mouth and his bigger dreams. Song imagined him settled in a new job, dressed in a white shirt and surrounded by books. He pictured an Englishman boss, pleasantly surprised at Hai's brilliant English, and who paid him a good wage and gave him a breezy room in his large house on a hill overlooking the sea. He imagined Hai in that room now, looking out of the window and watching the *Dartmouth* sail out to sea. He wondered if Hai was thinking of him, as he thought of Hai.

The voyage dragged on and Song fell into a lonely routine. Without Hai, he now had a full bowl of rice each day; he ate every grain deliberately, sipping his fresh water slowly. From time to time he was able to climb up the ladder with Li Bai, but otherwise he lay on his back in the dark, waiting. He had more time to think now. And he started to reflect more deeply on what the haircutter had told him, and what Hai had said: that Guiana was too far away to make it there alive.

The journey was taking too long. His body was getting weaker. He found himself crying in his sleep, but too quietly for anyone to notice. Memories of home flitted in and out of his head: Xiao Bo bleating for food; his sisters chanting little ditties; his mother calling out his name; his father's silhouette as he left through the doorway for the last time. Sometimes he woke himself up by shouting out loud in his dreams. He smeared away his tears and tried to force himself back to sleep. He didn't want anyone to notice, but he felt painfully alone in the cramped, crowded space.

Since Madras the sailing had been steady. There had also been no further outbreaks of fever. Many of the passengers from Madras had brought fresh chillies with them and they remained markedly healthier than the rest. It was those who had been on board the longest who looked the sickest. Their skin was increasingly pallid and breaking out in sores; some, like Song, had open ulcers around their mouths.

'I don't think I would have lasted if you hadn't started taking me with you up there,' Song said to Li Bai.

'You would,' Li Bai said.

Song shook his head. 'I'm not so sure.'

'You wouldn't know any different. I sometimes think it's harder for the two of us. We get to see daylight, we get to breathe, and then we have to come back down here again.'

'At least we see it,' Song said quietly.

'At least we do.'

'I don't think I'd . . .'

'I don't want to hear about it,' Li Bai interrupted. 'You need to stop talking this way. You can be collapsing inside but you gotta stand tall.'

There had been fewer trips up the ladder to clear the dead but Song had overheard enough to know that Guiana was the next and final destination.

'This better be the last,' Song heard one of the men say, as Li Bai heaved another limp body over the side of the ship. 'We've got to keep everyone alive from now on. No more ports to restock and it won't do us any good arriving with an empty ship.'

Song was surprised to hear that their survival was important to these men too. But he was glad of it. Daily rations of rice and water increased. Pails of salt water were even sent down to regularly wash out the hold. Hope started to creep back into Song's mind. Not since before Madras, when he had been trying to persuade Hai to stay on, had he thought about his dream of sugar and gold and diamonds. Now he again allowed himself to believe.

Then the weather changed.

The wind had dropped and the ship was becalmed. Not even a wave lapped against the outside of the hull. The temperature rose inside the hold. There was a far-off rumbling of thunder but no sound of rain.

The humidity made everyone drowsy. Song's head was pounding in the stagnant air. He found himself slipping between light uneasy sleep and strong preternatural dreams, and then a sudden terror of not knowing where he was. He thought he had drifted into another muddled nightmare. There was a man shouting. A young girl screamed. Swirling water. The noise grew louder. Women ululating like at a funeral. There was a crack of thunder.

The floor beneath Song shook. He jolted awake but still the noises persisted. A pulse of blue light streaked into the hold. The ship smashed against the water as if it was going to burst open.

'What is it?' Song shouted at Li Bai.

'The ship's breaking apart.' Li Bai was crouching on his haunches and retching between his legs.

In another burst of light the hold brightened for a second: a flash of flailing limbs, mouths open in fear, families cowering. Men and women bellowed like cows able to smell their own impending slaughter. The boat thrashed out of time with the rising sea and the shuddering wood vibrated through Song's body like a fever. It was then, amid this noise and terror, that Song realised how hard it would be to turn around and ever make the long journey back home.

Seemingly impossibly, the violence of the storm only increased. Song tried to flatten himself against the floor to stop himself from smashing into anyone else, or slamming against the walls of the hold. There were objects tossed in the air: buckets, utensils, boxes. Song took a hit just above his eyebrow. He reached up his hand and felt the hot blood trickling down his face, and then blacked out.

Nobody knew how long the storm lasted. Days, they said. Song could not be sure what he had dreamed and what he had lived. When the ship was finally stilled he wondered if they had sunk to the bottom of the sea.

Nobody moved much. There was a low groaning, and some sobbing. When Song got up, he noticed Li Bai sprawled unnaturally at the bottom of the ladder, as if he had deliberately put his body there, ready to be carried up to deck and cleared. Song went to him, already feeling the anguish of losing a friend. Song saw Li Bai's swollen misshapen head and a pool of dark blood around him. He crouched down and put out his hand to touch the soft tissue. It was still wet and sticky. The man's eyes were open but unmoving. Song brushed his hand down Li Bai's face, forcing his eyelids to close. He couldn't look at him this way.

'I won't go back,' Song said to himself. 'I will never go back.'

Song longed for an end to the voyage. Any end. Guiana or not. He wanted solid earth beneath his feet, like the raised pathways latticing the rice fields. He wanted to feel the mud between his toes and the sureness of ground underfoot.

He thought of Li Bai often. How he had asked Song to be tough, to focus on surviving. Song did. He ate, he drank, he washed the cut above his eye with his rationed water. He no longer went up the ladder to clear the dead but discovered something of the outside down in their bleak quarters. At the back of the ship, on the starboard side, there were some loose boards, and from time to time he went there to see the spears of light splitting open the darkness. He let his fingers play in and out of the sun and shadow, believing he could almost grab hold of the light, as if it was the gold he was trying to reach.

Then one day, Song heard the grating of the anchor unravelling. There was a great splash into the sea. It must be Guiana. He sniffed the air. There seemed to be the smell of land: something earthy and sweet, rather than the stench of their quarters or the salt of the sea. Like broken leaves and burned sugar.

From inside the hold Song could hear boats put upon the sea, but there was still no sign of the hatch opening. A day and night passed. There was a ragged edge to the long hours, an increasing desperation and the smell of festering wounds. But nobody was giving up now, not after all they had been through. There was less talking, less mixing, as if they were saving any shred of life to get them through these last days. Song stopped listening in on stories and observing those around him.

After another full day passed, people became restless. The following night a fight broke out. Everybody knew the signs. It started over a game of cards. Song heard the shouting. He sat up and peered into the gloom at the two men wrestling on the ground. He saw Wei Ling take up his knife and thrust it twice into Dai Jie's chest before someone pulled them apart.

Song knew the sound of dying. The shallow breathing. High wheezing. The choking gasp. Nobody touched the dead man. Wei Ling sat in a corner cursing his victim and the night. Song thought about how far they had come. Like him, both men had boarded in Guangzhou. To die now. After all these months, to die now. Song gritted his teeth and curled his hands up into small fists, as if his fight was just getting underway.

On the third day the hatch opened. There were orders shouted from above, and down in the hold there was a burst of activity. After all the months of waiting to arrive, suddenly nobody was ready to leave. Song looked around at the men and women hurriedly untying hammocks, clattering bowls, roughly folding clothing. He threw his shirt over his shoulder, and waited his turn. After this journey, a journey so many had told him was too long, he had made it to Guiana. He allowed himself a small smile, but at the same time closed his eyes, wary to witness this beat of hope that could be snatched from him.

From the deck of the ship there was little to see. But it was surely land. A green band of vegetation. Above it a stretch of haze wobbled in the air. A small group of figures was standing on the mud flats. Song hardly dared breathe. This was the Guiana he had been dreaming of. The beginning of his new life.

Song climbed over the railing of the ship, down the rope ladder and into a boat. The sea was creamy brown, more like the colour of river. He lowered his hand over the side to feel the cool water and brought his fingers up to his mouth. Salt. He wiped his face and then slipped his hand back into the sea, letting the water eddy about his fingers.

Before the small boat had slid to a halt on the shore Song was on the beach. He felt dizzy and stumbled. It was the same for those around him. They swayed like drunks on the solid ground.

Song sat where he had fallen and sensed the ground moving beneath him. Beneath his palms he speared his fingers down into the wet sand in the same way he used to plant rice seedlings. Rough granules rubbed against his skin. His first touch of Guiana.

The crowd on the shore swelled. They clung to their natural groups: families, brothers, friends. But there was the same unease in the air that there had been on the dock at Guangzhou. Song looked around him and realised how few had come all the way from there. Those with any choice had elected to leave earlier, such as Hai. Many more had been thrown into the sea. There was a handful of them, no more. He felt closer to those few, not that he showed it, and they didn't give any sign of feeling the same. He was still as alone as he had been on the day he boarded the cart to leave home.

Song looked back out at the ship and thought how small it looked now, and how still. It was sitting high in the water as if it was holding its breath. 'I won't go back,' he said to himself, shaking his head. He had shocked himself when he had first whispered those words after the storm. He repeated them again now. 'I will never go back.'

CHAPTER 3

The crowd started to grow agitated. Song felt someone shove him from behind. There was pushing and shouting as they were hustled towards the carts. A family was being split. An elder brother was yelling. The Englishman was telling him to shut up but the brother was panicking. He didn't understand. Song understood. He wanted to come to the brother's help, to tell him to be quiet, that he would translate for him, but before he'd had a chance the brother had pushed the Englishman away from his family. Three Englishmen moved in and one hit him on the head with the butt of his shotgun. The brother slumped to the ground. The rest of his family fell to their knees around him, wailing, but the Englishmen pulled them away, and everyone else fell silent, climbing quickly on to the carts. Song felt he had seen this all before: the rough treatment, the shouting, the impatience. He looked at the brother's unmoving body on the ground. To die now. After all this, to die now. He cursed himself for not speaking up earlier, but knew that he might have taken the hit instead.

'Name?' A man's voice interrupted his thoughts. He was taking note of each passenger. He looked down at Song. 'Name?'

'Song.'

'Forty-three,' the man said.

Song understood the number but didn't know what it meant. He wondered who forty-two and forty-four were, and where they were all going.

Song used the spokes of the wheel like rungs to climb into the back of the cart. They pulled away. The bumping of the wheels on the uneven road felt good after the swaying motion of the sea. Song hung on to the side, studying the tall trees and spotting bright squawking birds flying in pairs. He sniffed the dusty heat of the earth and the freshness of leaves. A man rode by in the other direction on a bicycle with a basket of okra and squash. There were odd ramshackle houses and children playing out front. Some pointed at the cart. Song and the others stared back unsmiling. But nothing could lessen the lightness Song felt, as Guiana unfolded, beating with life, so full of colour, so different to everything he knew.

The roads widened and there were trees planted neatly on both sides of the street. The grand whitewashed homes resembled those Song had seen in Guangzhou, with their large windows and wrap-around porches. One house they passed had rattan lounge-chairs and knotted hammocks on either side of the front door with gardens of rolling green lawns and beds of red and pink flowers. There was a young man in sky-blue clothes trimming a bush with clippers and Song thought how he would like such work, at least for a time, until he could go looking for gold. The cart rolled on by.

On the pavements women dressed in soft colours carrying parasols walked with men in pale suits wearing hats who looked like the sailors on the ship, but cleaned up and dressed well. They turned their faces away as the cart passed; Song didn't understand why.

The tree-lined streets narrowed again and the houses bordering the road became more modest. Paint was peeling off the walls. The front yards were filled with junk. Men slept in hammocks in the shade. An old woman rocked in a chair.

As the cart continued the sugar plantations came into view, just like Song had imagined. The fields spread out as far as he could see, rising and dipping, revealing huge stretches of cultivated land beyond. The crop was tall and green and dense. It whispered with the same sound Zhu Wei had described. It was as beautiful as Song had hoped.

They stopped at a clearing beside the road where there were several wooden buildings. Song was taken to the one furthest away.

There was a row of bedrolls running along each wall, each painted with a number on the floor. At one end was a table with a stack of metal bowls. Nothing more. Song looked for his number, 43, and laid his jacket down on the bedroll.

The other boys in the room also seemed to be the young ones from the ship. He recognised Jinda, the boy who had boarded in Madras but who he hadn't spoken to.

'I'm Song,' he said in English.

'I'm Jinda,' he panted. 'I saw you. On the boat.' He could only say a few words before running out of breath. 'I thought you were sick,' Jinda continued. 'You never said much.'

'Just sick of the boat,' Song said.

Jinda laughed and that made him cough. 'Me too.'

'Did you come on your own?' Song asked.

'I ran away. My father beat me. So after my mother died I left. One morning she stopped cooking. She sat down. Rested her head on the table. That was it. I watched her. So peaceful.' Jinda seemed to be in his old life for a moment. His breathing had become deeper, calmer. Song watched him visibly shake himself back to the present. 'That's when I left. My father came after me. But he couldn't find me. And you?'

'My father died in a flood. We lost our crop and there was nothing to eat. So I came to find work.' Song paused. 'I might go home when I'm rich.' His voice broke as he spoke.

'You're a long way from home now.'

'I'm a long way from being rich, too.'

Jinda laughed again, which gave rise to another fit of coughing. Song frowned. 'Are you all right?'

'I don't breathe so well,' he wheezed. 'Runs in the family.'

'Listen up.' There was a booming voice from the end of the building. Song looked up to see the hulking shape of a man against the light.

'I'm Mr Carmichael, the plantation manager, and I'm not interested in anyone who can't cut cane till their body buckles. There's work to be done around here. You're here to get on and do it.'

He paused and nodded at the man by his side. 'This here is Mr Nichols, your supervisor.' Mr Nichols could have been Mr Carmichael's younger brother. Both men were burly, with thick necks which seemed to melt into their rounded shoulders and slope off down to strong sunburned arms. Their large callused hands looked more like paddles. Song couldn't deny the pair of them were intimidating. 'Mr Nichols will be reporting to me on who's behaving right, and who's not,' Mr Carmichael continued. 'I advise you to choose the right way.'

Song was aware that most of the kids in the room wouldn't understand Mr Carmichael's words. But he knew Jinda had. He looked across at him, and Jinda gave him a knowing smile. Song thought how much braver he was than himself. He didn't feel much like smiling.

'Not all of you are going to understand what I'm saying,' Mr Carmichael continued, almost as if he had read Song's mind. 'That is no excuse in my book. Anyone that understands, you tell the others. If any of you step out of line, you will all be punished. I worked hard when I was young and you're going to work hard too. You'll thank me for that later in life.'

Song wasn't worried about hard toil or long days. He knew all about field work. Whether the crop was rice or cane mattered little.

But seeing these two men, he knew there wouldn't be much room for kindness in this place. And he'd do well to remember his father's words: keep your head down; don't say too much. Yet he also knew this wasn't always enough. There were people on the boat who hadn't drawn attention to themselves, but still failed to make it to the end of the trip.

The boys filed out of the buildings and were led up to the cane fields. Each was given a machete. 'You get one of these at the start of every day,' Mr Nichols spat as he spoke. 'And you return it at the end. We don't trust you not to put a blade in each other. So don't be taking one of these back to camp with you. You hear?'

That day Song learned how to cut cane, how to stack it in alternate directions and lift it onto his back. It was harder than rice. By nightfall his arms were aching and his hands rubbed raw, but somehow he felt renewed. On their way back to the camp, he and the others sucked the splintered, frayed ends of chopped cane. It tasted coarse and sweet, and Song's hands were sticky with the juice. He looked at the other boys, who were all savouring the taste of this crop. The fear hanging in the air had gone, at least for now. With his feet on solid earth, Song had not been this happy for a very long time. The land was sweet like he had been told, exactly as he had hoped.

In the half-light of morning when the boys awoke the air was still milky-cool. They rose, pulled on their clothing and stumbled out of the door, traipsing along the canals, past the fishing ponds to the cane fields beyond.

Song liked the freshness of the early hour and the birdsong. His skin felt tight from the previous day's sun but his limbs were rested and ready.

Song stayed close to Jinda. He had quickly realised that the boy, with his strained breathing, wasn't able to work as quickly as he needed to. Mr Nichols made regular visits to check on the boys' progress, poking their bundles with a stick and uttering sharp words if one looked smaller than the rest. Mr Carmichael also came up from time to time with a switch in his hand. He didn't say much, but he didn't have to.

Song cut more cane than boys twice his size and wanted to help Jinda. He felt sorry for him with his laboured breathing. And he loved his stories. He'd ask Jinda to tell him again and again about his mother's cooking, even when Song had belly cramps. Especially when Song had belly cramps.

'I'd be halfway down the street but could already smell the good smells of my mother's kitchen,' Jinda would say. 'Ah, the lamb curry with apricots, so tender and so sweet. Perfumed basmati rice with strands of saffron. Shiny okra with chilli; you think it's soft and then it kicks you in the throat. Cooled by cucumber diced in white buffalo yogurt and sprinkled in paprika.'

Song loved Jinda for the world of fantasy he painted. A world coloured in saffron and turmeric. Jinda drew elephant-gods in the dust and built up images of shore temples with congregations wading waist-deep in the surf. He conjured the sweet smell of rose water on the necks of women who danced with a hundred spark-ling bangles on their wrists.

Song discreetly added some of his cane to Jinda's bundle. At first they both ignored it, as if Song had merely made an error. But in time, Jinda said something.

'You know I wouldn't make it without you,' he said.

Song shrugged. 'You'd find a way.'

Jinda shook his head. 'You do it so quiet, nobody even notices.'

'I know field work. It's the only thing I know how to do.'

'Couldn't make it without you. If my mother knew, she'd fix you up a feast.'

'Just tell me about that feast now and then. Feed me with your stories.'

'I will,' Jinda said.

The truth was Song was worried about Jinda. He noticed how his breathing worsened at all the wrong times: if Mr Nichols approached, or Mr Carmichael; there were even some older plantation boys who could send Jinda into a spasm. At night, Song was woken by the noise of his friend's high-pitched wheezing. Song lay still, listening out for the next breath, afraid it might never come. He often fell asleep with the sound of Jinda's whistling in his head, mixing it up with the noise of his nightmares, whether it was the desperate screams or high winds of a storm.

'Watch out,' Song warned. Mr Nichols was walking down the line.

Jinda was leaning on the wooden butt of his cutlass, the point of the blade drilling into the dirt. 'Help me,' he panted.

'I can't, Jinda,' Song's voice was sharp. 'Stand up. Cut out that wheezing right now.'

Jinda made a great effort as the heavy footsteps of Mr Nichols passed by. Then Song watched as the boy's eyes fluttered and he keeled over.

In a panic, Song pulled Jinda to his feet. He slapped him about the face. 'Jinda, Jinda.'

Jinda half opened his eyes. 'Yes, I'm here.' He was still gasping for breath.

Another time Jinda wasn't able to pretend. It was Mr Carmichael walking up and down the line, flicking his switch in the air. Jinda was sitting on the ground trying to slow down his breathing.

45

'Get up,' Song whispered.

Jinda looked up and shook his head.

Mr Carmichael was getting closer. Without thinking, Song shouted out the word 'snake' to cause a distraction. There was pandemonium as the boys all fell over each other trying to get away.

Mr Carmichael was livid. 'Who's responsible for this?' he shouted.

Song lifted his arm. 'I saw a snake, sir. I thought it could have bitten any one of us.'

'Do I look like I care?'

'I was afraid it might bite you, sir.'

'I'll tell you what. I'll take care of me. You take care of your work. Got it?'

'Yes, sir.'

'And where is this goddamn snake now?'

'I think it's gone.'

'How inconvenient. We'll never know if it was ever here. Down on your front.'

'Sir?'

'You heard me. Down on the ground. Stomach down.'

Song did as he was told. He held his arms stiffly by his side, his eyes closed. The first blow came down harder than he expected. Song lost his breath. Another. Then another. Four. Five. Six. There wasn't a seventh.

'Get up.'

Song crawled to his feet. He didn't look Mr Carmichael in the eye.

'Let that be a lesson to all of you,' Mr Carmichael said. 'Disrupt the working day and you'll be thrashed. Now you know.'

Song was in pain, but he didn't show it. The other boys looked at him with horror, with pity. It had been the first beating.

Back at camp that evening, Song caught Jinda's eye. Jinda mouthed the words 'thank you'; Song shrugged his shoulders, as if to say it was nothing.

Song looked up in the branches at the astonishing bird. A huge beak, as large as the bird's body, and an eye ringed in a teal band bordered by a yellow stripe against black, and flashes of red around the tail. Then Song noticed the movement of a second bird. They were a pair. The other equally beautiful. The sight of these two made him suddenly feel alone.

'What are you looking at?'

Song jumped. There was an Englishman looking at him, not unkindly. He wore a cream suit, like the other men, except there was a black and white collar around his neck.

'Nothing, sir,' Song replied, embarrassed.

'It's a Guianan toucanet,' the man said. 'A medium-sized toucan. Part of the genus *Pteroglossus*. Lovely, isn't it? Extraordinary really. Not sure if there are birds where you come from but where I come from we have nothing like this.'

'Yes, sir,' Song said, overwhelmed by the way this man was speaking to him. As if the man cared about what Song thought.

'Do you understand English?'

'Yes, sir,' Song said emphatically, frustrated that it might have come across any other way.

'Then tell me what you like about the bird.'

Song hesitated.

'Go on,' the man continued. 'You don't have to be afraid. And call me Father, don't call me sir. My name's Father Holmes. Yours?'

Song's mouth was dry. 'My name is Song, Father. And there are two birds up there.'

Father Holmes looked up again. 'So there are. Sharp eyes. Well, Song, tell me what it is about this species of bird.'

'I like all birds, Father. I like them because they can fly away. They can fly anywhere they want.'

The man smiled. 'Freedom. That's a good reason. Might be the reason I like them, too. Although I didn't know it till now.'

Song studied this man who was talking to him with such keen interest. He had reddish hair and his skin was as pale and thin as paper. The tips of his ears stuck out and were turning pink; his eyes were the same faded blue as the handkerchief which he now used to mop his perspiring face.

'You're going to be seeing rather a lot of me here at Diamond,' Father Holmes said. 'I stopped by today to see Mr Nichols and I'm going to be coming to the plantation every Sunday to teach you boys to read. Fancy learning to read?'

'Yes, Father.'

'And where did you learn your good English?'

Song blushed. 'On the boat. From a boy called Hai. He got off in Madras. I gave him half my food rations and he taught me English.'

Father Holmes frowned. 'Well, you look pretty skinny. But your English is good, so perhaps it wasn't such a bad deal. Sounds like you're a boy with plans. That right?'

Song didn't know what to say.

'Or a boy with hope,' Father Holmes continued. 'Have you got hope?'

Song still didn't reply. But he warmed to the man and felt a great urge to please him. He was only ashamed that he had nothing to say.

'In time, perhaps,' Father Holmes said reassuringly. 'We'll get to know each other better in time.'

*

48

Father Holmes often arrived late on Sundays, running late on his way from church. The boys would gather at an opening of cleared ground where a pitched roof of banana leaves had been raised on stilts between their huts. On one such Sunday, they were sitting cross-legged in their pressed blue uniforms, waiting. Song looked around, noticing that some of the boys already needed clothes the next size up. Song did, too. But he didn't want to have to buy a set off Mr Carmichael and have his wage docked. He wondered if there was a way around it.

His thoughts were interrupted by Mr Nichols. 'You're getting into the carts today. Come on, hurry up.'

The boys loaded up. It was their first time leaving the plantation. Nobody said much. Song had overheard that they were all going to be dunked in the river but when he said so, nobody believed him. They remained nervous though. They crouched in the back of the cart and watched the road pass under them.

The cane fields drifted all around them. A light wind through the crop made the sound of a thousand sweeping brooms. Song looked out at the endless plantations and wondered if Mr Carmichael owned everything he could see.

The road turned right and ran alongside a wide river. The water was a rich orange-brown. A log was being carried downstream with a small white bird riding upon it.

They came to a halt and the boys set down. In front of them the riverbank was crowded with people from town. There were pretty women wearing long dresses in pink and yellow and pale blue. The men wore cream suits and hats. The boys huddled closer together.

There was Father Holmes coming towards them. He stopped in front of the boys and smiled: 'I'm sure you're all wondering why you're here on the banks of the Demerara.'

They were silent. Song saw Father Holmes' eyes drawn to an iridescent green bird skipping in flight along the bank.

'Now, there's nothing to worry about,' Father Holmes continued. 'Today you're going to become part of a big family. God's family.'

Song didn't want to become part of another family. Not that he dared refuse. Families only break and are lost, he thought.

The vicar bent down and began removing his socks and shoes. Song watched in astonishment as he rolled up his trouser legs high above his knees, revealing hairy calves, and waded into the river. As he did he lost his footing and his trousers became wet. Some of the children from town began to laugh. Song heard the higher pitched giggles of girls. It sounded like his sisters laughing.

By now Father Holmes was standing knee-deep in the river. He reached his arms up to the sky. The men and women from town bowed their heads and mumbled 'Amen'. Song saw Mr Carmichael with his pretty young wife by his side and two little girls in pastel dresses. There was also Mr Nichols with his family. He did not recognise anyone else.

Father Holmes held his arms out like the Jesus he had shown them on the crucifix. Song thought how lonely he looked, cast out in the river like that. The vicar was staring up at the sky chanting repetitive sentences. His clothes were splattered in mud and there was water seeping up his trouser legs.

'Take your clothes off, boys,' Mr Nichols ordered.

They looked around at each other. Song began to undress.

'Move this way,' Father Holmes said warmly. 'Come towards me.'

The boys filed down the riverbank. First in line was Jun, one of the bigger boys. Song watched as the vicar smiled at him, placed a hand on the crown of his head, and then suddenly pushed him

50

down into the water. Jun lashed out, panicking. But Father Holmes wasn't rough and he lifted him out of the water by his underarms.

Song waited his turn. As the boys emerged from the water spluttering, the crowd on the riverbank clapped. Song didn't understand or much care for what was happening.

He looked across at Jinda, who had already started wheezing. 'I'll go first,' Song said. 'Follow me.'

Song slid down the bank into the silty water. It was cold but felt good. He took Jinda's hand and they waded in together.

'My friend's sick, Father,' Song said under his breath.

Father Holmes looked across at Jinda.

'He can't breathe,' Song said. 'He won't be able to breathe if you dunk him.'

Father Holmes hesitated. He rested his hand on both boys' heads. Song felt himself pushed under and resisted, unsure if both of them were going under, and there was a frantic explosion of splashing.

'All right, Father?' Mr Nichols called out.

Song heard the men's voices and rushing air as he broke the surface. He looked across at his friend, who was still above the water line. Jinda smiled faintly.

'Yes, Mr Nichols, everything's all right,' Father Holmes replied.

Song caught his breath. He looked up at Father Holmes. His blue eyes were so pale they were almost colourless. They were fixed on Song; Song didn't flinch. It was as if they each seemed to know something deeper about the other in that instant.

When it rained in Guiana, work stopped. Song and the boys put down their cutlasses and sheltered under the thatching by the planter's office. The rain never lasted more than a few minutes but the supervisor usually went inside at that time and they were left alone. They lay on the cool dry ground, resting their aching shoulders and watching the falling raindrops.

The rain reminded Song of home. He used to leave the fields with his sisters and brothers, racing the rain until they reached the doorway of their house breathing hard and laughing. There they waited, watching the land stilled by the pounding raindrops.

'The sky's crying again,' Xiao Mei would say. 'Why is the sky unhappy?'

'Stop your nonsense,' their mother would reply. 'You'll bring us more bad luck than you already have.' She had always been hard on the daughter whose twin had not survived.

Song wished again he had brought his little sister with him. But she would have had to endure the boat journey and Song worried that she would not have made it. Maybe she was better where she was: alive, but hungry, and with the rest of his family.

That morning they had been burning the roots of cut cane in the next field. Song hated working in the smoke. His eyes stung and his throat itched. But Jinda had it much worse. He was doubled over, snatching breaths. Song saw he had propped himself up on the nub of his cutlass.

'Jinda,' Song called out. 'Watch out.'

Jinda raised his eyes, saw the figure of Mr Carmichael and then let his head fall.

'Come on,' Song begged him.

Mr Carmichael strode towards them. He was swatting at flies about his face.

Song heard the thud of his boots come to a stop. 'What the devil do we have here? Taking a day off are we?'

'He's sick, sir,' Song said.

'You again.' Mr Carmichael said. 'Am I talking to you?'

Song ducked the blow the man threw at his head. Then Mr Carmichael kicked out. He stumbled as he tried to bring the boy down. Song knew better than to dodge him again. He felt the hardness of the man's boot on the side of his knee.

'The rest of you, get back to work.'

On that warning there was a frenzy of thrashing cutlasses.

Mr Carmichael turned his eyes on Jinda. He kicked the cutlass out from under him. The boy thumped to the ground.

'Think you came here to take a rest on my plantation? Is that what you think?'

Jinda did not move.

Mr Carmichael pushed his boot beneath the boy and turned him over. 'What's wrong with you? Get up.'

Song willed his friend to get to his feet.

'I said, get up.' Mr Carmichael looked around him and saw the boys had stopped working again. A new and terrible expression twisted his face.

'Think you can bring the whole plantation to a standstill with your tricks, do you?'

The man grabbed at Jinda's shirt, pulled him to his feet and thrust him in the direction of the canal. Song looked down at Jinda's cutlass in the dirt, then up at the giant figure of the man dragging the crumpled boy along the track.

He ran after them. 'Mr Carmichael, please. He's sick.'

Mr Carmichael turned to face Song. His eyes were like an animal's. On the hunt. But from where he stood, he was unable to strike Song again. 'You get back to work, or you're next,' he snarled.

Song watched as Mr Carmichael hauled Jinda to the water's edge. He tossed him into the shallows. Song moved closer to watch what was happening. He could see one of Jinda's outstretched limp arms. And then Mr Carmichael put his hands upon him, holding him down and waiting. Song could barely breathe himself. He ran forward three or four steps, then stopped almost as quickly as he had started.

'No, no, no, no,' he cried.

It didn't take long. Mr Carmichael pulled back, wiping his hands dry on the back of his trousers. Song saw Jinda's back float up to the surface of the water. Then the back of his head bobbed up, his wet black hair reflecting the sunlight.

From that day forward Song kept to himself and the other boys were mindful to keep a distance. From little Binu to big Jun, everybody wanted to do right by Song – the one who had tried to stand up for Jinda.

Song lived by his own rhythm. He awoke early to lie in the cool darkness, listening to the cicadas subside and the birds waken. He ate breakfast alone. As the other boys were only stirring in their beds Song was already waiting for the morning call to move into the fields. He would have started working earlier, if he'd been allowed. He wanted to get on and earn a wage.

Song no longer needed to work as hard as he'd done when Jinda was alive and he'd cut cane for both of them. But Song preferred to push his body, bringing down the cutlass against the rigid shafts of cane, to feel the pain shudder through him. Sometimes the tears rose up and squeezed out of his eyes until he could no longer make out the shapes around him; there was only the glint of his cutlass and a blur of green. But he wouldn't let anybody see him cry.

As the days passed by like the swell of an open sea, Song became increasingly frustrated that they had seen no pay. Eventually he found the courage to speak to Mr Nichols.

'Sir, please may I ask when we are to be paid?'

Mr Nichols smacked him across his shoulder with his stick. 'Shut your mouth,' he said.

Song tried Father Holmes instead.

'Father, do you know when we are to be paid? I asked Mr Nichols but he wouldn't say.'

'Have you not been paid yet?'

Song shook his head.

'Not since you've been here?

Song shook his head again. 'No.'

'I'll find out.'

Meantime, Song was forming an idea about their Sunday uniforms. Instead of letting Mr Carmichael swap around their clothes and dock their pay, Song thought they could go about it themselves. It would be one less excuse to delay paying them their wages, he thought.

The following Sunday, Father Holmes stood in front of all the boys with an answer to Song's question.

'Good morning everyone. I wanted to address something that's probably been bothering a number of you for some weeks. About pay. I asked Mr Carmichael and he explained to me that many of you came here without paying for your passage – the boat journey – which means that your wages will be docked until that charge is cleared. In arrears, as it were.'

'How much is that?' one boy asked.

'How long will it take?' asked Song.

'I'm afraid I don't know. I did ask, but Mr Carmichael said that every boy had a different set of circumstances. I guess that means you came from different places. Some had shorter passages, some longer.'

Song wasn't satisfied with that answer. He tried Mr Nichols again.

'Sir, I wondered how long it might take for me to pay for my boat passage? And when I can start sending money home?'

Mr Nichols snorted. 'Do you know how lucky you were to get a free passage in advance? You'd never have been able to afford to come here. Count yourself one of the lucky ones. Then there's your beds, your uniforms, your food. We're not a charity, you know. You'll see a wage when I say you'll see a wage. No sooner than that.'

Hai had been right. There was no money to send home. Song struggled to believe it. They had been lied to. Tricked. And there was no escape from that truth.

At the close of the day, he went to bed before the others to try to think of a way out. Under his breath, he made a promise to his dead friend Jinda that he would break out of this place and live twice as hard for the both of them. He would yet live a life that was a story worth telling.

CHAPTER 4

It was a Sunday and they were putting on their uniforms before Father Holmes arrived. Song watched Jun struggling to fit into his clothes.

'It looks like you need a bigger size,' Song said.

Jun looked down at his clothes. 'Do you think?'

Song could feel his own shirt tightening across his upper back, pulling at his shoulders and puckering the cotton around his collar bone. His feet hurt, too. He had to curl up his toes inside the hard leather shoes.

'How about I get you a bigger uniform?' Song paused. 'It won't cost you a thing.'

Jun frowned. 'How are you going to do that?'

'Same way Mr C does. He just swaps our uniforms around and charges us for new ones. We should do it ourselves.'

Jun looked worried. 'I don't know. What if he finds out?'

'What's he going to do? Get rid of the lot of us?'

'How about beat the lot of us?'

'He can't beat all of us. Think about it. Who'd be left to work? Come on, Jun. I'll find you a uniform in your size.'

Jun was reluctant but agreed. 'I don't know why I have to go first. I'm going to be beaten first.' But he started to unbutton his shirt anyway.

'Thanks, Jun,' Song said. 'Who's next?'

'I think we're going to get caught,' Binu said.

'We're not doing anything wrong,' Song replied.

'That's not how Mr C's going to see it,' Jun said.

'You might be right,' Song said. 'I'll take the hit. It's my idea.'

'You already took the hit for Jinda,' one of the younger ones said.

'Jinda took his own hit.'

'Let's do it for Jinda,' Binu said.

'Jinda wouldn't do it if he was alive,' Jun said. 'He was too nervous about everything.'

'That's probably true,' Song said. 'But it doesn't mean he wouldn't want us to. We deserve to see our money.'

Suddenly everyone was undressing.

'Let's do it.'

'Maybe he won't even notice.'

'No chance of that.'

The boys switched around clothes to find the best fit. If there were sizes missing, Song said they'd have to buy that uniform collectively and share the cost. It was only fair. He hoped to ask Father Holmes to buy those uniforms on their behalf. What they'd have to pay would be a fraction of what they'd otherwise have docked from their wages, under Mr Carmichael's system. Song counted in his head how much they would be saving and felt a lightness for the first time in weeks.

It was early one Sunday morning when Song saw Mr Carmichael pull up on his horse. He had never come to the plantation on a Sunday. The boys were already amassed, waiting for Father Holmes.

Song watched as Mr Carmichael roughly tied his horse up to a post and then leaned forward as he paced across the yard. He swished his leather switch in front of him as if he was clearing a path. Song knew he knew. He felt his chest tighten.

Mr Carmichael stood in front of the rows of boys. 'So who's responsible for this little game, then?'

Nobody moved. The boys did not even exchange glances with each other. There was not a sound.

Mr Carmichael tapped the strap against the side of his thigh. 'Who's going to be the first to do the right thing?'

He slowly took off his jacket and threw it over the table they used as a makeshift altar. Underneath his shirt was transparent with sweat. He pointed his whip at Binu. 'You. Tell me what's going on.'

Binu was one of the youngest. Song could see his lips trembling.

'I'm sorry, Mr Carmichael,' Binu said. 'I don't know.'

'Don't know? Of course you bloody know. I'm talking about your uniforms.'

Binu had started to whimper.

'Do you really want something to cry about?' Mr Carmichael waved his whip in front of Binu's face. 'If you don't tell me now who's been selling you your uniforms . . .'

'It was my idea, sir.' Song heard the voice and barely recognised it as his own. 'But I didn't sell them. We swapped them around. We just wanted to be able to save some money to send home.'

For a moment Mr Carmichael did not move. Song let himself hope that everything might be all right.

Parakeets squawked overhead, bursting through the silence.

Then Mr Carmichael suddenly came at him. He felt the man's rough hand grab his collar. Song's head was spinning as he was dragged out to the yard and felt the first strike come down on the side of his head. He curled himself up. He could see Mr Carmichael's boots, the thick soles, the pale laces pulled tight, one frayed at its end. The switch cut through the air before he felt the second blow. There was a third. And then Song closed down.

*

Song felt the stinging cool on his back before he opened his eyes. He could smell lime and wood and mould. He peeped out between his eyelashes. There was a white blur of sheets, a green glass bottle upon a table and the smudged shapes of large furniture. Across from him Father Holmes sat in a red armchair, reading. Dressed in his usual cream suit he did not look as flushed as usual. He was more than halfway through the book in his hand. Beside him was a small wooden table, highly polished, with elegant curved legs. Upon it was a teacup and saucer. Through the window behind the vicar, the light was fading. Song could see some pink flowers growing close to the house.

Father Holmes reached out to feel for the cup and at the same time glanced up. 'Song, you're awake. Why didn't you say so? How are you feeling?'

Song scrunched his eyes shut. 'Sorry, Father.'

'There's nothing to be sorry about. I brought you to the vicarage this morning, after I found you. But I don't want you to worry about any of this. I want you to use your strength to get better.'

He walked to the door and opened it a crack. 'Amalia. He's awake.'

He turned back to face Song. 'I admit you had us worried. You've taken a beating, Song, but the doctor's already had a look. He says you should heal.'

The memories were fuzzy but they started to come back to Song. Mr Carmichael's swearing. The flicking of the switch. A taste of dust in his mouth. But nothing more. He didn't know how he had come to be here.

A woman walked through the door, carrying a large white jug. She was huge about the hips but with a tiny bosom. A white apron covered her white dress. She panted into the room, steam billowing about her face. Like the angels Father Holmes talked about, Song thought.

'Are we pleased to see you with your eyes wide open and some life back in you,' she said. 'You've given us a scare all right.'

She poured hot water into a deep bowl, splashing some on the table before wetting and squeezing out a rag. She leaned over Song, gently wiping his face and around his neck and shoulders. Her soft touch reminded him of Ji Liu, and he was glad of it. But she also made him feel more fragile, caring for him this way. Song saw the light catch some flecks of gold in her eyes. Amalia took another cloth and dried Song's shoulders. He winced. 'You'll be all right soon enough,' she said.

'You will with Amalia looking after you,' Father Holmes agreed. 'But you weren't good when I found you. Unconscious face down in the yard. There's one thing I need to know, Song, and then I want you to rest. Why did Mr Carmichael do this to you?'

Song felt the colour rising in his cheeks.

'I need to know,' Father Holmes said softly.

'It was my fault, Father,' Song said. 'I really need to send money back to my family and I had an idea to swap uniforms between us, instead of having to buy a new set from Mr Carmichael. But I should never have done it. I think I've gotten everybody in trouble . . .'

Father Holmes had raised himself from his chair and was reaching for his jacket.

'It's all right, Song. I'm leaving you with Amalia now. She's going to look after you. Get some more sleep.'

Song drifted in and out of a drowsy haze. He was puzzled by the soft voice of a woman above him. He felt someone fanning his back as he slipped into another semi-conscious drowse.

'Who's that?' Song asked, suddenly afraid. He recognised a voice in the next room.

'That there's Mr Carmichael,' Amalia said. 'Came here to talk to Father Holmes. Don't you worry about a thing. Father Holmes will make sure everything's going to be all right.'

Song listened intently. The conversation was faint.

'You try to get a good day's work out of them. Lazy bastards, the lot of them. Always trying to pull one over you. Got to keep your eyes open.'

'I'm sure you keep a firm hand,' he heard Father Holmes say. 'In fact that's what I wanted to talk to you about. I've had word that the children working at Diamond are being beaten.'

'Beaten? Well, I'm sure some of the planters get frustrated from time to time, and I can't blame them for that. There might be an odd thwack about the head for the cheeky ones. That's only natural. Sometimes it's the only way to keep order. Otherwise we'll have a rebellion on our hands. Don't want our wives and children being raped and killed, do we?'

'I'm not talking about thwacks to the head. I've seen bleeding welts on the back of one boy, Mr Carmichael. That is unacceptable. It is no better than slavery.'

There was now a sharpness to Mr Carmichael's voice. 'Let me give you a history lesson, Father. Slavery was abolished fifty years ago. These boys are indentured labourers who came here of their own free will looking for a better life. They are paid a fair wage. They are treated well if they work hard. They are disciplined if they do not.'

'By beating them within an inch of their life?'

'We would all like to live in a perfect world, Father. You more than most, it seems. I live in the real world.'

'A world where they beat children until . . .'

'You're a vicar,' Mr Carmichael interrupted. 'You could never understand the demands of running a profitable plantation. Labourers are rewarded for hard work. Not for slacking. This business wouldn't survive a week if it was underpinned by your ideals.'

'I'm not dreaming up a utopia. I'm asking for some basic, decent, civilised behaviour. We are talking about children as young as your own. The boy was almost dead when I got to him.'

'Is that right, Father? Well, rest assured I don't want anyone dead on my plantation. Think about it. That'd be one less worker. Now, let's put all this behind us, shall we, and look forward to better days.'

'I see these boys every week. I don't want to hear of, let alone see, another beaten boy.'

Mr Carmichael cleared his throat. 'Let's get one thing straight here. You come to the plantation on my invitation to give these wayward boys some good Christian instruction. But they are there to work. And one of my many jobs is to make sure they work. You stick to your job, Father, and I'll stick to mine.'

Their voices fell silent. Song strained to listen in.

'Now is there anything else?' It was Mr Carmichael again. 'Don't tell me you've brought me all the way here to rap me on the back of my hand.'

'The boy we are discussing,' Father Holmes said. 'I want you to release him from his duties on the plantation.'

Mr Carmichael laughed aloud. 'Do you think I just give them away? Valuable, these boys. Can't farm them out for nothing.'

There was a pause. 'A position has come up on the church committee that would suit Mrs Carmichael very well. As you know, committee members are highly respected in town and a number of people have already approached me about it.'

'And?'

'Mrs Carmichael is a highly committed member of the congregation. It must be hard for her living so far out of town with no female company, especially when the girls are at school.'

'It sounds like you've put a lot of thought into this, Father, and I hate to disappoint you. But I can't trade a boy for a committee position for my wife. With all due respect to your committees.'

'Well, then, Mr Carmichael, how do you suggest we make progress on this matter?'

'I'm sorry to say there doesn't seem to be a way, Father. I guess we can't always have what we covet, can we?'

'The vicarage only has a small budget, but I can ask the governor for some extra funds for a houseboy and to compensate you for the trouble. I'm sure he'd agree if he knew how much help this boy might be to the church – and what a nuisance he has been to you.' Father Holmes had slowed down his speech. 'If I explained the situation clearly.'

'You wouldn't be threatening me, Father, would you?'

'I am sure London wouldn't want to hear about the methods of discipline in the plantations of one of its finest colonies.'

'Fortunately, Father, I'm a man of favours and I'm in a good mood tonight,' Mr Carmichael said. 'You put Mrs Carmichael on the committee and I'll send the boy over. Think of it as a favour to you.'

'I'd be delighted if Mrs Carmichael accepts.'

'Pleasure doing business with you, Father,' he said. 'First time I've done a deal with a vicar.'

'There won't be any need to send the boy over,' Father Holmes added. 'He seems to have found his way to the vicarage already. I'll send someone tomorrow to collect his things.'

At that point Song stopped trying to hear the two men's conversation. He exhaled, letting himself breathe normally again. Burying his face into the pillow, lying front down because his back was too sore, he wondered what this all meant for him.

As Song grew well Father Holmes began reading with him. He followed the words on the page as the vicar recounted tales from the Bible: the turning of water into wine; how lakes became instantly full of fish; Lazarus brought back from the dead. Miracle after miracle. They all seemed ludicrous. But then Song wondered about his own miracle, ending up staying in a house like this one and being taught to read.

Song liked the stories but he preferred to hear Father Holmes speak about Wales, the country he was from. The vicar described how the weather was so cold the rain could turn to snow, falling like soft cotton or petals off a tree. He explained how water in ponds became hard enough to walk on; how there were fires inside the houses to stay warm with chimneys to carry away the smoke, and glass in the windows to stop the wind; the sun rose for only a few hours each day, skirting the horizon, before sinking again beneath the edge of the earth.

That is what Song loved so much about stories. A description of a place so real that he could smell or taste or feel what it must be like to be there. It allowed him to be taken somewhere else, even for a moment.

Father Holmes also described the birds which lived around his parents' house, sketching them for Song, detailing their plumage and the colour of their eggs. He impersonated their calls and Song learned to whistle like the thrushes and blackbirds that nested in the hedgerows of north Wales. He was pleased with the new sounds. So simple, so haunting. So different to the birds of Guiana. More throaty, strident, more powerful.

When Song was allowed out of bed Amalia brought a loose cotton shirt for him to wear.

Song looked at it. 'That's not my shirt.'

'It is now.' She held it up for him to see. 'I made it for you.'

'But where are my clothes?'

'You won't need your uniform any more, Song,' Father Holmes said. 'I've had a word with Mr Carmichael. You're going to continue to stay here with us. That is, if you'd like to?'

Song swallowed hard. 'But what will I do here?'

'You'll live with me and Amalia,' Father Holmes said. 'We'll read books. We'll study birds.'

Song began to feel nervous. 'But I have to work. I need to send money home.'

Father Holmes smiled kindly. 'Of course you do. You'll be paid for your work here. There's a lot to do around the vicarage and at St Andrew's. You won't be bored.'

Song looked at the white shirt Amalia was holding up for him. His head filled with memories of the plantation. Jinda dragged away. His friend's lifeless body in the canal. He remembered the hot sun, the ridged cane, the calluses on his hands, the tired walk back to the huts. He pictured Mr Carmichael's creased skin and thick boots. Song was glad to be out of there, but couldn't help remembering the faces of all the boys left behind. Row upon row of them. Lining up on a Sunday morning waiting for Father Holmes to show up.

Song put his hand up to cover his eyes and could not stop the tears. Amalia came to put her arms around him. He noticed how careful she was not to touch his wounds, but he still pushed her away. He didn't want to let himself crumble, not visibly. He remembered Li Bai's words: 'You got to start thinking harder about surviving.'

66

CHAPTER 5

Mornings, Song lay in the darkness. He pulled up the white cotton sheets to his nose, smelling the lime detergent Amalia used for laundry. The material was soft and worn from years of scrubbing. He listened to the aracaris in the gloom. As their chirruping grew louder he slipped out from under the mosquito net, folded back the sheet to air, and tugged on his overalls.

Down the stairs he padded softly on the polished floors and skirted around the rugs. He slipped out of the kitchen door to fetch eggs from the chicken coop, collect water for Amalia, and then took Father Holmes' large bicycle to Belle's bakery, happy to know he was trusted with money in his pocket to buy warm bread for breakfast. This was Song's favourite time of day, alone and carefree, before town had fully woken.

By the time he was back Amalia was boiling water for tea. She told him he moved more quietly than a shadow. Song polished Father Holmes' shoes and left them by the study door. Then he went to the church with fresh flowers, to sweep the floors, and to organise the prayer and hymn books. He loved being there in the cool emptiness, with all the responsibility on him to keep the church presentable – that's how Father Holmes had expressed it. It was up to Song to make sure that it was in a perfect state for every service and for every member of the congregation who might stop by at any time of the day or night. Song took huge pride in his work there. He came to know every dark recess, every loose hinge, every nick in the wooden pews, every crease in the cloth worn across the hips of the carving of Jesus Christ on the cross, which Song polished daily. He wanted it to be perfect for Father Holmes and anyone else who walked through the church's doors.

At the end of the month Father Holmes handed Song an envelope. 'You've worked hard, Song. Thank you.'

Song felt the hard coins through the paper. 'Can I send it home?'

'You can do whatever you want with it. It's your money. You can save it, you can spend it, you can send it home – whatever you choose.'

'Please can you help me send it home?'

'Of course. How have you sent it before?'

'I haven't yet. I was still paying for my passage.'

'How long was that going to take?'

'I don't know.'

Father Holmes shook his head. 'Slavery's over,' he muttered. 'What do they think they're up to?'

Song didn't know if he was meant to reply. 'Who, Father?'

'Never mind. What did the other boys do when they sent money home?'

'I don't know. I didn't know anyone who had.'

'Do you have an address?'

'Lishui. That's my village.'

'Any more than that?'

Song shook his head. 'I didn't know how to write the name of my village. I'm sorry. I never learned.' He began to realise the impossibility of what he was asking. He had come all this way to find work, to save his family, but he'd never understood how far he would be going.

'I'm sure we'll figure it out. I know Malcolm at the post office well. He'll help us. When the next boat sails we can find out where it's going and see how this all might work.'

Song felt the coins in his wage packet again and imagined his family waiting, hoping to see him walk back into town leading a pair of laden buffaloes. He thought of Xiao Mei and San San tangled together on the wet ground while he slept at the vicarage with a full stomach between white sheets. He was so far away now. Too far away.

'I want you to take the day off today,' Father Holmes said. 'No more chores. Go and do whatever you like.'

'Whatever I like,' Song repeated softly. He knew what he wanted to do. He slipped into the backyard and began climbing the mango tree until he was so high the chickens scratching in the dirt below were only brown and white smudges. He could cover the surface of the water in the vat with his thumbprint.

He stopped on a branch where there were a pair of yellow kiskadees. They cocked their heads from side to side, looking at him.

The branches hung heavy with fruit, just like Zhu Wei had described. Song plucked a mango and pierced an end, sucking out the sticky juice. Then he kicked his legs around and hung upside-down so that everything turned the other way and his mind was clear of anything except that the sky was the ground and the ground was the sky, and the mango tasted sweet in his mouth.

That evening, Song heard Father Holmes open the door to someone.

'Ah, Huw, I'm so glad you came.' Then he called for Song.

Song quickly padded into the hallway. 'Yes, Father?'

'I want you to meet my friend, Mr Rees-Jones. He heads up St Mark's Preparatory School – and is one of the more free-thinking men in Georgetown. He happens to be a Welshman, too, by the way.'

'Good evening, sir,' Song said. Mr Rees-Jones was a well-lined but handsome man with thick brown hair and dark-rimmed spectacles. He had a kind expression and engaging eyes.

'Good evening, Song. And how old are you?'

'Ten. Nearly eleven, sir.'

'Got some growing in you, I think.'

'Yes, sir.'

'Right, off you go,' Father Holmes said. 'I'm going to talk to Huw about something important – your education.'

Song didn't really know what Father Holmes meant but he felt honoured that these two men were going to be discussing him and that it was important. 'Thank you,' he said, although neither man heard. They were already inside Father Holmes' study.

Song could hear their conversation from the kitchen table where Amalia had sat him down to clean rice. He began to pick out the dark specks.

'So, Father, tell me what plan you're hatching.'

'I want him in school.'

'I can't deny I'd like him in school, too.'

'So?'

'I think you know the answer to that.'

'He's eager to learn. You can't shut the door on a boy who wants to better himself.'

'This is why I love you, Father. For your idealism. Your hope. Your faith in humanity.'

'Who's going to object?'

'Everyone! Everyone will object. The councillors, the teachers, the parents. They'd take their children out of school until the boy was removed. The whole affair would be a mess. Not least for Song.'

Song wondered what Mr Rees-Jones meant. Why might everyone object to him going to school? A plantation boy, that must have been it . . .

'They wouldn't dare speak out against you,' Father Holmes said.

'You flatter me, Father, but you don't know Georgetown as well as I thought. There'll be a queue outside my door all the way to St Andrew's.'

'It's not right.'

'I'm not saying it's right.'

'Shall I go to the governor?'

'I'd be more careful if I were you. His answer will be a much stronger no.'

There was a long silence.

'You know I'd do something if I could,' Mr Rees-Jones said. 'Keep him at home, Father. Teach him yourself. He will do as well under your guidance as he would under any of my teachers.'

'I don't know the first thing about teaching a boy. He barely even speaks to me. He needs to be around other boys his age—'

'Like it or not, no one in Georgetown is going to want their son mixing with a plantation boy. Your efforts will fail, and will only make life more difficult for Song.'

'What kind of community is this, which refuses an education to a boy who cannot change the circumstances of his birth?'

'I don't know. In truth, it doesn't feel like my community. It's definitely not yours.'

'But we can change it, Huw. If I can't ask you—'

'Please don't. It pains me to say no to you.'

'This isn't just about Song. This could change—'

'Change what?' Mr Rees-Jones interrupted. 'Georgetown

society? You think they'll be happy to send an entire plantation to school?'

'Is that so crazy?'

'Perhaps not. There have been rumours of a preacher heading down to Diamond every Sunday to teach the plantation boys to read. Just imagine, plantation boys reading. Whatever next?'

'I don't think I'm doing a very good job there.'

'Heed my advice, Father, and don't take this fight on. If this is truly about Song's education, use your energy to teach him, not to fight the system.'

Song longed for the opportunity to learn how to read and write. He would have loved to have gone to school, but maybe not like this, not with all of Georgetown objecting to him having an education. Perhaps Father Holmes would teach him. Or they'd find some way together, some way to better himself.

Song saw Father Holmes jump when he saw him standing in front of his desk. 'You move so quietly, Song, I don't even hear you.'

'Sorry, Father. Amalia told me to come and find you.'

'That's right. I wanted to tell you that we're going to start studying together.'

Song's heart began to beat a little quicker. 'Yes, Father.'

'Would you like that?'

'Yes, Father. But I'm not sure what it means.'

Father Holmes got up and strode across to the shelves. He picked up a slim weathered book.

'We're going to read Daniel Defoe's *Robinson Crusoe*. This was the first novel I ever read and it made me want to go to sea. Not that the voyage is an easy ride, nor the book an easy read. It's a story of a shipwrecked man who washes up on an island and learns how to survive. Sound familiar?'

Song nodded. He could hear the storm in his head. The boat thrashing out of time with the rising sea and the shuddering wood.

'It's a good place to start.' Father Holmes waved his arm across the shelves. 'But you're going to read every single book in this room, Song. What do you think about that?'

Song surveyed the room. There must have been hundreds of books, even thousands. Row after row after row. All unintelligible to him. But he found himself nodding, full of fervour. 'I'd like that, Father. I'd like to know I could do that.'

'You can. You will. We'll do it together.'

Song suddenly felt like this was his chance. Like the way he'd imagined Hai in Madras living in a large house overlooking the sea with an Englishman boss who paid him a good wage and gave him a breezy room. This was his chance: to stay here and learn to read every book in this room. To live a life that was a story worth telling, just like he'd promised Jinda.

'It's not only about reading,' Father Holmes went on. 'It's about studying what we read. We'll talk about the books. Discuss ideas. We'll look at the language, the melody of the prose, the structure of the plot.'

Song was lost. He couldn't follow what Father Holmes was saying. But he nodded again. 'Yes, Father.'

Father Holmes looked across at Song tenderly. 'Let's not worry about all that yet. All you need to know for now is that you'll read every morning on your own. We'll talk through the passages over lunch. I'll set you some writing. You'll have to fit in your chores. Then we'll study together again in the evening. How does that sound?'

'I'd like that,' he said, so softly he could barely hear the words himself.

'One of the first things you're going to have to learn, Song, is to speak up, to disagree with me. If you're not sure about something, you have to ask. If you don't agree, you have to say so.'

Song nodded again. But to speak out against something this man, who was helping him so much, might say?

It was like Father Holmes read his mind. 'Be brave, Song. Shout me down. This is the way you'll learn and grow. Me, too. I'll be learning from you too, you know. Right, let's make a start.'

Song read all the time. In the early light of morning, he reached out in his bedclothes to feel for the hard corners of the book he'd been reading the night before, and had inevitably fallen asleep with. He'd have a slimmer book in a back pocket during the day, to read a few pages between chores. On his bicycle he balanced a book on the handlebars, turning the pages with one hand, steering with the other. But he hid it away when he saw people approaching, aware that some believed it was not something he should be doing. Mrs Mills, one of the choir singers, had rebuked Song when she saw him the first time. 'I can see that's not a Bible, boy,' she shouted across the road. 'You should be ashamed of yourself, reading when you should be getting on with the work of a houseboy.'

But some were amused at how Song could read while he cycled. Scott, a houseboy for the governor's first secretary, said he was going to learn to read just like Song. 'Whatch you reading now?' he'd call out cheerily. 'I'm goin' to learn the same way as you, mark me.'

When Song had free time he climbed up the mango tree to sit on the branches and take in a chapter. Sometimes, when Father Holmes was out for lunch, Amalia let Song read at the table while he ate. 'I never learnt so you gotta be reading for the both of us,' she'd say.

Song was taken all over the world with Father Holmes' books, from smoky London streets to the winding lanes in a county called Dorset to the church towers of medieval Paris. He read about pirates and pilgrims and pickpockets. Song felt like he was travelling, no longer in a hold of a boat, but like a bird up among the clouds, to wherever he wanted to go that day. And yet he'd be back at the vicarage in time for supper.

Every evening Father Holmes and Song sat together in the study and discussed what Song had read that day. He loved Robert Louis Stevenson's *Treasure Island*. The black spot, Ben Gunn, the mutiny. Like Jim Hawkins, Song knew about nightmares of the sea and the lure of gold.

The pair spoke long into the night about, for example, why Stevenson chose Jim as the storyteller: a naive young boy who grew up to become a free-thinking, charismatic man. 'You're not fresh like him, Song, but there is still a lot to learn,' Father Holmes said. 'You have a great appetite for life, and a huge capacity to love; it's how we choose to use that life, that love.'

They discussed the complexities of a boy becoming a man, the forming of identity, and what it is to be human. Song found himself challenging Father Holmes, and sometimes even noticed a subtle smile on the vicar's face when he spoke up. 'But I disagree, Father. Long John Silver is not all villain. I think Stevenson is trying to tell us that it's not as simple as good or evil. Sometimes the two are mixed up together.'

On Sundays, Song arrived with Father Holmes at St Andrew's several hours before a service. Song placed a hymn and a prayer book at every place, and ensured the correct numbered hymns were displayed on the board.

He had begun to know where everyone sat, and who was who. There was Mrs Stewart, who helped arrange the flowers at the church. On one side was her husband, who worked in the tax office, and in between sat their daughter Millie. There was the governor's wife, Mrs Johnson, who ran the church choir, but it was Mrs Boyle who had the most beautiful voice. Mr Carmichael sat at the very front with his wife and daughters.

For the service itself, Song sat out of view of the congregation, but he could see Father Holmes. Song was becoming familiar with the language Father Holmes used, the refrains. He knew if this religion could make a man like Father Holmes it must have some good in it. But he also knew that there were people there, sitting in front of Father Holmes, who were just pretending to live a life faithful to the church's teaching.

One Sunday, the service had been particularly slow. The hush was as oppressive as the heat, and everyone was uncomfortable. Between the buzzing of flies was the constant flapping of painted paper fans. Song saw Mrs Burford, the committee secretary, approach Father Holmes. She had a pinched, determined look about her. Song moved closer but kept himself out of sight.

'There's something I need to talk to you about, Father. Now.'

'Yes, Mrs Burford, of course.'

Song noticed the droplets of sweat blooming on Mrs Burford's forehead.

'It's that houseboy of yours.'

'Song, you mean?'

'Everybody's talking about him.'

'How curious. I can't imagine why a slip of an eleven-year-old could be the subject of so much attention.'

Mrs Burford leaned forward and dropped her voice. Song missed what she said.

'You'll have to excuse me, Mrs Burford, but why might that be?'

'You haven't been here long, Father, and you don't know how

things work. I'm going to help you by explaining things. The problem is you're being too good to the boy—'

'Too good?'

'People aren't happy about it.'

'Not happy about me being too good to a boy? You can't imagine how puzzling that sounds to me.'

Mrs Burford dropped her voice again but Song could still hear. 'He's living with you. Houseboys should not be, well, living in a house the way yours is. It's not right.'

'Where do you think a houseboy should be living, if not in a house?'

'Houseboys don't sleep *upstairs* in our houses.'

Even if Father Holmes didn't understand what Mrs Burford was saying, Song understood completely. She didn't want Father Holmes to care about him.

'Is that what all this is about, Mrs Burford? Where in the house he is sleeping? I'm relieved to hear that, because I have a simple explanation as to why Song is sleeping upstairs. The thing is, I have a perfectly good room upstairs at the vicarage, and absolutely nowhere downstairs.'

Song was moved by this man showing such loyalty to him.

'The problem is it sets a precedent for the rest of us. Soon they'll all want to be sleeping upstairs.'

'Well, I'm glad you now know the simple reason why Song is upstairs, Mrs Burford. It's only a matter of space. I hope I've allayed your worries.'

'But he's a plantation boy, Father. He's not even a houseboy. And you've got him reading too. We on the committee don't feel, well . . . you know he has a book with him everywhere. We've seen him all over town with a book in his hand.'

'Mrs Burford, you're not telling me that the committee doesn't want him to read?'

'It's not just the reading. It's everything. You're making this very difficult for me, Father. I'm trying to explain how things work here and you're refusing to understand.'

'It is not a matter of refusing to understand, Mrs Burford. I am simply failing to see why the committee would prefer to see Song illiterate. After all, he organises the prayer books and hymn books in the church every day. I'm sure we'd all like him to know which was which.'

Song detected Father Holmes' slightly condescending tone and couldn't help but be amused.

Mrs Burford obviously heard it too. She raised her voice. 'I would have thought you'd have been a little bit grateful for me passing on to you what people are saying. I'm not the only one. Try speaking to any of your congregation. Mrs Boyle. Mrs Stewart. They all feel the same.'

'You tell the committee what I've told you, Mrs Burford. Song's a good, hard-working boy. If I can give him a decent start in life that must be good in God's eyes and it should be in ours too. Good day.'

That night Father Holmes called Song into his study. 'I've got some good news. I've heard of a man who's going to Hong Kong. It's a long trip and it's not certain when he will get there but I think he is a good person to trust. He's said he'll do what he can to help you and carry money back to your family.'

Back to your family. The words spun around Song's head. His family seemed so far away from where he was now. Even if the man reached Hong Kong, how would he find them?

'What do you think?' Father Holmes said.

'Do you think it will work?'

'We can only try. I'll give the man some recompense for his trouble and I'm sure he'll do what he can. We need to tell him the name of your family, the village, and the names of important people in the village. Perhaps how long it took you to get from your village to Guangzhou, and so on. As much information as we can pull together to help him.'

Song allowed himself to hope. Maybe it would work. He tried to imagine this man walking into his village with Song's wage packet, asking for a woman by the name of Zhang Je, pressing the envelope into his mother's hand, telling her it was from Song, and recording her surprise.

'But I suggest you keep some money for yourself, Song, just in case,' Father Holmes said. 'It's good to have something to fall back on. And a man cannot live on books alone. Talking of which, I have another project for us.'

Father Holmes walked over to his shelves and reached for a book. He laid it open in front of Song. There was an illustration of a bird. Its feathers were burnt orange with black tips. Its delicate feet were criss-crossed in a fine filigree pattern. The eye – a piercing yellow – stared out from the page. It was as if it had caught a glint of real sunlight. Like a first sight of gold.

Father Holmes pointed at the title on the page and Song followed his finger and read out the name: 'Double-feathered whistling drongo'.

'What a name,' Father Holmes said. 'And there's more. They're all as wonderful as that.'

The pages flashed with colour as they flicked through the book. 'Black-headed tiger finch,' Song read out loud. 'Salmon-jowled heron. Yellow-beaked fish hawk.'

'Mr Matthews, the author, was an Englishman who lived in

Tobago,' Father Holmes told Song. 'It's an island not far from here and many of the birds in this book are the same ones we can see here in Guiana. I bought this book on Charing Cross Road in London and the man who sold it to me knew Mr Matthews personally. He was a great ornithologist who spent more than half his life in the West Indies. He died falling out of a hide he had built at the top of a mora tree in Antigua. Now that, Song, is commitment.'

'Is it?' Song said. 'That sounds pretty reckless to me.'

Song saw Father Holmes' smile. 'You're right, Song,' Father Holmes said. 'It is rather reckless behaviour.'

He reached across his desk for another book. On the cover was embossed: *Birds of the Coastal Regions, British Guiana, Volume I, Part I.*

'Now, Song, do you know what this is?' Father Holmes asked.

Song shook his head.

Father Holmes opened the book. There were some hand-drawn sketches and notes written in ink. 'This is our book. I started it soon after I arrived here but haven't had time to do much work on it. We're going to document every bird we see in Guiana.'

Song took it in his hands and leafed through the pages. Father Holmes had organised his book the same way as Mr Matthews. There was an illustration and detailed below were notes on the bird's size, its habitat and call.

'I'm afraid I don't draw so well as Mr Matthews,' Father Holmes said. He turned to his last entry, about a quarter of the way through the book. Beyond, the pages were blank. 'You and I are going to fill this whole book,' he said.

'I'd like that,' Song said. He wondered if this might be a way he could prove himself to Father Holmes. To show him that he could take on something like this, something that mattered very much to

Father Holmes, and to do it well. 'I won't be falling out of a tree for the book, Father, but you can count on my commitment.'

The weather had been very hot and very still for several days. Everybody was suffering in the high temperatures.

'Let's go up to the sea wall tonight,' Father Holmes suggested. 'If there's any breeze at all, that's where we'll feel it.'

Song had never been up there after dark. He had only seen the boardwalk by day, when the sun was so hot the strip was empty except for the swooping gulls mewing like newborns. But in the evening, as dusk softened the glare, he knew this was where Georgetown came to lime – the term used to describe whiling away time, strolling, laughing, holding hands. You didn't see English folk up there.

The sea wall was nothing much to look at. It ran along the north shore of the city and was built of plastered brick and painted with advertisements for products such as Cadbury's and Ovaltine, the chocolate powder and sweet malt he knew Amalia used to buy with her wages but he'd never yet tasted. Beyond the wall the silty water of the Caribbean Sea stretched out into the darkness.

Song walked quickly to keep up with Father Holmes' loping stride. The vicar addressed by name everyone they passed. Song copied him before casting down his eyes. 'Strangers don't like strangers. If nobody notices you, nothing bad will happen to you,' his father had told him.

The moon was barely a sliver but its reflection shimmered from the shore to the horizon. The rest of the ocean was as dark as ink. It purred against the sea wall, occasionally kicking up a spray.

'I love it here,' Father Holmes said. Song was surprised to learn that he'd been here previously.

'Before you came into my life, Song, before we passed our evenings in the study reading, I used to come up to the sea wall to hear the water lapping at the shore and to remember how it was when I was a boy, standing on the docks with my father. That's a long time ago. And now I'm here with you.'

Father Holmes was immersed in his reminiscences when Song noticed the couple. They were sitting at the very end of the wall a good twenty feet ahead of them. The boy was holding the girl close to him and stroking her back. Song recognised her as Millie, the daughter of Mr and Mrs Stewart. Song knew the boy, too. It was Scott, the houseboy who wanted to read like him.

As Father Holmes and Song approached, the couple jumped to their feet. Millie covered her face in her hands.

'Father, I'm sorry.' She began to cry. 'Please don't say anything. I beg you.'

Scott tried to put his arm around her but she pulled away and ran across to Father Holmes, burying her face in his shirt. Her wailing became louder.

'Be quiet, Millie,' Father Holmes said. He peeled Millie's fingers from his shirt and steered her away.

Scott turned to leave.

'We'll all walk home together, please,' Father Holmes said. 'You too, Scott.'

'Best I go,' the boy said.

'No, Scott. We're walking back together.'

'Yes, sir. Father.'

Father Holmes turned to Millie, who was now sobbing uncontrollably.

'Pull yourself together and walk properly, like the grown-up you have been pretending to be.'

Millie fell into a coughing fit. Song hung back from the party.

He watched Millie move away from Scott and cross to the other side of Father Holmes. Her arms hung loose by her sides. She was kicking the ground as she walked.

'What in heaven's name were you two thinking?' Father Holmes said.

Millie wiped her face with her handkerchief. 'It's his fault,' she said, pointing at Scott.

Father Holmes turned to her. 'Do you know what you're playing at?' he said. 'What is the worst thing that could happen to you? Think about it. Now what's the worst thing that could happen to Scott?'

'I – I don't know,' Millie stammered.

'Think a bit harder then,' Father Holmes said. 'You might get a telling-off. You might have to stay home for a week. This boy might . . .'

Millie interrupted. 'But he made me do it.'

'Enough.' Father Holmes' voice was fierce.

Millie broke into a sob. 'Please, Father.'

'Hush, Millie,' Scott said. 'We've got trouble enough.'

'Don't you speak to me like that,' Millie said sharply. She turned to Father Holmes. 'See what he's like. Always telling me what to do.'

Song watched in horror as he saw Father Holmes suddenly grab Millie by her shoulders and shake her. 'How dare you speak about him that way?' he said. 'You mind your language. You mind your manners. If you can treat this young man half as well as he's treating you, then maybe you can hold your head up again.'

Millie flinched.

Scott stepped forward. 'Don't be hard on her, Father. She's frightened.'

'It's all right, Scott,' he said.

'You hurt me,' Millie said to Father Holmes. Her voice had risen to a shriek. 'If you say anything, I'll tell them how you hurt me.'

'You watch what comes out of your mouth, Millie Stewart. My, you have a long way to go before you deserve the attentions of this young man.'

As they approached the first secretary's house, Father Holmes turned to Scott. 'Go on, Scott,' Father Holmes said. 'Don't think about this any more tonight. Come and see me tomorrow, please.'

Scott slipped away into the darkness towards the back of the house.

Millie whimpered the rest of the way home.

'He forced me—'

'I don't want to hear another word. Go home.'

'But are you—'

'I hope you cannot sleep tonight, Millie, and that you do some hard thinking. Now go home.'

Millie pouted. She turned and ran off up to her house. When she opened the front door, lamplight spilled on to the porch.

Father Holmes waited a few minutes. He carried on staring at the house. 'I didn't hurt her, Song.'

'Yes, Father. I know.'

'There are injustices in this world, Song, and it is upon us to enable change. I don't know why I'm telling you this. You know a whole lot more about this than me.'

Song did know. And he knew he was a Scott in this town, not a Millie.

The man and boy carried on walking home, listening to the rise and fall of the cicadas, lifting to a crescendo, before droning out to a buzz.

CHAPTER 6

Father Holmes and Song were on the porch sitting in a pair of Berbice chairs when Governor Johnson stopped by. Song had long been curious about him. His word seemed to be law in town, and nobody dared cross him. Once when Song had asked Scott to tell him more about the governor, Scott had said that 'he couldn't risk his job by talking the truth'.

But he looked a pleasant enough man standing there in front of the vicarage. Not tall, a ruddied face, a quick smile.

'Ah, Father, I'm glad I caught you at home.'

'Good morning, Governor. What gives us the good fortune of a visit from the busiest man in Georgetown?'

'In truth, some rather important business.'

'We'll have to get on with this later, Song,' Father Holmes said. He turned to the governor again. 'This is my houseboy, Song. We're working on a bird book together. Song, Governor Johnson is a passionate bird man, too – with two full-time trappers and a large aviary behind his house.'

Song looked at the governor, who was sheltering his eyes from the sun and studying the sky for birds. 'Nice to meet you, sir,' Song said.

But the governor didn't seem to be listening to him or Father Holmes. Song quietly retreated into the house, but he was still in hearing distance of the men's conversation.

'Tell me more, Governor,' he heard Father Holmes say.

'Ah, yes. I will come directly to the point. Bloody hot, isn't it?'

'The good thing about this weather is I get a full house on Sunday. The church is the coolest place in town.'

The governor laughed. 'Sounds like God's own work. Now where was I? Unfortunately this is all rather sudden. I've just been informed that a new vicar, by the name of Father Francis, is – as we speak – sailing to British Guiana with his family. He'll be taking over your position here in Georgetown.'

There was a pause. The loopy whistle of a screaming piha filled the silence.

'And this is the first we've heard of it?'

'For some time there have been discussions in London about whether the colonies would be better staffed by men with families. We've been trying to get more families out here but haven't had a lot of luck. Too many bachelors, or married men on short-term postings who leave the family back home. All getting up to mischief, that kind of thing. London thinks we need to make the place more attractive to families. You know, ladies shopping, kids in school, a proper ladder at the tennis club. The kind of thing that will keep people here.'

'I see.'

'If we speed up the handover period it might mean you'll be back in England for Christmas. You'll have to remember us all sweltering here . . .'

Song could hear his own breathing above the clock chiming in the hallway.

'So this is nothing to do with my work?'

'Not at all. Although if you want to know the truth, Father, there have been some rumbling complaints from a few corners of the community. I'm sure you know what I'm talking about. Educating houseboys and all that. But let's not bother ourselves with any of that now. I'll be putting in a very good word for you back in London. Where would you like to go? Back to Wales? Or overseas again? How about India? I hear Ceylon is very popular now.'

'I can't imagine leaving Guiana. Not now.'

'I'm surprised to hear that, Father.'

'How about the interior? Bartica or Lethem?'

'You can't be serious?'

'Quite serious.'

'It's no Georgetown.'

'There's even more work to be done out there.'

'Interior, eh? It's a wild place.'

'I'm really not ready to leave.'

'I can hear that.'

'And think of the birds.'

'I was thinking of the mosquitoes,' the governor said.

'I feel a real calling here.'

'You are a special man, Father. A transfer, huh? Let me look into it.'

For so long Song hadn't let himself dare hope that his time with Father Holmes might last beyond tomorrow. But now he was suddenly afraid of losing him, that there was a real chance of them being torn apart. Song closed his eyes and willed them to be together for all time.

Malaria broke out in the east of the city. It started as a few cases of high fever, uncontrollable shaking, a drifting into unconsciousness. Not everyone died from it, but some did. The disease began to spread, moving across neighbourhoods like the shadow of dusk. The gloom was felt on every street. Whole households were left sweating and shaking.

Song knew about disease like this. And he knew about

surviving. What had his mother once said? 'Song'll make it. He came to us in a good year.' Song had beaten a fever once before. He could beat it again if he had to. But he worried about Father Holmes.

Father Holmes was hardly ever home at the vicarage during that time. Day and night he accompanied Dr Hew, the chief medical officer, on his house calls. They worked around the clock: Dr Hew recommending poultices and cold wraps; Father Holmes offering comfort and prayers.

Song tried to wait up for Father Holmes but sleep often over-took him. In the morning he would know if the vicar had passed by, however briefly. He would see with relief a partially eaten plate of food or carefully selected books laid out for him to read.

Amalia preferred Song to stay around the house rather than to be out exposing himself to the fever. 'Nursed you enough in my life already. There's no need for you to be to-ing and fro-ing around town for no reason. You stay put 'less I tell you otherwise.'

The only errands he was allowed to run were to the homes of the bereaved.

'Don't enter the house,' Amalia instructed him. 'No lingering. Be quick without being rude.'

Song was glad to obey Amalia. He hated hearing the sounds of the grieving, the wailing, the smell of medication, even the smell of death. Song knocked on the front doors offering condolences from the vicarage, bearing cut flowers and trays of sweet pine tarts, and then he swiftly left.

The rest of the time Song stayed at the vicarage reading the books Father Holmes had chosen, thinking up the questions he might ask him. He sometimes made up dialogues between himself and an imaginary Father Holmes, going back and forth, sitting in

Father Holmes' chair, even speaking in the vicar's deeper voice, then switching to sit opposite, back as Song, to talk about what he had learned and what he didn't understand.

One quiet, muggy evening he was eating supper alone when there was a noise on the porch. Amalia called out from the kitchen. 'Go on then. Must be him.'

Song ran into the hallway. Standing in the frame of the door was a pale-skinned woman wearing a dark roll-necked dress. Her face glistened with sweat. Song recognised her immediately. Mrs Boyle – with the most beautiful voice in the church choir. They stared at each other through the screen door. Even in the dark Song could see that she had been crying.

'Where is he?'

Song looked at Mrs Boyle's hands, clenched tightly by her side, and felt wary.

'Where's that coolie-lover of yours?'

Song was shocked by the woman's language and her tone. He knew only her sweet, light voice, as the woman who sang the starting note in choir practice for everyone to follow.

'Please, ma'am?' Song said.

'Good-for-nothing coolie-child.' She spat out the words.

Song felt himself recoil. 'Father Holmes isn't here.'

'You fetch him, you hear me. You tell him I want to talk to him.'

'He's not here,' Song repeated more firmly. 'He's visiting the sick with Dr Hew.'

Mrs Boyle let out a shriek of laughter. 'You're a liar. That's what you are.'

Mrs Boyle pulled open the screen door. 'I'm coming to talk to him. You get him.'

At that moment Father Holmes' voice came out of the darkness from behind the woman. He was just arriving home.

'Is that Mrs Boyle?' he asked. 'I was planning to come around this evening but you're already here. Will you come inside and join me?'

Mrs Boyle turned to face Father Holmes. 'Don't you "will you come inside" me.'

'I'm sorry, Mrs Boyle. I've just learned about your loss. I'm terribly sorry I could not be there.'

'You're not sorry.'

'We are trying to see everyone we can but we are living through a truly dreadful time.'

'Who is? You and your coolie-child?'

'Go inside please, Song,' Father Holmes said.

Song did as he was asked, but stayed in the shadows of the hallway. He heard Father Holmes steadying his voice. 'Mrs Boyle, perhaps you need some rest. Let me—'

'Don't you tell me what I need. You wouldn't know what any of us need. You spend all your time with a yellow-bellied coolie. He should be out cutting cane, not reading books.'

Song saw Father Holmes peer through the screen door and look down the hallway for him. He pulled himself back from the light. He didn't want Father Holmes to know he'd heard any more. He knew it would upset him. But Song himself didn't care what Mrs Boyle had to say. She could not stop him reading books now. He would always have the power to read.

'Mrs Boyle, please control yourself. I know you are upset but so are we all—'

Mrs Boyle's voice had risen to a scream. 'My baby's dead and you tell me to control myself. You didn't come to the house, did you? Not when you were needed? Too busy teaching that stinking coolie how to read. What about your own people? You forgotten why you're here?'

'That's enough, Mrs Boyle.' Father Holmes reached out for her hand. 'Let me accompany you home.'

Mrs Boyle took a step forward, raised her arm and struck Father Holmes across the face. 'Stay away from me,' she said. 'Don't you come near me.'

Song gasped. He could not believe what she had done.

'I'm not coming near you.' There was frustration in Father Holmes' voice. 'I want you to stay away from us, too. Go home, Mrs Boyle. It's late.'

Song was equally shocked at Father Holmes' response, even if she had hit him. His was the same tone he'd used on Millie that night at the sea wall when Song had watched on in horror, and Scott had told Father Holmes not to be so hard on his girl.

Mrs Boyle suddenly threw herself at Father Holmes, beating him about the face. Father Holmes grabbed her wrists. Song was torn between going to Father Holmes' aid, and remaining unseen. He watched in desperation. There was a struggle and Song saw the woman give up and collapse on the front steps. 'God will judge you,' she sobbed. 'You're a wicked, wicked man.'

There was a man's voice, out of breath and full of urgency. 'Father Holmes. I'm so sorry.'

Song couldn't see him in the shadows but he guessed it was Mrs Boyle's husband, George.

'I'm glad you came. Your wife was just on her way home.'

Mrs Boyle looked up at her husband. There was a fierceness in her voice as she pointed at Father Holmes. 'He killed her.'

'I'm sorry, Father. She's very upset. The baby and all.' He reached out to take his wife by the arm.

'Don't you touch me. You're as bad as him.' Mrs Boyle was still shouting.

'That's enough, Miranda. Come home now.'

Song looked away from the fighting and down the corridor towards the back door. He watched the shadows dance as the lamplight struck the branches of the mango tree. He would never go back to the plantation, he swore that to himself. But he feared everything had changed. Mrs Boyle had tried to hurt Father Holmes. Father Holmes had ordered her home, even though she has just lost her baby, with a tone Song had hardly ever heard him use. Song's faith in his new life was shaken. He knew he couldn't risk staying. Even with Father Holmes by his side, there were too many people against him.

Amalia walked down the hall to the front door mumbling to herself. She passed Song without noticing him. 'What's going on here?' he heard her say. 'All this shouting so late at night?'

After she passed Song slipped out of the back of the house. He moved towards the swaying branches of the mango tree and into the darkness. The voices on the porch became fainter. Then he heard Father Holmes call out his name. He ran into the night, glad of the darkness.

Song went straight to the church. He knew places there he could hide. There was a huge store cupboard where he could envelop himself between costumes used for the nativity play. There was also the altar, which was actually a table draped in cloth, that he could sleep under in the heat of the day. From there, he could hear footsteps, snippets of conversation, mumbled prayers, even the sound of a man sobbing. At choir practice, Mrs Boyle's soprano voice rose high above the rest, and Song cursed her. After dark, he ventured out to find food, bringing back to the church a clutch of bananas, handfuls of guava, mangoes.

Song had left the house so quickly, he had brought nothing except the book in his hand. *Moby Dick*. He read it slowly, studying the character of Ishmael, the outsider, the survivor. Someone without a family or a last name. The story underscored to Song that he didn't want to run further away. In fact, he longed to go back to the vicarage. He wanted Father Holmes in his life. But he struggled to find the courage to return.

By the time Sunday came around it had been four days. Song left the church early in the morning, before the hour Father Holmes left the vicarage. He walked up the steps, pulled at the screen door and winced at the whine. There was Amalia's voice. 'I'll go, Father. You carry on eating.'

Song padded quickly through the hall. Before Amalia had cleaned her hands on her apron he had reached the doorway to the dining room. Father Holmes looked up. Their eyes met like they had that day in the river. But this time it was more knowing. A bond already forged, there was a deeper understanding between the two of them.

CHAPTER 7

The cart heaved forward. Song sat atop their pile of possessions: boxes of books, rolled-up rugs, stacks of gloomy oil paintings, a typewriter. Up front Father Holmes sat next to Bento, whose donkeys strained forward with the weight of the load. Song thought back to the swing-basket of rice and the shirt on his back, the only two things he had when he left his family. It was so different now, yet he felt the same weighted sense of expectation, of a future unknown.

They reached the muddy Demerara, running swiftly and high. Song sat quietly to the side and watched the unloading, and then the loading of their effects on to the boat; the short crossing, and then the same on the other side. Once, twice, then another time. It took all morning to do the transfer before Song and Father Holmes themselves crossed the river, and continued their journey west.

The land opened up into miles of cane fields and Song watched the plantation workers burning the dried stubs. Searing sweet smoke clouded out the sun and rolled thickly across the fields. He blinked the scene in and out of his stinging eyes. He was acutely aware of the way the bodies moved of these men, how they raised their arms and slashed them downwards, something he knew how to do so well. He thought of Jinda. Then he thought of all the boys back at Diamond, toiling the same way, day after day. He felt sorry, even guilty. But then he thought of Li Bai's words: You got to start thinking harder about surviving.

The journey passed slowly. Song slept in bursts throughout the day. Sometimes his dreams crowded out the reality of where he was. He was running, out of breath, shouting his father's name, searching, unable to find him. There was the noise of the ship, which so often thrashed around in his head. The switch flicking in the air, the beating on his back. When he woke, he quickly looked across at Father Holmes, just to be sure he was there.

They stopped from time to time to stretch their legs. As they stood by each other's side, Song turned to Father Holmes. Something had been worrying him.

'Do you think we'll hear back from the man who went to Hong Kong, if we're in Bartica?'

'Course we will,' Father Holmes replied confidently. 'I've been checking with Malcolm regularly. He or someone else will send word.'

'We haven't heard back yet.' Song's voice was flat.

'That's true. Not yet. But it's a long way to go and a long way back, you know that.'

Song nodded because he thought it would please Father Holmes.

The two of them clambered aboard the cart and went on their way. Fields gave way to sparse brush before the foliage thickened again with shiny green fronds of banana trees. They were planted in small groves each bearing hundreds of tightly clustered bananas. Men with machetes hacked at the thick stems to harvest the fruit. There was a splitting sound of vegetation.

The road ended abruptly at the banks of the Essequibo. Song had heard about this mighty river. Amalia had told him it was as wide as an ocean with midstream islands as big as countries. A river, as strong as the rising waters of the Li, capable of taking away all the men of a village, yet also with the power and fury of the open sea. Song was afraid but he knew he had to keep going; he could not turn back.

He stood beside the boatman on the water's edge and peered to see the other side.

'How far is it?' he asked.

'Two days,' the man replied. 'All day for two days.'

'Without stopping?'

The man waved his arm across the great expanse of water.

'It's a long, long way.'

Song thought how that was not a long, long way. He knew much longer.

The boatman put out a hand, and Song shook it.

'Call me Fowl Man,' he said.

'Pleased to meet you, Fowl Man,' Song replied. The man was tall and scrawny but must have been strong given his trade.

Song turned back to their course ahead. Unlike the Demerara, the Essequibo's waters were clear, but they were rougher, too. Waves lapped against the bank, staining the shoreline with torn branches and shrivelled coconuts. Every so often a bigger one washed right up the muddy bank. Song felt a fear rising inside him.

He looked at the long wooden dugout that Fowl Man had started loading. It seemed very small and unsteady to be taking them all the way to the opposite bank, two days away without stop-ping. The silver lettering of *Marie Christine* shimmered on the side of the vessel. It lowered into the water as it was filled with the crates of books and belongings, and Fowl Man stretched tarpaulin across the boxes. Song worried the rough waters might lap over the rim, or that the boat might split apart, that they'd sink. He tried hard to strike out those thoughts.

'I'll have to come back for the rest, Father,' Fowl Man said. 'That all right? Bento will take care of everything until I can return.'

Father Holmes surveyed the numerous boxes remaining on the cart and nodded. Then he and Song stepped into the boat and hunkered down. Song peered over the side. The water was almost above his eye-line.

'Everything all right, Song?' Father Holmes asked.

'Yes, fine,' Song replied. His firm answer made him feel a little better.

They pushed out into the current. Fowl Man and his oarsman strained to dig their paddles into the river. Swifts angled across the surface of the water, catching flies. Father Holmes pointed out a grey kingfisher with a shaggy crest as they pulled away from the bank. Song was grateful for the distraction. The river stretched out wide ahead of them, restive and silver.

Fowl Man was right. It took two full days to reach Bartica. Father Holmes and Song passed much of the time bird-spotting.

'A rufescent tiger heron, no?' Father Holmes said.

Song nodded and made a note in their book.

'Ah, it's good to be on the move,' Father Holmes continued.

Song wasn't so sure.

'Or is it not?' Father Holmes said. He must have detected Song's hesitation.

'Yes,' Song said. 'But I liked the vicarage in Georgetown, too.'

'You'll like this vicarage even more,' Father Holmes said. 'Bartica's fascinating. Not so polished as Georgetown, but that makes for a more interesting place to call home.'

Song watched the water splash over the rim of the boat, but it didn't rock, instead gliding steadily through the rough water.

'Actually Song, I don't know Bartica myself. That's only hearsay. But what makes this an adventure is that neither of us do. We'll discover it together. It won't be you joining me in my home but us making a home together.'

Song thought hard about that idea: us making a home together. The words sounded sweet. 'I like the idea of that,' Song said, 'but how do we do it? How do we make a home?'

'We just live, Song. It's the easiest thing in the world. We just live out our lives, make friends, get to know the place, dream up new adventures. That makes for a home.'

Fowl Man might have been right about the duration of the crossing, but Amalia was wrong; it was nothing like an ocean crossing. They hadn't come close to capsizing, or falling foul in any way. When the opposite bank came into sight, the oarsman turned to Song and pointed. 'Bartica.' He spat out the word like chewed tobacco. 'For dreamers.'

'Not just for dreamers,' Fowl Man contradicted him. He winked at Song. 'There are real dreams there, too.'

Song studied the bank of mangroves. Even as they neared he could not see much of a town. There were three or four white-washed houses with tended gardens rolling down to the river. A dozen men sat on the jetty, some playing dominoes, two with a fishing rod. He noticed another had a line looped around his big toe. He lazed back on his elbows and tipped a brown-glassed bottle to his lips. Song was fascinated at how the man might catch something with so little effort; he knew Amalia wouldn't approve – 'I know that type, drinking in the day, nothing to show for it', she'd say – even if the man had gotten a tug and a fish.

Fowl Man threw a rope and it landed on the planks of the jetty. One of the men sauntered up to it and stood on the frayed end. Another fended off the boat.

The man on the dock was grinning. He had three gold teeth. 'Welcome to Bartica.'

'City of gold,' another said, wiping his wet hands on his cut-offs.

'Enough of all your welcome talk nonsense,' Fowl Man said. 'Where's the damn cart I ordered?'

'Take it easy, man,' the man with gold teeth said. 'Cart's coming now.'

'And when's now?'

'Now's late.'

'Damn right it's late. I could have told you that. This here gentleman ain't waiting around all day for a late cart.'

'Welcome to Bartica, sir,' another said.

Fowl Man corrected him. 'It's Father. Don'ch you know nothing. Look at his collar. This here is Father Holmes, new vicar in town. Young fella is Song.'

He turned to Father Holmes and Song. 'Gentlemen, please meet Joseph and Basil and Dory; they might seem slow in getting things done, but they'll share their last beer with you.'

'Been a long time since we had a Father around here,' Joseph said. 'Need some forgiveness in this town. Low on forgiveness, Bartica.'

Song listened closely. He'd need to toughen up even more quickly.

'I'm here to help however I can,' Father Holmes said to Joseph.

'You coming to St Ethelbert's?' Dory asked.

'That's right,' Father Holmes said. 'Hope to see you there.'

The men shrieked with laughter.

Song felt sorry for Father Holmes. Fowl Man scowled. 'Let's have some respect, boys.'

'Know why they call him Fowl Man?' Joseph asked Song.

Song shook his head. 'Maybe because his laugh sounds like a chicken?'

'More like sense of humour of a chicken,' Joseph said. The men fell about laughing again.

'You don't listen to them, Song,' Fowl Man said. 'You more right than them. Father had a chicken farm. I grew up with chickens. I probably do sound like one, come to think of it.'

Basil slid up to Song and put his arm around the boy. He smelled of shrimp and sweat. 'See them posts?' he asked. 'That's wood of the greenheart tree. Strongest wood in the whole world. Been holding up this dock since before Jesus was born.'

'How do you know that?' Song asked.

'My father told me,' Basil said. 'And his father told him. And his father's father told him. Right back to Jesus.'

A cart pulled up at the end of the dock. Joseph smiled his three gold teeth. 'What did I tell you?' Joseph said. 'Gotta be patient in Bartica, Fowl Man, or your heart gonna stop young. Things take their time around here but they 'ventually get done. Can't hurry them up. Get to work, boys.'

The men on the dock raised themselves and began to unload the boxes from the *Marie Christine*.

The man with the cart shook hands with Father Holmes. 'I'm Short John, Father,' the man said. 'On account of my height.' Song smiled. The man was a good head taller than Father Holmes, broad-shouldered and with a thick crop of hair that made him seem even bigger. 'Welcome to Bartica,' he said.

'Pleasure to meet you, Short John.'

'Sorry 'bout running late, especially seeing you'se a Father. Been working all night. I'se a drummer. We be the B Town Troubadours. B Boys everyone calls us. Steel music and smokin' songs. You'd be welcome any time at Ruby Lou's. Play there most nights. It might not be the kind of 'stablishment you usually show up in but Bartica's a colourful kinda place. Like pretty church glass. If you really want to get to know the town come one night to Ruby Lou's. Rest your head on our music.'

Song didn't understand what Short John was talking about but he loved the way his words fizzed. He wanted to go to Ruby Lou's and hear the smokin' music. Melodies, he imagined, that could make you feel like you were somewhere else, like Hai's or Jinda's stories, or Father Holmes' books.

'You'll be welcome anytime at St Ethelbert's,' Father Holmes said.

'I might just take you up on that, Father. Been a while since I stepped foot in a church and it wouldn't do the soul no bad to do so once in a while.'

Short John turned to Song. 'And you are?'

'I'm Song.'

'With a name like that you can join me on stage. I bet you sing like an angel.'

Song pulled a face. 'I can't, but I can whistle.'

'That'll do,' Short John said. 'The best songs don't have no lyrics. Lyrics just make the world a sad and lonely place.'

Once the cart was loaded Father Holmes sat up beside Short John and Song squashed himself behind them both. He did not want to miss a word. He loved the way this man spoke so melodically, like the poetry he and Father Holmes read together, but this was even more soulful because it was real life.

'Not an easy town for a man like you, Father, no offence mind,' Short John said, shaking the reins. 'Tinkers, traders, two-timers. Loan sharks who like to keep it in the family. Kill you for a tin pot. You'll get a lot of the brothel women down your way I should imagine. Wailing on your doorstep.'

'That's why I'm here,' Father Holmes said. 'My door is open to anyone who wants to walk through it.'

'Nice to hear that, Father. There's goodness even in the bad folks, but not everyone 'preciates that. Hope. That's what makes Bartica special. Might be a tough town but it ain't low on hope. Surprisin' really. So many people let down so many times. Hard to imagine there'd be any hope left here but they keep on going on hoping. And that's why they keep on listenin' to us B Town Troubadours, I reckon. That's my theory anyways. We dream up songs so sweet no man alive could fail to hope they might at least come part true.'

Short John turned his head to Song. 'That's what I mean about lyrics and songs, boy. You carry on whistling.'

Song smiled back at the big man he already liked. Short John talked enough for a congregation. Song thought about what he'd said about Bartica: tough but not low on hope. Like Song wanted to be.

The light was fading as they reached the bungalow beside St Ethelbert's. Short John pointed at the building. 'That's it. That's your new home.'

It was a small sleepy-looking building with a crumpled pitched roof. There was a hammock slung across the corner of the broad porch and rocking chairs on either side of the door. A woman came out, skinny and dark like molasses. She wore a white apron over a faded blue dress and her skin sagged in creased folds around her knees.

'Welcome, Father. And you must be Song. I'm Jingy. Now come in and eat. It's on the table. You can unpack tomorrow. Don't think about your things tonight. Short John will bring the boxes in. Short John, bring the boxes in. You must both be exhausted. It's good to have you here finally. Welcome to your new home. We've been waiting for you.'

Home. Song looked around at the dark wooden walls, the whitewashed ceilings, the big open windows, and thought with relief, with joy, how this was to be his new home. A place they would discover together, Father Holmes had said, where they could dream up new adventures.

That next morning after breakfast Song went out to explore his new neighbourhood.

'Don't go far, Song,' Father Holmes called out from his study. 'Be back by the top of the hour.'

Song set out, noticing first St Ethelbert's and its cemetery. The church was much smaller than the one in Georgetown. It wouldn't take him long to sweep the floor or tidy the books in the pews.

He continued down to the river where there was a row of shops: Golden Don's; Everlasting Street Stores; Ruthie's Best Roti Hut; Mickey's Perishables. There were sacks of rice outside Mickey's and Song picked up a few grains to chew on. Short John clattered past in his cart.

'You just wakin' up and I'se goin' to bed,' he yelled at Song. 'Long night playing songs with no lyrics.'

Song waved back and then crossed the road to another line of shops. Song peered into the darkness of the first. A man looked up. 'Buying or selling?'

'Just looking,' Song said.

'No use to me then,' he snorted.

On the back shelf of his shop Song looked at the large glass jars. They were filled with tiny clear stones.

'Diamonds, boy. I'll tell you something.' The man beckoned to him and opened his clenched hand. There were a dozen stones in his palm. 'The eight-sided cut. Light dances like flames. Take one.'

Diamonds. This is what Song had been looking for. He imagined his sisters' and brothers' faces as he might have reached into his pockets to share with them handfuls of these gemstones. They were more beautiful than he could have imagined. Transfixed, Song reached out to touch one, but the man snatched back his hand, laughing. Song blushed, grateful for the darkness in the room.

'No one's going to *give* you a diamond, boy, remember that. Don't come so easily.'

'I don't want anyone to give me one,' Song said. 'I'm going to find my own someday.'

'I like that,' the man said. 'Then you come and find Old Ivor and I'll give you a fair price. I'm a gold and diamond merchant, not interested in nothing else. Nothing else worth being interested in.'

'Can I see some gold?' Song asked.

'You don't know much, do you? Boy who's never seen gold, heh?'

'I've just arrived from Georgetown. With the new vicar, Father Holmes.'

'A lot to learn then, I'll say,' Old Ivor said. He reached into his pocket and pulled out a rolled-up swatch of cloth. 'Always keep gold on me,' he said. 'Can't trust your own brother in a town like this.'

Old Ivor unpeeled the cloth and Song watched on, hardly breathing. Inside was a misshapen lump of gold. Song was trembling inside.

'This here's a good-sized nugget. Keeping it on me till the price goes up. Don't want to keep it on you too long though. Set yourself a price, and sell it as soon as it comes around. Don't hang on to it for a minute longer. That's the difference between a good merchant and a bad merchant, being alive or dead.'

Gold. Finally. Gold and diamonds. This was what Zhu Wei had been speaking about all those years ago. This was the place. Now he had to find a way to put both in his own hands.

Song looked around Old Ivor's shop. A set of scales hung from string above the counter with small weights loaded on each dish. There was an open ledger on a table; written inside were long columns of numbers, and there was a sharpened pencil and an eyepiece resting on the page.

Old Ivor seemed to read Song's mind. 'You don't need much to set up as a merchant,' he said. 'That's the beauty of it. Just need to know when to buy and when to sell.' He tapped his nose. 'I can smell the right time.'

'I don't want to be buying or selling,' Song said. 'I want to do the finding.'

'Ah, a pork-knocker, that's what you're in the making, and you don't even know it.'

Song furrowed his brow.

'Pork-knockers. That's what we call gold prospectors here. Don't know why. Funny name come to think of it, must be the diet of salt pork upriver. Anyway, the name's stuck. They're a funny lonesome lot. Spend most of their lives in the interior, only coming back once in a while to cash in.

'Where do they go?' Song asked.

'Upriver, that's all,' Old Ivor said. 'Can't be more specific than that. A place for dreamers.'

'I'm going there,' Song said.

'You do that. You hurry up so you can come back with your diamond or nugget and sell it to me before I peg out. I'm getting on, you know.'

Song walked back outside into the bright light of the street and thought about the place Old Ivor called 'upriver'. He wanted to know how to get there. He had come this far, but there was further to go to make good on his promise.

Song carried on down the street. There was another shop with a sign that read: 'Old Copper Pence, Moneylender', followed by a dank rum shop. Heat billowed out from a blacksmith. Clunk-clunk-clunk, hiss. Song watched a glowing rod cool in the inky water. It smelled of tar and ash.

Stray dogs wandered the streets. One was almost bald and its pink skin was speckled black. A little girl carried a puppy close to her chest. She stuck her tongue out at Song. He smiled, and she pouted.

There was one very large house with its shutters pinned right back. A woman sat outside on the balustrade. She wore a green dress and her fingernails were painted.

'Hey child, what you doing out of school?'

'I don't go to school, ma'am,' Song said.

'How old are you, not to go to school?'

'I'm twelve.'

'Then you should be in school. School's more important than you might think.'

'We only arrived last night.'

'Where d'you arrive from?'

'From Georgetown.'

'Big city child, huh? What your father do?'

'I'm with Father Holmes at St Ethelbert's.'

'A preacher?'

'Yes, ma'am.'

'If this town don't need one thing— Say, what you make of this town?'

'I like it.'

'What you like about it?'

'Short John. And Jingy. Everyone talks a lot. Fowl Man with the chicken laugh. And Joseph's gold teeth'

'What's your name?'

106

'Song, ma'am.'

'You sing?'

'No, ma'am.'

'That's not much good then, having a name like Song. You should be a singer. Ever tried?'

Song shook his head. 'But I can whistle.'

'Can't make a living whistling,' she said. 'No lyrics in a whistle. I'm Lady. And this here is Ruby Lou's. If folk want to hear a song this is where they come. Sweet folk, tired folk, folk 'bout ready to finish up living – they all come here.'

'I know about Ruby Lou's,' Song said, pleased with himself. 'This is where there's smokin' music.'

'Smokin' music, that's one way of calling it. Burns you up inside all right.'

Lady started to hum, clicking her fingers, before she opened her mouth to sing.

'Life got you by the throat,
Life got me by the throat,
Life got us by the throat,
And then we all lie down and die.'

'That's sad,' Song said. He thought of his own family.

'People don't want to hear happy songs, you'll learn that. They want to hear how it's worse for someone else.'

'I want to hear happy songs.'

Lady laughed. 'You're a bit different, Song. With your pretty name and your pretty ways. You be careful about this town. It ain't always kind to boys like you.'

'Why's that?'

She lifted her left hand and showed him a ring. 'Diamonds,' she said. On her middle finger was a silver band. The clear stones caught the light. 'They say people drown in that there river for a single stone. I say, pushed more like. Pushed in for diamonds.'

'No one's going to push me in,' Song said.

'I believe it.'

Song walked home a little lighter of step. He liked this town. Coloured with all sorts of folk, living all their different ways. He felt all right here. Like he could call this place home.

Jingy didn't looked pleased when Song walked through the door. 'Where you been so long?'

'Just looking around,' Song said.

'You be careful just looking around,' Jingy said. 'Never know what can find you first. What d'you make of the place then?'

'I like it. I like it a lot.'

'Good. There's a lot of bad things said about Bartica but it ain't all that way. There's a lot of deep down kindness. Everyone looking out for everyone else. Until someone breaks the chain. Not breaking the chain, that's the thing.'

Song thought he understood. He wanted to be part of Bartica, looking out for everyone else, everyone else looking out for him. He wanted to believe what Jingy said.

She started to take off her apron. 'We goin' catchin' crabs now. You ready? I'm going to take a roundabout way to the river so I can introduce you to a few people.'

As they stepped out, Jingy raised her hand and waved at a man on the other side of the street. 'That there is Don of Golden Don's,' she said. 'Gold merchant, obviously. Not to be trusted but he won't do folks like us any harm. Ah, but here's one you can trust, at least with your dirty clothes. Afternoon, Mr Chow.'

The man was small, both short and slight, in fact not much taller than Song. He nodded towards Song. 'Afternoon. And who's this?'

'Song,' she said. 'Boy that came with Father Holmes.'

'You're a lucky boy. You got the best washerwoman in town, you know that? No gossip and doesn't leave a shadow of a stain. Too good for me. I've been offering her a job as long as I can remember but the lady thinks she's too good for this here 'stablishment. And she'd be right.'

Jingy smiled. 'Quit that.'

'Mr Chow runs the best laundry in town,' Jingy said, after they passed. 'And that there is Louis'. Town's main storekeeper.'

Song stared at the brute of a man by the doorway. 'Is that Louis?'

Jingy laughed. 'Louis is smaller than me. That's Bronco.'

'What does he do?'

'Helps look after the store.'

Song looked at the scars on Bronco's face. The left side of his mouth had been split at one time and hung lower than the right. 'Is he a fighter?'

Jingy tsk-ed. 'Nothing exciting about fighting if he was.'

A few doors down was a colourful shack painted sky-blue with yellow window frames and a pink sign which read 'Josie's'. The door and windows were wide open. Inside Song saw two young girls slopping the floor clean with mops and buckets of soapy water. He recognised one as the girl with the puppy that had stuck out her tongue at him. They both waved at Jingy.

'Hi Maia, hi Clio,' Jingy called. She lowered her voice. 'Rough bar. Josie's had it hard. Banged about all her life. She's done well to bring up three sweet girls alone. Poor mites. They don't stand much chance in life. It's hard to change the stripes of your family. You be friendly to them. They live only one down from us.'

Song thought of his own family. And how he had left them for a chance in life. 'Every boy should travel,' Zhu Wei had said. 'Go and see new places. See the world.'

Jingy interrupted his thoughts. 'You watch and do what I tell you,' she said. They had arrived at the edge of the river.

Song watched in amazement as the wiry old woman clambered down the side of the dock. She wedged the bony fingers of one hand into the niches between the wooden planks while with the other she snatched at crabs with a long net. Some got away, scuttling out of reach or falling into the water with a splash. Jingy swore blue each time she lost one.

Once she had one netted, it snapped and twisted, trying to untangle itself from the mesh. Jingy scooped the net upwards, passing the handle towards Song who, in turn, tried to flip the crab out into the basket.

'Use your hands,' Jingy shouted, as she watched Song banging the net against the side of the basket. 'It won't come out that way. And crabs with headaches don't taste good.'

Song obeyed, and yelped as the creature's snapping claws drew blood. He sucked the nicks on his hands.

Jingy laughed. 'You'll learn. Catch it on its back where it's smooth. Behind the eyes.'

Song tried again but another claw caught him.

Jingy laughed again. She had caught half a dozen females before the hour was out, throwing the males into the water in disgust. 'Make sure you get them with that triangle,' Jingy said, pointing at their soft underbellies. 'You don't want the males. Flesh's not so sweet and no eggs neither.'

They walked home with a full basket of six large crabs, each deep violet in colour. Song kept tapping at them with a stick as they tried to clamber out.

'You don't have to worry,' Jingy said. 'Let them be. One climbs up, another pulls it down. Crabs don't like other crabs getting up. Bit like folk. Gotta fight your way up against everyone.'

That night Father Holmes and Song ate crab backs for supper. 'Lovely,' Father Holmes said. 'Good job out there.'

'Jingy caught most of them. She's so quick.' Song lowered his voice. 'How old is she, Father?'

'You can't ask that, Song,' Father Holmes said. 'It's not polite.'

Jingy carried in a plate of pine tarts. 'Two hundred and thirty-seven.'

Song blushed.

'Serious,' she said. 'Oldest washerwoman in town but with the softest hands.' She put down the plate and spread out her pink palms for them to see. 'Only one sure thing you'll die with is your body. Got to look after it. Warm coconut oil every night.' She rubbed her hands together.

Before they'd finished dinner, two men had arrived at the house.

'Good timing, gentlemen,' Father Holmes said. 'We're just finishing up. Song, this is the police chief, Tom Jameson, and Mr Edward Hoare, who works at the taxes and weights office.'

Song looked at the two men. Tom was too slight to be convincing as the PC and his white uniform was a size too big, which shrunk him even more. He smiled a warm lopsided smile out of one corner of his mouth.

Edward Hoare was in better proportion except for his ears, which stuck straight out of the side of his head. His hair was slightly too long, perhaps to disguise the imperfection. He was wearing brown slacks and a cream shirt with the initials E.F.H. sewn on the breast pocket.

'Good evening,' Song said, rather overawed by the station of the two men.

'Bring us some crab backs out to the front porch, will you, Song?'

Song carried some plates to the three men, who had already arranged themselves on the porch and begun their conversation. Song retired back into the house but didn't go far. He wanted to listen in and find out more about the ins and outs of Bartica life.

'Gave up on this district long ago,' Tom sighed. 'Haven't given up on God, but gave up on Bartica a long time since. I'm afraid to say it straight, but this city's wasting your time, Father.'

'It's a city like this that needs me most,' Father Holmes said.

'He's right, Tom,' Edward said. 'It might be bad for a policeman but it's not the same for a vicar. And there's a kindness here you won't find in many places in the world.'

'Kindness? Are you kidding?' Tom said. 'Listen to me, Father. I know this town better than most. There might be only two hundred people living here officially but there's about five thousand passing through. We got thirty-nine licensed drinking stations. That's licensed mind you, imagine the real number. There's fifty brothels at least, and rum shops, bottle shops, late-night music halls, gambling houses, liquor windows. Liquor's cheaper than rainwater.'

'There's no point me working among a town of angels,' Father Holmes said. 'My door is open to anyone willing to walk through it.'

'Too busy whoring and gambling and killing to walk through your door,' Tom said. 'I'm being straight with you, Father. This town don't need a man like you and it don't need a man like me neither. That's the truth. Bartica takes care of its own troubles. Revenge. That's the law. Bobbing up and down in the river the next day, carved across the throat.'

Song remembered how people said that of the Pearl River, too. Perhaps it was true of all rivers.

'This man deals too much with murder, Father,' Edward said. 'It's eating him up from the inside.'

'The job can't be easy, Tom—'

'Just hate to see you wasting your time, that's all I'm saying. So many good folk out there. Who knows why they sent you here.'

'I asked to be moved here.'

The police chief whistled. 'Must be a man of God. No gentleman would come here of his own accord. Not who didn't have killing in their blood already. Some say it's the worst posting of anywhere. In the whole world.'

Perhaps Tom Jameson hadn't seen life on a boat, Song thought. He knew about men with killing in their blood. On the *Dartmouth*, just before the end of the voyage. Killed playing cards after months of scraping by. A quick knife in the chest and it's all over. Could it be as bad as that in Bartica?

'I'm here,' Edward said. 'Of my own accord.'

Edward's words made Song feel better. Another one of the surprising folk who made up this town, he thought. Edward Hoare wasn't a big man, nor a strong man, but he was clearly unafraid.

'That you are,' Tom said. 'And there are some things in life with no rhyme and no reason. You're one of them, Edward.'

There was a laidback looseness to the conversation between the three men, and Song wished he could join them eating crab backs in the evening cool. Perhaps in a few years, he'd be allowed to sit there rocking on the porch, talking back and forth like they were. Father Holmes asking him his thoughts, all of them sharing news of their day.

'You're here too, Tom,' Father Holmes said. 'Why are you still here? It sounds like you've done your time. You could get a transfer if you wanted.'

'You're right, Father. I'm ashamed to say I'm another one who can't explain their choices in life. I just can't imagine myself anywhere else now. Seven years. Seven years and it's worse than when I started. What does that say about the effectiveness of this police chief?'

'And the DC?'

'Nobody sees much of William Wright,' Edward said. 'He's a nice enough man but keeps himself to himself. He must be counting the days. He hates it here.'

'Waste of a salary, between you and me,' Tom added.

Jingy approached, and jumped when she spotted Song in the shadows.

'What you doing?'

'Just listening,' Song said.

'You be careful just listenin',' Jingy said, dropping her voice. 'Nothing less interesting than some rumour circulating like a roundabout breeze with no sense of direction.'

'They're just talking—'

'Maybes. Perhaps. Did you hears. Every whisper becomes a half-truth and a town's no good if it's built on half-truths,' Jingy said. 'It's time for your bed. You've done enough just looking and just listening for one day.'

Jingy's voice was firm and Song wasn't sure if he was going to be punished. 'I'm sorry.'

Then Jingy pulled Song to her and hugged him close. 'You ain't had much affection, had you? Squeeze 'em like a lime, my sister used to say. Add enough sugar and they'll taste sweet.'

Song felt relieved Jingy wasn't angry. But he also squirmed in her arms. She let go and pushed Song towards his room.

'You make sure you shut your window, don't forget. Or the bats'll come in and suck your blood.'

CHAPTER 8

T he first Sunday in Bartica was not that different to Sundays in
Georgetown. Father Holmes and Song arrived at church several hours before the start of the service. Song ensured the correct
numbered hymns were displayed on the board, and placed a hymn
and a prayer book at each place.

The difference was that the congregation here was small. Jingy
sat in the front pew in a dress printed with tiny purple flowers and
a wide-brimmed straw hat with a matching band of the same material. She pointed out the diminutive figure of Paul Nutt to Song,
'a weary, lonely, educated man' who, she told him, taught history
and French at the elementary school. There was also Edward Hoare
and the district commissioner, William Wright, who Song thought
disappointingly ordinary; he would have been tall if he had stood
up straight, but he was slightly hunched over and with a distant
look in his eyes. Tom Jameson showed up; Song remembered how
he'd said that he hadn't given up on God. Song didn't know himself if he had taken on God. He wanted to believe what Father
Holmes believed to please him. But the idea of a single man being
the son of God seemed too strange, too far-fetched. He preferred
the idea of praying to his grandparents, his own father, to help him
through life.

Halfway through the service, Short John turned up. He didn't
arrive quietly but knocked into a pew with his big frame, calling

out 'sorry' to Father Holmes mid-sermon, to apologise both that he was late and loud.

'Don't say I didn't tell you, Father,' Tom said after the service.

'It's only the first week, Tom,' Father Holmes replied.

'Hate to tell you this, but the town is still drunk from the night before. Church couldn't be scheduled on a worse day. Sunday morning after a Saturday night. Whose idea was that?'

Father Holmes smiled. 'The same one who created the world and needed a day of rest.'

'Day of hangover. You might get one or two women down here if they've had a slow night. They'll probably come praying for more business. That's what'll be going on in their pretty heads.'

'I'd be glad if they came, no matter the reason,' Father Holmes said. 'This town's getting you down, Tom. Perhaps you need some help at the station.'

Short John turned to Song and said in a lowered voice. 'What do you think, Song? I think he needs a woman.'

Song allowed himself a smile. Short John made him feel like he was a man already. Song nodded. 'I think he does.'

Song looked down at his cold scrambled eggs.

'You finish that,' Jingy said. 'You ain't leaving till it's all eaten. Nobody can think without food in his belly.'

Song's stomach was knotted. He rushed down the last few mouthfuls.

'You go and see Father Holmes when you're done,' she called out from the kitchen.

Song passed into the hall and glanced in the mirror. The knot in his tie was not sitting flat. He pressed it down, then licked his palm and parted his hair before he walked into the study.

'You look fine,' Father Holmes said. 'Nervous?'

Song shook his head.

'I have something for you.' Father Holmes opened a drawer and took out a fountain pen. He held it out. 'It's a serious matter, a first day of school.'

Song took it in his fingers. It was heavy, with a gold band around its middle. He gently removed the lid. The nib was fine like a needle. He felt a rush of gratitude, not only for this but for everything Father Holmes had given him. He managed a 'thank you,' but his voice broke as he spoke.

Song felt Father Holmes' hand on his shoulder. 'I don't have to, but would you like me to walk with you?'

'That's okay. I know how to find it.'

St Peter's was on the miners' road leading out of town. It wasn't a long walk but Song ran all the way; as he did, he beamed, and found himself shouting out loud: 'I'm going to school, I'm going to school, look at me, a plantation boy, a houseboy, going to school.'

He arrived early, so early that nobody else was there. The building was painted yellow with dark brown window frames and fretting along the eaves. Above the main entrance, painted in white, was a sign that read: St Peter's Elementary, Middle and Secondary School.

Song waited nearby in the shade of a rain tree until other children had arrived before he walked through the gate and into the grounds. His heart was racing. Many of the other children seemed to know each other; Song kept to himself until a teacher assigned him to the class of Mr Nutt, who Song already knew from church. 'Classroom M for Middle,' the teacher said. Song passed E and S, peering through the doors at the students sitting in rows and waiting patiently for lessons to begin, before entering his own classroom.

He took a seat beside a boy with a mass of black tangled hair – the kind Jingy would have warned was full of fleas – and a crooked mouth which made him look friendly. His uniform was clean but too small for him.

'So you're that vicar's boy?'

Song nodded. He had started to feel itchy.

'I'm Cecil Pereira. My ma owns Ruthie's Best Roti Hut. What's your name?'

'I know that place. I'm Song.'

'Song what?'

Song surprised himself with his answer. 'Song Holmes,' he said. It felt good to say it out loud.

Cecil nodded in approval. 'Do you know Mr Nutt's first name?'

'Isn't it Paul?'

'Paul. Paul Nutt. P. Nutt. Peanut.' Cecil grinned. 'Get it?'

Song smiled back at him.

Mr Nutt walked into the room and the children fell silent.

'Open your books, please,' he said. 'First page. Everyone read on your own. Look up when you've finished up to the end of the chapter so I know when you're all at the same point. Start now.'

Song took his index finger and followed the words on the page, line after line, left to right, as quickly as he could. He could barely contain his excitement for where he was and what he was doing. When he read the last word on that first page, he quickly looked up at Mr Nutt. Nobody else had yet done the same.

At break time Song sat on the wall and watched the boys play cricket. The bowler delivered a fast ball, and the batsman defended it. Cecil Pereira was wicket-keeping. As Song studied the game, a girl suddenly appeared before him who he recognised as Maia from Josie's bar.

'Hello. You're the boy at the vicarage. Why aren't you playing cricket?'

Song felt shy in front of her. 'I don't know how.'

'It's not very hard. So, how's it living with a preacher?'

'With Father Holmes? It's everything I could hope for.'

'Isn't it a bit strange? Is he strict? I think he's scary.'

Song was amused that Father Holmes could be scary. 'He's not. He's kind and patient and generous.'

'Still, it must be a bit strange,' she said. Then she ran off, as quickly as she'd appeared. 'See you around!' she called back over her shoulder. Song watched her from afar as she tucked her dress into the elastic of her panties and started flinging herself up on the palms of her hands, walking upside-down in figures of eight. Song stared at her skinny flailing legs and her arched back.

The schoolyard was an expanse of dirt mostly cleared of trees but with thick dark forest on two sides. One side faced the road. Every so often a cart trundled past loaded with miners and equipment. The men stared out into the schoolyard. Song thought how some looked no older than himself. He was glad to be there in the schoolyard, preparing to return to a classroom, but was also curious about where they were going, what they would be doing. One of the men called out a name, trying to get the attention of some kid too involved in a game to notice. Some of the smaller children waved back anyway.

In a branch hanging above him Song caught sight of parakeets the colour of fresh limes. He loved these birds. They were always so friendly, and he felt lonely sitting there in the schoolyard. He put his palm to his mouth and began to mimic their call.

The birds chattered back.

A boy walked over to Song. He had uniform trousers on but was wearing the wrong shirt. He stooped as he walked, like Jinda had, and at that moment Song wished his old friend was also with him on this first day of school.

'What you doing?' The boy asked.

Song pointed. 'Parakeets.'

The boy sheltered his eyes from the sun and looked into the tree. He looked puzzled. 'Can they understand you?'

Song brought his hand to his mouth and released a series of high-pitched chirrups.

Again the parakeets chattered back.

The boy turned to him with bright eyes. 'Who taught you that?'

'Father Holmes,' Song said. 'That's who I live with. I can do lots more impressions.' Suddenly Song felt the urge to tell his new friend everything. 'We've got a bird book, too. I can show you if you come over.'

'Sure,' the boy said. 'I'm Jon Swire. I can draw.'

'We need someone who can draw. I'm Song Holmes.'

Jon came over after school the next day.

'This is Jon Swire, Father. He can draw really well. He's going to illustrate our bird book.'

'What good news,' Father Holmes said. 'We need a proper artist for this book, Jon, and I'm glad to know you're one.'

Then Song took Jon into the kitchen to meet Jingy. 'Jingy, this is Jon Swire, my friend from school.' Song savoured those words.

'Nice to meet you, Jon Swire. Hope you've got a good appetite.'

'I do, ma'am,' he said. 'Always, anytime.'

'Good. I'm glad to hear that.'

The pair went to the front yard of the vicarage with the bird book. Song observed Jon's talent with amazement: how he could miniaturise the world around him on a blank piece of paper. The image of a bird lost none of its life on a page. He was quick and accurate. Song loved watching him sketch: the curve of a head, the point of a beak, the shape of a wing.

'How do you know how long to make the tail?' Song asked.

Jon flicked his wrist. 'You just look, and then you draw,' he said simply.

One day Jon asked Song over to his house after school. They took the long way round, stopping to see Lady. Of all the people in Bartica she was Song's favourite. He had taken to running her errands and bringing her cakes.

'Hey Lady,' Song called out, as the pair arrived. He could see her painted pink toenails peeping above the sides of the hammock. 'Cream pie or a pine tart?'

She raised her head and then let herself slump back down again. 'Nothing but a crust for me today. This woman don't deserve nothin' else.'

'I've bought one of each already.' He gave one to Lady.

'Now, what you doin' buying me something I don't need.' She bit into the pastry. 'Mmm, guava jam, sugar sprinkled soft like morning rain. Now, on your way. I'm too ragged to talk today.'

'How about a song?'

'Not from me. But you can peep inside and hear some real music.'

Song and Jon stepped up to the porch. They pushed the door gently. Haunting melancholic music swirled out, like smoke. Song was entranced. He felt he could almost touch the raw notes.

Lady's voice was drowsy. 'Makes me feel all the more worn. Hung out like laundry. Too many pork-knockers in town.'

'Anyone found any gold?' Song asked.

'Those men are as full of made-up stories as they are real ones. Telling me about places so far up the Rupununi you're no longer in British Guiana but in Brazil, where gold just about bleeds out of the ground. Cathedrals and tiered theatres deep in the forest bigger than anything in the cities of Europe; shops selling feathered hats and trinkets and reels of coloured ribbons long enough to reach the moon and back. Don't believe a word of it. Nobody cares about those good-for-nothings. Not the wives, not the kids. Not these women, neither. We all want to see the back of those men with their big stories and bad breath and bloodshot eyes. Let them fill up their boats with rice, salt pork and oil, and be gone. Good riddance.'

Song and Jon carried on down the road. They passed Louis' store and Bronco clipped Jon around the ear for eyeing a soursop. At the dock Joseph showed them his bucket of fish. There was an eel squirming among the catches.

Jon's house was on the poorer Mazaruni side of Bartica, furthest from the Essequibo. It was a large ramshackle house with broken boards and flaking paint. The yard was heaped with junk. Out front, Jon's baby sister Sonia was alone and crying. Jon picked her up and she grew quiet. Inside they heard a woman and man arguing.

'Sorry,' Jon said. 'That's Mama's friend Kiddo. We can sit out here for a bit. I told her you were coming.'

Song shook his head. 'It doesn't matter.'

'They don't always fight. Sometimes it's nice.'

The two boys played with little Sonia, swinging her around by her wrists. She wailed whenever they stopped, so Song swung her around again and again, happy to hear her endless chuckling.

'She's got worms,' he said, pointing at her bloated stomach.

'Maybe,' Jon said. 'The doctor that came by said she should have more milk.'

Suddenly Kiddo burst out of the house, thumping his shoulder against the frame of the door. He was tall, gaunt in the face and with thick wavy hair. Only one mismatched button of his red shirt was done up. There was a light fuzz on his chest.

Song stopped swinging Sonia. He lifted her up to sit on the edge of the porch.

Kiddo looked at Jon. 'What are you doing here?' He threw his empty bottle at Jon and it hit him on the shoulder, then bounced off and struck Sonia's face. She was still for a second, then her eyes widened and she screamed.

'Shut up,' Kiddo shouted at her.

Song was angry, but at a loss as to what to do. Sonia continued to scream, too little to know she had better stop or might face more abuse from this grown man. Song thought of Mr Carmichael. The same kind of man.

Jon's mother came out of the door. The skin above her eye was split. 'Baby,' she cried out, looking at Sonia. She turned on Kiddo 'What you do to her?'

'Leave off, woman.' Kiddo tripped down the steps of the porch.

Jon's mother picked up Sonia and bounced her on her hip. 'Who've you brought home, Jonny?'

'Song,' Jon said. 'Like I told you.'

'Did you? Don't remember.'

'I did.'

'Well, you're late. What you been doing?'

'Nothing. We came straight.'

'Don't lie.'

'Don't lie to your mother,' Kiddo shouted.

Jon pulled a face. 'I ain't lyin'. What you got for dinner?'

Jon's mother was patting the cut above her eyebrow with the back of her hand. She saw it was bleeding. 'That's nice, ain't it? You just come home and want dinner straight. S'pose you want some for your friend, too.'

'Damn charity,' Kiddo said. He had laid down on his back in the yard, squinting at the sky. Sonia was still screaming. 'Shut that kid up,' he said again.

Song and Jon both spoke at the same time: 'I told you he was coming, Mama,' Jon said, as Song said: 'It doesn't matter. I need to get home anyway.'

'Well, we ain't got nothing. What's your name again?'

'I'm Song.'

'Pleased to meet you, Song. I'm Jonny's mother. Now he didn't say we had guests coming, so we ain't got enough to go round tonight. You'll have to go on home.'

Song couldn't bear to leave Jon and Sonia there with Kiddo. But he was also glad to be ordered home. 'Yes, ma'am,' he said. 'I'm sorry if I bothered you.'

'Lady man,' Kiddo muttered.

Jon looked at Song. 'Sorry.'

'See you tomorrow,' Song said.

Kiddo tried to grab at Song's ankle as he passed but Song was too quick. He was running as fast as he could. But he felt smashed up inside knowing now that it was true, that Bartica had men like this.

Back at the vicarage, Father Holmes was eating alone. He looked up at Song and smiled. 'You were quick. Everything all right?'

'Fine, thanks,' Song said.

'You eaten?' There was a tureen of chicken stew on the table.

'Yes,' Song replied.

'Want to join me while I finish up?'

Song sat down in his usual place. 'Can Jon come and live with us?'

Father Holmes chewed slowly on his mouthful. 'Does he want to?'

Song hesitated. 'I don't know.'

'Why do you ask?'

'I just wondered if he could.'

'I would have thought Jon's mother needs him at home.'

Song said nothing.

'You can bring him for dinner as often as you like,' Father Holmes said.

Song looked at the dish of chicken stew and thought how much he had in his life now. There was always enough to eat. He wished he could do more for his friend. He knew Jon had it hard at home.

Song also thought of Lady. Forever saying she was all right, pretending she didn't need anything, but always glad, always grateful for something sweet. All these friends with so much less than him.

The next morning, still weighed down by the day before, Song stopped by Louis' to buy something for Lady. Outside the store, there was a girl untying trays of cakes loaded on the back of her bicycle. Song noticed the icing sugar down the front of her dress. She clumsily loosened the trays and Song watched a half-dozen biscuits fall to the ground. They broke on landing. He heard the girl grunt in frustration. He grinned at her funny ways, glad to smile. She was too busy to see Song. As he wondered who she was, he saw the words painted on the side of her bicycle: Mary Luck's Lucky Bakery. She must be Mary's daughter.

Song sped in and out of Louis' to pick up a bag of fritters. But when he came back out into the street the girl was already gone, and he wished she wasn't. He rushed on to find Lady. She was lounging on a Berbice chair with her knees on the leg rests. He handed her the bag of banana fritters. Before she'd had a chance to protest, he spoke. 'Lady, tell me what you think of Kiddo?'

'He's a dog,' she said.

'Why's Jon's mama with him?'

'That's what women do.'

'But he hits her.'

Lady nodded. 'Bet he does.'

'She should run away.'

Lady smiled. 'Where should she run away to?'

'Anywhere. Anywhere he can't find her.'

'She won't run. That's a fact.'

Song didn't understand. 'Why not?'

'Women don't run. Don't go nowhere.'

Song shook his head at her answer. Jon's mama had to run. She had to get away.

'You need to stop worrying about everyone else, and start worrying about yourself.' Lady licked her fingers and started to hum. Then she parted her lips and let the languorous words fall out.

> *'At the end of the day*
> *when your bones are tired,*
> *And you ain't no friend in the world,*
> *Hold your head high, don't give up, don't give in,*
> *And walk tall wherever you go.'*

'All the wisdom of the world,' she said, 'is wrapped up in a mother's lullaby. You remember that when you feel like the whole world hates you.'

Song thought of his own mother. He couldn't remember her ever singing to him. When he tried to picture her now, he couldn't see her face. Only the blur of her and his sisters' and brothers' shapes in the distance. He didn't want to forget, but he didn't want to try to remember if he wasn't able.

'You lost, Song? Whatch you thinking about?'

He shook his head. '"You can be collapsing inside but you gotta stand tall." A man once told me that.'

'I like that man,' Lady said. 'Kind of man for me. Where can I find him?'

'He's dead.'

'Course he is,' Lady said. 'Good ones are always dead. You come share your company, Song. It's good for a woman like me to remember there are folk left in the world like you, full of wonder and hope and truth. Carry on living that way and you'll be finer than most.'

'Wonder and hope and truth,' Song softly repeated Lady's words. He liked that. He wanted that to be true.

He continued to school and on his way he bought four pints of milk from Louis'.

He gave them to Jon. 'They're for Sonia. We had spare.'

'Mama won't take it,' Jon said. 'Kiddo told her not to accept any charity. When the doctor came around with medicine he wouldn't let her take any of it.'

'But this is spare,' Song said. 'Say you just got it.'

'From where?' Jon said. 'Maybe you give it to her. She was pretty nice about you after you left. Said she liked your manners.'

During their break the two boys walked over to Jon's house. His mother was on the front porch, her head in Kiddo's lap.

'You brought him again?' she said.

'Not to eat,' Jon said. 'He's got a present.'

Song held up the bag. His voice was trembling. 'We had some spare milk, ma'am, so I brought it for Sonia.'

Kiddo pushed Jon's mother's head out of his lap and stood up. 'Who d'you think you are? We got plenty of milk.'

'Now Kiddo, calm down,' Jon's mother said. 'Boy was just trying to be nice.'

Kiddo walked out from under the shadow of the porch. 'Who asked you for milk, eh?'

'Nobody, sir,' Song said. 'Just had some spare, that was all.'

'Maybe we don't want your spare.'

'Yes, sir.'

'Give that to me.'

Kiddo reached out and grabbed at Song.

'Leave him alone,' Jon cried out.

'You shut up,' Kiddo shouted back. 'You're next.' He held Song around the wrist and with the other hand snatched a bottle out of Song's bag. Then he turned and threw it at the front of the house. Glass splintered and milk splashed over the porch.

'Cut that out,' Jon's mother said. 'Jonny, why you bring him 'round again?'

Kiddo threw a second. It shattered by the door. Milk ran down the walls. Sonia woke up in the hammock and started crying.

'That's enough, Kiddo!' Jon's mother was yelling now.

As Kiddo pulled out a third from the bag, Song grabbed the last bottle and smashed it on to the ground by their feet. Glass and milk exploded over them both. Taken by surprise, Kiddo loosened his grasp. Song took his chance to turn and run. He raced through the yard, through town and towards home without looking back. Back in his room he threw himself onto his bed. His heart was hammering. He pulled his knees up to his chest to look at the nicks and cuts on his shins. In his head he could still hear Sonia's cries. He closed his eyes and tried to remember his mother holding his face between her palms; Ji Liu cradling him when he was so sick; Amalia, careful not to touch the welts on his back; Jingy drawing him close to her, squeezing him like lime.

Song was late leaving the house and Lady was not outside Ruby Lou's. He looked up at her window. The yellow cotton curtains were flapping loosely in the breeze.

'Lady?' He called up in a half-whisper.

Nobody came.

He waited for a few minutes before continuing to the bakery. He bought her a coconut cream pie.

On his way back Song saw a dozen people jostling in the street. He stopped, straddling the frame of his bicycle. All the boys from the dock were there. Neighbours had come out to see what the ruckus was about so early in the day. In the middle of the crowd Ruby Lou was screaming at Jameson.

'Ain't you meant to be running this hell hole of a hell town, Mr Jameson? And where's that goddamn DC? We got thievin' and murderin' strangers coming into 'stablishments like ours kickin' up one hell of a stink leaving us frightened for our lives, bloodying up the place like there's no good respect in these parts any more. D'you think this is law 'n' order, Mr Jameson, 'cause I for sho' ain't callin' it that.'

Ruby's girls were wailing on the porch. Sugar, the skinniest but the loudest, had joined in and was shouting down Tom Jameson. 'You find out who's responsible,' she yelled. 'And you find out quick. Or we'll be taking this into our own hands.'

'Now settle down, ladies,' Tom said. 'We need some calm and reason so we can get to the bottom of this.'

Song caught sight of Joseph. 'What happened?'

'Lady's wound up dead and nobody knows why,' he said. 'Some stranger took a knife to her neck. Of all the girls and it had to be Lady. She was the finest woman in there. Breaks my heart. She was my first, and the first of half the men in this town.'

Song pushed his way out of the crowd. The street was a blur in front of him. He could still hear Sugar shouting. He looked down at the cream pie he was holding and let it fall to the ground.

CHAPTER 9

Father Holmes had taken a trip upriver to do what he called missionary work. That's how he'd explained it to Song, not too unlike what he'd done at Diamond with the plantation boys. He said he'd be teaching the Amerindians who lived in the villages on the banks of the Essequibo. Song couldn't go; Father Holmes had told him he had to stay behind to attend school. Song didn't want Father Holmes to leave, not now, not ever, but he pretended to be unconcerned, even supportive. Privately he hoped that he might join Father Holmes on a trip upriver one day.

While they were apart, Song had been spending time at the jetty. He stopped by after school, or came on Sundays after lunch when the hours passed by slowly and the heat was high.

'Ah, that woman, Lady,' Joseph said, unexpectedly. 'Think of her too often. Some tramp who couldn't pay. Should have at least tried the tables. Can turn handfuls of pennies into handfuls of diamonds with one throw of the dice.'

Song didn't want to hear anything more about Lady. In fact, he was taking himself to the jetty hoping to get away from thinking about her. Of the way she'd been killed. Of the way she used to sing to him.

'Teach me the tables,' Song said, hoping to change the subject.

Dory nodded. 'Wei qi, that's the game. Not hard to understand but impossible to master.'

'Don't matter what it is,' Joseph said. 'S'long as you win. Don't be learning yet though, boy. Not at your age. Can run you into trouble if you know the tricks too young.'

'Teach him poker, man,' Basil said. 'Nothing wrong with a round or two of poker. Play for crabs.'

'Crabs?' Dory sneered. 'No point in that. Lose a crab and you just catch another. No risk, no sport.'

'I'm not teaching no preacher's son the tables' Joseph said. 'And that's that.'

'I don't want to play for money,' Song said, 'not ever.' He was thinking of Dai Jie, who had journeyed all the way around the world only to be killed over a game of cards the night before they left the boat. His death still haunted Song. 'I want to learn to play for fun.'

Joseph wagged his finger at him.

'Dory, teach me wei qi,' Song said.

'Can't neither. I'm a superstitious man. Don't want to end up in hell.'

'Like you not going anyways,' Basil said.

'You ask Mr Holmes. Father Holmes, I mean,' Dory said. 'He'll teach you.'

The rest of the boys fell about laughing.

'He doesn't know how,' Song said, hurt by their reaction. 'But you'd be surprised what he does know.'

'Bet he does know how to play,' Dory said. 'Every man knows, even if he don't admit it.'

'If every man knows,' Song said, 'then I have to learn, too.'

There was a voice from below the dock. 'I'll teach you.'

Song peered down. There was a man untangling fishing line on the lower deck. He was unwashed, wearing torn-off trousers and with a shirt tied around his head. He winked at Song and gave him a crooked smile.

'You don't be teaching him nothing, Jesus,' Joseph said. 'You ain't involved in this here conversation.'

'You come to me, boy. I'll teach you all you need to know 'bout anything you want to know. These boys don't know nothing about nothing. Limin' all day on the jetty, carrying a few tin pots about the place pretending they got a job. You want some edge to your life, you come see Jesus.'

'Stay out of it,' Joseph said. 'This boy's here with us.'

Song didn't know why the jetty boys were being so hostile to this man. Song kept quiet but he was curious. The man they all disliked, who he couldn't believe was called Jesus, seemed to have taken a shine to him.

'Make your choice, boy,' Jesus goaded. 'Wanna end up like this lot? Nothing to show for nothing.'

'Watch your mouth or I'll reshape it for you,' said Basil.

Song wanted to be loyal to the jetty boys but he was intrigued. 'I'm already late,' he said. 'Gotta go. See you all around.'

'You come find me, boy. I'll show you some real-life gamblin'. Not cards. Not tables. Upriver. That's gamblin' for real men. That's what dreams are made of.'

Song was awash with relief when Father Holmes returned home. He had tried to persuade himself each day that Father Holmes might be back before bedtime but doubts crept into his head, crowding out any hopes.

'No need to be so twitchy, sweet child,' Jingy said to Song. 'That grown man can look after himself. All he's doing is taking a boat up and down talking to folks, no different to what he does here 'cept it's on the river. Mark me, he'll come walking into this house some day soon looking for a meal and a wash.'

Jingy was right. That's exactly how it was. Song had just sat down for lunch when he heard the front door open and Father Holmes' voice.

'Song. Jingy. Anyone home?'

Song leapt down from his chair and raced into the hallway. 'You're back, you're back,' he cried out. 'How was your trip? Do you remember every detail to tell me? We're having crab for lunch. Are you hungry? I've been studying hard and I've read so many books; I've got so much to tell you. Jon and I have been working on the bird book. He has it right now but I'll get him to come over and show you.' Song was breathless.

Father Holmes laughed. 'I look forward to seeing it – and to hearing all your news,' he said. 'I've got a lot to tell you, too, Song. You'd have loved this trip. There's so much energy in the forest, so many sounds, the howlers, the screaming piha, I woke up every day to the noise, the frantic rhythm. It's another world out there and it makes you feel so alive.'

He opened his arms and Song hesitated for a moment before stepping forward. Father Holmes wrapped him in his arms and Song allowed himself to be held close.

'I've missed you,' Father Holmes said.

Song couldn't find the right words. 'You were gone so long,' was all he could say. He hoped Father Holmes might have known what he hadn't said.

'I'm back now.'

Some weeks later, Song was out catching crabs when Jesus pulled his boat up alongside the bank. Song was pleased to see him again. He had been thinking about real-life gambling. Gold and diamonds. Upriver: that's where Old Ivor said he'd find it.

'Give me one of 'em,' Jesus said, pointing a finger at Song's basket. 'Pastor's son can't turn away Jesus himself.'

Song laughed 'Go right ahead. I've got more than I need.'

'Welcome to the kingdom of heaven, my friend,' Jesus said, peering into the bucket. He pulled out the biggest.

Song noticed the man's skin was breaking out in sores.

'What happened?' Song asked.

'Kabauras,' Jesus said. 'Damn things so small you can't even see 'em. Bite starts tiny too. But itch you so bad you can't sleep.'

Song stared at the scabs. Some had broken open and were infected.

Then he scanned Jesus' boat. 'So did you find anything?' Song asked.

'Me? Sure. The only thing worth looking for.'

'How much?'

'Wouldn't like to say.'

'Come on, Jesus. Show me.'

Jesus cast his eyes around the bank. He pulled a filthy bunched-up rag out of his pocket and unravelled it. A knob of gold glinted against the cloth.

'How much is it worth?'

Jesus sucked the air in between his teeth. 'Twenty bits. Maybe twenty-five. Never one to wait on a price. Crazy dogs the ones who wait. I get it off of me fast as I can. Dangerous to carry gold on you, 'specially in Bartica. Bon Success, Boa Vista, Ciudad Bolivar. I've been to 'em all. But nowhere's for the killing like Bartica.'

'How long were you gone?'

'Found all this in under an hour,' Jesus said. 'Course I been gone a couple weeks. But when you see that first fleck looking up at you like a sunrise you know there's a lot more where that came from.'

Song looked again at the small lump of gold.

'I can teach you everything you need to know about life upriver,' Jesus continued. 'Life of a pork-knocker ain't easy. You're gone

134

most of the year. Come back to cash in, spend a bit of money. A couple nights at Josie's and a few bottles of cassiri. Or buy the room a round at Ruby Lou's. I take three girls upstairs at a time. Spend the rest on supplies for the next trip and then you're gone again.'

Song couldn't follow everything Jesus said but he was beginning to understand the life of a pork-knocker, the high risks, the hand-to-mouth existence. He looked again at the gold in Jesus' hand. 'So this is a lot, is it?' he asked.

'More than your basket of crabs, boy.' Jesus lifted out a second crab. It snapped as he held it up in the air. 'Nothing as beautiful as yellow gold. And there's plenty more out there. Wanna join me, boy? I could do with a hand. Give you a battel for sifting out the gold and you'll soon be on your way.'

Song couldn't deny that he was captivated by Jesus' talk. But he didn't want to bare all. He knew Jesus would keep at him if he thought Song still needed persuading. And Song wanted to learn more about the ways and wiles of a pork-knocker. 'I'll think about it,' he said.

'Best job in the world. Worst job in the world. Any day could be your lucky day. Strike gold and you'll never have to work again. Or you might be found floating down the river. Men kill for half an ounce 'round here. Some less than that. Important thing is never to tell anyone how much you got; only a fool brags.'

Song picked up his basket. 'I'd better be going.'

'They'd be conditions taking you on,' Jesus added. 'Hate talkin'. Kill a man who talks too much. But I'm as fair as they come. I'd give you a wage from the start, and let's face it, you wouldn't be much good to me first off. Couldn't be fairer than that. I'd teach you the rules.' Jesus flashed him a gold-toothed smile. 'The rules are there are no rules.'

Every line Jesus uttered seemed to grab Song harder by the throat.

'Gold in your blood, boy,' Jesus said. 'Fire in your eyes. I know 'em when I see 'em, and I ain't never been wrong.'

Song hurried home. He felt like he'd already shown too much of his hand.

Jingy was on the porch talking to a tall man in a suit. There were trunks and cases beside him.

'Where you been chil'?' Jingy called out. 'That basket better be full.'

'It is,' Song said.

'What took you so long?'

Song hesitated. 'I was talking to Jesus.'

'You don't be speaking to that scoundrel. 'Specially when we got guests. That man's nothin' but trouble. Now this here's Mr Robert Leigh. Come from America to see Father Holmes.'

The man was handsome, clean-shaven and with a broad smile. He wore his cream shirt open at the neck. He put out his hand to shake Song's.

'Pleasure to meet you, Song. So you've been consorting with scoundrels named Jesus? It sounds like I won't be bored in this town.'

'Pleased to meet you, sir,' Song said. 'He's not really a scoundrel. Jingy thinks so because he's a pork-knocker. They're people who look for gold. Are you moving to Bartica?'

'He's a scoundrel all right,' Jingy interrupted. 'That man just got the wrong name. What was his mother thinking? I'd say you're asking for trouble naming someone Jesus. No one's going to live up to that.'

'It's Spanish,' Song said. 'It's common in Spanish. It's actually pronounced "hay-zuz".'

'I don't care if everybody in Spanish is called Jesus, it don't make it no better he got that name,' Jingy said. 'Blasphemy is what it is. You don't go spending time in that man's company. You've got enough to do just looking after yourself.'

'Wise words,' Mr Leigh said. 'Women are the wise ones, Song. That's something you'll figure out. We're just a side-show.'

Song liked the man's slow certain voice. 'Are you really from America, sir?'

'I'm from Buffalo, New York. Know it?'

'Yes, sir. It's on the east coast. I've read *Uncle Tom's Cabin*. Your president is McKinley. The country's built on steel and oil.' Song looked across at Jingy. 'And gold.'

'You're an encyclopaedia, Song,' Mr Leigh said. 'Sounds like you're getting a fine education.'

Song felt his cheeks grow warm. 'What brings you to Bartica, sir?'

'You could call me a pork-knocker of sorts,' he winked at Jingy. 'I'm a metals man. Here to look for new mining opportunities. Silver, tin, bauxite,' Mr Leigh paused, 'and gold, of course. Mind you, I wouldn't turn my nose up at diamonds. I hear they're no harder to find here than your crabs.'

Father Holmes came into sight and Jingy called out to him. 'Mr Robert Leigh's here from America.'

Song watched as Father Holmes hurried towards the house. He was out of breath when he arrived.

'Good morning, Father Holmes,' Mr Leigh said. 'Pleasure to meet you. Robert Leigh's the name. I'm hoping you were expecting me? Governor Johnson said he had written a letter to you.'

The two men shook hands. 'The post in these parts can be unreliable,' Father Holmes panted. 'I've received no letter from the

137

governor, but welcome to the vicarage, Mr Leigh. What can I do to help?'

'The governor suggested I might join one of your trips upriver. I'm researching the mineral resources in the region.'

'I'll do whatever I can to help. You're welcome to stay with us. What are you looking for in particular?'

'From what I hear, the same thing most men roll into this town for. Gold.'

It was a few weeks before the next trip upriver, and in the meantime it was Song's job to introduce Mr Leigh to Bartica. He felt proud to show the American how well he knew the town's streets, its characters, its rhythm. They visited DC William Wright about land registration and Edward Hoare at the taxes and weights office. Song introduced him to the boys at the jetty; Bronco outside Louis'; Louis himself; Mr Chow; Old Ivor, Golden Don and all the gold merchants along Central Street. Everyone was curious. Some claimed the American was just a big-talking small-timing fraud. Others heard he had enough money to buy all the land upriver and kick every pork-knocker to kingdom come.

Each evening, before the mosquitoes rose up in clouds, Song headed to the promontory with Mr Leigh to go fishing, carrying a rod and a bucket of worms. He liked hearing his stories: of buildings so tall they took an hour to walk up; ships made of metal that could carry a thousand people, and a country so big you could walk for a lifetime and still not have even covered one per cent of one per cent of its size.

'Girl's calling out to you, Song,' Mr Leigh said, nodding down the street.

Song looked up. It was Maia. Song could see she was wearing one of her older sister's dresses; it trailed below her ankles and she was tripping up as she walked. 'That's Maia. She's goes to the same school as me.'

Mr Leigh winked at him. 'Maia, huh?'

Song shrugged. 'She's only waving at me because of you, Mr Leigh. She wouldn't have otherwise. She doesn't notice me usually.'

Mr Leigh also waved at Maia, but she didn't wave back. 'I'm not so sure.'

'She's just shy,' Song said. 'Her mother runs Josie's bar so I don't think she likes strangers much. The place is always full of drunks. Jingy says it's the worst kind of bar.'

'Everyone's got to make ends meet, remember that. Anyway you can tell your girl that I'm no drunk.'

Songs squirmed. 'She's not my girl.'

'Treat her nice, Song. That won't cost you anything. Father Holmes won't be teaching you much about one thing, and that's women. Sweetest thing on the planet. Might knock your pride from time to time but that's no bad thing for any man. Find a sweet one and stick with her. Treat her right and she'll stick by you forever.'

Song turned back to look at Maia. She was swinging back and forth on an open gate. He loved watching her play, wildly yet so innocently, unaware of him or anyone watching.

He saw her head turn, as someone called out her name. It was her mama. Song saw Josie beckoning her little girl back home. Then he noticed Josie was outside the bar with Father Holmes. She said something to him, and he laughed blithely. They seemed to be sharing a joke. Song waved but neither noticed him.

'Tell me about your family, Song,' Mr Leigh said.

'What about them?' Song said, still looking down the street.

'I'd like to know more about where you're from. How old are you? How many sisters and brothers do you have? What about your parents?'

139

Song pictured his family sitting in their one-roomed house. His mother. The memory of his father. His sisters and brothers. By now there'd be Xiao Song, too. He took a deep breath before he answered Mr Leigh.

'My father passed on. I have two sisters and two brothers. My mother was pregnant when I left so there'll be one more now. I left when I was nine. I'm thirteen now.'

'Your father would be very proud if he could see you now.'

'I don't know. He's dead anyway.'

'Do you think about them very much?'

'Not really,' Song lied.

'Do you write to them?'

'They can't read. Father Holmes helped me send money home once but I'll never know if it ever arrived.' Song felt sad to hear himself say that out loud, but it was what he thought. The man going to Hong Kong probably died on his ship. It was too far away, too long a trip.

Mr Leigh pressed him. 'Do you want to go back one day?'

'No, sir.'

'Not ever?'

'My family could have come with me, if they had wanted. There were lots of families on my ship.' Song remembered what Hai had said to him: 'Anyway, at least by my leaving it was one less mouth to feed.'

'You weren't just a mouth to feed, Song.'

Song swatted away the comment. He didn't want to answer any more questions. It churned him up too much. He turned the line of questioning on Mr Leigh. 'What about your family?'

Mr Leigh smiled. 'Well, I have a beautiful, unfaithful wife who I still love. And four boys who adore their mother. And a beautiful daughter who had polio and cannot walk very well, but she's an angel. Everybody knows about my wife's philandering except the children. Or perhaps they do know and they're trying to protect me because that's what children do. I guess they know their parents only talk to each other in public. When we're all home she doesn't even look at me. She resents me for taking away her freedom. She resents them, too, for getting in the way of her dreams. She never wanted to raise a family. She wanted to see the world. And now I get to go off to far-off lands, and she has to stay at home. You see, Song, no family is perfect. Like mine, like yours.'

Song was surprised at Mr Leigh's candour, but pleased that the man trusted him enough to confide in him this way. He talked about children as if Song wasn't one himself. Perhaps he was no longer a child, or at least didn't seem to be one to Mr Leigh. Maybe he was toughening up, as Li Bai had told him to.

'I thought you of anyone would have the perfect family,' Song said.

'We ask too much of life,' Mr Leigh said. 'I'm lucky to have five wonderful children. I live in a nice house. I like my job; it pays me well. I'm lucky to have met a fine young man like you, Song. You're lucky too. Remember that. If you believe hard enough that you're lucky, you will be.'

Father Holmes came to Song's room late one evening. Song put his book to one side.

'What are you reading?' Father Holmes asked.

'*Moby Dick.*'

'Again?'

'I love it. I've read it seven times.'

'It's a wondrous, imaginative, extraordinary book. What do you love about it?'

'Ishmael. A wanderer, like me. And Queequeg the harpooner. Do you mind me saying that he sometimes reminds me of you?'

Father Holmes shook his head. 'I'll have to study him more closely.'

'Can I read you a passage?'

'Of course. Please.'

Song had slipped strips of paper between the leaves of the book at points he wanted to return to. He opened it at the one he'd marked with a Q. Then he took a breath and began to read: 'I had noticed also that Queequeg never consorted at all, or but very little, with the other seamen in the inn. He made no advances whatever; appeared to have no desire to enlarge the circle of his acquaintances. All this struck me as mighty singular; yet, upon second thoughts, there was something almost sublime in it. Here was a man some twenty thousand miles from home, by the way of Cape Horn, that is – which was the only way he could get there – thrown among people as strange to him as though he were in the planet Jupiter; and yet he seemed entirely at his ease; preserving the utmost serenity; content with his own companionship; always equal to himself. Surely this was a touch of fine philosophy; though no doubt he had never heard there was such a thing as that. But, perhaps, to be true philosophers, we mortals should not be conscious of so living or so striving.' Song looked up. 'I thought of you when I read that,' he said.

'And I think of you.'

Song blushed. 'Not me, Father.' But Song was touched Father Holmes thought so. Not that he might be like Queequeg, but like Father Holmes. Song continued, trying to deflect the attention. 'Do you remember what it says about where Queequeg from? "It is not down in any map; true places never are." That's how I feel about home. I think if I wanted to get back there, I could never find it.

That's why I can never send money home. Nobody can ever find it.'

'That's not true, Song.'

'I don't think that man who went to Hong Kong found it. We waited, but we never heard back.'

'You're right, we didn't. But we cannot assume he never got there. We must believe he did.'

For a short moment, and for the first time, Song let himself believe the man travelling to Hong Kong had found his family. He closed his eyes and imagined their happiness, his mother's relief, his brothers' and sisters' incredulity, and all the food they would buy with the money the man gave them. But then, too fast, the shadow of doubt fell across Song again. He didn't want Father Holmes to see him falter.

'Maybe he did,' Song said positively, for Father Holmes, not himself, before he lightened the conversation. 'Although let's hope he wasn't on the *Pequod*. That boat makes me feel better about the *Dartmouth*, you know. I wouldn't have much liked to have been aboard that vessel.'

Father Holmes smiled. 'You know so much now, Song. Talking of boat trips, I'm leaving in a few days to go upriver. Mr Leigh will be coming on this trip and I was wondering if you would like to join us?'

Song sat straight up. 'Really?'

'I've wanted to take you on the river for a while now. I know how fond you are of Mr Leigh and it might be nice for you to spend some time upriver together before he leaves. These trips can sometimes be rough though. Do you think you can handle it?'

Song wasn't afraid, not of going upriver. It was so different to going to sea. 'I can handle it.'

'I thought you might say that. You can work on the book. There are hundreds of new birds upriver.'

Song thought about his best friend. This was an opportunity to get him away from Kiddo. 'Do you think Jon can come with us?'

'Jon? Why not? If you think his mother will let him.'

'If you ask her, she will.'

Father Holmes smiled. 'Then I'll ask her.'

Father Holmes reached into his pocket and pulled out something small wrapped in newspaper which fitted snugly in the palm of his hand. 'I think you might find this useful.'

Song unfolded the paper. Inside there was a black-handled pocket knife.

'It's horn,' Father Holmes. 'Open it up.'

Song swivelled out the blade. He thought how this wasn't the kind of present you gave to a child. Mr Leigh's adult talk. Father Holmes' knife. Perhaps nobody saw him as a child any more. He pressed his finger against the sharp edge.

'Careful,' Father Holmes said. 'I'll get the boys to teach you how to skin a labba and scale a fish. The fish upriver are thicker-skinned. The scales can slice off a hand. There's a special technique to avoid cutting yourself. I love the river, Song, and I hope you will too.'

'I will,' Song said.

'You know I was about your age now when I entered the seminary,' Father Holmes said. 'All I wanted to do was to go off and find some adventure. Like this. I'm glad we can do this together.'

'Did you not want to be a vicar?'

Father Holmes became wistful. 'Just not so young, perhaps. I lost some freedom. I don't want you to lose yours.'

Song looked again at this man who had opened up his home, opened up his life to him. He choked down the feelings of love rising inside, not worried about losing his freedom but about losing Father Holmes.

'Going upriver has its risks,' Father Holmes continued. 'You've probably been ready for this trip for some time now. It's me that hasn't been ready to take you. Gosh, you've come to mean an enormous amount to me. Do you know that?'

Song looked steadily at Father Holmes. He didn't reply, but he did know that and he hoped Father Holmes understood how much he meant to Song, too.

CHAPTER 10

Morning slowly coloured the dark river. The depthless water lightened to a pearly grey. The smudge of trees began to create patterns of green. On the bank a family of capybara came to drink, their coarse hairs silvery through the layer of mist. They lapped at the water, eyeing the narrow boats that glided past. Above, a lonely indistinguishable stork sailed against the light. Song felt like he immediately belonged to this mystical place he'd always called 'upriver'.

The party of twelve left before sunrise. This is what Song had long dreamed of. Upriver. Ever since hearing about it from Old Ivor, then Jesus. This is where he'd wanted to be.

In the first boat Song sat with Jon and Father Holmes. Behind them in a second boat were Jim Groves, Bartica's post office clerk, and Dr Foo, who was the town's medical practitioner. Song didn't know either man well. Jingy called Jim Groves a 'bad sort', and said she held him personally responsible for any parcels that went missing at the post office. Which they often did. 'Not to be trusted, that one,' she'd say, when she and Song passed him in the street. He was tall and balding with an awkward gait, usually carrying large sacks of mail on him.

Dr Foo was a large, round-faced man with an easy smile, though he was missing half a dozen teeth at the front. Song always wondered how he could be in charge of helping people get well when he himself looked so unkempt.

Behind their boat, Mr Leigh followed with two fixers. There was a fourth boat laden with supplies roped at the rear. At the back of each boat an oarsman steered with paddles or a pole.

Song munched on dough sticks Jingy had fried earlier that morning. There was a claggy chill in the air. He picked out the quiet whistling of drongos between more unfamiliar cries and cackles. A pair of macaws flapped across the strip of sky above him but the light was still too grey to make out their colours. Monkeys tore up the air with throaty howls.

Around him the trees towered as if they might uproot and morph into beasts. They soared up from the thick dark mulch in search of light. At their ends a filigree of leaves breathed out a swirling mist. Specks of birds billowed up, chattering from their roosts. Like the forest was exhaling, Song thought.

As the hours passed the sun rose higher and beat down on the river. The boats kept close to the banks for shade. Song had drifted off, lulled by the ripple on the surface of the water, to be woken abruptly by light laughter. He looked up and saw more than a dozen children waving and dancing, some with infants on their hips. The women were bare-breasted carrying swaddled babies close to their bodies. Song felt shy seeing the women without clothes, and he didn't stare.

As the boats drew left and slid into the mud, Father Holmes leaned backwards to whisper to Song.

'This is Yupukama,' he said. 'One of the most resourceful villages I've come across. I've been looking forward to bringing you here.'

Father Holmes stepped out and the children crowded around him, calling his name and clapping. He led them across to the open ground and began a service in the clearing. The children started to sing.

Song watched on. It surprised him to come across all these children who felt comfortable enough to call out Father Holmes' name in this way, and who clearly liked him so much. An unfamiliar wave of jealousy passed through him, but he was also grateful to be the boy living with a man so loved. He felt a welling up of pride, increasingly aware of how he had come to think of this man as a father. He loved him.

He turned to the task of the bird book, hoping this might be a way to show him his word, his love. He skirted the edge of the village listening for new calls. Yupukama wasn't large. It was a collection of a few dozen huts, flanked on every side by thick rainforest. The river offered the most light, and the bank was steep down to the water. A few small boats were tied to a short jetty. Song scanned for movement in the branches, venturing deeper into the trees, before he turned back to the village.

Father Holmes was still taking the service. Dr Foo was conducting medical checks, child by child. Mr Leigh was busy speaking to some of the villagers, putting together a smaller expedition to survey the area. Jim Groves was handing out large packages. Song approached quietly. 'Who are they from?' he asked.

Jim looked up. 'Some of the villagers take jobs in town. They buy stuff in Bartica and send it home. Oil, soap, sugar, that kind of thing. I'm a busy man. You run off now.'

Sending things home. Song wished he could be sending things home in the same way. He thought how he would like his family to be receiving a large package of oil, of soap, of sugar.

Back among the huts, Song saw that Jon had found three toucans with clipped wings hopping about the cooking area. They had never seen these birds so close. They clacked their luminous beaks and Jon took his time sketching their form, their colours.

Some of the children were curious. They approached to watch Jon drawing, looking on in wonder.

'I'm Sammy,' one of the boys said in English. Song thought he must be about his age. They were about the same height but Sammy was slightly heavier. His hair was shaggy, long over his eyes, and he had a habit of flicking back his head so that he could see. There was only a cloth tied around his waist.

'I'm Song. This is Jon.'

'So why d'you come?'

'I live with Father Holmes. He wanted to show us upriver. And we're putting together this book on birds. There are so many more birds upriver than in Bartica.'

Sammy nodded. He wasn't the biggest of the children but Song sensed he was the unspoken leader.

'You can come with me, if you like,' Sammy said. 'We're off hunting for labba and tapir. We can teach you how to make curare, if you don't know how.'

'What is it?' Song asked.

'Kills an adult with one drop,' Sammy said. 'Kills a child with a sniff. You need to mix together a hundred different plants. Then you dip in your arrowhead and shoot. You better not touch the poison though. Or you'll be dead like the labba.'

The boys did as Sammy said, mixing together the ingredients he had harvested before dipping in their arrows. Jon hit a monkey which instantly fell out of a tree with a plump thud. The power of the poison shocked them both. Going forward they were even more careful with the sticky black liquid. Song looked down at the dead monkey and felt sorry for it.

'Can you eat it?' Song asked.

'If you get the arrow out quickly. Otherwise, the meat becomes poisonous.'

That evening they waded in the creek pools to catch peacock bass with wire trace using live minnows as bait. They roasted their catches on embers and used the thick bones of the fish to pick their teeth while inspecting each other's skin for leeches and ticks. Song had never felt freer. He wanted to stay on, living out the same life as Sammy and his friends.

'We'll see them in a few days, Song,' Father Holmes said, when they had to leave Yupukama. 'We'll be coming back in a week or so to pick up Mr Leigh.'

Song was glad to hear they'd be returning. Meanwhile he and Jon and the rest of the Bartica party slowly got on their way to head further upriver. For the next week, they passed through a dozen villages, sometimes spending a few hours, sometimes a day.

They travelled along the western bank of the Essequibo, setting up camp on the riverbank, stringing up hammocks between trees. The drapes of mosquito netting hung like thick giant cobwebs in the gloom of the forest. Song lay in the darkness listening to the noise of the bush and the sound of the river. He felt a strange sense of belonging here. Upriver. Like he knew this place from another time, from another life. It was an unusually settling feeling. Believe you'll be lucky. That's what Mr Leigh had said. Believe you'll be lucky and you will be.

On their way back to Bartica they stopped at Yupukama again. Song was happy to be back.

'How was it?' he asked Mr Leigh.

'Indian knowledge, that's what you want,' he said. 'There's plenty of gold here, that's for sure, and they know how to find it.'

'Where is it?' Song asked.

'In the rivers,' Mr Leigh said. 'Deep in the ground, too. Seems like it's everywhere you look. I'll be coming back.'

'I'm glad about that,' Song said.

Mr Leigh gave him a friendly shove, and Song felt pleased to be on such terms with the American.

Then Song saw Sammy. He ran up to him. 'We're back, Sammy.'

Sammy smiled. 'Everyone says they're coming back but not everyone does.'

'I'm always going to come back,' Song said. 'Say, you going hunting sometime? Or fishing?'

'No. Just back. Do you want to find gold instead?'

Song could hardly believe the words he was hearing. 'How?'

'Follow me.'

Song trailed Sammy into the trees till they came across running water. 'Got to find a bend in a stream,' he said. He took up his battel and swirled it around and around, rinsing the shingle from the riverbed in the shallow wooden dish.

'See, here?' he said. Sammy pointed at a glimmer in the dark dish.

Song could see the fine flecks. 'That's it?' He could feel his mouth go dry.

'That's it,' Sammy said. 'It's heavy so it sinks to the bottom.

Song plucked it out of the sediment. It shone in the sun. He felt a lightness pass through his body.

Then Song copied Sammy's actions, mixing a small amount of water with shingle from the riverbed. He swirled it around and around, dish after dish, until Song also saw a glint of gold in the base. He touched it, studying it on the end of his fingertip. It wasn't so hard to find gold, he thought. He could do this. This was only the beginning.

The boys melted their finds together, cooling it quickly in river water with a fizz. Song rushed to show the bead of metal to Robert Leigh who turned it over in his palm, bit it between his teeth and nodded in approval. 'Not quite heavy enough to put on my scales, Song, but you're on your way.'

The plan was to leave later that day and return to Bartica, but Jim Groves came down with a sudden fever. Song watched on as the man sweated and shouted, seemingly in his sleep. At times he shook violently, and thrashed about his arms.

'We're going to stay on and sit out his fever,' Father Holmes said to Song. 'It's serious and Dr Foo says it's the only way he might get better. Are you doing all right though? This is a much longer trip than I expected.'

'Don't worry about me, Father. I love it upriver. I've never been happier.'

'I worry about the risks. Exposing you to fevers like this. After everything you've already been through.'

'There are no more risks here than in Bartica.'

'You're probably right.'

Meanwhile Jon and Song made great progress with the book. Jon spent his days with his pencil in hand. Song tried to concentrate on supporting him but often found himself tagging along with Sammy. He learned to speak a few simple words of Arawak – greetings and niceties. And Sammy improved his English, which was already good; he'd learned what he knew from his father, who he'd accompany from time to time to Bartica for supplies.

'I've never seen you in town,' Song said. 'Where do you stay?'

'On the boat.'

'At the dock?'

'We moor upstream. Dad gets worried about getting too close to town. We only come by to get supplies, things that Jim Groves don't bring. Everyone knows him as a swindler.'

'That's what Jingy says, too,' Song agreed. 'She lives with us at the vicarage. She knows everybody in Bartica and their business.'

'Nobody likes that man. He barters cigarettes, liquor and salt for our gold. But he don't give nobody a fair price. There's some who think he opens our parcels, and sells us what's inside. That man's a full-time cheat.'

'I'm going to tell Jingy that. She'll say she told me all along. You should come and stay with us at the vicarage next time. You'll get to meet her.'

'Dad doesn't like town. Says you can catch fevers there, like the one Jim Groves has. They'll smoke out that room after you've all left. Everyone's afraid of town.'

'That's funny. Everyone in town is afraid of upriver. I guess everyone's afraid of something. Especially if it's something they don't know. Will you try and change your dad's mind? Bartica's not as fun as here but you can come with me to class one day.'

Sammy nodded. 'I'd like that, but I wouldn't be allowed. Dad's strict. Not like Father Holmes. He lets you do anything.'

Song was amazed to hear Sammy say that. 'Does he?'

'Lets you go to school. Lets you come upriver. Lets you come hunting.'

'Guess you're right,' Song said. On reflection, he realised Father Holmes did give him lots of freedom.

'You should ask him if we can spend a night away,' Sammy continued. 'There's a place I could show you and Jon but it's more than a day away.'

'What is it?'

'It's a surprise.'

'Sure you can go,' Father Holmes said when Song asked him.

'It's high time these two boys saw the "smoking place" we call Kaieteur,' said Sammy's father. 'You take Molson and Kai with you, Sammy.'

Molson and Kai might have been older and bigger than Sammy,

but they paid attention to Sammy like he was an older brother. They seemed like quiet sorts, but that was mostly because their English wasn't good. Kai told Song he was actually named after the 'smoking place'.

The five boys left after breakfast and walked the whole day through the forest. Mr Leigh had loaned Song his compass, but Song had already lost all sense of direction.

'You know I don't have any idea where we are,' he told Jon.

'Don't say that.'

'It's okay. We've got the boys. Kai knows where we are.'

Kai was leading the group. He raised his hand as if to acknowledge the statement.

'Sometimes you feel like you're lost but you never are,' Sammy said. 'Trick is not to change your mind. Just got to stick to what you think is the right way. Don't double back. Don't hesitate. Push on.'

While they moved through the forest, they came across birds that neither Song nor Jon had ever seen, even in Mr Matthews' book. The sound was more like an aria than birdsong, as if the birds were improvising scores. Sometimes the boys might catch a glimpse of plumage, but the songbirds never lived up to their melodies. The finest singers were always the dullest creatures: small and dark with indistinct markings, like the loud but tiny dusty-throated antshrike or the extraordinary lowing of the capuchinbird, which was one of Mr Matthews' favourites.

As the afternoon rains approached the light began to fade. Song could hear a low steady rumble.

'Thunder,' he said.

'Not thunder,' said Molson.

Molson was right. It didn't sound like thunder. It sounded like heavy rain, the kind you can hear before you can feel. 'What is it?'

'You'll see,' Sammy said.

They continued walking for another ten minutes before they broke out at a riverbank. The rumble had grown louder.

'This is the Potaro,' Sammy said.

Kai pointed downstream. 'Your thunder.'

Song followed Kai's gaze. 'What is it?' he asked.

'You'll see.'

'Perhaps we should go back,' Jon said. He looked worried. Song put his arm around his friend's shoulder.

The five of them pulled a boat out of the trees which had been hidden in the foliage. Kai and Molson steered them downstream. The river was wide but the current was strong and they kept close to the bank.

The noise continued to grow louder, like the rising calls of a thousand howler monkeys.

'What is it?' Jon asked again.

Song looked ahead. He could see a mist rising on the water. 'Rapids.'

Kai shook his head. 'Not rapids.'

Molson started steering the boat sharply towards the bank and tied up.

'It's too dangerous to get any closer,' Sammy said. 'We'll walk the rest of the way.'

The rumble became a roar. 'If it's not rapids, why can't we use the boat?' Song asked. He was full of anticipation but becoming irritated with the boys for acting so mysteriously.

Molson pointed ahead. 'Kaieteur.'

Song looked ahead. He didn't see anything at first. The river seemed to be moving even more slowly here. There were few rocks to break its flow and there was no indication of rough water ahead. The river was carrying a heavy trunk in its current and suddenly

Song saw the tree tip up and disappear. It was like how he'd imagined the edge of the world might be.

He stared, and then started to run along the bank. Jon was right behind him. As they approached, they saw the river stop suddenly. There were clouds of spray and rainbows like diamonds.

Sammy, Kai and Molson lay on their stomachs and crawled up to the edge of the cliff. Song and Jon copied them, shuffling forward to peer over the edge. The river fell so far down Song couldn't see where it ended. In the mist were tumbling swifts; swooping, rising, darting, sometimes passing through the torrents of water. Song had the sensation he was also flying. Above everything below.

One morning Dr Foo said there was probably nothing more he could do for his patient; they may as well begin the journey back to Bartica. There was a sombre mood among the party but Song didn't feel much for Jim Groves after what Jingy and Sammy had said about him.

As they carried the post office clerk's limp body down to the riverbank, Song turned to Father Holmes. 'Do you think we could stay on?'

Father Holmes raised his eyebrows. 'You and I? Here?'

'I don't mean for ever,' Song quickly added. He didn't want Father Holmes to think he didn't love the home they'd made together in Bartica. 'Just until we finish the book.'

'I think we need to get Jim back.'

'Jim could go back with Dr Foo.'

'I think you two need to get back to your studies. Don't you miss school?'

'Yes,' Song said. He did miss school. But he thought that when he was back at school, he'd miss being upriver more.

'We'll come back another time,' Father Holmes said.

Song fell quiet as their boats pulled away. Sammy and the others stood on the bank. Song watched until the boats turned a bend and the village was out of sight.

Jim Groves died a day before they arrived back in Bartica. Father Holmes gave him the last rites on the river. For the rest of the journey, Song stared at the fourth boat carrying Jim Groves' wrapped body and thought about the clouds of water above Kaieteur, rising like angels. These were his angels now: not cherubs with wings like in Father Holmes' Christian books but instead swirling clouds of water rising up from the falls, darting swifts, macaws flying free in the big skies above.

Bartica seemed oddly quiet after their time in the forest and the unceasing sound of birds and monkeys and insects.

On Robert Leigh's last day he took Song swimming on the Mazaruni side of town where the current was strongest. They battled in the rough water just to stay still, before digging with sticks in the muddy banks looking for worms. Then they caught a few crabs before lying down upon the grassy verge, catching their breaths and slapping at mosquitoes.

'I'll miss you, Song,' the American said. 'You've been a fine host. I want to thank you for that.'

Song felt a wave of sadness pass through him. Nobody had said something like that to him before. Praise that seemed more intended for an adult. 'I hope you'll come back,' he said.

'I hope so, too. But setting up a mine is a big investment. The risks are high. The rewards can be high, too, of course. I'll file my report and then it's up to the company. They'll make the final decision.'

'And what do you think they'll do?'

'I've no doubt they should invest. But the funny thing is that after I bring back all the facts and figures, they'll pore over my report, but it will still come down to one thing.'

'What's that?'

Mr Leigh hit himself in the stomach. 'Gut.'

Song thumped himself in his stomach. 'My gut says you'll come back.'

Mr Leigh laughed. 'That's not your gut. That's your heart. Now before I go, Song, I want to know your big plan. What are you looking for from life?'

Song didn't know if he had a good answer to that, at least not one that he wanted to share. His plan was to go back upriver, simple as that. Until now that had been a figment. Now it was something tangible. What he was looking for from life was harder to say. Gold, diamonds, but beyond that, who knew? Song didn't want to think about that, let alone talk about it out loud. He'd known too many dreams that didn't come to pass.

'I'm sorry, sir,' he said flatly. 'I don't know.'

'You're only, what, thirteen, fourteen? It's a wonderful thing to have your whole life ahead of you, but it's a crime to waste it. Remember you can do whatever you want. Anything. Mining? Teaching? The church?'

Song shook his head. 'Not the church.' He surprised himself with how strongly he felt.

'You could go to sea.'

Song shook his head again. He knew he couldn't do that. 'I've been to sea.'

'Then what?' Mr Leigh was pressing him.

'I guess I'd like to go upriver again,' Song said.

'If you choose to go upriver, you make sure you hit the big time. I don't want to hear of you pork-knocking a few specks of gold dust out of the ground. Don't be one of the many. Set yourself apart, Song. You're smarter than all of those pork-knockers put together, with a battel in one hand and a bottle of liquor in the other. You can read and write, you can figure things out differently. You need to discipline yourself, build some structure. Think about buying land. That's what my mining company will be doing if they choose to invest. There's no reason you can't do the same. Save enough and buy land. Then you know you'll own everything you find, no questions, no disputes.'

'I'll remember that,' Song said. 'I'll write and tell you how I get on.'

'Do that. Tell you what, I'm going to leave you my set of brass scales so that I can be sure you're weighing something of note. That sound good?'

'You don't need to leave me your scales, sir. I'll make sure what I find will be worth weighing.'

'I'm sure, too, but it'll be a good reminder. I'd like you to have them.'

'Thank you, sir,' Song said. 'Perhaps the one thing I do worry about is what Father Holmes might think.'

'Don't worry about what you can't control. Worry about what you can. Choose a life that will make you happy.'

'But pork-knocking? Jingy says it's for drunks.'

'She's right. I'm sure there are some drunks. But there's more than one type of pork-knocker. You're not going to be the kind chipping away at a rock for the rest of your life. Besides, would you enter the church because it might make a preacher and a cook happy? That's a big gamble. Now, tell me your biggest dream, Song.'

'Same as yours.'

'Which is?'

Song hesitated, nervous to say it out loud. 'You're chasing gold, too.'

Mr Leigh sighed. 'Gold is only a tool for me. If I bring the company here and they strike it big, I get a promotion and a raise. And a small part of me hopes it might help win me back the love and respect of my wife. That's why I want to find gold.'

Song toyed with the crabs scrambling over each other in the basket.

'And you?' Mr Leigh asked. 'There must be a good reason you want to find gold. Gold isn't an end game.'

Song shrugged. 'For a life upriver,' he heard himself say, as if it was someone else's voice. 'For the freedom it will bring.'

They walked back to the house without saying much more to each other. As they approached the vicarage Song saw Father Holmes on the porch. He thought how lonely he looked. Song felt sorry, like he had betrayed Father Holmes by sharing his dreams with Mr Leigh and not him. Song broke into a run. When he reached the steps he tilted the bucket forwards to show off the contents. 'Look what we dug up.'

Father Holmes looked inside. 'Good job.'

'Mr Leigh caught most of them.'

'He must have had a good teacher.'

'The best,' Mr Leigh said.

'I didn't teach him,' Song said. 'There are crabs in America too.'

'Not like these,' Mr Leigh said. 'Might have to take some of these indigo shells back. My boys wouldn't believe the colour.'

Mr Leigh moved to sit down beside Father Holmes. 'Tobacco?'

Song made to take the basket inside to Jingy but he lingered in the hallway.

'No, thanks,' he heard Father Holmes say.

'Virginian, mind.'

'You go ahead.'

'Makes me miss my family, sitting out here on a porch like this.'

'And they miss you, Mr Leigh. I know they'll be glad to have you back but we'll miss you here, especially Song. He's very fond of you. I can see you've opened his eyes to a bigger world than I could have shown him.'

Song felt guilty. He didn't like to think Father Holmes felt second best next to Mr Leigh.

He heard the striking of a match and knew Mr Leigh must be lighting a cigarette. At the same time the cicadas suddenly struck up their soft hum. 'He's a wonderful boy,' Mr Leigh said, 'and he knew something about the big world before I ever got to him.'

'That's true. He makes me feel like I've only lived half a life.'

'You've got him questioning, too. It's impressive.'

'I sometimes worry if it isn't too much. He's making me question myself and my work, too. Like my missionary trips. He's right. Upriver, they look at the birds, the trees, the mountains, the world around them; that's what they believe in. Who am I to say that's wrong?'

'I don't know many vicars who'd say something like that. You're a special man, Father, and Song knows it; he cares a great deal about you.'

'He's got nobody else.'

Song realised Father Holmes was right. He didn't have anybody else, but it hurt Song to be reminded of that.

'He couldn't hope for better in you, Father.'

'That's nice of you to say, Mr Leigh. All I know is that he deserves some shot at a childhood after the ride he's had, and I would like to give him that. The rest will be up to him.'

'Song's got dreams, Father. That's all he needs to get on in life.'

Song squeezed his hands tightly together, as if it might be a way of holding on to his dreams and not letting go.

*

The vicarage was very quiet after Mr Leigh left. The American had been a good talker with a resonant voice that could be heard a street away. After his departure Jingy sang louder than ever as she went about her work, as if the notes might fill the space he left. Song wrote him long letters, proudly labelling the front of the envelope with Mr Leigh's address in 'The United States of America'. He relayed to him news about all the people Mr Leigh knew in Bartica. He described catching crabs and hooking big fish and swimming in the river with Jon at dusk. He even sent Mr Leigh updates on pork-knocker gossip he overheard at the dock or outside the bars: there was word that someone had found a thick seam and there was so much gold coming out of the ground it was causing the price to drop.

Every afternoon when he came home from school he asked Jingy if he had received any post. Nothing arrived. As the months passed Song wrote with less frequency. Jingy cursed the man who she said had taken advantage of her cooking and all of their hospitality without so much as a written word of thanks. When people asked Song if he had heard any news from the big American, they nodded knowingly at Song's negative response.

'As soon as they leave they forget everything we done for them,' Joseph said. 'While you're useful they couldn't be nicer. Once they're done, you're done. That's how things work out there in the rest of the world.'

Father Holmes insisted that Mr Leigh was a good man and said if he did not write, there must be a very good reason. 'Trust your judgement, Song. It's more reliable than the postal service. Anything could happen to a letter over a few thousand miles.'

Song well knew what could happen over a thousand miles. He didn't want to imagine that Mr Leigh's ship had gone down, or he had died of a sickness on board. Perhaps a lover of his wife had taken a knife to him, or Mr Leigh had taken a knife to the lover and wound up in jail. Song didn't want to consider any of this. He was alive to Song, that was all that mattered. A part of him wished he knew the real reason why Mr Leigh had never replied, but another part was grateful not to.

Still no letter came. Life returned to how it had been before the American visitor arrived, although there were good memories of him throughout the house. He had left Father Holmes his elegant yellowed globe, which now stood in the study. To Song he had given his compass and the fine set of brass scales he'd promised him. Song turned over the smooth cold metal weights in his hand, letting the heaviest rest in his palm. He stacked them up in each dish, trying to find as many different combinations to balance both sides as he could. Over and again he read the small plaque fixed to the wood, embossed with 'Pittsburgh, Pennsylvania,' and thought how far away the place sounded.

Song didn't want the memories to fade. He wanted to remember freshly everything Mr Leigh had said to him: 'It's a wonderful thing to have your whole life ahead of you, but it's a crime to waste it'; 'If you choose to go upriver, make sure you hit the big time'; 'There must be a good reason you want to find gold. Gold isn't an end game'; 'Your father would be very proud if he could see you now'; 'I'll miss you, Song.' Song didn't want Mr Leigh not to be in his life any more. But he switched on his resolve, telling himself how when a cloud passed overhead, the sky was the same again on the other side.

CHAPTER 11

The following year slipped by. Father Holmes and Song became so much a part of Bartica life that nobody could remember a time before the pair lived at the vicarage. 'You two might as well have been born here,' Short John told Song. 'But then you wouldn't be so nice.'

'Father Holmes is nice,' Song said. 'I'm not sure I am.'

'Course you are. Never seen you do a damn thing wrong.'

Song wondered about that. He'd left his family and never gone back. He hadn't saved them, in spite of his promise. He hadn't even managed to send money home. And now he spent his days dreaming of going upriver; that seemed wrong, too, after everything Father Holmes had done for him.

But he had also been studying hard at school and getting through the books in Father Holmes' library. With Jon, they had finished the first and a second bird book, and had started a third volume. Song had learned a lot about life upriver, too. From Sammy, he had grasped some survival skills – and how to look for gold. Indian knowledge, that's what Mr Leigh had talked so passionately about.

Song had made some good friends, and he and Father Holmes knew many of Bartica's residents by name. Father Holmes had taken on the task of personally inviting every living soul to his services. Together they went down streets that had never seen the shadow of a man of the church.

'The church should be open to everyone,' he said to Song. 'In fact, everything should be open to everyone. It doesn't matter where people are born or who their family is or what their prospects are, they shouldn't be treated any differently to anybody else. Don't forget that.'

Song watched Father Holmes repeatedly trying to persuade another tired mother or another drunk to come to St Ethelbert's on Sunday. At times, he wished Father Holmes wouldn't. The vicar just got knocked back again and again. Tom Jameson had probably been right. Bartica didn't need Father Holmes. But there were other times when Song wondered if they were making a difference. If Bartica was becoming a kinder, gentler place.

The congregation sometimes swelled, but then the next week shrunk – on a whim, it seemed. There were some who became regulars that nobody would have expected, like Dolly from Ruby Lou's and Old Ivor, who initially said he was too tired of life to care about being saved to live another one. Josie also attended, sometimes with Ella, rarely with Maia, and never with Clio. She'd had a baby boy, Vivi, who usually screamed through the service, but she nevertheless always brought him, no matter; nobody knew who the father was and nobody asked.

Bronco said he would've come more but couldn't leave his post. One or two of the jetty boys turned up from time to time; Mulay from the post office, and Odd-job Bunny, an albino who could turn his hand to anything. The town's affection grew for Father Holmes and the boy by his side.

'Town's a better place with you in it,' Edward Hoare said to Father Holmes. He and Tom Jameson came around most Sunday evenings now, and Song always made sure to listen in to their conversation from the study.

'Turned that boy around too,' Tom added.

Song stopped reading his book and listened harder.

'There was nothing to turn around,' Father Holmes said.

'Well, you've made him the man he's becoming,' the policeman said. 'And there's not many good ones in these parts.'

'He's still a boy, Tom. Give him time.'

Song reflected on how Mr Leigh hadn't thought of him as a boy.

'There's younger than him working in the mines,' Tom said. 'Learning a trade. Making a living.'

'I'd like to keep him at the vicarage for as long as I can. After everything he's been through.'

'No use growing up too soon,' Edward said in agreement. 'Would you like to see him in the church?'

Song held his breath.

'He's too smart for the church. He doesn't take anything for granted. He's even got me questioning things I've made vows about.'

They laughed. 'Then why are you teaching him to read all these books?' Tom asked.

'Because he's good at it.'

'That's a reason,' Edward said.

'But what good will it do him?' Tom asked. 'A houseboy who can read books.'

'Reading changes everything. Writing will give him a step up. Whatever Song chooses to do in life he'll do it better with a pen or a book in his hand.'

Tom whistled. 'All what you're giving to him and you're not even grooming him for the church. I don't believe it.'

'Church isn't for everyone.'

Song felt relieved. He didn't know why he'd ever doubted Father Holmes, or been anxious that he'd disapprove of his plans.

'When did you know it was for you?' Edward asked.

'It wasn't my decision,' Father Holmes said. 'My mother had me down for the church when I was a baby. I was as sick as a runt at birth and she swore – holding me up to the heavens, as she told me a thousand times – that if God allowed me to survive childhood I'd be in the seminary at thirteen. A gift from God given back to God, she used to say.'

That was a revelation. Song suddenly felt sorry for Father Holmes.

'And you were all right about that, were you?' Edward asked.

'I didn't have a choice,' Father Holmes said. 'In truth I wanted to go to sea. When I was small my father used to take me down to the docks at Liverpool where his brother worked and we'd watch the stevedores loading and unloading cargo. We tried to guess what was in the boxes and where all the boats might be going. I looked enviously at the sailors boarding the ship dressed in uniforms with shiny buttons, adventure flashing in their eyes. I had dreams to be an engineer and build boats and take myself to far-off places.'

Song heard the men put down their glasses. Tom smacked his lips. 'And instead you ended up at a seminary. A mother's curse, I swear.'

'It didn't turn out so bad. I still went to sea. I loved the journey here. I spent my whole time with the crew, not the passengers. And here I am living on the banks of one of the world's great rivers. Who'd have known?'

'Guess mothers get it right more often than we think,' Edward said.

Song thought about his own mother. She had not got it right. She could have come, too, with his younger sisters and brothers; on the boat they would have all had at least a bowl of rice every day. They would have been saved, without him having to save them.

'I don't doubt that I have a richer life because she sent me away,'

167

Father Holmes said. 'I could be hedging in Wales or watching over a dozen sheep in the hills. And I wouldn't have Song.'

Song was stilled by Father Holmes' words. His was also a life enriched. He had lost a father, but by leaving he had found a father, too.

Later that evening Father Holmes came to say goodnight to Song.

'Father, can I ask you something? It's about what I should do after school.'

'You've got lots of time to decide, Song. Study hard and you will have many choices.'

'Will you not mind whatever it is?'

'I'd like you to do whatever you want to do.'

Song hesitated. 'I'm ashamed to tell you.'

'Ashamed?'

'Embarrassed.'

'I know many people who spend their lives doing something they don't want to be doing. Follow your own dreams, Song.'

'Even if it's pork-knocking?'

'If that's your dream.'

'Don't you mind? Some say it's just gambling.'

Father Holmes sighed. 'Gambling is the roll of a dice. You can get lucky upriver, but that doesn't make it gambling. You need to make something of your life, Song. The average pork-knocker does not.'

'When I save up enough, I was thinking of buying land. Then I'd own everything I found. No one could take it away from me.'

'I know you won't do it the usual way. And if that makes you happy . . .'

'Are you happy you're a vicar?'

'I don't indulge myself with that question, Song. I am a vicar. I'm happy.'

'But if you could do it all over again, would you be a vicar again?' Song probed.

Father Holmes sighed. 'I think I've taught you to ask too many questions. Would I do it all again? I think I would. But I'd need you to turn up along the way.'

'I'd turn up.'

'That's settled then. I'd do it all again and you'd turn up. Goodnight, Song.'

Father Holmes leaned across and put his arms around Song. Song closed his eyes and could not help but imagine the emptiness if Father Holmes' arms were not around him. He lost everyone he loved. But he also believed Father Holmes would never leave him. They would be together always.

Song and Jon Swire continued to spend much of their free time together. Song had moved up a class mid-term but they still met after school every day to work on the book. Early evenings they went to the Mazaruni side where there was more bird life. Song cherished these excursions. He and Jon had spent so many hours together, learned so much alongside each other.

One evening Jon said he wanted to try to finish his sketch of an unusual duck. They took out the boat and spent a good hour spotting lapwings but had not yet seen a mandarin. The light was going and they would have to head back soon.

'I won't come for dinner tonight,' Jon said. 'Kiddo's been on at me about spending too much time at yours. Not helping enough at home, that kind of thing. Not that he does a damn thing, of course.'

'But you can't get your homework done there.' Song also knew there wasn't enough food on the table.

Jon closed the book and put away his pencil. 'I better go back tonight though. I have a feeling he'll take it out on Mama otherwise.'

A yell startled them both. 'What you boys up to?'

They looked up and saw Kiddo shouting at them from the bank.

'You shirking your family again. Know who your family is? It's not some goddamn preacher man and a Chiney boy. I'm coming to give you some reminding.'

Jon dropped his voice so even Song could barely hear him. 'You the hell not my damn family.'

'You bring that boat here,' Kiddo shouted.

'Don't answer,' Jon said to Song. 'He's drunk.'

'You hear me, boy. You're going to feel it tonight.'

'I ain't your boy,' Jon shouted back.

'You're mine enough to beat the living hell out of you. You get that boat back here.'

Song watched Kiddo pacing up and down the bank of the river. There wasn't a location either side they could dock safely. Then he thought about going around the promontory where the two rivers met. He looked at the ripples on the water and knew they'd struggle to turn the boat back upstream. But there was no way he was letting Jon face Kiddo. He looked at his friend's pale face.

'Jon, let's go downstream and then around. I know we can do it.'

'That's too dangerous. We'll never make it.'

The light was almost gone. 'We have to. It's the only way.'

Song turned the boat towards the middle of the river to pick up more current. They started to move swiftly downstream.

'What you boys up to?' Kiddo shouted; his voice was becoming increasingly agitated.

'We can't miss the turn,' Song said to Jon. 'When I shout "turn", you dig in your paddle.'

'Do you think we'll make it?'

'Too late to change our minds now. Just twist in your paddle when I yell.'

The boat was moving quickly now. They had already travelled too far to hear Kiddo's shouting. They could still just see him moving along the bank, but his figure had become shadowy in the gloom.

'Now,' Song yelled suddenly. 'Turn.'

The two boys shoved their paddles into the water on the right side of the boat angling the flat sides of the wood against the current. The nose of the boat twisted sharply to the right.

'Dig,' Song shouted. 'Don't stop.'

As they lifted their paddles in and out of the water, trying to pick up speed around the promontory, the current caught them again. The boys fought. They were managing to stop themselves moving further downriver but they were making no headway. They kept it up but Song could see Jon tiring. His own arms hurt, too.

'Stronger, Jon,' he shouted, but at that instant, a wash of rough water tipped the boat. Both boys were catapulted into the river.

Song had barely caught his breath before he started kicking his legs towards the bank. At the same time he yelled out Jon's name. It was almost too dark to see anything now.

Song trod water while he scanned the surface of the water. He saw his friend further out. Jon was floundering to stay afloat. Song let the current carry him towards his friend.

When Song was near, Jon lurched towards him, pushing down on his shoulders. Song found himself being held down. His chest was burning for breath. He inhaled a mouthful of water but managed to break the surface for a moment to take a gulp of air. Jon grabbed at him again. Without thinking Song punched his friend in the face. Jon cried out and loosened his grip. At that moment

Song seized Jon from behind, dragging him into the crux of his elbow, and then started to kick them both back to land.

'Kick,' he shouted at Jon. 'I can't do this on my own.'

Song thrashed his legs, trying to steer them both in the direction of the bank. He could feel Jon weakening.

'Damn it,' Song shouted. 'Help me.'

With relief Song felt his friend start kicking. Swimming backwards, Song turned to see the dark shadow of trees behind him. They were almost there. He put his feet down to see if he could touch the riverbed but there was nothing. It was fully dark now. He pushed on. And with relief felt solid ground underfoot. He pulled Jon up on the bank and turned him on his side. He was coughing up water. Song flopped down beside him.

The two boys lay in the darkness. Only the sound of their heaving chests broke the stillness. As Song heard Jon's breath calm, he felt his own body relax.

A squawk of parrots burst through the air. The flapping of wings halted as the birds settled to roost in the trees above them.

'The book,' Jon said, still gasping. 'We lost the book.'

Song thought about Jon's beautiful birds: the lustre of their feathers, the light in their eyes. 'We lost Kiddo,' Song said. 'That's what matters.'

'Maybe I should have taken the beating. I'll only get it later anyway. And we'd still have the book. And the boat.'

Song shared Jon's regret at the loss of the book, like a chapter of their life was gone. But he took it as a sign: he could no longer only observe, now he had to make his own story, to live a life that was a story worth telling.

Song felt Jon's hand reach for his own. He squeezed his friend's hand back.

*

Jon wasn't at school the next day. Song's heart sank when he saw his empty desk. He walked past Jon's house on his way home but there was nobody about. Jon didn't show up for a week. When he finally came back to school, Song could still see the bruising on his face. Song winced. There was a cut above Jon's eye that was infected.

'I'm going to kill Kiddo one day,' Song said to Jon.

Jon gave Song a half-smile.

'What did your mama say when he did this?' Song asked.

'Said I needed to stop provoking him. She can't say anything to Kiddo. He'll hit her if she does.'

'He's got to go, Jon. She has to get rid of him.'

'She won't. I don't know why,' Jon touched his forehead. 'Is it bad?'

'You need to keep washing it. Jingy's got some brew she uses when there's an infection. You could come by and she could treat it.'

'Mama says I've got to go straight home after school now. Don't give Kiddo a reason, she says. So, what did Father Holmes say about the book?'

'He was more worried about you than the book.'

'That's nice of him.'

'We still have two, remember. We hadn't done so much in the one we lost. We were less than halfway through.'

'Guess I should have taken the beating there and then. Saved us a lot of trouble. But thanks for what you did that night.'

'I probably got you a harder beating.'

'Would have been hard either way.'

When Song saw Father Holmes on the porch with Edward Hoare he went around to the back of the house.

'What you sneaking up on me for?' Jingy said when she saw him come padding through the back door.

'Thought I might steal one of your pine tarts without you seeing.'

Jingy smiled. 'On your way.' She shooed him out of the kitchen. Song went to the study where he knew he could hear the men's conversation on the porch. He picked up *The Count of Monte Cristo*, which he was halfway through.

'. . . I'm not going to do it,' Father Holmes said. 'He shouldn't be asking this of me. I'm not suggesting the church should condone prostitution. But I do believe it is exactly these women who need our help most.'

Song thought about Josie, and of all the girls at Ruby Lou's.

'Father Francis is a man clearly out of touch with the real world,' Edward said.

'If I shut this church to all the sinners on his list I may as well leave Bartica altogether. Or apply for a job as a policeman.'

Edward chuckled. 'Tom Jameson could do with an assistant.'

'I'm serious. His letter says that nobody should have the privilege of attending church who drinks, who listens to music, who prospects for gold . . .'

Song thought about the pork-knockers at Ruby Lou's doing all three. There was a strange part of him that felt slightly pleased the church took this view. It helped him justify even more his decision to turn away from it, even in private.

'Maybe you should invite him here to take a look at the place for himself,' Edward said. 'Not that he would come of course. I've been in the colonies long enough to know his type. I'd tear up his letter if I were you.'

'I'm subordinate to Father Francis, you know that.'

Song hated that. He thought of the time when he himself was

answerable to Mr Carmichael. There and then, he swore he would never be answerable to anyone again.

'Write back and say you'll try to put all his ideas into practice,' Edward said. 'Give him what he wants to hear. Then forget about everything he's said. He won't be any the wiser. It's your parish. He'll never come here. You can run it however you see fit.'

'It would be breaking rank.'

'Follow your heart. Not the church. Hark at me giving advice to a clergyman.'

'I'm grateful to you for listening, Edward. There are not many who I could talk to about this. The truth is I'm already seen as something of a troublemaker. As much as a vicar can be, at least. The governor agreed to this posting because it would get me out of Georgetown. He said I was neglecting St Andrew's; I was spending too much time with sinners and not enough time with good Christians.'

Song wondered who the good Christians were. Not Mrs Boyle, who'd struck Father Holmes. Nor Mrs Mills, who'd been against Song reading. Both women were in the choir and everyone thought they were some of the finest churchgoers. And then there was the committee secretary, Mrs Burford, who didn't want Song living upstairs, who said the whole congregation felt the same way.

Edward Hoare snorted. 'I could tell them a story or two about so-called good Christians sinning right under their noses. Married men and married women behaving like rabbits. The drinking at the club puts Josie's in the pale. Hypocrites. Preaching one thing, practising another. If he wants to get serious about shutting church doors he'd leave out in the cold half of Georgetown society.'

'You might be right.'

'At least Bartica's more honest. They hang out their dirty

175

laundry instead of trying to hide it away. It's why I can't stand Georgetown. The niceties and nonsense. They couldn't be sweeter to your face. Turn your back and they're sleeping with your wife or knocking off your business partner. Nobody there ever said congratulations and meant it. They twist themselves up at anyone else's good news. At least in a town like Bartica you know where you stand. No pretences. If someone's going to kill you at least he has the decency to tell you first.'

Father Holmes laughed. 'I might leave that out when I write my reply.'

'They're all reading from a script,' Edward said. 'I could cite it from memory. Complaints about the insufferable heat and the mosquitoes and the lazy locals while lording it up with houses full of staff, good wages and sex in the afternoons. Back home they would be masturbating mediocre civil servants. Here they're sleeping with their best friend's wife – while she's throwing up her hands about the promiscuity of the local population. Do me a favour, Father. Rip up the letter. I don't know another man who can put his hand on his heart like you can.'

Song was shocked at Edward speaking that way to Father Holmes. For the first time, perhaps, he realised that Father Holmes was more man than vicar and he loved him all the more.

'You think too highly of me, Edward. None of us are perfect – and that's my point. If we're demanding perfection before people walk through our doors we'll have very empty churches.'

'Don't let this man get to you, Father. You carry on listening to whatever voice has been in your head all this time.'

'I just wish it was always loud and clear. My head is noisy with questions. Maybe this town's changing me, like Tom says. Maybe I'm afraid I myself am no longer good enough to walk through the doors of my own church.'

'Eternal doubt of the eternal man. We wouldn't be men if we were sure of our position in the world. Faith is built on doubt.'

There was a long pause. Song waited.

'I'll rip it up,' Father Holmes finally said.

A few weeks later, Jon joined Song for an early dinner at the vicarage. Both boys knew he couldn't stay long; he'd have to run home straight after his last mouthful.

At the table Father Holmes handed Jon a letter. 'Song tells me you've been having a rough ride at home. So I took some liberties. Figured you needed to plan a future.'

Jon looked at the envelope addressed to him. 'Thanks, but I'm okay, Father.'

'Open it,' Song repeated. He was excited for his friend.

'I sent some samples of your artwork to Governor Johnson. He loves birds.' Father Holmes continued. 'This is his reply.'

Jon looked at the envelope. 'For me? A letter from the governor?'

'It's good news.'

Jon took out the letter and read its contents. His face lit up.

'What does it say?' Song asked.

'He wants me to draw some sketches of birds for Governor's House. He's going to pay me.'

'Exactly,' Father Holmes said. 'You've a professional future in drawing, Jon. You'll be able to make a good living this way.'

'What else does it say?' Song asked.

'He wants me to draw every ibis and spoonbill,' Jon said. 'He wants them on linen paper and framed.'

'Don't worry about that last part,' Father Holmes said. 'I'll help you with the materials.'

'How much is he going to pay you?' Song asked.

'You don't have to tell us, Jon,' Father Holmes said. 'It's your business.'

'He says a shilling,' Jon said. 'We can put it towards a new boat.'

'Now, I have something else to talk to you both about,' Father Holmes said. 'I want you both to apply for a scholarship to Queen's College in Georgetown to finish your secondary school. Song, you have a good chance of an academic scholarship, and Jon, I absolutely insist you try for an art scholarship. The education there is first-class and you'd both benefit from the experience. I've already made inquiries and you can sit the examinations here.'

Song stared at Father Holmes. 'Georgetown? You mean we'd leave Bartica?'

'My mama would never let me,' Jon said.

'Let's not get ahead of ourselves,' Father Holmes said. 'Neither of you have got it yet and the exams are not easy. Let's apply first. If either or both of you get it, we can then think about what to do next.'

Song considered the idea of a scholarship to Queen's College. It was beyond what he'd ever hoped he might have achieved at school. Then he thought about his dream to go upriver. That's where he believed he really belonged. Like the feeling he had looking over the cliff at Kaieteur. Answerable to no one. Entirely free.

Both boys sat the examination after school one day. It was only the two of them in an otherwise empty classroom. Mr Nutt stood vigil.

Song felt the weight of the occasion, filled more with awe than anxiety as he stared at the exam paper before him. As luck would have it, one of the questions asked him to explore the opposites of good and evil in *Treasure Island*, which he and Father Holmes had discussed together at great length. Song chose to write about the duality of the character of Long John Silver, a bold adventurer yet a ruthless criminal, and a man who became progressively vulnerable and therefore likeable, yet it could not be denied was also a manipulator and murderer. They were the blurred lines of good and evil, Song contemplated. He outlined something Father Holmes had said to him, suggesting some readers might be outraged if Long John Silver was hanged even though he had killed a man, and how it was much more adroit of Stevenson to let the pirate escape, rather than be brought to justice.

Another question on the examination paper asked him what was the greatest adversity he had ever faced. Song responded by writing about the voyage from China to British Guiana, bringing in elements from *Moby Dick* about Ahab, the 'grand, ungodly, godlike man', his depthless courage and drastic single-mindedness.

Song was determined to do well for Father Holmes, but he didn't believe he would ever attend Queen's College, even if he won a place. He didn't want to abandon his dream of going upriver. After he put his pen down, he dismissed the idea of Georgetown altogether.

CHAPTER 12

Father Holmes handed the letter to Song. 'It's from the Arch-bishop of York.'

Song scanned the page: 'It is on my recommendation that you have been invited to represent your region at the Annual General Meeting of the Synod which will this year be built around the theme of Rural Missionary Work. I understand the great distances of our world but I consider your attendance essential. This conference will map out the missionary work of the church for the next ten years.'

'It sounds like an honour,' Song said. 'Or at least they want it to seem that way.'

He read the rest, quickly absorbing key sentences: 'attendees from every continent'; 'your contribution would be highly valued given your experience in the field'; 'I am well aware of the import-ant work you are doing among the rural communities of British Guiana'; 'the conference will be held in London this coming November'.

Song looked up sharply. 'Will you go?'

'I am obliged to accept. But this presents an opportunity for us, Song. For a while now I've been wanting to talk to you about a trip to England. Together. Will you come with me?'

'To England?'

'To England. To London. To Wales. To the museums. The art galleries. The theatres. All the places we've read about.'

Song stared back down at the letter. 'I don't know—'

'There are so many places for us to see. We'll go to the British Library, where there are more books than we could read in both our lifetimes. We can visit the Royal Ornithological Society, where there are thousands of plates of birds. We'll see all the world in the British Museum: Egypt, India, Greece. We can think of the trip as an integral part of your education.'

Song did not look up.

Father Holmes' voice softened. 'Does that sound terrible?'

'No, it doesn't,' Song choked.

'What is it then?'

'I can't go back to sea.'

'It would be nothing like the last time, I promise.'

Song shut his eyes. 'Please don't ask me to.'

There was silence in the room.

'It's all right, Song.'

'Will you go?'

Father Holmes' voice was quiet. 'I have to. In truth I'm not even sure what I think about rural missionary work any more. Do you know why? Because of you, Song. Because you help me to ask myself hard questions.'

Song didn't want to talk about any of that. 'Will you come back?' he asked simply.

'Without a doubt.'

Song folded up the letter and pushed it back across the table.

'It won't be long,' Father Holmes said, seemingly trying to calm himself as much as Song. 'You'll have the important job of looking after things here while I'm away. Can you do that? We'll write. You'll study. I'll do the conference. It will be no time before I'm back and we're together again.'

'Yes, of course,' Song said, unflinchingly. Inside he was hurting but he buried that. 'I'll be waiting here for you, Father.'

Father Holmes reached out his hand to Song. 'I'll miss you. I miss you already.'

With Father Holmes gone there were fewer chores around the house and even fewer visitors. Father Francis did not come to Bartica to hold a service and although Song continued to keep the church clean and tidy, it became a sorrowful place to be.

Month after month passed and there was still no news from Father Holmes. There were moments when Song was filled with panic, not doubting Father Holmes would write but that he would survive the long sea crossing. To steady himself, Song focused on his studies and read until his eyes could no longer strain to see the words in the dark. He wrote frequently to Father Holmes, sometimes every day. He also began a new volume of bird book. From time to time, he saw Jon, but otherwise he kept himself to himself.

He had avoided entering Father Holmes' room, only glancing at the closed door and wishing it would soon be flung open. But one day when he missed the vicar terribly, for no particular reason he could explain, he approached his room and turned the handle. His hands shook as he pushed open the door. He felt the blast of Father Holmes: in the smell of the room, seeing his shaving brush by the bowl, a notebook by his bed with a pen lying diagonally across it. Song could not help himself. He broke down in sobs.

The first news came three months after his departure. A dozen letters arrived altogether, which Father Holmes had written over the course of his sea voyage. It had been a slow crossing, he said, with light winds. He had painted every day to pass the time. The last letter was written shortly after the boat had docked. Father Holmes had described the biting wind on England's south coast and the crunch of snow underfoot. Song imagined touching the fallen snow and the cold wind on his face.

Cheered, Song wrote to Father Holmes every evening. He detailed the birds he and Jon had spotted and their progress with the new book. He did not mention that the church lay empty. Nor did he say how badly Kiddo had beaten up Jon's mama and then knocked out Tom Jameson, who had been called to sort out the fighting. Song did not skip only the bad news. He wanted to save the fact that he had moved up another grade and that he had won the Latin prize.

One month later another batch of letters arrived. Song arranged them in chronological order before reading them. In one Father Holmes wrote how the conference in London had been fascinating and attended by people from all over the world. He expressed how, whether he agreed with it or not, there would be a push to increase missionary work in rural regions like Bartica. In another, he wrote that he had received Song's letters which had given him 'immeasurable joy'; he missed Bartica, he missed Song.

He also described how he had dropped off the first two volumes of their bird books at the Royal Ornithological Society, protecting them under his coat against sleeting rain. The weather had been bitterly cold and he wrote how much he missed their warm evenings together on the vicarage porch.

Song touched the writing paper, trying to imagine Father Holmes touching the same paper. It didn't seem possible.

The last few letters were not written in London but in Wales, where Father Holmes was visiting his sick mother. There were descriptions of the damp draughty cottage and the winter gloom; he wrote that it was already too dark by lunchtime to read without a lamp. His mother was not well and he spent long evenings by her bedside reciting passages from the Bible.

The next line jolted Song. Father Holmes explained how his mother's illness might force him to delay his return.

Song could feel a rising fear inside of him. He imagined the vicar's sick mother gripping Father Holmes' hand and charging him never to leave her bedside, just like she had sentenced him to a life in the church.

It was with dread that Song picked up Father Holmes' last letter. After reading the first sentence a shiver of guilt passed through him. The old woman had passed away. Song held the letter to his chest. Father Holmes wrote that he would be leaving shortly after the funeral. The *Falmouth* was sailing. He hoped to be back by Easter.

The boat was late, as boats always were. March rolled into April. May came around. Still the *Falmouth* did not arrive. Song remembered his same mounting fears when Father Holmes was gone upriver the first time and he had waited anxiously for his return. 'That grown man can look after himself,' Jingy had assured him. And she was right. Father Holmes had come strolling back into the vicarage just like she'd said he would. Nevertheless Song's uneasiness kept him up at night. He saw storms in his head. Screams on the wind. The splintering of wood. Choking on salt water. Bodies floating on a flat calm. He awoke from his nightmares embalmed in sweat and gasping for breath.

Song had never imagined Father Holmes would not be back for his last day of school. He felt his absence acutely, watching the friends in his year with their mother or father or both. Jingy was there, of course. Edward Hoare turned up, too, to congratulate him on his graduation.

'Least I could do for Father Holmes. He'd be very proud to see you today. So, are you heading to Queen's College for your last two years of school? Father Holmes mentioned something about that. And you must be, what, sixteen by now?'

'I haven't heard back. I'm guessing that means I didn't get in.'

'Bide your time, Song. You don't know till you know. Any more news from Father Holmes?'

'That's one I'm biding my time on, sir.'

Edward Hoare smiled. 'You're more patient than I am. We all wish he'd hurry back. Let me know when you hear.'

'I will.'

Across the schoolyard, Song saw Josie, her daughters and their younger brother Vivi, who'd grown up a lot since Song had last seen him. He clutched a book in one hand and held a ball in the other. Maia came running over to Song. She had her hair pinned back and looked more like a schoolgirl than ever, less like a daughter of Josie's bar.

'Do you want to join us? What with Father Holmes being away and all.'

Song looked at Jingy. 'Of course,' Jingy said. 'We'd love to. I haven't been up all night baking for any other reason than getting together and celebrating with everyone.'

Song was grateful to Maia for including them. 'Thanks, Maia.'

'Come on, then. Mama's brought banana cake and all sorts.'

Song and Jingy joined Maia and her family, along with Jon and his mama and Sonia.

'Any news from the Father?' Josie asked.

'Not recently, ma'am. But when I do hear from him I get a bundle of letters all in one go. His mother was poorly, that's why he's delayed. He'll be back soon.'

'You think he's really coming back?' Jon's mama asked.

'You stopped trusting men a long time ago,' Josie said. 'I don't blame you for that. But rest assured, Father Holmes is coming back.'

Song was happy to hear Josie sound so confident about the vicar's return.

'Father Holmes will be proud of you when he gets back,' she continued. 'All grown up and graduated. Like I'm proud of you, Maia.' She tweaked Maia's ear lobe affectionately. 'So what you all going to be doing now? Jon? You first. What about all those draw-ings for the governor? You going to be one of the famous sons of Bartica.'

'I've already done those pictures,' Jon said. He looked across at his mother. 'I don't know. I guess I'll be sticking around for a bit.'

'You got to do what you got to do,' his mama said.

'Wise words,' Jingy added. 'You just see what comes up. Don't say no to nothing.'

'What about you, Maia?' Jon's mama asked her.

'I'm going to see the world,' she said, as casually as if she'd announced she was off to buy bread.

Song would always love Maia. He knew that then.

Clio snorted. 'Ridiculous.'

'I believe you, Maia,' Vivi said. And Song warmed to him, too.

'And you, Song?' Josie asked.

'I'm waiting for Father Holmes.'

'Course you are. Aren't we all? And when he's back, what then?'

Song hesitated. 'Upriver. I think I might go upriver.'

Jon's mama whistled. 'Pork-knocker.'

'You let him alone,' Jingy said. 'He'll be doing it his own way, no matter what he chooses.'

'If you go upriver, don't be gone too long, you hear,' Maia whis-pered.

'I won't,' Song whispered back. He remembered his first day of school, so nervous and excited at the same time, with Maia doing handstands in the yard. Now, as Josie said, they were all grown up and graduated. For the first time in months, Song allowed himself to feel happy, surrounded by friends who he knew cared about him.

On his way home Song went to collect the week's mail. Odd-job Bunny was in front of him talking to Mulay, the clerk.

'Did you hear the *Portsmouth*'s in?' Mulay said.

Bunny nodded. 'What it bring?'

'Don't you know what that means, fool?' Mulay said.

Bunny looked up from the sorting. 'Nestlé for me. Lifebuoy for the lady.'

Mulay rolled his eyes. 'Fool! It means the *Falmouth* is lost. They said it sailed months before them. Should've been here in March, or April latest. Bottom of the sea. Most all white folk too. Families. Georgetown's a zoo with all the wailing.'

Song turned. He felt for the doorframe to steady himself as he moved out of the dark office. It was unbearably bright outside. Like the first time he climbed the ladder behind Li Bai and found himself on deck in the sunlight. Song was taken back again to his passage: the storm churning, the screams, the slamming of the boat against the water, the choking. He had dreamed it. Like a premonition. Like he had known it all along. As if he had brought it upon Father Holmes himself. Mulay's voice was a noise echoing about Song's head. He broke into a run and tripped on the edge of the path, sprawling across the gravel. He lay there, pushing his face into the stones. He could not believe it. Would not believe it. He never wanted to get up.

After the news of the *Falmouth*'s sinking, Song moved into Josie's bar. Jingy went looking for him the first night he did not come

187

home. Through his drunken daze he saw her arm swing back. Her hand landed on the side of his face but he barely felt it.

He soaked himself in liquor the same way he had seen other men do until they hit the floor. He tried his best to forget everything good he had ever known. The instant he came around, he ordered another drink to push away the stink of his own sweat, the stale liquor burning in his throat, the thunder in his head.

Maia took him one night. She was gentle, as if to give him comfort. Song did not need to pretend he knew anything. He lay on his back half drunk as she moved up and down his body like a slick of oil. She was as soft as Song was hard. He watched the blur of her face above him. Her long dark hair swinging about her shoulders. Her small hands gripping his shoulders as she rocked to and fro. Song's head was spinning from the drink. He felt a flood of heat between his legs. He could barely breathe. It was as if he was drowning. His voice cracked as he called out her name. Maia collapsed upon him and then rolled off onto the matting.

Neither moved as they caught their breath. Song drifted. When he came around he reached out for her but she was gone. He put out his other arm to feel for the bottle he had left by the bed but he instead knocked it over and liquor spilled across the floor. He cursed the darkness.

Hours or days later, Song wasn't sure which, he saw Jon walk through the door. Song was in the bar, his head resting on its side on a table.

'Song, it's Jon,' he heard his friend whisper. 'I've come to get you out of here. I need you to come home with me. Now.'

Song tried to open his eyes more fully. The light from the open doorway cut into the darkness.

'I got a new book for us. You should see the birds I been seeing. And drawing. There's nothing written though. You need to do the writing. All I got is lots of pretty pictures. It ain't a book if there ain't no writing.'

Song squinted in the light. He could see Jon's outline. His throat was dry. 'I can't,' he croaked.

'I didn't come here just to have a look about the place,' Jon continued. 'I could guess how a place like this'd look. I came to fetch you and I'm not leaving 'less we're leaving together. This whole town seems to be going down without Father Holmes in it. But I'm not letting you be part of that.'

Song covered his head with his hands as if he was holding his skull together. 'I need a drink.'

Jon smashed his fist on the table. Song winced. 'You know who says that?' Jon said. 'You know who says those very same words, just like you are now? I'll tell you. You won't like it but I'll tell you. Kiddo. Kiddo says that same damn thing that you're saying to me now: I need a drink.'

Song slipped the hand on his head downwards to cover his eyes.

Jon's voice softened again. 'I don't like it either, Song, but you need to know. You carry on like this, you'll be no better than any other drunk in this town. I've come to get you out. You gotta stand up and walk home with me right now.'

Song felt Jon's hand on his shoulder.'Come with me,' Jon said.

Song groaned.

'I'm gonna help you and we're gonna do it together.'

'I can't.'

Jon thumped on the table again. But he spoke in a whisper. 'This is the last thing Father Holmes would have wanted. You know that.'

Song thought of himself with Father Holmes in the study of the vicarage. It was as if Song could hear their voices now, discussing books, agreeing, disagreeing, laughing together.

Song let Jon steer him out of the bar. In a strange way, he felt like he was holding the arm of Father Holmes. They passed Vivi playing in the front yard. The little boy stared at Song. There was something about his expression that Song recognised, but he couldn't place. His young face was full of wariness, even fear, horror. Song hated himself. They continued slowly all the way back to the vicarage.

Jingy did not say a word as the pair arrived through the front door. Song saw her nod at Jon. Jon took him upstairs, undressed him and put him into bed. Song didn't know how long he slept. From time to time he reached out for a sip of the sweet black tea Jingy had brought to his bedside.

Then late one afternoon, he padded down the stairs. Jingy was rinsing rice on the back steps. She barely looked up.

He crouched beside her and poured some water in a bowl. He wetted a cloth and pressed it against his face before scrubbing behind his neck and ears.

'Make sure you're whistle-clean before you sit down at my table.'

Song looked across and nodded.

'There's lunch when you're done,' Jingy said.

'I'm sorry.'

'Every man's entitled to lose his way. Takes a while for a boy to become a man. Not my place, nor anyone else's, to go rushing you.'

'That's generous. Not sure I deserve it.'

Song dried himself, fingering the soft fuzz on his face.

'Father Holmes forgot his razor,' Jingy said. 'I blame myself for that. It's beside his washbowl. Since wondered to myself what that man looked like with a beard.'

Song filled a jug with clean water and climbed the stairs to Father Holmes' room. He turned the handle and walked in, more boldly than the last time. But a year on and the room still smelled of his shirts and polished leather. Song felt it like a blow to the head.

Beside the ceramic bowl at the window was Father Holmes' shaving kit, swathed in cloth. Song opened up the folds and poured some water into a bowl. He looked at his face in the small hand mirror. It looked thinner than he remembered. His cheekbones had sharpened and his jaw had a harder edge to it. The whites of his eyes were red. He blinked at his reflection. He reached up and felt again the soft bristles on his upper lip and chin. It was like he was looking at someone else's face.

Song took up Father Holmes' razor to shave off the new growth. He nicked his skin but it felt good. His face burned against the scraping metal and stung with the lather of caustic soap. He used Father Holmes' scissors to cut the fringe away from his eyes, bending forward to let the tresses hang down above the bowl. Then he lay flat on Father Holmes' bed, staring at the ceiling.

He had lost his greatest friend. He had lost himself for a while, too. He thanked Jon for rescuing him. And Jingy for being so quick to forgive him. Li Bai's advice swirled around his head. 'Get on with your own life now, Song. You got to think harder about surviving.' There was Mr Leigh's booming voice: 'Remember that if you believe hard enough that you're lucky, you will be.' 'I'd like you to do whatever you want to do.' That was what Father Holmes had said. 'Follow your own dreams.' Song remembered Father Holmes putting his arms around him after that conversation, and Song imagining a time without him, yet willing it never to be. But the time had come. He had lost everyone he loved. That was the curse of his life. So now he would leave everything behind and go and find his freedom. Upriver.

CHAPTER 13

There had been weeks of hard rain and the river was high. Jesus had not stopped complaining since the first day. The wet clothes, the insects, the food. A month in and they hadn't found a grain of gold.

The pair didn't speak much. Song was careful to remember what Jesus had said about not liking talkers. Instead he watched on from a distance, studying Jesus' technique as he took up each of his tools. Jesus worked slowly, swilling the water around his iron battel, filtering the riverbed matter. When he had time between his chores in the camp, Song copied him. It was a similar technique to the one Sammy had shown him.

'Gold in your blood, boy,' Jesus said. 'I know 'em when I see 'em. You were born to do this.'

'Glad you think so.'

'Never been wrong.'

'Seems like you need a lot of patience though. I've always thought I've been short on patience.'

'Patience.' Jesus snorted. 'Luck. That's what you need. Good, ol' fashioned luck.'

That was the first conversation they'd had in a week. Jesus wasn't teaching him everything he knew, like he'd promised. In fact, he wasn't teaching him anything. Song felt more like a camp hand than a pork-knocker.

At the end of the day Jesus threw himself in a hammock. 'Where's the goddamn food? Late and cold.'

Jesus was in a worse mood than usual. His body was covered in welts from the tiny bêtes rouges insects which had burrowed into the creases of his skin: his armpits, the backs of his knees, his groin. He set about trying to squeeze out the tiny critters and then took up a burning log from the fire to run across his skin. Song knew how the sweep of a flame could offer some relief from the itching.

After they had finished eating, darkness came swiftly. Song threw some wet wood upon the embers and lay back in his hammock, scooped into its comfortable moon shape. He did not feel tired tonight. There were howler monkeys calling from afar, their sound so strange it was hard to believe they were part of this world. He loved nights this dark. He could pretend he was alone upriver. Without Jesus. Only himself to depend upon.

Jesus was stirring again, restless with the fiery itching. Song shut out the man's stream of abuse. He heard him at the fire taking up another burning log.

Suddenly Song's hammock was flipped and he landed with a thump on the ground. Before he had recovered his breath he felt the weight of Jesus land hard on his back. He tried to turn over but Jesus struck him across the side of his head.

'Don't try it,' Jesus said.

Song twisted his body, trying to jerk Jesus off him. Instead he felt the man press down heavier on his buttocks. There was a torrent of pain between his shoulders and he smelled the burning of skin.

'One more move. One. You wouldn't be the first man I've known to burn to death.'

Song could hear Jesus' close breathing. There was another blow to his back. He felt a thump, and then smelled the burning as his skin crisped.

'You stay still if you know what's good for you.'

Song could barely breathe with the weight of Jesus upon him and the pain of his searing skin. Jesus was yanking at the string waistband of Song's trousers. Song heard the cloth rip and he cried out before Jesus struck him again across the head. Then came the burning log another time upon his back. Jesus pressed it down hard. Song's skin pinched and tightened. He screwed up his face. Tears squeezed out of his eyes. It was as if he was already somewhere further along in his life and not where he was at this instant lying on the ground. He knew he would always remember the smell of his scorched skin.

An image of Jinda being dragged to the river came into his head. He remembered seeing his back float up to the surface. He could hear the sound of his own machete moving through the air. And then the switch as Mr Carmichael came down again and again upon his back. There was that pain once more between his shoulders as he lay, face pressed down in the dust. He remembered fighting then not to black out, like he was fighting now. As Jesus came down upon him again and again. Song heard the cries, unsure if they were Jesus' or his own. He let his consciousness slip away because there was nowhere else to go.

When Song woke the sun was already high. It hurt to open his eyes. Through the blur of his eyelashes he saw the fire was out. There was no sign of Jesus.

He tried to pull himself up off the ground but gasped at the pain and lowered himself again. Then he made his way towards the ash of the fire, dragging himself forward on his elbows. There were ants all over the plates and in the pot he had used to cook the beans but he had put a lid on the leftover rice and he now ate the remains.

He again tried to haul himself up off the ground. As he did he drew his torn trousers up around his waist and loosely knotted the frayed string. He reached behind him and let his fingers move lightly across the skin but it was too raw to touch. On his feet now, dizzy with the pain of every movement, he began to tidy the camp. He tried to close off his senses, close off the memories, but he could still smell his burned skin.

Jesus woke Song with a kick to the side of his ribs.

'Get your man his dinner,' he yelled. 'What the hell have you been doing all day? No lunch. Now no dinner.'

Song got to his feet. It was nearing nightfall already. He must have slept most of the day. He set about making the fire.

Jesus threw himself into the hammock. 'That's right,' he said. 'You get on with it and get on with it fast. Now you know why a man needs a boy in his camp. No good sleeping away the day and feeling sorry for yourself. This is the way the young 'uns learn. We all go through it. Gets you ready for the hard world out there. You'll learn to appreciate that I took pity on you and taught you what a man needs to survive upriver. As luck would have it, boy, you found Jesus.'

As the rice boiled Song roughly descaled a fish with the knife Father Holmes had given him. He gripped it in his hand, feeling less alone knowing that the vicar had once held the same black horn handle. Then Song fried the fish on both sides in a pan of oil. He had not said a word.

'I like 'em when they're quiet,' Jesus said. 'Don't think you're bothering me by your quiet. Hate a boy who talks too much.'

Jesus began to eat. The only sound from the camp was the

scraping of his metal spoon and the odd belch. When he was done Jesus threw his plate down.

'Best food you've made so far,' he said. 'You're the kind that needs a bit of a beating to get you working, isn't that right? Not the first time you've heard that. Seen the scars on your back. Well, you got some more now, boy. You can show 'em off to some whore and say you got 'em fighting a caiman. Get you laid that kind of talk. You'll be thanking me later.'

Jesus was chuckling to himself. He reached out to the fire as if to pick up one of the burning logs.

Song jumped to his feet.

'Got ya,' Jesus hooted with laughter. 'You scared of a bit of burning firewood?'

Song shook his head. 'I'm not scared.'

Jesus' voice hardened. 'If you not scared, boy, sounds like I got some teaching to do yet.'

Song did not move.

Jesus laughed again. 'You try and be all tough. You're learning the river, boy. That's what you're doing. Tough is how we want 'em. Now get on and clean up and tell me then how well you can sleep with that new fear in your belly. You've slept your last good night's sleep.'

Song collected the plates and went down to the river to wash up. As he squatted by the water's edge he felt the pinched tautness of his back's burned skin. His head was pounding. He stood up, steadied himself, and slowly walked back to camp.

Jesus was already in his hammock. Song was on him before the man had a chance to move. The pots and plates clattered to the ground. Song's knife was open and he carved it across Jesus' throat, pressing the blade deep into the hard flesh. The way Song held him down Jesus could not put up a struggle. His breathing turned to wheezing, then choking. Song knew the sound of dying. He felt the heat of the thickening blood between his fingers. He did not give up on the pressure. He pushed himself and his knife harder into the man, and waited.

It surprised him how fast it had happened, how easy it had been. In only a few minutes Jesus was dead. Song eventually lessened his force but his body remained tense. He wanted to be sure there was not another breath of life in the man.

Song carried Jesus's body down to the river across his raw shoulders. Jesus' swinging arms thwacked against Song's back with every step but Song drove on in the darkness. When he reached the bank he let Jesus fall off him, and heard the splash in the water. He remembered that same sound as Li Bai tossed dead bodies into the sea, and how Song had wished for those deaths every night just so he could go up on deck.

Song pushed Jesus' body towards the faster flowing current and watched the dark shape carried away. Bartica takes care of its own troubles, Song thought. That's what Tom Jameson had once said. Revenge. That's the law. Someone wrongs you, and they'll be bobbing up and down on the river the next day. Song got into the water himself to wash off the blood and rinse out his clothes.

By the next morning the river had risen sharply. Song walked down to where they had been working and where he had dumped Jesus' body. Dead Man's Bend, he called it in his head, as a warning to himself. He had taken a man's life. It was easy. That made it all the more horrific.

Song collected the tools together. He felt inside the pouches of Jesus' leather belt and checked inside the battel. Nothing.

Song studied the site. The river was rough here. He knew Jesus hated working in strong current; the man had not even known how to swim. Song undressed and slipped into the shallows, remembering what Sammy had taught him about studying the shape of the river and the feel of gravel underfoot. Song's eyes flicked around the lines of trees. He felt as if he was being watched. By some God he no longer believed in. Probably never had.

He wiggled his toes deep into the riverbed, probing for more grainy material before diving down to grab handfuls of earth. He flung the wet gravel onto the bank. After a dozen dives he pulled himself out and lay on his back to catch his breath. The mating call of a hermit hummingbird drew his eyes to the trees and he blocked out the sun with his hand. As he did he caught a glint of light under his nails, still stained around the cuticles with the blood of Jesus. He flicked out the dirt and smeared it across his forearm. There was a glimmer in the dark streak. He rubbed the dirt into his skin and saw again the flicker of reflected sunlight.

He looked at the piles of wet earth by his side and took up the sieve. Removing the larger pebbles he searched among the finer material. Nothing. Again he sieved the filtered matter, swirling around the water and shingle. He squinted down into the battel, shading it from the bright sunlight. Was the sun tricking him? There were a hundred specks of golden light between the granules. One was about the size of a sesame seed. He plucked it out and bit it between his teeth. Gold. Finally. This was rough justice, Song thought. He surprised himself at how he was without feeling towards Jesus. He had killed a man at the age of seventeen with a knife given to him by a vicar, but he felt nothing.

Song spent another two days panning the bend of the river. At the end of the day he melted his finds down and sewed them inside the hem of his shirt. He was going to close up camp and head back to Bartica.

Before he left Song made discreet markings on each side of the riverbank and sketched out a rough map of the site in the pages of his book. Then he loaded the boat and headed downstream.

Song always knew the journey back to Bartica would be difficult, even though he had made rigorous notes on the journey out. He stuck to the smaller rivers. If he started down one waterway and lost his nerve, he'd continue anyway. That's what Sammy had said: don't change your mind, push on against your fears. Song was determined and tired in equal measure; he found himself nodding off even as he rowed. By the time he arrived in town he had been gone sixty-two days. It was not two weeks since he had killed Jesus and thrown him into the river like scrap. Before he arrived back in Bartica he scrubbed himself once more and rinsed out his clothes. He tried to dig the dried blood out from under his fingernails. He wanted to be sure there was no sign when he arrived at the jetty.

'Look at you,' Dory said. 'Skin an' bone. Done with life, boy?'

'Ain't you been bothering to eat?' Joseph asked.

Dory threw him a guava from the dock. 'Where's Jesus?'

Song didn't reply to any of their questions.

'Looks like you 'bout ready to die, boy,' Joseph said.

'Maybe I am,' Song said, cracking open the guava and sucking at the flesh.

'Boy's become a man, that's for sure.'

'Where's Jesus?'

'Is he here?' Song asked.

Basil whistled. 'Ain't he with you?'

Song shook his head. 'I thought he could be back here.'

'Ain't seen no Jesus for a couple thousand years,' Dory said. Everyone laughed.

Song threw a rope to the boys. Joseph helped him up to the jetty.

'I lost him,' Song shrugged.

Basil whistled again. 'Kill 'im?'

Song didn't flinch but he felt his throat tighten. He needed to get away from the dock and all their loose banter.

'Shut your big mouth,' Joseph said. 'This boy's the son of a preacher.'

The son of a preacher. Song couldn't bear to hear their talk. He shuddered to think what Father Holmes would think of him now.

'Lost him to the river,' Song said. 'The current was rough. Don't think he could swim. Maybe he didn't make it. Maybe he did.'

'Drowned?'

'I waited around but he never showed up.'

'Ain't gonna resurrect himself, boy,' Dory said. 'Even if he was called Jesus.'

Song turned to go.

'If I was you I'd be hoping he wouldn't ever show up again,' Basil said. 'He'll be 'bout ready to kill you.'

'You don't know nothing, Basil,' Joseph said. 'The man's dead and gone and about time, I say. Jesus lived too long as it was.'

'Never found his body, eh?' Basil said. 'Just like Jesus, son of God. Preacher's son'll know all about that, of course.'

Song didn't want to be reminded again. 'What's going on here?' he asked.

'Bad times. Ever since Father Holmes gone, place has gone back to its old ways. Like a boat without a mooring.'

'He couldn't keep this place in check either,' Song said.

'Used to be better with him in town. Kind of a compass telling us which way to point. He made you feel like you didn't want to let him down, you know.'

'Yes, I know,' said Song.

'So you find any gold?' Dory asked.

'A bit.'

'Sounds like a lot. Let's take a look.'

'Give the boy a break,' Joseph said. 'Look at the state of him. He deserves everything he got.'

'It's not a lot,' Song said. 'But I'll be going back up.'

'Course you are, boy. They always do.'

The vicarage seemed smaller and quieter. Song fingered the gold in the seam of his shirt to be sure it was still there. He went around to the back of the house.

'Hey, Jingy.'

Jingy slapped her chest. 'Whatch you doin' giving me a heart attack? Look at you, what's left of you.'

Song bent his head to walk under the doorframe into the kitchen. He smelled the burned brown sugar of pepper pot. The lid of boiling rice rattled. 'You got guests?' Song asked.

'Look like one just walked in. Don't you think there's people worryin' 'bout you? Sit yourself down. I'm gonna break my own rules given you look like you do.' Jingy steered him out of her kitchen. 'You eat before you wash to save me from being accused of murder. Can count your ribs through your shirt. What you been doing, starving yourself? Growin' up and not out. I've letters for you.'

Song thought how the dining room looked like a framed still-life. It seemed like it hadn't changed since Father Holmes was last there. Jingy handed him the post before heading back into the kitchen muttering. Song looked over the letters. The first was from Queen's College. He tore open the envelope. He had won the scholarship. A full bursary for tuition and board. Term had started a month earlier. He slipped the letter back into the envelope.

Father Holmes would have been proud he'd won a place, but not if he had let it go.

The next one was from London. It had a stamp from the Royal Ornithological Society. Inside was a single sheet of paper.

> *Royal Ornithological Society*
> *London*
> *14 February 1887*

> *Master Song Holmes, Esq.,*
> *The Vicarage,*
> *Parish of Bartica,*
> *British Guiana*

> *Dear Master Holmes,*
> *We have studied your commendable books regarding the Birds of British Guiana, gratefully received from your guardian Father Holmes (Vicar, Parish of Bartica, British Guiana) on 24 November 1886.*
> *We were most interested in the observation of species Number 11. Given the professional nature of the recordings in these books, The Royal Ornithological Society has taken upon itself to confirm the existence of the 'Whiskered white-headed song warbler', so named as per Father Holmes' request.*

Song stopped reading. The page blurred through his tears. He began to sob uncontrollably, like the day he had walked into Father Holmes' room, missing him, willing him to return. He missed him again now, unbearably.

A scholarship. A letter from the Royal Ornithological Society. A bird named after him. And he had killed a man.

*

The following day Song went to see Old Ivor. He remembered their first exchange all those years ago, the old man teasing Song with a handful of diamonds.

'Ah, so the boy finally made it upriver. Not looking so good though. How long were you gone?'

'Couple months.'

'That'll grow you up. How much you come back with?'

Song put the lump of melted gold on the table.

Old Ivor whistled. 'Work that hard for only this and you'll be in your grave before long. You didn't have much luck up there, did you?'

'Never much believed in luck.'

'Wrong business you in then.'

Song wanted to get in and out of there quickly. 'How much?'

Old Ivor weighed the gold and slid a few groats across the table. Song picked up the coins one by one. He felt their weight, the cool metal, the worn edges. Hard-earned. This money hadn't come easily, but it felt good.

He then headed to market to buy oil, sugar and pulses for Jingy. While he was there he ran into Jon and his sister, Sonia. Song greeted them awkwardly. Seeing Jon reminded Song of his childhood, more innocent times. He felt like he'd betrayed all of that by committing an act reserved for grown men. Sonia mustn't have noticed Song's uneasiness because she reached up and hugged him.

Jon looked him over. 'You okay?'

'Fine. Long time on the river, but I'm fine.' Song was impatient to hear about Jon's art scholarship. 'Did you hear back from Q.C.?'

'Yes. I got it.'

'You did?'

'Full scholarship. Mama wouldn't let me go, of course.'

'No. You can't waste this. Go anyway. Even if it means going against her.'

'You know how hard she has it at home. I can't leave right now.'

'But this is big, Jon.'

'Don't blame her. I don't think she really knows what it means. I did worry what Father Holmes would have thought though.'

'He'd have persuaded your mama, I guess,' Song said.

'You're right, he would.' Jon had a faraway look in his eyes, as if he was imagining that life.

'I could try and talk to her,' Song said.

Jon shook his head. 'What about you?'

'Same.'

'You got it, too? Then what are you doing here?'

'I only read the letter yesterday. I missed the deadline by weeks.'

Jon became animated. 'They'd still take you if you explained. You could easily catch up. You probably wouldn't even need to catch up. You'd be ahead of half the class. You've got to go, Song. For both of us. You've got nothing keeping you here.'

'Haven't I?' He'd heard words like that before. Father Holmes had once said he'd got nobody else. 'Maybe you're right. Maybe I haven't. Anyway it's too late.'

Jon shook his head. 'It's not too late.'

Song shrugged. He felt tired suddenly. Tired of trying to justify his choices.

'I can't believe we both got it and neither of us took it,' Jon said. 'He'd have been crushed.'

Song flinched. 'Would he?'

'I think he would, yes,' Jon said solemnly.

'Poor Jon,' Sonia said, sensing the sadness in the air.

Song changed the subject. 'I came back to Bartica on my own, you know.'

'What happened to Jesus?'

'He's dead.'

'Dead?'

Song suddenly wanted to tell Jon everything that had happened. To confide. To share his dark secret. But then he looked at Sonia and all her sweetness, and couldn't bear to sully her with that kind of talk.

'How'd he die?' Jon asked.

'Just on the river.'

Jon nodded and asked no more.

Song picked Sonia up and looked into her eyes. He remembered the little girl as a baby. He recalled the milk pouring down the walls of Jon's house. It seemed like a hundred years ago but it was five. 'It's so good to see you both again.'

Sonia tried to wriggle free and Song set her back down again.

Jon whistled. 'How the hell was travelling back on your own?'

'Hell,' Sonia repeated.

'Shh,' Jon said to his sister.

'Thank our time with Sammy for getting me through. Remember what he said? How the ones who hesitate are goners. Push on against your fears. Wasn't easy but I wasn't about to give up neither. Caught a labba, which saw me through those last days, although, hell, I was almost too weak to skin the thing.'

'Hell,' Sonia repeated again.

Jon rolled his eyes at her.

'I'll be going back up,' Song added.

'You always loved it upriver,' Jon said. 'It always scared me a bit.'

'Town scares me more,' Song said. 'Give me birds over people.'

'You're right about that.'

'So what are you going to do next?' Song asked.

'I'll finish school. Then maybe Georgetown. How's this? I wrote a letter to the governor asking if he might need an illustrator. Not just for birds but other stuff, too. Documenting Guiana life, that kind of thing. I'd never have had the courage without Father Holmes.'

'Braver stuff than going upriver,' Song said, wanting to sound a note of encouragement to his friend. 'Father Holmes would have been proud of you.'

There was silence between the boys.

'You get any gold?' Sonia asked.

'Sure,' Song said crouching down to her height. 'Everyone does. It's how much that's important.'

Sonia's eyes widened. 'Can I see it?'

Song lifted his bag of shopping. 'It's here. Oil and lentils. Sorry. Next time I'll show you before I sell.'

She pouted. 'Hell.'

The boys laughed.

'What do you think Father Holmes would've thought about you going upriver?' Jon asked.

'I don't know. Said he wanted me to do whatever I wanted to do. Even gold.'

'He was the one who first took us upriver, you know. You could even pin it on him.'

Song smiled. 'Thanks. I'll remember that the next time I have to defend my choices.'

Jon was lost in his own thoughts. 'Those few weeks were the best of my life, I swear.'

'Come join me anytime.'

'I'm only good for sketching,' Jon said. 'But if you ever need someone to draw you striking it rich you give me a holler.'

When Song arrived back to the vicarage, Jingy was scrubbing his clothes. He watched her from the fence as she flung a shirt into a bowl of bubbles, raising the garment up to the heavens before rubbing the cloth against itself with clenched fists. He had a sudden surge of sadness, as if he was remembering the scene after Jingy had died. Song didn't know why. Perhaps it was his way of steeling himself, preparing for all the people he loved to pass on.

She looked up. 'So when you goin' off again?'

'Who said anything about that?'

'I no fool. It's a fever.' She rinsed the next garment, slapping it down on a slab of stone, like dough. Her hands gleamed wet and raw.

'I don't have the fever, Jingy.'

Jingy let out a laugh. 'A man's got to live the life a man wants to live. It's a foolish woman who chooses to get in the way of that.'

'Could say the same thing about you, Jingy. What if I got in your way in the kitchen?'

'Father Holmes put wisdom and judgement inside a' you. Now you got to decide your path. Whatever that path may be.'

Song reflected on the path he'd already chosen. Murder. Revenge. He didn't dare think about that too hard, not with Jingy watching on. She was so intuitive she'd probably figure it out.

'What do you think he'd have thought about my pork-knocking?'

'Ain't no worse than nothing else.'

Song smiled. 'I'm going to pay you, you know.'

'For what? Saying what you want to hear?'

'For washing and cooking and everything.'

She laughed. 'Sho' you will. If you got money to pay me, pay me. Some days you can pay me twice over to make up for the days you broke. Tough life pork-knocking. And you won't need me to remind you a' that.'

CHAPTER 14

Song had heard that Jesus had a few kids running about the west side of town. He tried to find out but nobody knew, or cared to know. Instead he went to Jesus' favourite at Ruby Lou's and put some money in her hand. He closed her fingers around the notes.

'What you givin' this to me for?' Lila said. 'I ain't family.'

'I'm taking on his boat, his rusty tools,' Song said. 'I've got to give someone something for his old junk. And since he's not here . . .'

'He might yet turn up,' Lila said. 'Then he'll show up on my doorstep wanting his money and I won't have a penny of it left. You causin' me more trouble than I already got.' She reached out as if to give it back to Song.

He pushed her hand away. 'He's not showing up again, Lila. Take the money.'

'Nothing could kill that man, I swear. Hard as greenheart.'

Song remembered Jesus' hot blood between his fingers and pushing the knife in harder. 'He owed you more than he paid you, I'm sure of that,' Song said. 'Take a night or two off.'

Lila smiled. 'You're a good man, Song. I know you're not taken with visiting us, 'cept for the music, but I'm here if you change your mind. That goes for any of the girls. We like gentlemen. Ain't many in these parts.'

She leaned towards him and kissed him on the mouth. Song

could taste liquor on her lips, and he thought of his time at Josie's on the bottle. He vowed he wouldn't let himself fall apart like that again.

She pulled away slowly. 'If you change your mind . . .'

'Only for the music, Lila, that's why I come.'

Song continued to Louis' store. Song nodded at Bronco, who blinked slowly but gave him no more. He pushed open the door. The store was empty except for a short man buying ice. Louis was shaving the block and chips darted into the dark air.

'Morning,' Song said to the men.

Louis looked up. 'Morning.'

The other man glanced across. Song recognised him by his profile. After all his visits around town with Father Holmes, Song knew most people by sight if not by name. This man was an odd-jobber. Upriver time to time. Didn't drink much. Pretty wife but the skinny sort. The kind where nobody knew how she had managed to survive so many babies.

'That's enough,' the man said to Louis.

'Won't be enough,' Louis said, 'but I'll stop if you want me to. Cheap is cheap. Don't come running to me when your drinks are warm and you're breaking a sweat. Cigarettes?'

'Nope,' the man said. 'That's it.'

There were two bottles of white rum on the counter. Louis started to wrap the purchases up.

'Party?' Song asked.

The man looked up through a ragged fringe of jet hair. 'Yan's sister is in from Berbice,' he said. 'Having a few drinks if you're passing by. Was sorry to hear about the Father.'

Song nodded his thanks. They both watched Louis put the wrapped bottles in a bag.

'Word is you found something,' Louis said.

There was a long pause.

'You talking to me?' the man asked.

Louis nodded in the direction of Song. 'Was talking to him. But he don't seem to be telling.'

'Me?' Song said. 'I imagined you were talking to the man throwing the party. Looks like he's the one celebrating.'

'Them that don't care to talk always got something to say,' Louis said.

'Not always,' the other man said. 'I know plenty of men who don't find nothing and don't want to talk 'bout finding nothing.'

Song looked again at the figure by his side in his tattered blue cotton shorts and white vest. He was wiry, but his shoulders looked like they'd been lifting and carrying all his life. His legs bowed out in the shape of a barrel. He looked hungry.

'You know the river?' Song said.

'Sure I know the river. Know the men on the river too. Some talk, some don't. Don't mean nothing. Some just like talking more than some others, that's all.'

'You going upriver again soon?' Song asked.

'Upriver, downriver, wherever. Am waiting for work.'

Song liked the man's unassuming manner. 'Name's Song. Not sure I remember yours.'

'Chi.' He pulled open the door and sunlight spilled into the store. 'Come by tonight if you like.'

Song's eyes followed the man outside.

Louis interrupted his thoughts. 'You going up again?'

'Guess so,' Song replied.

Louis grinned. 'Fever burning you up, boy. You just got back. You going again.'

'It's just a job, Louis, not a fever.'

'You found something?'

'Not a lot. But I will.'

Song put on a clean shirt and walked over to Chi's later that night. He could not remember the exact house but neighbours pointed the way. It looked nice in the dark, but most houses did when the cracked paint and slumped roof were disguised by the night. There was a Tilley lamp on the porch throwing buttery yellow light on the damp skin of a few figures who were softly laughing. Song set to turn back. He wasn't sure he wanted to be taking it easy that evening; he preferred to hide away with his raw memories a bit longer. But Chi caught sight of him.

'It's this house,' he shouted. 'You got the right one.'

He handed Song a bottle as he stepped up onto the porch. 'Am I interrupting?' Song asked.

'You're welcome to join us,' the other man on the porch said. He stretched out a hand. 'Gloster.'

Song took it. 'Song.'

'I'm Dorothy,' the woman said, lifting a hand. Her skin was the colour of honey and her hair curled under like Song had seen in advertisements for soap. He thought she was too beautiful for him to be around. Like he belonged somewhere else.

'Gloster's a businessman from Berbice,' Chi said. 'Dorothy's Yan's sister.'

Song nodded at them. 'Nice to meet you both. How's Berbice these days?'

Dorothy spoke first. 'Breezy,' she said, with a voice that sounded the same. 'Ever been?'

'Never been,' Song said.

'Mangoes and fresh fish. That's Berbice,' she said.

'I've heard about those sweet mangoes.'

'They'd make anyone feel better about life,' Dorothy drawled.

Gloster continued with his story. Song noticed some kids in the shadows. Then Yan emerged from the house in a white cotton dress. She was skinnier than her sister, like Song remembered, and the dress hung from her shoulders like from a clothes hanger.

'Hear you're just back from the river,' she said, leaning against the frame of the door. 'You need some help?'

'You offering?' Song said.

Yan smiled. 'I'd like that. But take my husband. He ain't as lazy as he looks. Word is you've found a string.'

'Hush, woman,' Chi said. 'Leave him alone.' He turned to Song. 'She's a straight-talking one. No offence.'

'None taken. Word travels quickly round here.'

'Defreitas sisters say it as they mean it,' Gloster said with a chuckle. Song saw him wink at his wife, and they shared a smile. Unexpectedly, suddenly, Song wished he had someone to do that with.

'We'd be grateful for the money.' Yan patted her rounded belly. 'Ninth on the way.'

'Just not sure I need help right now.'

'You'll excuse my fast tongue,' Yan said. 'Only thinking of the children and our next.' She patted her belly again. 'Chi's come back from long trips before with nothing. Nothing don't feed nothing. I've a feeling you're a fair man.'

'Nobody's called me fair before.'

'A fair man don't have to be fair every day of the week,' Yan said. 'That's too much to ask of anyone.'

Dorothy's voice was soft. 'Stop and start like a breeze, that's more usual.'

'You seen the red-eyed woman then?' Gloster asked.

'Not sure I have,' Song replied.

'You don't know about her?' Dorothy asked.

Song shook his head.

'She'll have seen you even if you ain't seen her,' Dorothy said. 'The patron of pork-knockers. She lives in the river. Flashing red eyes. Come close to her, and you catch the fever. She'll take everything off you that you find.'

'It's a story,' Song said.

'There's truth in it though.'

The evening rolled by. It was warm and soft on the porch. Yan and Dorothy brought out plates of crab. The five of them crunched the shells, sucking the juices out of the pincers and spitting aside the splinters. Song wanted to feel at ease but couldn't, and wondered if he ever would again.

Gloster continued with his tall tales of life on the coast. He had more stories than someone who had lived a hundred lives. He spoke of boats docking in Berbice with a thousand turtle shells for ballast; he explained new schemes for buying sugar in the future that could double your money; he told them about a Lebanese man found swinging on a rope outside his shop after he wronged a drunk seaman with the finest of fingers who could tie every sailing knot in the book with his eyes shut.

Song wanted to listen to all of Gloster's stories yet at the same time he didn't want to hear a thing. He looked across at Chi again. Song thought how he didn't want to be going back upriver on his own right now. Maybe he could do with some company for this next trip.

After he left Chi's house he wandered down to the river. The moon was up, reflecting chopped-up light on the water. He looked upstream into the darkness. Somewhere up there, he'd killed a man. Somewhere up there he was going to find gold.

As he walked back to the vicarage, he passed Josie's. There was laughter inside, and shouting. He hesitated and then entered. It was busy. Maia was behind the bar, staring into the distance as she often did, with a misty look in her eyes.

'Hello,' Song said softly.

Maia looked his way. 'You. Took your time. Been thinking about me?'

Maia could make him feel good with a half-dozen words yet Song didn't want to be there. 'Just checking on you, that's all.'

'Well, I'm checked.'

'I'll be on my way then.'

'You not staying?'

'Maybe another time.'

'No time like the moment.'

'I'll be on my way.'

'Another time then.'

A week later, Song and Chi left Bartica. They met at first light down at the dock. Chi was there first. He lifted his head as Song approached but continued to pack the boat. Song passed him the last few boxes down from the jetty, a canister of oil and some stacked sieves. Within a few minutes they had shoved off the bank and the boat slid into the river. Song threw back the rope. It landed with a thud, coiled on the jetty. Song felt nervous about returning to the place where he'd killed Jesus, but he had too much to lose to show it. He gripped the oars tight to stop his hands from shaking.

A paleness was arching into the east of the sky and seeping into the dark river water. A layer of mist hovered. The croaking frogs heard only at nighttime were missing a beat now and then, lessening in strength, yet the birds seemed wary to break the day. The river was silent save the water off the two men's paddles.

They steered the boat close to the bank where the current was slowest as they moved up the Essequibo. Neither man spoke. They were concentrating on keeping the rhythm of their paddling. Chi was at the back, ploughing the water and choosing their course. Song sat at the front, keeping up the speed but stopping now and then to look at his notebook. He plotted any changes, wrote down where they stopped for the night, where the soil was softer or the rock exposed, and any changes in plant life. In between, he scribbled down notes about the birds he saw: dusky parrots and green-and-rufous kingfishers and stripe-backed bitterns. He wrote all day until it was too dark to see. This was how Song wanted it to be. Not random and faintly hopeful. He remembered what Mr Leigh had said to him. 'You're smarter than all of those pork-knockers put together. You can read and write, you can figure things out differently.' Song echoed that line to himself: he was going to do things differently.

As the light faded they pulled into the bank for the night. Chi moved around knowingly in the darkness, as if he already knew each place. After the hammocks were strung up, Chi crouched by the fire where the rice was boiling. He dug a spoon into the pot and lifted out some grains.

'You know it all,' Song said. 'Why haven't you set up on your own?'

Chi swallowed the hot mouthful before he shrugged.

'You'd make more money,' Song said.

'Sounds like Yan's got your ear,' Chi said. 'Rice?'

'Sure.'

Chi passed him a plate. 'You think I'm here on account of the gold everyone thinks you found?'

'Well, that'd be as good a reason as any . . .'

Song heard Chi chuckle in the darkness. 'I'm smart enough to know that if you were so sure you'd found it, you'd be fetching it yourself.'

'Maybe sure.'

The two men fell into silence. Song could no longer make out Chi's outline in the dark folds of the night. But he ignored any jitters he had about Jesus coming out at him of the darkness, the weight on his back, the smell of burning skin.

For nearly a week, Song cross-referenced the notes he'd made on the previous expedition, navigating his way down the smaller channels, trying to remember the way one river bend looked compared to another. There were times when everywhere looked familiar, and others when nothing did. But Song pushed on, trying to ignore his doubts, just like Sammy had taught him. He used Mr Leigh's compass for directions, and his own rough measurements of distance and time. By the end of the week he had found the site.

'Here,' he said, pointing with his paddle at the bank. 'Turn in here.'

Chi dug in his own paddle to turn the boat. Song leapt onto the bank and tied them up. His hands were trembling. He scanned the trees, out of habit, as if he was looking for birds. He could feel his breathing quicken. Perhaps he should have come alone after all. Perhaps Chi would guess what he had done. Song cast his eyes over the area.

'Time to unload,' Song said, trying to ease the tension.

Chi was already unpacking. 'How long you spend here then?' he asked.

'Not long,' Song replied. Chi was making him nervous. He was nosing around like a dog.

'I'll show you where we're going to set up camp,' Song said. 'Not here but further in.'

Song walked through the area where he had camped with Jesus. He flicked his eyes around, checking to see if there were any remains of the fire, any sign of the scuffle, of the dark patch of blood on the ground.

'Keep following,' Song said. The once-beaten trail was overgrown, almost impossible to find. Song cleared the way with his cutlass. It felt good to be doing something physical. He took a swipe at a vine even though it was not in his path. It sliced clean in half but in the thick vegetation the loose stem did not fall to the ground.

'Rough water,' Chi remarked as they approached the tributary.

'It was rougher before. Dead Man's Bend, I called it.' Song said. 'Last place I saw Jesus.'

'I think it needs a new name. I'm not superstitious but . . .'

'Been thinking about that myself,' Song said. 'Omaia. I have a friend called Maia. Let's call it Omaia.'

'I could love this place more than my woman.'

'Sounds like you've always loved the river more than your woman.'

It didn't take long for the two men to find their rhythm. They spent their days at the river with their battels, swirling around the wet gravel from the riverbed. Song felt like time was passing in the same way, like the hands of a clock moving slowly around and around. It gave him time to think, perhaps too much time. Too much time to relive what he'd done at this place. They were working day in, day out, at the very spot he'd let go of Jesus' body.

'Never seen gold giving itself up like this,' Chi said.

'That right?'

'We find something every day. Most days.'

Song shrugged. 'Don't feel it's that much.'

'It's more than I've known.'

'Good.' Song knew he wasn't making conversation easy for Chi.

'River can swallow you up, can spit you out, but in the end it offers up what you deserve.'

'Not sure I believe that,' Song said, but he felt some vindication in Chi's words. Jesus, the man who'd raped him, had also revealed this place to him.

For those first couple months Song and Chi had found gold in their battels by the close of each day. But as their food supplies dried up, so did their finds. Song asked Chi to cut down their daily rations so they could stay out longer. Chi didn't seem to mind. He was in good spirits with what they'd already found. Song was less so. 'If you choose to go upriver, you make sure you hit the big time.' That's what Mr Leigh had said. 'Set yourself apart.'

'Time we had a break, I think,' Song said one evening. He'd been counting; they'd been out ninety-two days.

Chi raised his eyebrows and continued to stoke the fire.

'It's already been three months,' Song continued.

'Been out for double that time before, and longer,' Chi said.

'Can't be easy for Yan.'

'She knows what it's like. She'll be happy enough s'long as I come back with heavy pockets.'

'We've been out of rice and oil for weeks. I can't live off raw fish and labba. We'll come back and make a fresh start. With fresh luck.' Song didn't really know what he meant by this. Maybe he was tired. Swirling the battels, time passing around and around. He felt he could be trapped into doing this forever. Like Jesus.

'Just don't want us quitting on account of my family,' Chi said.

'No one's quitting. I need to do a bit of thinking. Away from here. I want to sell what we've found. There'll be some for you, some for supplies. With the rest, I'm going to register the land.'

Chi frowned. 'Dangerous. Better we keep it to ourselves. This is a good spot.'

'I don't want to risk losing this land. What if some American company comes along and buys up half the Essequibo, including here? I need to get in first. I want the deeds. With all the paperwork in order. No disputes.'

'We'll have everyone on our back if you do,' Chi said. 'They won't waste a minute. Place'll be crawling with pork-knockers by the time we'd return here.'

'I won't be registering only this parcel of land. Land is cheap. I'll buy as much as I can. Acres. Hundreds of acres if I can. They wouldn't know where to look first.'

Chi was sullen. 'Nobody else registers land.'

'That's because most pork-knockers can't read. They couldn't even point to where they are on a map. But if we register the land, everything we pull out is ours.'

'You the boss. Just don't like the idea of everyone knowing where we are. Heard about whole gangs found crawling over registered land. No mercy upriver. Bodies wash up in Bartica every month and nobody sheds a tear.'

Song wondered if he'd already shared too much. There was a voice inside telling him not to be too quick to trust Chi. But after three months upriver with him – working together, eating together – Song wanted to believe he was the steady sort.

'We won't stay in Bartica long,' Song said. 'I'll need you to prepare supplies for the next trip.'

'I'll be ready to leave as soon as we get in.'

Song was beginning to understand the gulf between him and

Chi. Chi pork-knocked because he loved nothing more than being upriver with a fever burning him up. The chance of getting rich was only a bonus. Song wanted more. He wanted to live up to what Father Holmes might have wanted for him. Not just to go upriver. Not even just to get rich. He wanted to set himself apart, that's how Mr Leigh had put it. To live a life that was a story worth telling . . .

'We'll return after the paperwork is sorted, after I've the deeds in my hand,' Song said.

'I ain't here to tell you nothing 'bout nothing. Just telling you what I know about the ways of the river. But sounds like you've got it all worked out—'

'I'll get a decent area with the gold we've found,' Song said. 'Then we'll be safe. Anything we find from then on will be ours.'

'Less they kill us,' Chi said.

'Guess that's true. And there's always the chance we don't find another grain, And then I'd own enough barren land to found a new country.'

CHAPTER 15

Song wanted to arrive in Bartica after dark to avoid drawing attention. They tied up a hundred yards from the dock and unloaded. The pair parted without a word, moving off in different directions like strangers. Each took half the boat's load but there wasn't much. There were clean out of supplies. They had only their bags and their battels.

Song walked slowly towards the vicarage. His footsteps were quiet. His free hand rested on the handle of a cutlass tucked between his belt and trousers. The street was in darkness and nobody seemed to be about.

As he approached the house he saw a light at the window of Father Holmes' study. Song put down his load in the yard and stepped silently upon the wooden porch.

There was a young man sitting at the desk writing. He was leaning over his papers, just like Father Holmes used to, his hand moving quickly across the page. His eyes glanced up and down between his script and there was a book held open by a magnifying glass. Around his neck was a dog-collar.

Song pulled back from the window. He tried to calm his quickening breath and reached out his shaking hands for the frame to steady himself. He moved quickly now, travelling to the back of the house to scale the mango tree. He knew every branch, even in the dark. His fingers probed for the knot he'd hollowed out. When he found the space he reached for the seam of his shirt, tearing at the fine stitches and feeling for the nubs of gold wrapped in a shred of shammy. He pressed them deep inside the hollow.

He released himself from the lowest branch of the tree and moved back around to the front of his house to retrieve his load. Then he slipped out through the gate. There weren't many places he could go. Josie's.

Song slipped up the back stairs. Clio was in the corridor. She jumped when she saw him.

'Goddamn it. What you doing walking around like a ghost?' She lit the cigarette in her left hand and inhaled deeply. Then she looked him up and down. 'You come to see Maia? You can clean up in there.' She swept the glowing end of her cigarette in an arc towards the door to his left. 'I'll tell Maia you're here.' She hesitated. 'She got smashed about last week. Does it matter? Ella's here too. I'm busy tonight.'

'Who hit her?'

'What's it to you? Nothing more I hate than a man getting all protective over us. Like you trying to take ownership or summink. We can look after ourselves thank you very much.'

Song put his finger up to his lips. 'Not tonight, Clio. I'm tired.'

'Look it, too.' she said. 'Go clean yourself up.'

She moved off and Song gently pushed open the door. The room was empty. He lifted the load down from his back. His body had started to hurt. He scrubbed himself with the first soap he had seen in over a month. The dirt was deep. He rinsed off with the half-full bucket of water in the corner. There was a film of mosquito eggs on the surface.

Maia pushed open the door without knocking. She was wearing a coffee-coloured shift and he could see the points of her breasts through the cotton. There was a white shawl around her shoulders but he could see bruises. There was a cut below her eye.

'Came back then?'

'Just to stock up, get some supplies.' He pointed at his bag in the corner. 'Clean out of oil for weeks now. And soap.'

'Didn't miss me then?' Maia's voice was firm but Song could hear the fragility beneath.

'Always miss you.' He didn't mean it until he said it out loud. Then he felt like he'd been missing her all his life.

Maia allowed herself a quick smile. 'Find anything?'

'Not as much as I'd like.'

She laughed like a bird. A four-tone staccato he remembered from their childhood. 'Name me a pork-knocker who's found as much as he'd like.'

Her eyes flicked over his body. She pulled a torn bolt of cloth from a line strung up across the room. 'Wanna come next door?'

She slipped out and shouted from down the corridor. 'Better bring your stuff with you. Won't last a minute in this dump. Thieves and liars and drunks.'

Song patted his face with the cloth. In the lamplight his shadow was thrown a half-dozen times across the room. He barely recognised himself. It was the body of a man undernourished but stronger about the shoulders and neck. He looked like how he remembered his father – standing in the doorway of their home before he left for the fields. A silhouette, a shadow. He was nearly eighteen, no longer a boy. In his head he could hear Lady singing to him: ... *don't give up, don't give in. And walk tall wherever you go.*

Song stayed at Josie's for a couple days. Without even stepping into the street he learned everything that had gone on in Bartica over the previous three months. Ella, the youngest sister, loved to talk.

'There's a new vicar come all the way from England, too scared

223

even to leave the house,' she said. 'Paul Nutt has been in Ruby Lou's. On a Monday because he figured fewer people would notice. With Lila, I think. Cecil Pereira lost his virginity to his mother's sister although he's pretending she's a half-sister.'

Song laughed. He hadn't heard himself laugh that way in a long time.

'Don't laugh; it's all true,' she pouted.

'Am sure it is. You could have been saying this same thing, just different names, when I left three months ago. Bartica doesn't change much.'

'Jon left, that's a change.'

'Where's he gone?'

'Georgetown. Got a big job at Governor's House.'

Song smiled. 'Drawing?'

'I think so.'

Maia was too much of a daydreamer to hear the gossip, or if she did she was too wrapped up in her own thoughts to remember a scrap of it. Clio did not have a minute for anyone but herself. If any of the three was going to last the long road it was going to be Clio.

Song's first outing was to collect a portion of gold from the mango tree. He slipped there under the cover of darkness and went on to sell it at first light. He knocked on the door of Old Ivor.

''Bout time you walked in here again,' the old man said. 'Was beginning to wonder if you were one of those fellas that slip up at the start. They say pork-knockers either die very young or very old. You'll probably last the course now.'

'So you're a fortune-teller, too, huh?' Song teased. 'How much is that service?'

'Free with every transaction,' Old Ivor said.

Song put the gold on the table. It was only a quarter of what they had found.

'That's more like it,' he said, setting the gold on his scales. As they wobbled, he whistled. 'Very good. You keep coming to me, I'll look after you.'

He slid some groats across the table and Song pocketed them. It felt different this time. His hands felt clean. This money had nothing to do with Jesus.

Song went to market and bought some of Jingy's favourites: Lifebuoy soap, lime astringent, Lyle's golden syrup. He waited for her by the dock early evening hoping she would come by to catch crabs. He saw her figure from a distance, bucket in one hand, fishing net in another. She was sharply on time, just before the mosquitoes rose up.

'You don't look much better this time around and I heard you had a cook with you,' Jingy said when she saw him. 'What's he feeding you?'

Song handed Jingy the bag of gifts. 'Labba mostly.'

'Labba mostly,' Jingy repeated, taking the bag from him. 'Call that a healthy way to go about living. You need to stop dying and start thinking about living.'

'I've thought the same,' Song said. 'That's why I'm back.'

She looked into the bag. The can of golden syrup was on top. She softened her tone. 'I ain't forgiving you just by you bringing me nice things. This woman can't be bought. You taken your time to come see me. I hear you've been in town a few days already. I'm old you know. I could've dropped dead by now and how bad would you have felt?' She lifted the can and saw the soap underneath. 'Now you've spent all your money on these frivolous things. Anyway I don't care to listen to excuses. I've enough to do. Crabs are waiting.'

The two continued to the river just like they used to, and Jingy clambered down the side of the dock passing the net up to Song to empty her haul into the bucket. The crabs were being artful to-night.

'Damn sneaky things,' she said. 'So you heard about the new vicar? Totally unexpected, as it always is in these parts. People arrive before the post. How d'you figure that? Just suddenly turned up. I had to clear out your rooms. Almost broke me packing up Father Holmes' things. Still think of the vicarage as his and your home, nobody else's.'

Song thought back to when Father Holmes talked of making a home together. Then he thought of Father Holmes' room at the vicarage, untouched since he left for England, and his own room and the many hours he lay in bed there waiting for the morning light to dissipate the gloom so he could read. It was another life.

'What you heard about Father Lovett, then?'

'Not a lot. Heard he's living scared, that's all.'

Jingy tsk-ed. 'Course you have. This town likes to put someone down before they know a thing about them. He's not so bad. No Father Holmes but he's worth getting to know. Nice name. Young though. And a bit serious for someone so young. Believes everyone should live by the book. Not an easy thing in a town like Bartica.'

'I'll come meet him later in the week,' Song said.

'Course you won't. I'll send your things. And Father Holmes'. All packed with your name on. And don't go asking me to send them to Josie's. I want a proper address.'

Song took a room above the Bits & Bobs pawnshop, across the street from Louis', and paid Bronco to watch his door. The room was empty save one table and a mat on the floor. Later in the day Short John turned up with the boxes from Jingy. Inside were Father Holmes' books, his typewriter and shaving kit. There was the globe and the brass scales from Mr Leigh. One of the boxes was filled with letters and other papers. He caught sight of Father

Holmes' neat handwriting and he ran his fingers over the words. Song closed the box again, trying to shut out the sadness he felt.

The next day Song woke early and made his way to the district commissioner's office. William Wright was the person to speak to about land registration, or in fact anything official in Bartica. But in truth nobody saw much of him. He kept a distance, and was more likely to be spotted on the ferry back and forth to Georgetown than on the streets of this town he was meant to be running.

When Song entered the office, Wright's assistant Harrington was hunched at his desk staring into space. He was strangely uncomfortable to look at – all jutting shoulders and bony elbows – and had a twitch of licking his lips over and again nervously. There was an aimlessness about him. Like he was just marking time through life.

'Is Mr Wright in?'

Harrington jumped. He looked up at Song and his eyes fell on the rolled-up map Song was carrying.

'What's your business?'

Song lifted up the map. 'Land.'

'Mr Wright's a busy man and won't be able to see you today.'

'We're all busy, Harrington,' Song said. 'But I've got a lot of land to purchase and I think he'd like to know.'

Harrington got up slowly. He knocked on the inside door leading into Mr Wright's office, entered and closed it behind him. Seconds later he returned. 'As I said before, Mr Wright is a very busy man, but you'll be grateful to know I've persuaded him to see you. You'll have to wait till he's ready.'

Mr Wright shouted 'come in' from inside his office. Harrington jumped. 'He's ready now. Follow me.'

Mr Wright's office was small and stuffy. There was one small window but it was closed. On the walls were hand-drawn maps with tracts colour-coded in red hatched lines, green dots and blue shading. Mr Wright was writing at his desk. Several pens sat in grooves carved into the wood. By his elbow was a half-drunk cup of tea. The shelves around the room were cluttered with reference books.

Mr Wright did not look up.

'Good morning, sir,' Song said. 'I'd like to see you about some land.'

'I've told him you're a very busy man, sir,' Harrington said.

'Take a seat,' Mr Wright said.

'Shall I take minutes?' Harrington said.

'Don't be ridiculous,' Mr Wright said.

Harrington pulled a face and left the room slowly. Song waited for the door to shut behind him. 'Thanks for your time, sir. I've been keen to get myself a piece of land. I have money saved up from working at the vicarage and thought it might be a good time to invest it. Father Holmes taught me that land was the best place to put money and I wanted to ask you what you thought of the timing. I hear the market is favourable.'

'A good man, Father Holmes. Not many of them in these parts. Smart, too. You could do a lot worse than buy land. Cheap, too. I don't know why more don't. Land is one thing they're not making more of. Where are you looking?'

'May I?' Song asked, as he unrolled the map he had brought and flattened it evenly upon the desk. 'This is one of Father Holmes' old maps,' he said. 'I've marked the area.'

Mr Wright looked at the great swathe of land Song had marked. He whistled. 'Buying up half the country? When I talked about speculation I didn't mean you had to buy up the Essequibo. What do you plan to do with it?'

'My plan is to survey the land before prospecting it, sir. I've got a fixer. Chi knows the interior a lot better than me. I figured the more I buy, the greater chance I have.'

Mr Wright studied the boundary. 'I haven't seen an application of this size in years. Mind you, we see so few applications. Nobody's much interested in speculating on land. That's the problem with most pork-knockers. They're just in it for the day. No long-term thinking. You've had Father Holmes' influence, of course. By the way, what do you think of this Father Lovett fellow. Have you met him yet?'

'Not yet, sir.'

'He's very young. Nineteen. To be a vicar in these parts.'

Song thought how he and Father Lovett were just a year apart. 'Young might be good. He will need the vigour.'

Mr Wright took out his wooden ruler and was marking points on Song's map. Song had deliberately drawn an irregular shape.

'I'll have to straighten out these lines. Too complicated other-wise.'

Mr Wright started scratching some sums on a scrap of paper. Finally he took off his spectacles. 'Well, if there are no other claims, it'll be about a shilling an acre.'

It was close to the number Song had in his head. 'You know what, sir, I might have enough money to buy a bit more – if that's all right with you.' Song took a pencil out of his pocket and extended the lines. The area almost doubled in size. The land Song really wanted fell into the extension.

Mr Wright sucked the air in between his teeth. 'More that gets surveyed the better for us. You know the rules. As long as you declare all your finds.'

'Yes, sir.'

Mr Wright sat back in his chair. 'A man in my profession knows when he meets someone with more than a hunch. People don't go buying up land in the hope it will make them rich.'

Song nodded. 'You're right, sir. As well as Chi I'm looking to some old friends. Father Holmes and I used to spend a lot of time in one particular village when we went upriver. We got to know the families there well. They taught me everything I know about the interior. I've asked them to guide me.' That wasn't strictly true but Song did have plans to call on Sammy and his friends.

'Ah, now you're talking. But they'll kill you for a grain of rice I hear. Not to be trusted.'

'Can't trust anyone in this business,' Song said.

Mr Wright had stopped listening. He was looking at the map and smoothing out the creases. 'You couldn't cover this much land in a lifetime.'

'I'll be hiring hands,' Song said.

'Pay them well, that's my advice. A bitter man shows no mercy. You don't want to end up floating down the river.'

Song wondered again about Chi and whether he was a man who would ever turn on him. He didn't think so. It didn't seem to take much to satisfy him. But Song needed to be cautious. The throes of gold fever could subjugate the usual manners of a man.

'I'll be careful,' Song said.

'I'll send confirmation as soon as this is authorised. Payment is cash only.'

Song left the room to find Harrington squatting on the other side of the door.

Harrington dropped his voice. 'I can make sure nobody finds out about this if you make it worth my while. Remember it was me who persuaded Mr Wright to see you.'

'Good day, Harrington,' Song said loudly.

'Otherwise word'll get out . . .'

*

Song had two copies of the deeds drawn up. He gave one to Jingy to put inside the box under her bed where she kept her wages, and he gave the other to Yan, who hid it in the biscuit tin on the top shelf of her kitchen. Song kept the original document between the pages of Father Holmes' Bible. He wondered what Father Holmes would have thought about that. Song was following his dreams, that was for sure. Every now and then he flicked through the pages until he reached halfway into the Book of Leviticus to read the document through again. He pored over maps charting the area he was buying. Mr Wright was right. It would take a lifetime to survey. But Song's eyes were trained on one location that was burning a hole in his mind. He wanted to believe that was the place that would change everything he knew.

CHAPTER 16

Song and Chi had to stay in town longer than they hoped, waiting on oil to arrive from Georgetown.

During that week Song spent much of his time in his room reading. At night he went to Ruby Lou's to hear the B Boys play. He didn't touch a drop of drink. Never again, he'd said to himself. But he listened to the music and let his mind wander. From the river to the sea to the river, remembering whatever it was that came into his head. Evenings with Father Holmes. That's what he missed most. Their tos and fros on books, local politics, the injustices Father Holmes wanted to redress. Back and forth in the glow of lamplight.

One afternoon Song met Father Lovett on the street. Thin, pale and freckled, he looked younger than Song remembered from his glimpse through the vicarage window. Song introduced himself.

'Father Lovett, you don't know me, but I was Father Holmes' houseboy. I used to live in the vicarage. My name's Song.'

'Ah, yes, I've heard about you.' His tone wasn't friendly. 'I'm surprised not to have seen you on a Sunday morning. I was under the impression Father Holmes put a lot of work into you. But I hear you're on the river now.'

Jingy was right. Father Lovett would struggle in Bartica.

'It was Father Holmes who first took me upriver, in fact. He loved the interior.'

'He wasn't looking for gold though, was he? Saving souls. That was his business. I hear there are a hundred wretched souls for every mile. Is that true?'

'I'd examine my own soul before I judged another. My world up there is more about birds. Recording with illustrations and descriptions . . .'

'Well, I'm not here for birds,' Father Lovett interrupted. 'I'm here to build a congregation. And I'm not impressed with where the town is with regard to that. I hope I can count on you this Sunday?'

'I'll be back upriver by then.'

'Disappointing.'

Father Lovett was not the only one on Song's back. Tom Jameson also had a turn. 'Do you know how much you meant to Father Holmes? What would he say if he could see you drinking in the bars?'

'I'm not drinking in the bars. I'm there for the music.'

'I don't deny that we all need a bit of entertainment. I'm not about to cut that out of a man's life. But I couldn't live with myself if I didn't ask you at least once to consider Father Holmes, that's all.'

Even Bronco pestered Song. 'Fever'll take you downriver if you're not careful,' he warned.

'Not me.'

'You be careful.'

'River hasn't taken you yet, Bronco.'

'I'se bigger than you.'

'That's why I've got you watching my door.'

'Just saying.' Bronco's voice was gentle for such a big man. 'Don't matter what happens to a man like me. Different for a kid like you.'

'I'm not a kid any more.'

'Everyone's smaller than me, so they're a kid. And like I said you'se different. You got promise.'

He wanted Bronco to be right. Promise perhaps, not luck as Mr Leigh had said. 'It's a wonderful thing to have your whole life ahead of you, but it's a crime to waste it,' he'd told Song. Song wasn't about to waste it, not with the plans he had. He wanted to do something that would have made Father Holmes proud.

Perhaps Jingy knew that, because she was the only one who let him be. She just inspected the state of his collar and pinched him hard in the stomach to see if he was eating enough. Not since the time he was passed out in Josie's bar, when she hit him hard across the head, had she called him in on his behaviour. She had never again mentioned those drunken few weeks.

In the evening Song could be found at Ruby Lou's and nowhere else. He'd cross the threshold just as the B Boys began their first set.

The big room was yellowed by candlelight and sweat and hard sad music. The girls were sometimes tired and sometimes drunk and sometimes angry but whatever their mood they could always talk like honey. Not that they ever approached Song. They might offer up a nervous smile as they passed his table but only Ruby Lou ever sat with him. Song came for the music. He drifted into a dream as the boys hit their notes: Jackson on the stand-up piano, Short John strumming a banjo and Boney singing ratchety tunes with his beat-up smoky old voice.

Song rolled the sounds around in his head, mixing them up. He heard in the mix the chanting of a times-table; Mrs Boyle singing 'Ave Maria'; Amalia's sweet humming while she cooked; Lady's voice, of course.

One-two, one-two. The rhythm beat on. Song could hear his sister Xiao Mei calling out numbers in her sing-song voice in the days before she had stopped talking. She hopped on one leg as the numbers increased and switched legs to count down. Then after the flood she didn't make another sound. Song recalled her silence the day he left, and the figures of his family diminishing. 'I'll be back with sugar and gold and diamonds, I promise.' Those were his words. 'You wait and see.'

Some nights, when the memories were too raw, too bloody, Song went straight home. It was too much. He'd yearn for Maia but could not bear for her to see him so broken.

Song made his way over to Chi's. He had heard the oil from Georgetown was arriving later that day and he wanted Chi to be ready to receive it on the jetty. If everything else was in order, they could head upriver the following day.

Nina, Chi's eldest, was on the porch shelling peas.

'Hello, Nina. Your papa around?'

'I thought he was with you. Said he was meeting you at the dock.'

'Missed him then. Yan in?'

'She's gone to market.'

Song pulled up a chair. 'Strange to see the house so quiet.'

'Hell glad for half a minute. 'Bout driving me crazy.'

Song laughed.

'You can laugh but you never had to run after a brother or sister. Just you being spoilt by that Father man. Teaching you fine and everything.'

Song thought how Nina didn't know the half of it. But he was amused by her straight talk.

'You lucky to be living in a nice quiet room in town,' she continued. 'Can do what you want anytime of the day or night. No one to think about or worry about or fret none.'

Song watched her hands deftly squeeze each pod as the peas popped into the bowl.

'Some might feel sorry for me, that I've got no family,' Song said.

'Not me,' Nina said. ''Bout done with family.' She held out a handful of peas. 'Want some?'

'Sure.'

She trickled a handful of peas into Song's cupped palm.

'Where's everyone else?' Song said.

'I don't know and don't care. School. Bibi's with Mama. I sent the rest of them playing. Hope they fall in the river and drown.'

Song laughed again. 'Nina, what's up with you? Yan giving you a hard time?'

'Everyone's giving me a hard time,' she said. 'I want my own time that I can choose what to do with. Why can't I go upriver? Like you and Papa.'

Song thought back to when he'd barely even noticed Nina; she'd been just a shadow on the edge of the porch. 'I don't see why you shouldn't,' he said.

'Tell that to Papa.'

He upturned his handful of peas into his mouth. 'We can take you on the river one day.'

Nina snorted. 'When?'

'I don't know. That's not up to me.'

'Will you ask Papa?'

'Ask him what?'

There was irritation in Nina's voice. 'If I can go upriver?'

'Sure.'

'Promise?'

'Sure, I promise.'

'I got dreams, you know. I'm not spending the rest of my life on a porch shelling peas.'

'I can see that.'

'Can you?'

'I can. I like your spirit, Nina. It's good to have dreams.'

'What else do you like about me?'

Song heard a slight change in her tone. He got up to go. 'Ah, I like all the things I see in your mother and father. Your mama's straight talk. Your papa's sense of adventure.'

Nina also got to her feet. The bowl fell and peas rolled across the floor. She giggled. The sound of a girl, not the woman she was trying to be.

Song bent down to collect them up but Nina caught his hands. 'Nobody's here,' she said. 'Let's go inside.'

'No, Nina. Not me. I don't want to be the same as every other man in Bartica. I'm off to find your papa. You look after yourself, you hear.'

Song and Chi left the next day. They were wary of being followed and planned a late departure, when most men would already be drunk or on their way. Only the jetty boys were around and most of them were fuzzy in the head.

'Hey, leaving in the dark,' Basil said. 'You two got something to hide?'

'We like counting stars,' Chi said.

Basil laughed, rubbing his hands together. 'I'm banking on you boys. I'm putting in my order for some of that gold – but a dose of luck'll do just as well. God help us, we need some luck around here, too.'

Neither responded. They went quietly on their way.

'It feels different this time,' Song said to Chi, under his breath. 'Feel different to you?'

'Sure it feels different,' Chi said. 'Feeling jumpy. Knowing everyone knows where we're headed.'

'They don't.'

'They know more than they did before. That good-for-nothing Harrington mouthing off about town.'

'The only thing they know is that we made a purchase.'

'Still.'

'You're the one making me jumpy, Chi.'

Silence enveloped them. There was the sound of their paddles dipping in the water and a nightjar's call, like 'who are you, who are you' – and Song wondered himself. From the outside a pork-knocker, but he had much more in him than that. This was more than prospecting, more than even discovering gold, but instead finding a sense of worth. He didn't want to ever feel hungry again, yes, but he had also promised to live a life that was a story worth telling. Whatever that story might yet be.

Song was glad for the darkness. The night was moonless and soft high cloud obscured the stars. He and Chi fell into a good rhythm and they drove the boat forward on memory and hope.

It was six days and five nights before they reached camp. They had been moving slower than usual, travelling only at night.

Chi got a fire going. They drank hot strong sweet tea and chewed stale churros. The first of the screaming pihas whooped just as the sun threw its first blades of light into camp.

Song spent a night with Chi before he left on his own for Yupukama. Chi was to stay behind and make a start.

Song carried with him a gallon of cooking oil, two jars of molasses, four bars of soap and a sack of sugar. He had a basket of cooked rice for the two days he should be on the river.

It was several years since Song had visited Yupukama but the villagers welcomed him back like a son. 'They'd share their last bowl of rice with you,' Father Holmes used to say. 'They're more Christian than the Christians.'

When he saw his old friends he was thrust back to his first trip upriver, when Jim Groves had gotten sick. When Father Holmes was alive and Mr Leigh was visiting from the United States of America. Both men lost to him now. But he didn't feel alone. He felt their company with him, even now.

Song spotted Molson and Kai first, then Sammy. Song had grown taller than him, but Sammy was stockier. His hair still hung in front of his eyes. He squinted through the tresses, and smiled.

'Where you been?'

'Finding my way,' Song said.

'Good to see you again.' He turned to the girl by his side. 'This is my wife, Veronique. You got yourself a wife yet?'

Song was taken aback that Sammy might have a wife. She seemed much younger than either of them with her adolescent figure, but she held a steady adult gaze. Like Sammy, her hair fell about her face. She smiled at Song.

'Hello,' he said.

'Hello,' she replied.

'Never thought of a wife,' Song admitted. The idea of a woman forever by his side was a strange new idea. He couldn't help but stare at her – intrigued and wary in equal measure.

Sammy continued, seeming not to notice Song's reaction.

'We heard about the Father's passing,' he said. 'Sorry for that.'

'His ship went down,' Song said simply.

'Never trusted the sea. Trust the rivers.'

'I like that,' Song said.

'How's that friend of yours? Still drawing?'

'Jon? He's doing all right. Found his calling. That in itself is a lot to be thankful for.'

'And the American?'

'Never heard from him again after he went back.' Song tried not to show his hurt. 'Another reason not to trust the sea, I guess.'

'Some come back, some don't.'

'You come back,' Molson said.

'It's been a long time,' Song said.

'You still come back,' Molson said.

Song handed out the gifts he had brought. Jars of dark brown molasses. 'It's thick and extra sweet.' He gave the soap to Sammy's wife. 'This kind doesn't use up so fast.'

Song dug into a bowl of hot stew sweetened with cassareep but declined a second serving in spite of his hunger. He didn't need to be eating their food. Then they stayed up late talking about Omaia. The others got drunk but Song stayed sober.

'Had a run-in with the stuff,' he said. 'Not touching it again.'

'That's a reason,' Sammy said.

'Gotta keep a clear head. Too much to lose now. Too much to live for.'

Sammy travelled in Song's boat. Kai and Molson took a second, lighter vessel. The women made them enough food for a week. The children ran down to the bank to see them off, clapping as the boats eased away. Song watched them wave until the boats turned out of sight.

The party moved stealthily along the river. Song observed the three men navigating, their eyes almost turning back on themselves. They noticed everything, from the first flies rising to the slight ripple of a skulking caiman. They travelled through the night.

Song paddled while Sammy slept, and then they switched. Kai and Molson did the same.

When they reached camp, the sun was not yet at its highest. Chi was out already but the embers were still warm.

They tied up the boats. Song grabbed some extra battels and the four men headed down to the bend.

Song saw Chi swing around when he heard their footsteps.

'Feeling jumpy?' Song asked.

'Hah! Actually I was expecting you to show up about now.'

'Any visitors?'

'Not a soul.'

'You found anything?'

'Found a lot of time,' Chi said. 'A man can't do enough thinking, my mother used to say. Think too much and nothing gets done, my father used to say. Must be why they were always fighting.'

Song rolled his eyes. 'You've been on your own too long.'

'Looks like I got some company now.'

'This is Sammy, Molson, Kai. I've known them for years.'

The three men nodded at Chi.

'Found anything?' Song asked.

'Nope.'

Chi's reply was very quick, Song thought to himself.

'All this time and nothing to show for it?' Song asked. 'You sure you haven't been lounging about in a hammock all day?'

'Look at these hands,' Chi said, turning his palms open. 'Worker's hands.'

Kai and Molson started walking up the edge of the river and within a few minutes they were out of sight. Sammy stood on the bank scanning both directions.

'What d'you think?' Song called out to him.

'Water's not moving well here.'

When Kai and Molson returned they agreed. 'It's better up-stream,' Sammy said. 'Not far. Just a few hundred yards.'

'It's not for panning though,' Molson said. 'You'll need to dig.'

'How deep?' Chi asked.

'Can't say.'

The five men left Dead Man's Bend and walked upstream. Here was another bend in the river, but swinging left, and the rock was similarly dark along the bank.

Song looked at the ground. It was mulch on top but it would be hard rock a couple feet below.

'We'll start digging, then,' Song said.

'Gold ain't the sun,' Sammy said. 'You never know when it's going to come up.'

'Dig up half this jungle if we have to,' Chi said. 'This boy's not satisfied with a grain or two.'

That night, as Chi was at the river getting water, Song found him-self rifling through Chi's things. He'd had a bad feeling – and discovered he was right. There, in a shammy, he found a nugget the size of a thumbnail. He felt deflated and angry in equal measure, cursing himself for trusting Chi so quickly.

Dinner had been quiet. Song didn't feel like speaking. The Yupukama boys never had a lot to say. Chi was the talker, if anyone was, but nobody was giving him much in return. Song turned in earlier than usual.

That night he hardly slept. He lay in his hammock listening to the raucous night. He was glad of the noise of the birds, the frogs, the insects. It helped drown out the thoughts in his head. There were the short hoots of a mottled owl, gwot gwot gwot.

Song thought back to the day he met Chi at Louis'. The evening at his home, Yan's warmth, Dorothy's honeyed voice, Gloster's stories. He shook his head at how he'd been taken in. It wasn't the worth of a single nugget, but that Chi had shattered Song's hopes for a partner, even a friend, upriver. He vowed that this would be the last time he'd open himself up to someone. He wouldn't be so easy going forward, that was for sure.

Morning came and he heard Chi get up. Song cursed him again under his breath – before Chi made him jump. He was peering into Song's hammock. 'You up?' he said. Got something to show you.'

Song slowly sat up, swinging his legs out. 'What's up?'

Chi reached into his pocket and pulled out a shammy. Song dared to hope. Chi dropped his voice. 'Didn't want to tell the boys but I found this a few days ago. Only just before you came. Right here on this river. Like you said we would.'

Song looked at the nugget, as if it was the first time. But it wasn't the first time. Song felt a wash of relief – and guilt. He'd learned more about himself than Chi.

'I'm glad you told me,' he said to his partner.

For the next few weeks they smashed their tools into the hard rock trying to make some headway. It was backbreaking work. Every swing of a hammer or chisel on rock jarred through their bones.

Kai and Molson were stronger but Song worked the hardest. He was the first up and often worked till well after the light had gone. Sammy sometimes came out with him but he didn't always take himself inside the pit. He'd stand by watching, telling all three which direction to dig. Song assigned Chi to camp to make sure there was always enough food. He didn't want the boys to go hungry.

The weeks passed and they hadn't had much luck. The pit was so deep now they could no longer see the tops of each other's heads and they were working calf-deep in groundwater. The men started to dig sideways, widening the mouth of the pit. They made new tools with the same rock they were trying to break apart. By evening their bodies ached but nobody complained. They were all used to physical work. In the morning they were as stiff as dead men.

If anyone it was Sammy who was keeping to himself a bit more.

'We'll be off after breakfast,' he said one day.

Song was surprised. They hadn't given him a sense they were tired, or ready to return.

'Have I asked too much?'

'Stay if we could. But gotta get back to the village. Veronique and the others will be waiting.'

'Can you at least stay one more night? Chi can cook up a feast.'

Sammy shook his head. 'We should get back. And besides,' he smiled, 'you ain't got nothing for a feast.'

Song was dispirited. He needed Sammy, but he pretended he didn't feel that way. 'Okay, Sammy. We'll be all right.'

'Course you will. You're going to find what you're looking for, you know that?'

'Sure,' Song said, encouraged by his friend's certainty. Amerindian knowledge, he hoped.

'I mean it,' Sammy said, shaking his finger. His narrow hunter's eyes trained on Song. 'It's just a matter of time.'

It felt much quieter around camp even though none of the Yupukama men had been talkers. Song and Chi pressed on. Within a week they were clean out of oil and sugar. A few days later, the last of the rice was gone. But they were not ready to head back to Bartica. Not yet. Not with so little. They worked harder and skipped meals.

It was around lunchtime. Song was feeling pangs in his stomach. He reached into his pocket for a handful of leaves and stuffed them into his mouth to chew on. That's what he used to do when he was little, too. He had never wanted to be that hungry again. He picked up his hammer again, positioned his chisel and slammed it down.

The rock split off like shrapnel. Song felt a sharp pain in his left eye. He cried out and reached up with his hand; the wound was wet with blood. His head was spinning. It was then, as he stood there leaning against the wall of the pit, that he noticed the exposed rock. The surface shimmered.

Trembling, Song reached out and felt it with his fingertips. A memory surged up inside him: the shards of light cutting into the darkness of the ship. He remembered how solid the light used to look, something strong and firm from the world outside. As if it was the gold he was trying to reach. The stripe in the rock in front of him reminded him of that chance of light. His fingers moved over the rock. He could hear his hard breathing even above the noise of the future in his head.

Chi appeared at the top of the pit. 'You all right?'

Still cupping his bloodied eye Song looked up and pointed at the rock.

Chi moved swiftly down to Song's side. He stared at the rock and whistled. Then he looked at Song and his smile collapsed.

'What happened?'

'Is it bad?'

'Looks really bad.'

'Both of them?'

'The left ain't good. The right seems okay.'

'Everything's blurred. Both sides.'

'We need to bathe the left one.'

Song pulled himself up. He reached out in his darkness to touch the rock once more.

'I can see it all right, Song Holmes,' Chi said. 'And my oh my, we got gold on our hands.'

CHAPTER 17

By the time they returned to Bartica it had been five and a half months. They had lost half their body weight. Song's bad eye had become infected. Chi had broken out in sores around his mouth and nose.

'Man,' Basil said. 'You boys the walking dead.'

Dory threw them a rope. 'You better have hit a goldmine to come back looking like this.'

'You need a good meal and a good doctor,' Joseph said. He helped Song up. Then Chi. Neither man had spoken yet. They had barely said a word to each other over the last few days.

'What's the news?' Chi asked.

'You two's back in town,' Basil said. 'That's the only news I got.'

'Yan all right?'

'Given up on her man for dead,' Dory said. 'Like most of town had given up on you two.'

'How long you been gone?' Basil asked.

'Nearly six months.'

'Jeez,' he said. 'Yan's going to have you. 'Less of course your pockets are full.'

'She'll be having me then,' Chi said.

'I ain't buying that,' Basil said. 'Six months, two dead men walking and empty pockets. No, sir.'

'Basil, quit your talk and let these two men go on,' Joseph said. 'We'll have two deaths on our hands if you stall 'em any longer.'

'You ain't got no news for us?' Chi said.

'Yan's well enough,' Joseph said. 'Had the baby. Boy I think.' He turned to the others. 'Was it a boy?'

Nobody could remember.

Joseph offered them each a cigarette but they both refused. 'Otherwise it's the usual,' he said. 'Wouldn't be Bartica without a few killings, of course. Tom Jameson. Were you here for that? Flat disappeared. Never seen again. Word is it must have been an outta-towner who saw the uniform and didn't know any better. Not even Mad Dog'd do something like that.'

'That's bad news,' Song said.

'All we got is bad news,' Basil said.

'New DC, too,' Joseph said. 'Calls the place lawless, like that's news to us.'

'What happened to Wright?' Song asked. 'Not another Bartica death?' William Wright had been an ally of sorts, or at least not someone against Song.

'Got a transfer. Finally. He'd been waiting for one ever since he arrived.'

'New one equally absent?' Song asked.

'He's around. Flexing. Rubbing people up all sorts of ways.'

'The vicar's still falling over himself trying to draw a crowd,' Dory said.

Song already felt a stirring to be back upriver. Not for the lure of gold, but for the silence. Or for the sound of the interior and his beloved birds. Without the noise of town and all its viciousness.

'Can one of you bring our stuff?' Song asked.

'Leave it with us,' said Joseph.

Song nodded at Chi before taking up his satchel and heading towards town. There was Bronco. His face twisted into a smile when he saw Song. 'Man, it's nice to see you. Kind of. Not lookin' so good though.'

'Any trouble?'

He snorted. 'Over my dead body. Jingy's been in and out of course. Flings open all the windows to air the place. Been bringing fresh flowers every week for the last how many weeks. Think she's mourning you.'

'Is she doing all right?'

'Looking better than you. But she had a fall by the dock catching crabs. Man, those crabs are in for it now. Still catching them even with her gammy leg. Twice as keen.'

Song smiled. He missed Jingy. Missed her cooking. Missed her sharp tongue.

'Say, what happened to your eye?' Bronco asked.

'Just grit, I think. Didn't wash it out at the time and everything rots upriver. Even the eyes in your head. Gotta get it seen to.'

Song unlocked his door and entered the room. It was pitch dark save a few splinters of light through the shutters. He went to the windows and unhooked the wooden latches to let in the cool morning air. The sunlight swallowed up the room. There were flowers in a glass on the table. The water was yellow. Song poured the water out of the window and put the flowers back in the empty glass. Then he went to the shelf to open Father Holmes' Bible. The deeds were still there. Song wondered again what Father Holmes would have thought of him slipping a set of deeds between the leaves of his Bible. 'Good safe place,' he might have said with a smile. Song thought he wouldn't have minded. Perhaps he'd have been amazed at Song charting land upriver, buying it up, finding gold. Song was doing it his way, and that's what Father Holmes had told him he'd do. Song closed the book and took off the shirt tied around his waist. It was heavy. Chi had stitched the gold in individual squares. There was probably three pounds. Song cut open a couple of squares and emptied the contents into two leather shammies. Then he knotted his shirt back around his waist.

Out of his satchel he pulled out his tools and books which were wrapped in dirty clothes. He went back down to the street to drop off the couple of shirts and a pair of trousers at Mr Chow's.

'Sure I can't catch anything from this?' he said, holding up the drawstring trousers. 'This stuff's more alive than you.'

'Jungle dirt's clean, Mr Chow. You've seen a lot worse.'

'Won't be as good as Jingy.'

'I'd heard she hurt her leg.'

'She's all right. Hasn't slowed her down. The Father's family's arrived now so she's got her hands full. Did you hear we got a new DC?'

'Seems like that's what everyone's talking about.'

'Crazy man. Says he's going to close down the bars. No hookers. No liquor. Then what'll everyone do to make a living? They'll start robbing and thieving. Then he'll see real lawless. Man's got no sense.'

'I'll keep my distance,' Song said.

'Rumour is,' Mr Chow dropped his voice, 'he himself got rid of Tom Jameson. Thought he was too soft. White man kill a white man. Thought makes you shiver. They say he's got his sights on shutting down Ruby Lou's.'

'It sounds like he won't be around long—'

Mr Chow held up his left hand. 'You be careful what you say out loud. That man's got spies. Say, you should get that eye seen to.'

'On my way.' Song left the shop and headed to Ruthie's Best Roti Hut. He bought a super deluxe with chicken and sank his teeth into the stuffed curry roll. Ruthie watched him eat. 'Never tasted so good, I'll bet,' she said. 'Even I can't make them taste so good as when you ain't eaten for a month.'

Song took a second bite and choked.

'Take it easy, son,' Ruthie said.

Song could feel the texture of the meat and potatoes between his teeth, and the heat in his throat. It tasted of the dishes Jinda used to conjure up in his head. Descriptions so evocative it was as if he filled their stomachs. Song was heavy-hearted that Jinda couldn't taste the food he was eating now. How he hadn't had a chance at life. But he promised again to his dead friend that he would live twice as hard for both of them.

'Need another?' Ruthie asked. 'On the house. Just 'cause you need it.'

Song shook his head with his mouth full, tried a smile and gestured 'later'. He wanted to see Edward Hoare before he knocked off for lunch.

Father Holmes used to say Mr Hoare was the kind of man Bartica was short on. He was mild-mannered, modest and straight as a ruler. He re-calibrated his scales with lead weights that he kept in a safe and used the most recent price of gold from Georgetown. You could be sure of those scales, unlike the lousy ones at Stein's, Slicker's or Ashkanzi's, which were always out but never out in your favour.

Song pushed at the door of the office and a bell attached to the hinges tinkled. Mr Hoare came out from the back room. He was wearing bankers' sleeves, rubbed grey with pencil lead, and his glasses rested on the end of his nose.

'Song Holmes. It's been a long time.'

Song smiled at the sound of his full name. 'I just got in, sir. Six months upriver.'

'Looks like it, too,' Mr Hoare said. 'More important things than eating, I guess. Jingy won't be pleased.'

'You're right about both. How's everything with you, sir?'

'Me? I'm always the same. Work's work. Bit of fishing. I've been heading up to Georgetown more often since what happened to Tom. You'll have heard by now I'm sure. The town was in shock, and you know how hard it is to shock this place. The thing is that man didn't really have an enemy. Imagine that. A PC without an enemy.'

'He was a good friend, wasn't he? I still remember when you and Tom used to come around to the vicarage and sit on the porch in the evenings. I spent more time listening to your conversations than I did doing my homework.'

'Hah! I miss both of those men. The world gets smaller as you get older. Did you hear the new DC's missing too?'

'You're joking? I heard he just arrived.'

'Didn't last a month. But you wouldn't be surprised if you'd heard his rhetoric. Bartica has no room for a man like him.'

Song whistled. 'This town's not got a shred of mercy.'

'Didn't have any for Tom neither.'

'No PC and no DC,' Song said. 'Guess Bartica will run itself then.'

'Like it always has done.'

'And how's business, sir?'

'Gold is just bleeding out of the earth as far as I can tell. Not that I see much of it passing through my doors.'

'Who's up on their luck?'

'It's always the same names. I believe you're either born with it, or not. Don't try to tell me pork-knocking is a trade. There's nothing to learn, not really, not as far as I can tell. It's a lottery.'

Song didn't agree but he let it go. He thought it might be better for him if Mr Hoare took this line, so as not to be suspicious when there were some weeks when Song chose not to declare any gold.

'I've got something today.' Song reached into his pocket and opened up the shammy. It was only about a quarter of what he had on him.

'I should hope so, after six months.' Mr Hoare pushed his glasses further up his nose to have a look. He rested the amount on his scales and added lead weights to the other side. The needle moved in jerks before steadying near the number nine. 'This should keep you off the river for a while. Or perhaps not.'

'Do you have the latest price?' Song asked.

'Latest I have is Tuesday gone. Thirty-five point three seven.'

'Where's it moving?'

'It hasn't moved much over the past few months. Slight shifts both ways. Would you rather wait?'

Song shook his head. 'I'll cash in. I need some food in my belly.'

Mr Hoare prepared the bill. 'Officially you have three days to pay your tax from today's date but I always suggest sooner. Money doesn't last long in Bartica.'

'I'll come back this afternoon,' Song said. 'I'm going to hire a boat to take me to Georgetown in a few days; if you need anything or want to join me, I'd be delighted.'

'I might take you up on that. Don't get paid enough to hire a boat. And the ferry's a bore.'

'I'll send word.'

'I'd appreciate that. Are you going to get that eye seen to?'

'I'm on my way.'

Song left the office and went to Slicker's. It was closer than Old Ivor's. Slicker often stood outside the front of his shop, hustling for business, and he was there today. Mouthful of gold teeth and hair greased back; some say that's how he got his name.

'You buying?' Song asked.

'Never not buying.'

'How much?'

'You looking for cash?'

'What else would I be looking for?'

'Right now I got cash 'n' diamonds.'

'Cash, Slicker,' Song said. 'I don't want your filthy diamonds.'

'Half cash today, half tomorrow?'

Song shook his head. 'We might both be dead tomorrow.'

'Give me thirty minutes?'

'What price?'

'Better than Stein's or Ashkanzi's. Whatever they offer you, I'll pay you point-one more.'

'I can wait thirty minutes for point-one more.' Song turned to move off down the street.

But Mad Dog was in his way, drunk. 'Hey, l'il Chiney boy. You still pretending you a man?'

'You still failing at being one?' Song snapped back.

'What you been selling?'

'All I got.'

'Sounds like you got something to share then.'

'Slicker hasn't paid me yet. I'm no good to you.' Song knew he could outrun Mad Dog in the state he was in.

Mad Dog spat on the ground. 'You think Slicker's gonna give you money later, you dreaming. What you doin' trustin' him?'

'That's where you and me are different, Maddy,' Song said. 'Got to trust someone.' Even as he said it, he wondered if he did. He remembered sharply how he had lost his trust in Chi in one mixed-up moment; the doubts he'd had that night still haunted him. He was determined to give everyone a chance to walk through his door, so to speak, like Father Holmes used to, that was the way he wanted to live.

Mad Dog hooted with laughter. 'Trust? You the son of a preacher all right.' He took a swipe at Song. Song ducked out of his way and Mad Dog fell on the ground. 'Watch it,' Mad Dog slurred. 'Know what happens to people like you – getting too ahead of yourself. You the ones end up floating down the river, belly down.'

'You before me.'

Song walked on to Ashkanzi's. Inside the shop it was very dark. There was a rotting smell in the air. He made out Old Man Kuros sitting on one side of the till in a rocking chair. He was blind but his fingers were playing with the ebony beads of an abacus. Click, click-click, click. His son Farad sat behind the table.

'Who is it?' Old Man Kuros asked.

'Father Holmes' boy,' Farad said.

Old Man Kuros looked astonished. 'He had a boy?'

'The sugar Chiney,' Farad said.

Song wanted to shake Farad, as if that might help shake off the tag and his history. He turned to the old man first.

'Good morning, Mr Ashkanzi. I'm Song.'

'Do you sing then?'

Song remembered what Lady had said. 'With a name like that I bet you sing like an angel.' He could hear her humming, her voice rising out of the folds of her hammock.

'I can't sing,' Song said. 'But I once knew a lady who could sing like an angel.'

Old Man Kuros snorted. 'Angels are for storybooks.'

'Don't disagree with that,' Song said. It sounded like he already had something in common with the old man.

'Selling?' The son asked. 'Or here for a chat?'

Song put his leather pouch on the table. Farad felt it from the outside and purred in approval before emptying its contents. He lifted it on to the dish of his scales.

'Not bad for someone so young,' Farad said.

'Young?' Old Man Kuros asked. He turned to Song. 'How young?'

'Some days I feel older than you.'

The old man snorted again.

'Nearly twenty,' Song said.

'Bad rate right now, as you probably know,' Farad said. 'Should have come last week. Some men might hang on to it and wait for the price to climb. 'Course it might drop. I'll give you a good price though, since you're new to the business. I'll want to see all your finds first, mind. Not doing it for nothing.'

'How much?' Song asked.

'Depends what kind of deal we have,' Farad went on.

'No deal. Just a straight price. I'm going to Georgetown next week, so that's the price you're competing with.'

'I'm not competing with next week, boy,' Farad said. 'Hang on to this and you'll have a knife in your belly. I'm buying today.'

'What'll you give me?'

Farad plucked the larger nuggets out of the dish. He held them up. 'See those impurities? I can't give you the weight but I'm feeling generous since you're new an' all. Ninety-eight per cent. Everyone needs a bit of help.'

Farad started to write numbers down on a pad. The pencil was blunt and scratched against the paper. Song could hear the ticking of a clock hanging on the wall. The brass pendulum swung calmly as if it would forever.

As Song's eyes became accustomed to the darkness, he noticed the stuffed birds on the shelves. They were in poor condition but beautifully crafted. There was a huge harpy eagle staring down at

Song with milky eyes. Cleverly stilled by the taxidermist, a golden warbler had been positioned by a nest as if it was feeding its young. They seemed alive, like Li Bai had looked when Song found him at the bottom of the ladder. Song had brushed his hand down over his face to close his eyes. Dead, yet somehow alive. That was how so many seemed to Song. Living on in some way.

Old Man Kuros spoke. 'You name the price you're looking for. What do you want for it?'

'Sorry, sir,' Song said. 'I'm looking for a price, not calling it.'

Old Man Kuros laughed. 'Listen to the boy, Farad.' He turned back to Song. 'Talk like you been doing business all your life.'

Song thought how much it did feel that way to him. Like he'd been negotiating since he could remember. To broker English lessons from Hai. To accompany Li Bai up on deck. To swap uniforms at the plantation. To find himself upriver with Jesus. To buy land.

'Just about have,' Song said.

'Sounds like you've never come across a bit of kindness either,' Old Man Kuros said. 'We're trying to help you.'

'I don't want help. All I want is a straight price.' Song made out as if he was going to leave.

'If it's cold business you're after, we can do cold business,' Farad said. 'One hundred dollars the lot.'

'Two hundred,' Song said.

Both men laughed. The son's was a grumble from his belly. His father's laugh was up in his nose like an extension of the way he snorted.

'If that's the best you can do—'

'One twenty,' Farad said.

'Not a chance,' Song said.

'Let me teach you something, son,' Old Man Kuros said. 'This is called negotiation. Ever heard of that? You negotiate in this business. You don't dig in your heels so you got nowhere to run.'

'All right,' Song said. 'Let's negotiate. Give me one-eighty, plus—' he paused. 'Plus the birds.'

'The birds? My birds?' Old Man Kuros said, tapping a shelf with his cane.

'All of them,' Song said.

'Are you trying to tell me you think all these birds are worth,' Old Man Kuros muttered a sum to himself, 'no more than twenty dollars?'

'Not like this,' Song said. 'Not in this damp room. They're rotting. I could smell them when I first walked in. The harpy's eyes are milky. The warbler is off its perch. They're filthy. They need re-fixing and I know someone who can do it. A man with the sharpest eye in the world for the way a bird looks and the way a bird moves. The emerald bee-eater's lost its colour. There's no green in its wings. Someone needs to look after these beautiful creatures.'

Old Man Kuros' mouth was hanging open.

But Farad was losing his patience. 'Leave out the birds. How much do you want?'

'You be quiet, Farad,' Old Man Kuros said, recovering himself. 'Who taught you about birds?'

'Father Holmes and I had several volumes of recordings. He took two to the Royal Ornithological Society in London. We identified the whiskered white-headed song warbler. These birds shouldn't be rotting here on your shelves.'

Old Man Kuros was silenced.

Farad tried again. 'How much?'

'Shut up,' Old Man Kuros said to his son. 'Who do you know that can fix them up?'

'A friend of mine called Jon Swire. He's no taxidermist but he's

257

the finest illustrator in British Guiana and his speciality is birds. He works in Georgetown. He worked on the books with me. He can draw any bird in the country – how the light reflects off their feathers, how they raise their wings to fly, if they lift their head to sing. He has delicate hands and a sharp eye. He'd bring life back into these.'

'I wasn't a taxidermist either . . .'

Song was taken aback. 'You did these?'

'Of course I did these,' Old Man Kuros said.

'They're beautiful.'

'A minute ago they were rotting,' Old Man Kuros said.

Song smiled. 'I didn't know they were your handiwork. They are rotting, but they are also beautiful.'

'Glad to find someone who appreciates them,' Old Man Kuros said. His voice was sharp and directed at his son. 'Give the boy the money, Farad. Two hundred. The birds aren't for sale.'

'If you give me two hundred, sir, I'll get them fixed up for you for nothing. I'll take them to Georgetown and get Jon to work on them. You might have to wait a while, but he's meticulous.'

Old Man Kuros mumbled a reply. 'I can't even see them.'

'You can feel them when they're done,' Song said. 'Like this you can't. They're falling apart. Jon would do a fine job.'

'All right,' Old Man Kuros said. 'Take them then, if it makes you happy. But take them one by one. Don't like to think of all of these shelves empty. Pay the boy, Farad. Take the harpy, if that's the one you want. Fix his eyes. Don't like to think of anything else not being able to see.'

Farad had stopped listening and was adding a column in his ledger. 'You've made me lose count,' he said, irritably.

'I said pay the boy,' Old Man Kuros said more loudly.

'One eighty, was it?' Farad said.

'Two hundred,' Old Man Kuros said.

'Two hundred! That's the profit for the month gone then.'

'Just pay him,' Old Man Kuros snarled.

Farad counted out the money, a first time, a second time backwards and a third time along the width of the notes. He pushed the money across the table.

Song took the money and counted it once. There was a twenty missing. He counted it again. 'It's short,' he said.

'Is it?' Farad counted more slowly a fourth time. 'Funny that. You sure you didn't slip a note in your pocket by mistake?'

Song didn't reply.

'I'll make it up this time,' Farad said. 'You remember that. Don't forget where you got your start. Two hundred dollars. Everything you asked for. You remember where you got your start when you find that goldmine. We buy diamonds too.'

'And the harpy,' Song said, pointing at the bird.

'Which one?' Farad said.

Old Man Kuros snorted in the corner. 'There's only one.'

'Be careful with it,' Song said, as Farad brought it down from the shelf.

'You watch yourself,' Farad said. 'Don't you forget who's on which side of the table.'

Song picked up the bird off the counter. It weighed little more than its feathers but it was a mighty size.

'Bring it here to me first,' Old Man Kuros said.

Song carried it across to the old man. He took up Old Man Kuros' hands and put them on either side of the bird's wings. He watched as his arthritic fingers sunk into the feathers. 'It's facing me,' Old Man Kuros said, feeling the direction of the feathers.

'Yes,' Song said.

'It's looking at me about as well as I can look at it,' Old Man

259

Kuros said. He spoke tenderly. 'Take her with you then. Bring her back with her eyes cleared up.'

Song picked up the bird and went out into the hard sunlight. There was no one in the street. He paused at Slicker's but the merchant still did not have the money.

'Next time, Slicker,' Song said.

'What's a few hours?' Slicker called out. 'I'm just saving you from getting drunk quicker.'

'I'm not here for liquor. I came back for the music.'

Dr Foo stared at Song's left eye. 'We can stitch it up and patch it,' he said. 'Or you can get a glass eye in Georgetown. They're good from a distance. Close up I don't think they're the best looking things.'

'Stitch it up if you would, Doctor,' Song said. 'I'd rather patch it.'

'Closing it up won't be pain-free but it's an easy procedure when the wound is clean and dry. Come back every day this week so I can change the dressing. Then we should be able to close it up.' He paused. 'I'm sorry I can't do any better. I could have saved your sight but not this late, not in this state.'

So this was the cost of finding gold. An eye for an eye. Another thing he had to give up, another thing he had to lose.

'It was worth it,' he said, trying to convince himself.

'Worth the loss of an eye? Not sure I would give up half my sight for anything. And you be careful with the other eye. You need to rest it from time to time. You can lose your sight completely after an injury to only one side. They act like a pair.'

'Strange that,' Song said.

Dr Foo shook his head. 'Not really. It often happens like that in the body. Like when one half of a couple dies and the other dies straight after. They live like one and die like one.'

260

CHAPTER 18

Song had seen a bee-eater on the roof above Louis' store. He was pleased to know he could still notice birds so sharply, in spite of his injury. The wound had healed well, albeit slowly. Dr Foo had spent nearly three weeks changing the dressings every day. When it was finally clear of infection, he stitched the eyelid closed and Song began wearing a black patch. Song observed how his field of vision had been halved and how it was harder to see depth and distance, but he was relieved the other eye had not been affected. He could live with this, he thought. Perhaps his patch would help shut out everything he didn't want to see in the world.

'What happened to your eye?'

Song swung around to see who was addressing him. It was a young woman who'd stopped to talk to him, legs straddling her bicycle. She was heavy-set with wide hips, as if she had already borne children. But her face was that of a child's, soft and rounded and unblemished. A few strands of hair had come loose. Song felt flustered – trying to think where he had seen her before. Then he saw the cake trays tied on the back and remembered. The one with the icing sugar down her front. Clumsily letting cakes fall to the ground. The daughter of Mary Luck of Mary Luck's Lucky Bakery.

Song looked at her eyes. One was green, like the wings of the bird he had been watching. The other was pale brown.

'I lost it,' Song said.

'Forever?'

Song smiled at her question. 'I guess so. Yes.'

'I'm sorry. What were you looking at just now?'

'An emerald bee-eater. It's a bird.' Song looked up again. 'It was on the roof but it's gone now. Its feathers are the same colour as your left eye.'

'That's nice. So you noticed my eyes are different colours then?'

'I did.'

'I better be on my way. Am running late. See you around.' The girl smiled and pedalled off.

Song watched her go. Halfway down the road she turned to look back. Her bicycle wobbled. He thought about her mismatched eyes. How beautiful they were because they were at odds. Not unlike his own life, from where he was seeing the world.

After that encounter Song looked out for her from his window. She pedalled along the street in the early morning. Bronco always nodded at her. She'd release a hand from her handlebars to wave at the big man. Song could not understand how he had not noticed her before with two eyes, and now she was all he could see with one.

One morning she stopped in the street and Song watched her offer Bronco a crescent-shaped biscuit. It obviously was not the first time. She held it up in front of his face and blew. A puff of icing sugar shrouded his face and he sneezed. She laughed. It was a melodic childish laugh for such a womanly figure.

'Who's that girl with the biscuits?' Song asked Bronco later.

'On the bicycle?'

'The one with the funny eyes.'

'Hannah. Mary Luck's daughter. Of Mary Luck's Lucky Bakery. She used to supply Louis till he got a better deal from that woman on the west side. Known Hannah since she was a baby. Tough mother. Not a tyrant but tough.'

Song tried to remember something about the Lucks. Her bakery was not on the good side of town and Jingy wouldn't have approved. Song had probably walked along their street before, mostly late at night when he took the long way from Chi's to Ruby Lou's. He tried to picture the street in the day, searching his mind for a bicycle leaning against a fence. For the glance of a girl as she pedalled off down a road, turning once to look back.

Song wanted to meet Old Man Kuros alone. He asked Bronco. The big man knew everybody's routine, which was a near miracle since all he did was stand outside one shop in one street almost every day of every week.

'Do you want to see him inside or outside of his shop?' Bronco asked.

'Doesn't matter. I just don't want Farad around.'

'Try the shop between twelve and two on a Wednesday. Farad plays bridge with Nutt that day. But sometimes they close the shop and the old man sleeps. Depends how he's feeling. Out of the shop, ask Sugar. He pays her to walk him around town. Not that he pays her a lot. She ain't got no loyalty to him so she'd tell you anything you need to know. You know he buys one pack of cigarettes a month from Louis. One pack! Says he doesn't like to smoke more than that. Bad for his eyes. Bad for a blind man's eyes, I ask you? Truth is he's tighter than a drum. Takes a puff, pinches the end; won't take another till the next day.'

Song went to see Sugar. The girls at Ruby Lou's would do anything for him, and told him as much. Song was different, they said; Ruby Lou treated him like a son she'd never had.

'Sure, lover boy. I got it,' Sugar said. 'I get a message across to you about where we's goin' so you can just turn up somewhere and it seems like we're plum running into you. That right?'

263

The next day Bronco whistled up to Song just after lunchtime. Song came to the window. Bronco pointed west down the street and held up ten fingers. Ten minutes. End of the street.

Song was there early. He saw them coming.

'Good afternoon, Mr Ashkanzi. It's Song.'

The old man stopped. 'What you doing waiting at the end of the street?'

'How did you know that?' Sugar snapped.

Song talked over her. 'I'm waiting for a friend, sir.'

'How did you know he was waiting here?' Sugar asked again.

'Man without eyes got feel,' Old Man Kuros said. 'He wasn't walking when we came upon him, was he?'

Song tapped his finger on his lips to signal to Sugar to be quiet.

'I heard you lost an eye,' Old Man Kuros said. 'That true?'

'Only one.'

'Don't go losing the other.'

'I'm not planning on it.'

'You lose the other and you have to rely on some untrustworthy fella to be your eyes. Like me. I've got my own cheating son to look out for me. Cheat his father? Surely not his own father, you say? In a heartbeat, I say. That boy stole from me the day he was born. Took his mother from me. That was the start of it and it's never stopped. If he could steal from me when the two eyes in my head were as quick as a cat's just think what he's doing now.'

'It can't be that bad,' Song said.

'My own son, I tell you. My own flesh and blood.'

'Can I walk with you?'

'I thought you were waiting for a friend.'

'I am, but I won't take a minute of your time. He'll wait.'

'Be my guest.'

Song held up five fingers to Sugar. She nodded and dropped back.

Song took Old Man Kuros' arm. 'Do you know anyone in Georgetown I can trust?'

Old Man Kuros snorted. 'I don't know anyone in the world you can trust.'

'I want to set up a direct channel to Georgetown. I need a big player. I want them to be able to take everything I bring out. Ideally a sole operator.' Song dropped his voice. 'Someone who's willing to see gold undeclared and split the difference. I can pay you for the introduction or a commission – without going through the shop. Farad doesn't need to know about it.'

Old Man Kuros chuckled. 'You asking me to cut out my own son?'

'That's up to you.'

'How much gold are we talking about?'

Song hesitated. 'How much would it have to be?'

Old Man Kuros muttered some sums. 'What you brought into the shop – half a pound. Every week.'

'No problem,' Song said bluntly.

'Every week. Not one week good, one week bad.'

'Every week. That, sir, I can do.'

'Mr Ebenezer is the man you want. I'll write you a letter of introduction. You take it with you. Sealed. It'll cost you two hundred dollars. You can pay me when you bring back the harpy. I'm not interested in taking a bit here and a bit there. Two hundred flat.'

'With the harpy? It might take a while getting her fixed up. Are you sure you want to wait that long?'

'You bring the money when you bring back my bird. I'll get Sugar to bring the letter across.' He snorted. 'Now go and meet your friend.'

*

265

Song had chosen to take the long way to Chi's that day, which would take him past Mary Luck's Lucky Bakery. When he turned into her street he felt nervous, even a wave of shyness, something he hadn't felt since he was a little boy. He tried to hold his head up, to walk tall, following the lyrics of Lady's song.

There were kids playing cricket in the street. The ball came near Song and he picked it up and threw it to one of the boys. He chipped it deftly at an angle back at the bowler but one of the street dogs rushed in and grabbed it in his mouth and bounded off. They chased him down, shouting till he dropped it.

Song continued down the street. He studied more closely the neighbourhood where she lived. The houses had all been pretty at one time. Each was painted a different colour, like teacakes, but the lemon yellows and pastel pinks were faded now. The roofs sagged under the weight of age and the fretwork needed fixing, but the front yards were not heaped in scrap wood or junk, and on every porch neighbours sat out in rocking chairs drinking something soft from tall glasses or swinging in hammocks with a leg hanging out, pushing from time to time at the side of a pillar to keep swaying.

Song startled himself when he saw Hannah. He had lost count of the houses he had passed and he was suddenly in front of hers. She was sitting on the porch brushing her mother's long undone hair. Mary Luck noticed him first and Song could tell by the way she looked him over and slightly lifted her head to speak that she was asking her daughter about him.

Hannah looked up and saw Song. She did not wave but smiled. Song's heart lifted. He raised his hand as if to say hello.

Then he saw her lean down and say something to her mother, before she continued brushing her hair, softly pulling the bristles downwards.

Song continued walking past her house, until he could not see her out of the corner of his good eye. He longed to turn around and catch sight of her one more time. But he didn't want to rush in. He needed to take it slow, like when he was sifting sand upriver; the only way to win something precious was with patience.

The next afternoon Song walked again to Mary Luck's Lucky Bakery. Hannah was not yet back from her deliveries but her mother was there.

'You're the one who walked past the house last night,' Mary Luck said.

Song saw where Hannah got her directness from. 'Yes ma'am.'

'And you're back again.'

'Yes. I wanted to place an order.'

'For?'

'For one of everything you sell?'

'One? *One* of everything? I hope you're kidding.'

Song took a deep breath. 'I'm not.'

'What do you want with one of everything? You setting up a business? Trying to steal my ideas?'

'No ma'am,' Song replied. 'I was looking to find out what I liked best so I'd know what to order in the future.'

Mary Luck gave a big sigh. 'It's a lot of fussy work to pack one of everything. Never had an order like that before. When do you want it?'

'Tomorrow?' Song said.

'Tuesday,' Mary Luck wrote down in her book. 'Well, we don't make everything every day. So tomorrow you can have one of everything we make tomorrow. On Wednesday you can have one of everything we make on Wednesdays except what you've already had on Tuesday. And Thursday you can have one of everything that you haven't already had on Tuesday or Wednesday. And we can do that until we're all exhausted and clean out of ideas. What do you say?'

Song laughed. 'Yes, please.'

'Orders around here getting crazier and crazier,' Mary Luck said. 'People around here getting crazier and crazier. What's your name?'

'Song.'

'Pretty name.' She wrote 'Song' down on the receipt. 'Address?'

'Opposite Louis'.'

Mary Luck pursed her lips. 'Don't mention that man's name to me,' she said. 'You know where he gets his cakes now? Some heathen who keeps her sugar in a vat outside her door. *Outside* the door, I tell you. I've seen drunk men pee in that vat, mark me. You ever seen sugar stuck together in clumps? That's what it is. Sugar stuck with pee. Nothing to do with nothing else, don't let anyone tell you neither. Louis is a mean old man who goes for price and not quality. That's why he has that big man out front. Worried customers'll get sick and come banging on his door. You can tell him I said so, too.'

'I think I will,' Song said.

'You should.' Mary Luck handed Song the receipt. 'You going to be eating all this yourself?'

'Yes,' Song said.

'Well, looks like you need to. Why you so skinny? And what happened to your eye?'

'I lost it.'

'Well, don't go losing the other. Hard to get by in this world without your eyes, one or two. My mother went blind, although it was a fall that eventually killed her. But it was the blindness that made her fall. If you can't see where you're going, you'll fall over and die and that's the wrong order. We should be dying and falling over, not the other way around.'

Hannah walked into the shop carrying a dozen empty baking trays.

'About time,' Mary Luck said. 'What you been doing? Taking a sight-seeing tour of the neighbourhood?'

'A darn dog got in my way,' Hannah said, 'and everything went flying. It took a good half-hour to stack up all the trays and fix 'em up tight again. Took me another half-hour to get the chain back on.'

Mary Luck tutted. 'She spends her life falling over,' she said to Song. 'Wrong way round, mark me.'

Song was looking into Hannah's face trying to see her mismatched eyes again. There was a streak of black grease on her cheek.

'You want to hear what this young man wants?' Mary Luck said to her daughter. 'It's the one who was on the street last night. He just walked on in here and ordered one of everything. What do you make of that?'

Hannah looked at Song. 'I'd say he has good taste.'

'I'd say so,' Song replied.

Hannah's green eye flashed.

Song knew Mary Luck saw the look that passed between him and her daughter.

'You two know each other?'

'You know him, too,' Hannah said. 'He came by here with Father Holmes years ago. Don't you remember?'

Song didn't remember, but he was glad she did.

'How'm I supposed to remember something that happened years ago when I can barely remember what happened this morning?' Mary Luck was examining the corners of the trays. 'You've dented them. You'll have to hammer them out. You make more work than you do, chil'. Can you stop wasting time chit-chatting in the shop when there are trays to scrub out the back? Excuse me, mister, but you'll have to go now. We'll send your one-of-everything order tomorrow. Then you can figure out what you like and what you don't like.'

Song wanted to stay there rooted to the floor forever, listening to this mother and daughter banter. He knew what he liked. He already knew what he wanted.

CHAPTER 19

Song saw Hannah every day that week to receive his order of cakes. She was always late, her face damp with sweat, and she would rush off before they'd had even a minute's exchange. But it was enough time for Song to notice more about her. There was a lightness to her. She was playful, almost childlike in nature with her clumsy ways and sticky hands that she'd lick or wipe on her apron that was already smeared with the pink of guava jelly and the yellow of pineapple jam. She was always on the move, running late but always smiling. Entirely natural, free. She reminded him of the swifts darting about the waterfall at Kaieteur.

On Friday afternoon Song went back to Mary Luck's Lucky Bakery.

'You should be pleased to know you're looking fatter,' Mary Luck said, looking him over. 'So you decided which recipes you're going to steal from me?'

Song laughed. 'I like them all. I've got another strange order for you, ma'am. Can you just send me something sweet every day. Anything. I'm not there all the time but Bronco can have it when I'm gone. I live across from Lou—' Song stopped himself mid-sentence.

'I know exactly where you live without you telling me *again*. Been sending enough cakes there this week to buy myself a new house. Problem is we now go from twenty-two cakes on one day down to one. How's a woman meant to run a business like that?'

Song laughed again. He wondered if there had ever been a Mr Luck.

'Don't tell me you came all this way to place an order for one cake a day? Have you got nothing to do with your days except eat cakes?'

'I also wanted to ask you,' Song hesitated, 'if I could take Hannah for a walk tonight?'

Mary Luck looked up. 'Ah, I see. Would this be a short walk or a long walk?'

'Not too long.'

Mary Luck did not reply for a minute or two. Then they both started to speak at the same time.

'I—' said Song.

'I—' said Mary Luck.

'Sorry,' said Song. 'Excuse me.'

'I don't know why you're asking me,' Mary Luck said. 'You're not asking me to go for this walk, are you? I'd certainly say no if you were. Hannah's got a mind of her own to be deciding if she wants to go for a walk, long or short. With you or anybody else. There ain't a man in this family to stop you asking her direct.'

'Thank you, ma'am.'

'And who's your family?'

It had been a long time since Song blushed. He felt awkward telling her his story. He hoped it was good enough. 'Father Holmes looked after me, ma'am. You might have heard he was on the *Falmouth* three years ago. That was the boat that went down. Before that I came on the *Dartmouth* from China. My mother let me go so I might find work. My father had already passed on.'

'Well, they'd be proud to see you today – even though you're skinny and lost an eye on the way. You can't have everything.

Friends can be as good as family, especially in a place like Bartica.'

'I think you're right, ma'am. I have friends here I'd trust with my life.' Song thought of Jingy and Bronco, maybe Chi, although he wasn't sure there was anybody else.

'Well, just because you've got nice friends doesn't mean you have to go trusting them with your life, or forgetting your family either. At least you have some family you know about. There's plenty of chillun running around here who don't know where they come from. You know who your family is, at least.'

Song nodded. 'I do, you're right.' But he thought how far away they were. How his memories were fading. He wondered if they were even alive.

'Ever think about going back?'

'I promised I'd go back, but I couldn't face that journey again.'

Mary Luck nodded. 'Fair enough. You wouldn't get me on a boat either. But it don't matter. Your mother knows you're safe and well. Mothers are smart like that.'

'I've sometimes hoped that she believes me to be dead, rather than the son who never came back after promising everything.'

Mary Luck scoffed. 'Those kind of promises don't count. Never have. Never will. They're just said out loud for drama. She'd rather you were alive, trust me. Mothers want what's best for their children, not what's best for them.'

Song felt heartened by her words, but didn't know if it was the truth.

'Best thing you can do is fatten yourself up and take care of that other eye of yours. Now you go and find Hannah to see if she wants to join you on that not-so-long walk of yours. That girl seems to think she's got more time on her hands, mark me, than the laziest stray in Bartica. Always late for everything. I've no doubt she'll think she's got time for a walk, too. I on the other hand can't be talking all day. Remember I got one whole single cake to be making for tomorrow.'

That evening Song arrived at Hannah's house just as it was getting dark. He stumbled as he walked down the path, nervous but awash with hope. Hannah emerged from the house before he'd even put his hand up to knock. He noticed how she'd put on a clean dress and let her hair down. There were beads of sweat on her nose. She shone.

'You look lovely,' he said, overwhelmed.

'You look nervous,' she said.

'I am,' Song said, because he didn't know what else to say. Her frankness disarmed him. He collected himself. 'It's because I've got a surprise for you. I'm not really taking you for a walk.'

'You'll remember that's all I agreed to.'

'It's still an outing.'

'Of course it is,' Hannah said. 'We're out.'

'And it's still a walk of sorts,' he said.

'Well that's not much of a surprise then.'

'Come with me.' They headed down the street and took a left down to the riverbank. Tied to a post was Song's boat. He had brought it around the point earlier in the day. There was a cushion on the seat and two bottles of soda by the paddles.

'I'd like to take you on the river.'

Song thought she looked pleased but couldn't be sure. 'Let's see,' Hannah said. 'That's definitely not a walk as far as I can tell. I mean, we wouldn't be on dry land.' She paused. 'And you can't drown going for a walk. But we might drown on the river.'

'Don't you want to go?'

Hannah softened. 'Is it safe? I can't swim.'

'I'll save you.'

Hannah looked at the boat and out into the river. 'If I agree, you have to allow me to do one thing.'

'What's that?'

'I'm not saying.'

'I have to agree without knowing?'

Hannah nodded.

'Sure,' Song said. 'Anything.'

'You sure about that?'

'Anything,' Song said again.

She made to run down the bank. 'Let's go.'

Once Hannah was sitting balanced in the middle of the boat, Song pushed them off. The boat wobbled and Hannah let out a nervous laugh.

'It's all right,' Song said. 'Just stay still till we get going.'

Song started to paddle slowly into the current. He looked behind him. Hannah was looking up at the sky.

'What do you see?' he asked.

She whispered, 'Sky.'

Song smiled. 'Anything else?'

'More sky.'

Song looked up. 'What do—'

'Shh,' she interrupted. 'I want to hear the river.'

Song stopped paddling. He turned around to face Hannah and put his finger on his lips. 'Shh,' he echoed her. 'Listen to the river. It has a message for you.'

She laughed. 'What's the message?'

'The river's inviting you to the sea. Far out. To the point where it meets the sky so you can see the sky close up.'

'Shall we go?' Hannah asked. 'Will we ever come back?'

'Never,' Song said.

Hannah laughed again. Song wanted to take those laughs and

have Jingy put them inside the same big glass jars she used for preserving peaches so he could keep the sound forever.

'So you said anything, right?' Hannah said.

'I did?' Song said. 'When did I say anything?'

Hannah sharply drew in a breath. 'You lying cheating scoundrel,' she said. She held on to the sides of the boat and started
rocking the vessel. 'My limp wet body will wash up in Trinidad and
the whole island will know you lied.'

Song laughed. 'Anything. I said anything.'

'So tell me about you.'

'That's it?'

'No. The anything's later. Tell me about you first.'

'I sense the rules are changing.' Song asked. 'What do you want
to know?'

'From the beginning,' Hannah said.

'You first.'

Hannah screwed up her face. 'I was born with two different eyes.
Crazy strict fierce crazy again mother. My father died before I was
old enough to remember him. Maybe that's why Mama's so stir-
crazy. We run a bakery. I do the deliveries. That's it. Your turn.'

Song sighed. 'I'm not very good at this.'

'I'm waiting.'

Song sighed again. 'I was born with two eyes. In China. Took a
boat to Guiana. Worked. Taken in by Father Holmes. Moved to
Bartica. Went to school. Found gold. Lost one eye. Met you.'

Hannah blushed.

'That all right?' Song asked.

Hannah shook her head. 'Why did you leave China?'

Song shrugged.

'Don't you know?' Hannah said.

'There wasn't enough to eat. I wanted to save my family.'

'Did you save them?'

'This is hard to talk about.'

'I'm sorry,' Hannah asked. She put her hand on his hand. 'Am I not allowed to ask you anything more?'

'You are,' Song said. 'Just saying it's not easy. I want to be perfect for you.'

Hannah smiled a soft smile. 'So tell me where you worked.'

'When?'

'Before Father Holmes.'

'In the plantations. I was one of the sugar Chinese.' Song paused. 'Does that bother you?'

'Why should it?' Hannah asked. 'Do you mind that I deliver cakes?'

Song smiled and shook his head. 'You ask a lot of questions.'

'I haven't finished yet,' she said. 'How was it? The plantations.'

'Harder than rice. Rice was all I'd ever known. Sugar was tougher and heavier. We sometimes had to work in smoke. Burning the fields. They treated us rough. I guess I learned how to fight back.' Song's voice had softened. 'I made good friends there, too.'

The river sounded louder to Song. He noticed the light was fading. 'We should be getting back.'

'Before we go there's still the "anything".'

'And there I was thinking you'd forgotten,' Song said.

Hannah turned coy. 'Please can I look under your patch?'

Song furrowed his brow. 'Do you really want to?'

'Only if you don't mind,' she said.

'I don't think it's very nice for you,' Song said.

'I'd like to.'

Song thought about what she wanted to do. She was taking all of him on. Song lifted the black felt so Hannah could see his scar.

She put out her hand to touch it. 'It's so neat.' She ran her fingers over the eyelid, and Song jerked back. 'Did I hurt you?'

'No,' Song said. 'It's just nobody's touched it before.'

'The stitches are so tiny. It looks like your eye's just shut. I like it. It's like you're winking at me.' Hannah leaned forward and kissed Song's closed eye. 'I'm sorry if I hurt you.'

'You didn't,' he whispered. Song felt something source from so deep inside him he thought he might cry. He passed his hand over Hannah's mismatched eyes so they closed. Then he leaned forward and took it in turn to kiss both of her shut eyes.

CHAPTER 20

Song asked Fowl Man to take him to Georgetown. The *Marie Christine* had sunk but he had a new boat called *Mimi* painted yellow with pink ribbons tied to the tiller.

'Bigger too,' Fowl Man said. 'Could've taken all of Father Holmes' books 'stead of doing two journeys. Bit slower, mind. Heavier wood. But in a brisk breeze mid-channel you'd be pressed to tell the difference.'

Song thought back to the journey he and Father Holmes had taken when they moved from Georgetown to Bartica. To make a home together, that's what he'd said, and that's what they'd done. Now he was directing his own journey. He wanted to make a home with Hannah, in the same way.

Good as his word, Song had informed Edward Hoare of his date of departure and the two of them travelled together. Song asked Jingy too but she said her bones were too old for travelling now except for funerals.

'I'll make a journey for the dead,' she said, 'but I'm not going anywhere for the living. Besides, someone's gotta stay here and open up your room once in a while. Save the place from rotting.' She gave Song a shopping list and forced money into his hand, refusing to listen to his protests.

It had been nearly four years since Song's last trip to Georgetown. That had been with Father Holmes to see him off on his trip to England. He was churning inside as they approached Parika.

Wishing Father Holmes was with him today. Imagining them walking these streets together, maybe buying their own boat to go upriver, on the lookout for birds.

The three men split when they docked. Fowl Man shuffled off to the Boathouse Bar. Edward Hoare was staying with the Stewarts. Song went to the vicarage to find Amalia. He had sent word ahead asking her to find him a place to stay. He had money in his pocket and gold still sewn in the seams of his shirt.

'She's out shopping,' Father Francis' wife told Song when he knocked at the door of the vicarage. Two children peered around the pleats of her long skirt. One started whimpering. 'If you find her tell her to hurry up home. That woman talks too much.'

Song ignored her comment. He knew where to find Amalia. He headed to Stabroek Market. As he suspected she was haggling over a price, standing among the pulses. She halted mid-speech when she saw Song and then screamed with delight.

'Look at you. Taller than me now. But a good deal skinnier. And what happened to your eye? What you been feeding yourself? There a war on I don't know about? Don't they have something called food in Bartica?'

'If you think this is bad you should have seen me a month ago,' Song said.

'Glad I didn't. You been upriver then?'

'Of course. That's all you do in Bartica. Go upriver. Come back for supplies. Go upriver again.'

'Ready to come back to this big city?'

'That's why I'm here,' Song said. 'Did you find me somewhere to stay? I'm walking around like a homeless.'

'Follow me,' Amalia said. 'I've found the perfect place right around the corner. Bit pricey but you can afford it from what I hear and that's what you get for a clean quiet place with no whores running around squealing in the middle of the night.'

Amalia led Song to a whitewashed boarding house. 'I've got you the best room,' she said. 'Biggest windows and a sea breeze although it might be a bit noisy early mornings with the market around the corner. I got them to swap the best mattress into this room.'

Song was touched by Amalia's help. He had come so far since she had cared for him those first few days at the vicarage.

'Now when are you coming to eat my food. Sunday at my sister's?'

Song smiled. 'Pepper pot?'

'Still as sweet as ever,' Amalia said. 'I want to hear all your news and why you're here and don't kid me you're moving to Georgetown with that small case and what's going on in Bartica and the ladies and so on but we can save all that for Sunday.'

Song didn't waste any time in Georgetown. He knew where he needed to go first. Edward Hoare called Mr Hing 'the finest jeweller in town'. Amalia murmured in agreement. 'I'm not one to know much about jewels but I hear he's one of the best. Doesn't follow trends like some of these upstarts coming in and copying all the fashions in the magazines from England as if that'll make us pay more, and then the next year it's a whole 'nother thing with green stones instead of red stones.'

Song stopped by Hing's. There were no other customers in the shop. He did not even think Mr Hing himself was there until the man bobbed up from his low seat on the other side of the counter where a strong oil lamp hung. He was not as old as Song had expected. He had a brass magnifier pressed deep into his eye socket and he was delicately holding something with tweezers.

'Good morning, Mr Hing,' Song said quietly. 'I was looking to buy something and I've heard very good things about your work.'

Mr Hing put down the gem he was examining on a swatch of black cloth. Then he relaxed his eye and caught the magnifier as it dropped into his palm.

'I was the boy Father Holmes took in,' Song went on. 'My name's Song.'

'Yes. I seem to remember hearing something about a houseboy done good.' He stood up and surprised Song with his height. He was at least a foot taller than Song. His head was shaved close and he wore a crisp white shirt.

'For a lady?'

Song hesitated. 'Yes.'

'A ring?'

'Something like that.'

'I work on commission, but I have a few pieces finished you can see. They're not for sale but it'll give you some ideas.' Mr Hing paused. 'You live in Bartica?'

'Yes,' Song said.

'And you're still alive?'

'So far.'

'You a pork-knocker?'

'In a way.'

Mr Hing smiled. 'Pork-knocker in denial. They say they're the worst.'

Mr Hing pointed out some of his bespoke pieces. There were textured gold bangles for a baby; polished rectangles of jade; a silver band set with diamonds; a charm bracelet that dangled with nuggets; pendants of Chinese characters and an animal tooth with a gold setting.

'How much is this?' Song asked, lifting a jade pendant.

'None of this is for sale. All on order. That's for Mr Ting-Lee's wife.'

There was a loose silver bracelet set with small pretty diamonds. It was modest enough.

'White gold,' Mr Hing said. 'For Mrs Patel.'

Song fumbled as he picked it up. 'How much if I ordered something similar?'

'This is costing her twelve dollars.'

'Can you make the same but two strands? Twenty dollars?'

'Can you pay now?'

Song nodded. 'If you can get it done in time. I leave in five days.'

He waited as Mr Hing prepared a receipt. He wrote it in Chinese.

'I was wondering where you source your stones?' Song asked.

'Lebanese. On the west side of town. They send the rough diamonds to Europe to be cut. I set them. They sell them right back to Europe for a profit. Some end up in the hands of royalty, I hear. I buy a few stones for my own pieces.'

'Might you be interested in a direct line from Bartica?' Song said.

'Might be,' Mr Hing said. 'Are you selling diamonds? That's what the ladies want.'

'Maybe. They say gold and diamonds run within the same soil.'

'Come back to me.'

'I don't want any in-betweeners taking commissions.'

'You watch yourself. It's the in-betweeners who have all the power in this town.'

'Who should I be looking out for?'

'Everyone.'

Song took the receipt and studied the Chinese characters.

'Don't you read?' Mr Hing asked.

'Not Chinese. I left too young.' Song felt ashamed not to be able to read the language of his motherland. But he also knew if he'd stayed, he wouldn't have been able to read at all.

'I can write it in English if you want,' Mr Hing said.

'That's okay.' Song handed over the deposit. 'Have you ever sent money to China?'

'Impossible.'

'Is it? I once sent money back.'

'It would never have got there. You either go yourself and put the money in the hand of the person you want to give it to, or you keep it in your own pocket and send them a prayer.'

Song felt some relief at Mr Hing's words. A man of trade, Song thought he must know the odds more than most of sending money halfway across the world.

'Come back on the day you leave,' Mr Hing said. 'The bracelet will be ready.'

'One more question. Is there anybody you can suggest I speak to about property in Georgetown?'

'Easy,' Mr Hing said. 'Mr House, that's his nickname. No idea of his real name. Or Ian Tilby. Nobody else worth talking to.'

'Mr House?'

'Houses by name, houses by nature – that's his line,' Mr Hing said. 'And he's as big as one.'

'And Ian Tilby?' Song asked.

'The rich man's choice with access to all the right neighbour-hoods. Bears a heavy grudge though. Meet Mr House first.'

'Where can I find him?' Song asked.

'Daytime I can't be sure. By night he plays dominoes up at the sea wall.'

Before that Song went to the next man on his list, Mr Ebenezer. He had in his pocket the letter from Old Man Kuros.

Mr Ebenezer did not have a shop but worked from his home on the second floor of a dilapidated building overlooking Stabroek Market. Song found nobody home so he went for lunch and returned an hour later.

Mr Ebenezer's maid opened the door.

'Good morning,' Song said. 'I'm here to see Mr Ebenezer. I have a letter of introduction from Mr Ashkanzi Senior of Bartica.'

The woman sniffed. She took the letter and shut the door behind her.

Song tried to listen through the door but could not hear anything until her approaching footsteps. He stepped back.

'He'll see you,' she said. Song followed her through a small hallway into an office that occupied the corner of the apartment. Here was clearly another man who loved to read. There were books on every shelf: upright, leaning and flat; piled like totems on the floor; scattered like cushions on a sofa; all over Mr Ebenezer's desk; books held open with the weight of other books or a conch shell or a brass hand barometer. On the wall was a landscape painting of a goatherd in rocky scrubland. It reminded Song of Father Holmes' painting of the Welsh shepherd.

Mr Ebenezer turned his chair around and motioned Song towards the cluttered sofa. 'Make space,' he said.

Song gently moved some books to the side and sat on the lip of the sofa. 'Sir, I wanted to introduce myself—' he began.

'Nanny gave me the letter. Father Holmes' boy.'

'He was the vicar—'

Mr Ebenezer interrupted again. 'Not a church-going man. Haven't got all day.'

'I have gold to sell, Mr Ebenezer.'

'That's more like it.'

Mr Ebenezer reminded Song of a toucan with his alert eyes, his large nose more like a beak and the jerky way he cocked his head from side to side.

'I'm looking for a direct channel from me straight to the hands of a broker in Georgetown. I don't want to sell in Bartica. I want to come directly to someone here. Nobody in between taking cuts or commissions. I'll declare some to make sure it's seen as above board. But I'll split the saving. I need someone to work quickly and take everything off my hands. They'll need to take it all – and pay cash.'

'Glad you got to the point,' Mr Ebenezer said. 'What I can't understand is why he's taken such a shine to you.'

Song shifted on the sofa and a book fell to the ground. Mr Ebenezer grimaced. Song picked it up and gently put it back on the seat.

Mr Ebenezer stopped looking at the painting and turned to face Song again. 'What did you say to him?'

'Mr Ashkanzi Senior? I met him at the shop once when I was selling. He and his son Farad. His price was lower than fair but we made a deal.'

Mr Ebenezer sneezed and took a large handkerchief out of his pocket. 'There must be something else . . .'

'I'm half-blind,' Song volunteered.

Mr Ebenezer snorted.

Song paused. 'We both like birds.'

'That's it,' Mr Ebenezer said. 'An amateur ornithologist.'

'I can't call myself an ornithologist, sir,' Song said. 'But with Father Holmes and a friend, Jon Swire, we drew up four books on the birds of Guiana. We were the first to identify the whiskered white-headed song warbler; the Royal Ornithological Society allowed us to name it.'

'That old man would like nothing more than someone who

could understand his passion for birds,' Mr Ebenezer said, blowing his nose. 'It was always more than a hobby to him. He could have devoted his life to birds. But his parents wouldn't have it. His son doesn't take an interest either. Never took an interest in anything except money. Easy money, too, that's the kind he likes. Lazy son-of-a. That's it, though. Didn't take me long to get to the root. It's the birds, of course.'

The two men were silent. Nanny was clattering metal dishes in the next room. Through the windows drifted in the holler of a stall-holder calling out the price of roti rolls; words hung on the air like the smell of good cooking.

'Do you know what you are?' Mr Ebenezer said. 'You're a fast talker. You make it sound like you have a new story. It's not a new story. You've got gold to sell. You want it out of the system. You want me to buy it at a good price. I need to sell it at a better price. And the world keeps turning.'

'There's one difference,' Song said. 'I've got enough gold to make us both very nervous.'

'How much are we talking about?'

'It will keep us both busy.'

'Where is it?'

Song smiled.

Mr Ebenezer was irritated. 'I'm not asking for X marks the spot.'

'It's on my land,' Song said. 'I bought fifteen thousand acres. I have the deeds.'

'You bought land? Not your average pork-knocker then. Who else is involved?'

'Nobody yet. I have a loyal fixer called Chi who gets paid very well and who I will continue to pay well. I plan on asking him to run the site.'

'You better pay him well. Loyal ain't a word I hear much about life upriver.'

'The business does well, he does well. He knows that.'

Mr Ebenezer pulled himself up from his chair, walked to the wall and stared into the dusky oil painting of the man tending his goats. He tapped the frame of the picture.

'This is a boy who lived in the mountains of Yemen. His father was a goatherd and he watched him head to the hills every day. But when the boy came of age he moved down to the city. He was a hard worker and had a sharp business mind. Within thirty years he owned most of the shops and controlled all the coffee and qat coming into the country from Ethiopia. Some said he was richer than the Sultan. Then one day he woke up and walked away. He left everything. His big house, his indulged family, his string of businesses. He went into the mountains and nobody heard from him again. Some say they saw him from time to time up in the hills with only his goats. The same life his father had lived.'

Song drew a breath. 'I like a good story. Was that your father?'

Mr Ebenezer didn't answer Song's question. 'It's a lesson against greed.'

'I'll remember it,' Song said. 'Not having enough, having too much, both have their problems.'

Mr Ebenezer nodded. 'I'll take you on. Jews of the East, they call the Chinese. Different eyes. Different noses.' He tapped his temple. 'But the same heads.'

Song didn't understand the comparison, nor did he like it, but he didn't speak out. He was aware he was choosing to follow his dead father's advice this time, to stay quiet, to keep his head down, and that didn't make Song feel good. But he knew he wanted to do business with this man and was conscious that speaking out might put the relationship in jeopardy.

'Where do you live?' Mr Ebenezer asked.

'Bartica.'

'Well, if you can survive Bartica . . .'

'I'll be back and forth from now on. I'm buying a house here.'

'Are you?' Mr Ebenezer cocked his head to the side again. 'Ashkanzi and I have something in common, you know. We like ambition. That's why he sent you to me. When the gold starts coming out thick and fast you bring it here and we'll talk some more.'

'It's already coming out thick and fast. Do you have a pair of scissors?' Song pulled his shirt outside of his trousers and let the hems hang in his hands. 'It's sewn into the cloth.'

'Nanny,' he yelled. 'Bring scissors.'

Nanny walked in with wet hands and a pair of scissors. 'No need to shout.'

'Make sure the door downstairs is locked,' Mr Ebenezer said to her.

'You know I find that entirely unnecessary.'

'Go on,' Mr Ebenezer said. 'Lock it.'

Song took off his shirt and laid it out on the desk. He started cutting the stitching around the borders of the squares Chi had arranged so carefully.

'Hurt your back?' Mr Ebenezer said. He was looking at Song's scars.

Song dismissed his comment. 'Long time ago,' he said. He felt more anger than shame. Angry at the men who had left their marks.

Mr Ebenezer nodded. 'Hard to forget with scars like that.'

'They're out of my sight. I don't notice them.'

What Song said was true. He was glad not to see those reminders daily, yet they also represented for him a fight he had to keep fighting – not to be answerable to anyone ever again. To better himself, to rise above, to leave that all behind him.

Song continued to unpick the stitching. He gently shook the cloth; three nubs of gold fell into his palm. He held them out to Mr Ebenezer. Mr Ebenezer took Song's wrist, flicked it and emptied the contents of his hand into his own.

'Very nice,' Mr Ebenezer said. His hands were trembling. 'How much is in this rag?'

'Just under three pounds. Took us two days to take this out and we haven't even started.'

Mr Ebenezer put a piece of gold in his teeth and bit it. 'How about we make this the first of many happy trades?'

Song put out his hand and Mr Ebenezer took it. They shook firmly. Song sensed he had found a match in this outspoken old man who was unafraid to say exactly what he thought. In many ways, more a Bartica type than the hypocrites of Georgetown. Brimful of prejudice perhaps, but not pretending to be otherwise. Song felt he knew what he was getting himself into with this one.

That night Song went up to the sea wall. It was hot and the mosquitoes were biting. Song recalled the last time he'd been this way – with Father Holmes by his side. They had come across Scott and Millie, and Song had seen a new side to Father Holmes, a vicar, or more simply a man, trying to fix the injustices of the world around him. His wrath at Millie, his concern for Scott. Song understood Father Holmes' reaction even more clearly now. Scott, the houseboy, like Song had been then. And in some ways, newly back in Georgetown, Song felt similarly now. He couldn't risk making a mistake, like Scott.

'I'm looking for a Mr House,' Song said to the man selling ice lollies. 'You know him?'

'Up there.' He nodded down the line of tables. 'You want a house, you got the right man. He's the big one. Nicer than he looks.'

There were a dozen wooden tables set out along the seafront with men playing draughts and dominoes. The onlookers were gambling, clutching the neck of a bottle and slapping at mosquitoes. Men looked up as Song walked by. Some touched their hat. One offered to take a bet. Song shook his head. 'Thanks, but I don't gamble.'

Song moved down the line and stopped where there were two men playing dominoes and five watching on. The player with his back to Song was huge and he guessed this was Mr House. His head became his neck became his shoulders which sloped down to his flabby arms. His white vest bulged outwards, tugging at the stitching.

Song joined the crowd to watch the game. Someone offered him a drink; he shook his head. No one spoke. Everyone watched the two men clackety-clack the ebony pieces around the tabletop.

The big man lost. There was clapping and cries of delight from some quarters. Others moseyed off into the night. The big man scraped his chair back. 'Can't win 'em all. Sorry boys.'

The winner asked him for a cigarette. Mr House handed him two. As the big man started to walk away Song touched his arm. 'Mr House?'

He turned his head slightly.

'My name's Song. I'm from Bartica, but I'm looking to buy myself a place in Georgetown.'

'Found the right man,' Mr House replied. 'What you looking for?'

'Something in a nice part of town.'

'Just for you?'

'Bigger than that.'

'I'll meet you at nine under the clock.'

'I'll be there.'

Mr House turned and headed back towards town. Song watched the huge figure slope off. It had been brief but congenial.

Song continued along the sea wall. The breeze had picked up and the salt air was cooling. He looked out across the water and listened to it lapping softly against the wall. The night was inky and starless. He could not see a horizon in the darkness. He imagined the *Dartmouth* moored offshore and remembered how small it had seemed that day they disembarked and he looked back. How much further away was his family? Beyond the edge of the sea, an impossible distance away. Blurred images came to him of his sisters and brothers. He watched their undefined silhouettes diminish as the cart rolled away. A family fading. Then he thought of Hannah. A strong clear image of her face, her smile, her figure on a bicycle. He hoped to show her a house in Georgetown. A new home. He pictured children running in the yard, hearing their voices carried through windows into the house. The hope of another family, another life.

The next morning Song arrived at the clock ten minutes before nine. Mr House was already there, sweating in spite of the coolness of the early hour. Song glanced up at the time.

'You're early,' Mr House reassured him. 'Just like to be earlier. Promptness is a sign of respect for other people's time.'

Mr House was wearing more clothes than the night before and looked bigger in daylight. He filled his shirt but not uncomfortably. His glasses were too narrow for his head and splayed over his ears. Droplets of sweat trickled down his temples and were absorbed into his shirt collar, which was cutting into his neck.

'More than a room, you said?' Mr House said.

'Yes,' Song replied. 'But it's the location I care about. I want a good address.'

'Where you living now?'

'Bartica.'

'Bartica, eh? Won't be hard to improve on that. Well, assuming you make it back here alive from time to time you'll want something nice here. And you won't be on your own forever. Man cannot live on bread alone. It's whether you want to live for the present or plan for the future.'

'For the future,' Song said. 'What's Georgetown's most respectable neighbourhood?'

'Outside of the English neighbourhood?'

'I don't have my bearings. Is the vicarage in the English neighbourhood?'

Mr House raised his eyebrows. 'On the edge of. But if you want to live in the vicarage you've come to the wrong man.'

'I did live there once, you know. I was Father Holmes' houseboy.'

'Ah, making sense to me now. I remember. Sugar boy come good. Not your average pork-knocker then?'

'I hope not. Otherwise I'd be poor, drunk and dead in ten years. So, the best neighbourhood?'

'I'd suggest by the law courts. A good area for a new boy in town. Don't want to tread on anyone's toes.'

'By the law courts,' Song repeated to himself.

'Of course it depends on how much you're prepared to spend.'

'Depends on how much they're charging,' Song said.

Mr House had organised a donkey cart and the two men rode around town. Memories were stirred up for Song at every street corner. He remembered the tree where he had hit a gecko with his slingshot and cried himself to sleep that night; the canopy where he had sheltered from the rain and was so late home Amalia walloped him, then kissed him, while he stood there puzzled; the plot where a house burned down and a married woman, stark naked, jumped out of the window to escape. Her lover had done the same and broken his neck on landing. She had walked off with her head held high and without a shred of clothing on her body.

But most of all Song remembered simply walking these streets with Father Holmes. He wished Father Holmes could see him now and what he was dreaming up.

Mr House pointed out all the favourable parts of town and explained what was for sale and for how much. His commission was what he could negotiate off the sale price; if he couldn't cut a sharper deal from the seller he'd walk away with nothing, that was his deal.

'Thing is not everyone has a price,' he said. 'Tilby – the biggest real estate racket in town – thinks he can get anyone to sell any-thing. A dying grandmother's bungalow. A family home. Probably thinks he could buy a damn church if he wanted to. You got to respect people. That's the rule I live by.'

Song pointed out one house close to the law courts. It was a huge whitewashed stand-alone house with a wraparound veranda on the ground and first and second floors. There must have been twenty shuttered windows, some bay, some bow, with fretwork and deep overhanging eaves. There were lanky palms and hibiscus bushes in the large garden.

Mr House raised his eyebrows. 'It's not for sale, as far as I know, but I can look into it.'

Song looked at the man working in the front yard of the house.

He recalled his first day in Guiana, when he looked out from the cart at the wide avenues and grand houses with their rolling green lawns. He remembered his hope that he might one day work in a garden like that. So much had changed for him since that first day in Guiana. His reality now was that he was buying the house, not hoping to work for the owner. Yet Song felt strongly that he still had more to do. He had been alone then. He didn't want to be alone any more.

'What should I offer?' Song asked.

Mr House said a price. Song named a figure 15 per cent lower for cash. They moved towards each other and shook hands.

By the end of the week, Mr House had secured the purchase. Song had the house and people had started to talk.

Song had one more person to look up before he left town. He had waited more than an hour outside the colonial administration building at the end of the work day before he caught sight of Jon. His old friend was wearing a nice shirt and pair of slacks. He looked relaxed, at ease in himself.

'Jon Swire. Look at you.'

'Song Holmes. Been wondering how long it would be till I ran into you. I been hearing rumours.'

'Rumours seem to follow me like a bad smell. How the hell are you?'

'Not bad. Got a good job. Thanks to Father Holmes, but you know that. I'm drawing sketches of birds for Governor Johnson, but also of Georgetown life for the library, and all sorts.'

'I couldn't be more pleased. You deserve it.'

'And you? Whatch you do to your eye?'

'Lost the sight in it.'

Jon flinched. 'Sorry to hear that. Must've hurt.'

'You know what it's like upriver. There are no second chances.'

'And whatch you doing in Georgetown?'

'I'm thinking of moving. Tell me, how's life here?'

'I don't do much except work and feed myself and send money home. I miss the family. Don't get to see them so often. They don't visit so I have to go up when I can.' Jon looked slightly flushed. 'And I'm seeing a girl.'

'It sounds pretty good,' Song said, and he meant it. He couldn't yet say he was seeing a girl. And although he had money, it would never be shared with his family. He found himself envying Jon, not with malice, but because his life sounded joyfully uncomplicated, true to himself and his family.

'How's your mama and little Sonia?'

'Sonia ain't so little. They're both doing okay, I think. I wanted to stick around for them but I had to leave. I couldn't be around Kiddo any more, couldn't watch Mama taking it from him. Either he was going to kill me, or I was going to kill him. And sure as hell he'd be better at killing than me.'

Song nodded. 'It was best you got out of there.'

'And now you're getting out, too? It'll be good to have you in the same town again.'

'Meantime I've got a job for you.'

'Upriver?'

Song raised his eyebrows. 'Would you really come? No, not upriver. And it's not a sketch. Believe it or not, I've got a stuffed harpy eagle back in my room. It's not beautiful but it was once. I need you to get it back to how it was, or close.'

'How sad. They're sad anyway, but a dead, badly stuffed harpy eagle.'

'It needs life, like you give life to the birds in your drawings.'

'I can't promise it'll be any good, but I'll try.' Jon paused. 'So, you been finding any gold? I heard it's going well.'

'We hit a seam.'

'This town's talking of nothing else. You should hear it: "Remember that sugar Chiney taken in by the pastor, that's the one"; "That boy became a pork-knocker out in Bartica and he's struck gold"; "He's buying up Georgetown, did you hear?"; "What'd that pastor think of him now?"'

'What would he think of me now?'

'He'd be proud.'

'Maybe.'

Then Song thought about what his own father would have thought. 'Keep to yourself.' That's what he'd have said. 'Trouble only comes to those who stand out.' Song didn't believe in those warnings anymore. He was tired of keeping himself to himself. Instead he was beginning to feel it was his time.

On his last day Song went to collect the bracelet. Mr Hing handed him a brown leather box. Song pressed the small metal button on the front. It clicked softly and Song opened the lid. It was a double strand of square-cut diamonds twisted around each other.

'It will sit better on a wrist than in the box,' Mr Hing said.

'It's very fine, thank you,' Song said. He wanted to be bound with Hannah the same way. 'Find a sweet one and stick with her,' that's what Mr Leigh had said. 'Treat her right and she'll stick by you forever.'

'I hope she says yes,' Mr Hing added.

Song was startled by Mr Hing's intuition but then realised how obvious it was. 'I hope so, too.'

CHAPTER 21

When Song returned to Bartica he went straight to Mary Luck's Lucky Bakery. Hannah's bicycle was not there so he waited in the yard. He could hear Mary Luck stacking trays inside. He reached up again to feel the smooth hard box in his shirt pocket and his stomach knotted.

There was a whir of bicycle wheels and suddenly she was in front of him. Her hair was tugged back and her face was glistening with sweat.

'Hannah,' he said. 'I'm back from Georgetown.'

'I can see that.' She stood in front of him, straddling her bicycle. 'How was it?'

'Busy.'

'How so.' Then she put her hand in her pocket and brought out some shelled Brazil nuts. 'You hungry?'

Song nodded. She let some fall into his open hand. 'I've been keeping them for you.'

'I have something for you, too.' Song reached into his pocket and took out the box.

'What is it?'

'Open it.'

'Will you hold the handlebars?'

Song held the bicycle steady. She rubbed her hands on her apron and took the box from him. Her eyes flashed. 'What is it?'

Song could barely wait. 'Please open it.'

She pressed the little metal button and there was a click. She looked up at him and smiled, before lifting the lid. The bracelet shone in the sunlight with tiny dancing rainbows like waterfall spray.

Song thought how much more beautiful it was in her hands. Rainbows, like a life with Hannah.

She shut the lid and pushed the box towards Song. 'I can't.'

'Why?' Song said.

'It's too much, Song. It's not right.'

'But it's for you.' Song's voice broke as he spoke. 'I had it made for you specially.'

'It's very beautiful but I can't accept it. Mother wouldn't allow it.'

'It's not for your mother to allow.'

Hannah hesitated. 'Yes and no.'

'She told me it was up to you if you wanted to go for a walk with me.'

'A walk maybe,' Hannah said. 'But not—'

'I want to marry you.'

Song hadn't planned to say it so soon.

Hannah stepped back sharply. As she did she lost her balance. Song tried to hold on to the handlebars but Hannah, her bicycle and the cake trays crashed to the ground. Mary Luck came to the door. 'What's going on?'

'Sorry,' Hannah said, pulling herself up. 'Everything's fine. The trays were empty anyway.'

'If they're empty there's more to deliver,' her mother said.

'Good morning, ma'am,' Song said.

'Fine time of the day to be making a visit, when we're delivering,' Mary Luck said to Song. 'Customers are waiting while you're both chatting away like there was all the time—'

'Let them wait,' Hannah cut in.

Her mother gasped. 'What's gotten into you, chil'?'

Hannah was looking at Song. Her one green and one brown eye were locked on to his one good eye. She smiled a small smile that nobody but he noticed.

'Song came to ask me to marry him, Mama,' Hannah said. 'And I said yes.'

Within the month, Song and Hannah were married at St Ethelbert's. Weddings were the best of times in Bartica. The women put on wide-brimmed hats and their biggest diamonds. The larger ladies wore billowing flowered dresses and the skinny ones straight shifts. All of Ruby Lou's girls came with ribbons in their hair and painted nails showing through open-toed shoes.

Weddings were also the best way to fill a church. Father Lovett took advantage of the chance to speak to so many people. His sermon lasted over an hour, preaching about the sin of drink, of music, of a life without meaning. He seemed to condemn most of the town to hell, foretelling consequences, perhaps not in this lifetime but at its end. Everyone was polite enough to stay the course but not enough to refrain from fidgeting. Parents pinched their babies hard in the backside to make them cry so they could excuse themselves and get some air. Song squeezed Hannah's hand to try to express how insufferable he thought Father Lovett was.

Of course the real reason everybody was attending the ceremony was for the party. Leading up to the wedding Jingy told Father Lovett she was taking the whole week off and she took charge of catering. The crab population of Bartica was just about extinct by the time she had finished crawling up and down the side of the dock filling up buckets. In addition the air was filled with the squawking of strangled chickens and their plucked feathers. Bartica was not going to see a chicken egg in a long time.

There was more food than anyone had seen on one single day. If half of Georgetown had come too there would still have been leftovers. As Song looked around he remembered how it was to feel hungry – and the conjured-up stories of food that had sustained him. Here it was for real. There were baked chicken legs in molasses; chicken wings in forest honey; bass with onion and ginger; cauldrons of pepper pot; rice coloured with strands of saffron; blackened barbecued pork; potato and pea curry with turmeric, and a dozen dishes of stewed okra and fried tomatoes.

Mary Luck closed the bakery for three days before the day of the wedding and kept the ovens hot through the night. She woke every few hours to take out trays of warm golden biscuits and to replace them with trays of uncooked pastry. There were enough currant cakes and pine tarts and cream pies for every man, woman and child three times over.

While the guests feasted the B Town Troubadours played through the night until dawn the following day. Everybody danced. Everybody sweated. Everybody drank the free-flowing rum. A couple of fights broke out in the early hours but nobody was badly hurt. Song could not have been happier, as if the best time of his life might be just beginning.

Song and Hannah left the party before Short John had played his last tune, but it was already so late none of the guests noticed. Song led her home to his Bits & Bobs room. Bronco was outside Louis' and he gave them a shy smile. He had insisted on keeping guard even if it meant missing the wedding. 'If I was a thief it would be exactly the moment I'd strike,' he said. 'Just make sure you save me some of Jingy's curry and I'll be a happy man.'

When Song unlocked his door there was a wave of perfume.

Jingy had decorated the room with flamboyants and frangipani, garlands of jasmine, and with bougainvillaea petals scattered across the bed. Hannah walked around the room smelling all the different flowers and looking at Song's few things. She touched the yellowed globe Mr Leigh had given Father Holmes, and looked surprised when it turned on itself. Then she ran her fingers along the spines of the books. 'Have you read all these?'

Song nodded. 'More than once.'

She leaned forward to smell the jasmine.

'We can always have flowers if you like,' Song said.

'Always? How long is always?'

'For all time. Forever.' Song leaned forward to take the frangipani from Hannah's hair. 'Why is it, Hannah Luck, that you married me?'

'That's Hannah Luck Holmes to you,' she said. 'And I married you, Song Holmes, because I love you.'

Hannah's words snatched Song's breath. 'And why is it that you love me?' Song asked.

'Another why.' Hannah said. 'How many whys shall I allow you tonight?'

'Please tell me.'

'Because of the way your one eye looks so deeply into my mixed-up eyes it makes up for the other that hides itself. It looks at me strong and curious and soft all at the same time. I love you, Song, because you are strong and curious and soft all at the same time.'

He kissed her on the lips. She tasted of papaya.

'And I love you also,' Hannah whispered, 'because you love me back.'

For an instant they simply looked at each other in the milky light. Then they began to loosen each other's clothes, unbuttoning and pulling at ties. The garments fell to the ground. Hannah picked up and carefully laid her red dress on Song's desk. She was standing in a white cotton petticoat that held her in so tightly it looked as if it had been sewn upon her. Her round breasts were pressed flat. The cotton tugged around her broad hips. Fine darts of stitching drew in her waist.

He led her towards the bed and pulled back the sheet. Petals rose up in the air in a cloud of colour and Hannah laughed. As she lay back her petticoat became trapped and there was the sound of seams tearing. There was her lullaby laugh again, sweet and drowsy.

Song put his hands on Hannah's body and felt the dampness of sweat through the cotton. He tried to slide up her petticoat and there was another gentle tear.

'Tear it off me,' Hannah whispered. 'I don't think it will come off any other way.'

Song took a seam between his hands. The threads ripped apart easily. The sound stirred him. His hands travelled over her soft buttery body. Then he moved upon her. She was motionless, looking at him with her mismatched eyes. For a moment they paused. Then they began to rock together back and forth as if to comfort each other after a lifetime apart.

The next morning Song woke to feel the light touch of fingers running across his back. He whispered her name. 'Hannah?' Her name was so soft, like breath. He found himself wanting to cry at the sound of her name. He could feel her lips on his back. She was kissing his scars.

CHAPTER 22

A few days after the wedding Song went to see Chi. Nina was in the front yard with her younger siblings. She was carrying Bibi on her hip. Song had not spoken to her since the afternoon he had cut her short and walked away.

'Hands full again?' Song asked.

Nina shrugged. 'Always.'

'Chi around?'

'Probably.'

She turned away from him and yelled. 'Papaaaa!' Bibi, clinging to her, jumped.

Chi came out in the yard in his underwear. It was Bibi's turn to shout. She mimicked her older sister. 'Papaaaa!' The other children laughed.

Song was glad for the break in the tension. He went up to sit on the porch and Chi straddled his hammock. 'I thought you'd forgotten your old river mate.'

'We're going to set up a goldmine, Chi.'

Chi rolled his eyes. 'You should be making babies, not talking about goldmines.'

'There'll be time for that later,' Song said. He wanted to make sure he could provide for Hannah and a family. He never wanted anybody to be hungry again.

'Gold first,' Chi said. 'I like the way you do things.'

'We'll need a team,' Song said. 'Maybe ten or twenty.'

'You want even more people to know about this? You're killing me.'

'What do you want to do? Have the two of us chip away at the wrong rock for the rest of our lives?'

'Of course that's what I want.'

Song ignored him. 'Will you run it?'

'Is it gonna make me a rich man?' Chi asked.

'You'll be a rich man whether you choose to run it or not. I'm taking my job to make you rich very seriously.'

Chi laughed. 'What's the catch?'

'You'll need to spend a lot of time upriver, but that's probably not a catch for you. We'll need two teams working on say, three-month rotations. You'll get to choose the men. We can ask Sammy and the boys but as we know, it's not for them all the time. We'll have to find a deputy to cover you when you bring the gold back to Bartica. That journey will have its risks but I'll have Bronco meet you before the dock. That'll be the gold we declare. The rest I'll take from the mine to Georgetown. I've found someone to work with directly. Says he'll take everything we pull out.'

Chi stared at Song.

'What?' Song said.

'There I was thinking you were falling in love and getting married,' Chi said, 'and all that time you were doing deals.'

'I'm thinking of your future, Chi, while you laze about in a hammock and walk around your yard in your underwear.'

'You know, there's such a thing as too much gold,' Chi said.

'Really?' Song asked sarcastically. 'Tell me about that.'

'Too much can weigh a man down.' Chi's voice was serious. 'All we really need is enough to buy a round or two, to pick up a super deluxe at Ruthie's, to buy a trinket for the wife and the whore. That'll do. A bit of change for the biscuit tin so we're allowed to leave again. Everyone's happy. Bring back too much and you're headed for trouble. Wife'll pester, wanting to rise up. She'll bother about why you need to leave so soon. You don't need to leave so soon, she'll say. And there goes the life we love.'

'So what are you saying?'

Chi smiled. 'I'm not saying nothing. When are we heading back?'

'Is that a yes?'

'What else am I going to do? Chip away at the wrong rock for the rest of my life, as you put it? Waiting around is making me jumpy.'

'Fever's rising in both of us.' Song wasn't sure this was true any more. The fever was stronger when there was nothing to lose. Now, with Hannah by his side, he was aware how much was at stake. He was responsible for both of them now. Lives bound together. Entangled with each other like the strands of a bracelet.

Chi met Song to tell him he'd hired ten men for the next expedition.

'Just wandered around my neighbourhood talking to the young 'uns,' Chi said. 'They're all hungry for adventure, eager to learn. None of them have one jot of pork-knocking experience. I like it that way. Clean slate. We can teach them our way. Besides hard to take the wanderer out of most pork-knockers. They'd like the company but they're no good at working for someone else, not for all the wages in the world.'

Song hired Joseph to do some of the boat transfers up and down the river. He would have liked to have taken him on full-time.

'Flattered to be asked,' he said, 'but I couldn't leave the dock. The boys might drive me crazy but this here little patch of the planet is where I'm set to live out my days.'

Song also hired Bronco full-time. Louis could not argue. He could never match the wage Song was offering the big man. But Song had given Louis a good deal on the side. When Bronco was in town – which would be most of the time – he would continue to stand outside Louis' store, while keeping an eye on his own room across the street. No charge to Louis.

Song had to fend off all the gossip. Harrington caught up with Song one morning.

'So I been hearing it's all a sham. Buying land just to boost land prices. Well, it won't happen. I know about land. Been working in land before you were born.'

'You're probably right, Harrington.'

'I know what land you bought. Too big an area for one man.'

'Not for this man.'

Harrington snorted. 'You getting too full of yourself. It's people like you who end up getting washed downriver.'

'I'll make sure I watch my back.' Song didn't dismiss Harrington's words. He was aware he was putting some people out. But neither was he going back to his old ways. He felt more self-assured. Maybe it was Hannah. Maybe it was age. He didn't want to keep his head down forever.

Dr Foo also questioned him. 'Some say you're buying gold straight from the Amerindians, not pork-knocking at all,' he said. 'That right? Need to be careful, if so. I know you got friends up there, but they don't live by the same rules as us.'

'And what rules does Bartica live by, Dr Foo? I don't see any rules here.'

'True, true. Just want you to look out for yourself, Song. Telling you what Father Holmes might have told you if he was alive.'

Song thought how Father Holmes would not have said anything like that if he was alive.

'Remember you only got one eye now. Use it well. Look out for yourself as much as you can.'

The jetty boys also pestered him. 'Hear you buying up Georgetown, too,' Dory said.

'I bought a place to stay when I'm there, that's all.'

'Not what we're hearing. Some say it's the biggest building in the city.'

'That's not true.'

Town was talking. Chi was buying up enough provisions to last a year. He cleaned Louis out of rice and maize. Ten five-gallon cans of oil and heavy gas burners were sent for directly from Georgetown. Song had been researching new methodologies of panning for gold, without the need for manpower. It was too slow to rely on ten men on the banks of a river with a battel in their hands, swirling water around day after day. Song wanted a more effective, more efficient way of working. He'd heard about equipment that could do the same job ten times more quickly: step-filter machines that used the energy of running water to separate different sizes of gravel. Piling up on the side of the dock were slender wooden planks, long coils of thick rope and huge bales of canvas tarpaulin. Children peeped inside crates to catch sight of the newfangled equipment. There were bottles of mercury, the colour of the moon reflected on the river, and strong-smelling pots of turpentine and white spirit.

The night before Song left, he lay in bed with Hannah and held her hand in his.

'It's never been this hard to leave,' he said. 'But I'm doing this for you now, you know that. You will be on my mind every day. Wait for me, won't you?'

'Where do you think I'd go? Take your rowboat and head downriver to the big open sea to see the world?'

'Don't joke about that.'

'I'll be here, Song. I want you to go upriver. It's what you do. I knew that when I found you.'

'I found you first. I saw you outside Louis' and you didn't even notice me. You were just a girl. Covered in icing sugar. Cakes falling off the back of your bicycle.'

'I found you before that. I saw you with Father Holmes walking down my street years before, and you can't even remember. The boy with the vicar.'

'Who's to say which came first?' Song said.

'Let's call it a tie,' Hannah said. She squeezed his hand. 'I'll be here waiting.'

The expedition set off early the next morning in fourteen boats. A crowd on the bank watched them leave. Nobody – not even the new recruits – knew where they were heading or how long they might be. Song and Chi caught each other's eye. Chi winked. Upriver. They were on their way again.

Song's navigation was sharp and they arrived at the site in under a week. Song was surprised to feel the dread rising in him as they neared their destination. His fears hadn't diminished out here. The ghosts of the past lingered. He knew the approach so well now: every bough of every tree, every rock breaking up the flow of the river. He'd even notice a new log caught among vegetation by the bank, or a new nest.

As they pulled up, Song jumped out of the first boat and tied up. Again, he noticed his hands trembling and he tried to block out the darkness of the past.

They secured the rest of the boats. There was not enough room to pull all fourteen up the bank, so they tied a half-dozen to each other and moored them out on the river.

Without wasting any time, they began to set up right away, felling trees and clearing a good area of forest to construct the camp. Cover was the first priority. They put up one closed shed for dry stores and five open-sided shelters: three for storage, one with hammocks and another floored with matting for meal times. Song wanted working conditions to be comfortable. The cooks were under strict instruction to provide generous meals. After the fresh food ran out, one cook was to stay in camp and prepare food while the other went off fishing and hunting.

After the first buildings were standing, half the men began work on widening the mine pit. As they burrowed sideways into the rock, parallel to the seam, they constructed supporting wooden beams to prevent collapses.

Song had sheaves of illustrations on how to assemble and operate the new equipment. The filter system was thirty-foot long and used a step technique every six feet to separate the finer granules from the coarser matter. This refined material was then transferred to mechanised trays of sand which vibrated vigorously, using the power of the river's current, which forced the gold to accumulate at the base of the trays. It was then collected on wet muslin sheets.

Song thought about what Mr Leigh had said. 'I don't want to hear of you pork-knocking a few specks of gold dust out of the ground.' He could now, hand on heart, answer that call.

Song stayed with Chi upriver for nearly a month to help organise the site. Then he went to Yupukama to see Sammy and the others. He found them recently returned from a long successful hunt, and the village had been feasting.

'Celebrating?' Song asked.

'More interested to know if you're celebrating,' Sammy said.

'You were right,' Song said. 'It was just a matter of time. We're celebrating.'

'Glad you found what you were looking for. Happy now?'

That was a good question. Was he happy now? Because of finding the gold?

'I'm married, Sammy. That makes me happy now.'

Sammy smiled. 'You've figured it out then.'

'I have.'

'But you're back.' Sammy said. 'Looking for more?'

Song nodded. 'Yes. Will you come back with me?'

'Sure,' he said. 'We'll come. Can't promise how long we'll stay, but we'll come.'

Song wished Mr Leigh could see him now. Getting local insight. Buying land. No disputes.

Chi had put together a hard-working team. Some learned more easily than others, but nobody slacked. That night Song spoke to the group and outlined his plans for the mine.

'You will always be the ones who were with us from the start. That's not down to luck. I don't believe in luck and you should not rely on it to get you anywhere in life either.

'Chi hired each of you because we believed you had something more to give than the average man on the streets of Bartica. Not just muscle and might. You should know by now that we're looking for more than that. It's no coincidence that none of you were pork-knockers before you joined our team. Experience isn't essential. What is essential is drive. All of you want to do well in life. We want you to do well in life, too.'

There wasn't a whisper among the young men. Song could sense their thrill at being here, for the opportunity to work hard, to share in the spoils.

'I'm leaving tomorrow to find a way to get the best price for the

311

gold you all find here. The system doesn't make that easy. The system goes against people like you – the ones plucking the gold out of the ground. I don't think it should be that way. You're key to this team. Without you I wouldn't have anything to take with me to Bartica tomorrow. I need you to get the gold out of the ground as effectively as you can. I want us all to get richer. If you stick with me, I will stick with you.'

'I'll stick with you,' someone said.

'Me, too.'

There were murmurings of support among the young men.

'As the operation grows so will the team,' Song continued. 'When I get back from this trip I am going to bring more bright young workers like yourselves. That's because you'll all need a break from time to time and we can't close the mine in your absence. You'll want to spend the money you earn. Just don't go telling me how.'

There was a ripple of laughter in the darkness. The light had faded. It was just the beat of the frogs in the night and Song's steady voice.

'Chi is your boss here. If you can be a tenth as solid as this man, we're in business. Hard work will be rewarded. If the mine does well, you will do well. This isn't about a wage, it's about commission. That's how it will work here. If we all work harder, we all do better. Not just me. Not just Chi. All of us.'

Song could feel the surging excitement in the group. The fever was rising in all of them. He hoped his words would get them thinking bigger than battels and liquor.

CHAPTER 23

Song arrived back in Bartica in the dead of night, light of step, moving swiftly from tying up the boat to being back at his room where he knew Hannah would be sleeping. He knocked on the door softly so as not to frighten her. But when there was no response he let himself in. He looked to the bed and saw her shape under the sheet. He breathed with relief.

'Hannah,' he said.

She sat up sharply.

'Song. Am I dreaming?'

He came to her. 'I'm back.'

'At this hour?'

'At any hour, you are my most precious thing in the world.'

'I missed you.'

Song took her in his arms and they held each other. He didn't want to make love to her, only to hold her close.

'Tell me how you are.'

'Bereft without you. Happy now.'

'And how is Mary Luck?'

'Complaining that I married a man who is never here.'

'Of course. And Bartica?'

'This town loves a mystery. And you're the mystery right now. Nothing people here like more than not knowing something. Gives them an excuse to make it all up and then tell you what they know for sure, no doubt, definitely. Some days you're thieving and murdering upriver, the next day you're as good as dead, the day after you've bought up half the interior and are selling it to some big-time American company and have moved to Venezuela. Been standing up for you, Song, fighting like a wounded jaguar, like only a woman knows how.'

'My woman. How is it that you're by my side of all the sides you could be beside in the world?'

'Because I am. You know I think I even enjoyed shouting down all the nonsense I heard, the roundabout ramblings. This town's half built on lies, the rest is built on sin. Still, I'm going to hate to leave this place when the time comes.'

'Can we talk about that, Hannah? When can we leave?' There was almost five pounds of gold burning a hole in Song's pocket.

'So soon?'

'Georgetown is the next step. It's where business is done. Besides,' he winked, 'this cramped room isn't the place to raise a family.'

'I'll throw that straight back at you. I think,' she paused, 'I might be pregnant.'

Hannah's words caught Song's breath. This is what he'd let himself dream about. He had wanted to show Hannah how much he loved her with a baby. A family.

'Silenced,' she said, clapping her hands 'Got you.'

'You have, Hannah Luck Holmes. In every way.'

Later that day, Song visited the weighing station to declare a half-pound of gold.

'We're moving to Georgetown,' Song told Edward Hoare. 'You're welcome to join us on the boat, but be warned: this time Hannah and Mary Luck and all of Mary Luck's life will be in tow, so I won't be offended if you turn me down.'

314

Mr Hoare laughed. 'The ferry sounds like it might be less crowded. We won't be seeing so much of you around here then?'

'I don't think I could ever leave Bartica entirely,' Song said. 'This was my home for so long, where I grew up, where Father Holmes taught me everything I now know. I'll be keeping the room. I'd like to continue to declare my finds with you, if that's okay, although I'll get Chi do it from time to time. I've hired Bronco; I don't want my neck broken for a penny weight.'

'A penny weight? They'd kill you for a grain here. Well, don't go abandoning us altogether, Song. Bartica wouldn't be the same without you. Besides, the selfish truth is I couldn't bear to lose my private charter to Georgetown. You're the only one who can afford it.'

Song headed down to Ashkanzi's, accompanied by Bronco.

'Glad to have you here, Bronco.'

'You better get used to it,' the big man replied. 'Town'll kill you for a lot less than you got. And less than that again.'

The pair walked into the shop together. Farad nodded at Bronco. 'Why you brought him along?'

'He's helping me.'

'You living scared?'

Song passed him the gold. 'I'm sure not dying scared, Farad.'

Farad scowled. 'This ain't the lot. I'm no fool. You couldn't pay a dozen wages on this.'

'What are you suggesting?'

'I'm not as stupid as you or my father think.'

'I've never thought you were stupid,' Song said. 'I just don't trust you. Like you don't trust me.'

'My father didn't trust me from the day I was born.'

'Maybe you haven't given him a reason to change his mind.'

'Maybe. Maybe not,' Farad sneered.

Farad handed over the money to Song, who headed off to pay the tax on what he'd declared. Sewed into the hem of his shirt, tied around his waist, he still carried more than four pounds of undeclared gold. He swore to himself that he wasn't going to be giving everything he pulled out to Governor's House and their lot. Not after all he had seen, all that had passed. He would find a way to get the better of them.

Song watched Hannah prepare for the move. Overall she seemed excited, in spite of her expressed mixed feelings about leaving. And Song discovered she had never left Bartica. He wondered how he would have been if he had never left Lishui. Not so perceptive as Hannah, but perhaps as kind. A simpler life. Or perhaps he wouldn't have made it. Too many hungry children. Life for him had taken a different turn and perhaps, in fact, he was the lucky one. He had survived. With only a shirt on his back and a swing-basket of rice.

He was surprised at how little Hannah had, too. A few dresses, and a matching hand mirror and hairbrush made of mother-of-pearl. It made Song want to buy her anything she set her eyes on.

Mary Luck made up for her daughter's modest luggage. She boxed everything she had ever owned, never mind if it was rusty or broken. She might have packed the bakery itself had there been a box big enough. Short John spent three days to-ing and fro-ing between her house and the dock and did not hold back on his jibing. He laughed out loud when he picked up a cage with two brown hens clucking nervously inside.

'They got chickens in Georgetown, you know,' he said to Mary Luck.

'Course I know they got chickens,' she said. 'I already been twice to that city. You calling me stupid? I'm taking them because I like *my* chickens. Bartica eggs taste different to city eggs.'

'Do they?' Short John asked. 'Eggs is eggs. I'm going to fry you one of each and see if you can tell the difference.' He strained to lift up the next box. 'You mind me asking what you got in this one, ma'am? You trying to snap my back in two.'

'You don't mind what I got and what I not got,' Mary Luck said. 'This is personal stuff. You just pack it up like you was packing bone china. I don't want nothing to break.'

'Other than my bones,' Short John grumbled. 'This ain't china, ma'am. Hey Song, I reckon your mother-in-law's been popping your pieces of eight in these here boxes.'

'They're rocks, if you want to know,' Mary Luck said.

'Lordy, Lordy,' Short John said.

'Don't you be complaining,' the old woman said. 'I should be the one complaining. Lived here all my life only to be uprooted by my own daughter. If I can't take some of my Bartica roots with me then I ain't leaving. You tryin' to deprive an old woman of her rights?'

'Ma'am, I'll box up and carry your whole darn yard for you, if you want me to,' Short John said. 'Not saying I won't grumble 'bout it 'long the way though.'

The journey was longer than usual because the river was high and fast, and the rains had cut up the road. Mary Luck insisted the box of chickens be on her lap all the way, even when the birds were flapping in panic on the boat. She was agitated, and hardly stopped talking to Short John up front.

Hannah slept most of the way. She'd become tired with the pregnancy. Song sat close to her so she could rest her head. He thought how different this journey was to the one with Father Holmes when they were travelling from Georgetown to Bartica. That was more than ten years ago. So much had changed. This time he was the one being turned to, the one promising a new home.

As they approached Georgetown he felt full of trepidation, yet hardly able to contain his excitement to show Hannah the big house he'd bought. She stirred from her sleep as the cart slowed down and the beautiful whitewashed buildings came into view.

'What's that?' she asked Song, pointing to their right. The building was fringed with delicate fretwork, with jalousie shutters propped open.

'The colonial administration building. And over there, the clock tower sits above Stabroek Market. It's open every day.'

'And that?' Hannah asked.

'Those are the law courts.'

'The law courts,' Hannah repeated softly.

'And that,' Song said, pointing to the opposite side of the road, 'is our new home.'

Hannah and her mother looked at the enormous white house. 'We're going to live there?' Hannah said. 'Opposite the law courts?'

'Have you not told me something?' Song teased. 'Do we need to be afraid of the rule of law?'

Hannah became shy. 'I didn't think we'd be living opposite the law courts. Did you, Mama? Such a nice neighbourhood, Song. Such a beautiful big house. Why did you buy a house so big?'

'For all the grandchildren you're going to give me, of course,' Mary Luck chimed in.

Song laughed. 'Do you like it?'

'Now I know why I didn't shed a tear when I sold the bakery,' Mary Luck said with some satisfaction. 'I didn't know at the time but I do now.'

Hannah squeezed Song's hand. 'I love it already.'

A woman called Little A welcomed the party at the door. Song had asked Amalia to find him a housekeeper and the woman she suggested was also called Amalia.

'I'm younger than Amalia at the vicarage so folk here call me Little A,' she said. Little A was also a quarter of Amalia's size.

'I don't think that's the only reason, Little A,' Song said. 'This is my wife Hannah and my mother-in-law Mary Luck.'

Song smiled as he spoke those words. He had never needed to introduce these two women to anyone before. Everybody in Bartica knew everybody.

'You bake?' Mary Luck said to the young woman.

'Yes, ma'am,' Little A said. 'My grandmother taught me to bake and she could bake so light that folk said her cakes could get up and fly.'

'Careful,' Song said. 'You're talking to Mary Luck of Lucky's Bakery.'

Little A blushed. 'I baked a lemon sponge this morning, if you would like to see if it's to your liking, ma'am.'

'I would like to see if it's to my liking, indeed,' Mary Luck said. 'You look pretty tiny to be good at baking. Don't you eat your own cakes?'

'I'm sure we'll love it, Little A,' Hannah interrupted. 'Now I'm counting on you to teach me all about this city. I've never been here before. In fact, I've never left old Bartica for anywhere.'

Amalia visited their first day to make sure they found everything to their liking. Song was amused at how nervous she became in front of Hannah and Mary Luck.

'It's nice to meet you, ma'am,' she said. 'You too, ma'am. I won't stay long. I know you're with child, ma'am, congratulations ma'am; I know you need to be getting some rest.'

Amalia was softer with Song, too. 'She's a lovely lady,' she said. 'Who'd have thought it? Song found himself someone very fine.'

Amalia's timidity around the family was offset by the way she bossed about Little A. 'Do you know who this family is?' Song overheard her. 'That there man owns a goldmine. Know what that is? You can't go serving him up any old food you think of at any old moment. You got to plan. Days in advance. He'll be entertaining, too. And that old woman, she was the best baker in Bartica. Bartica ain't so big but she was still the best at it. So you don't get no high horses about your baking skills. Act sharp now. Just because that new lady's being nice to you doesn't mean you can slack around the house. When she's expecting, you need to feed her twice as good.'

Hannah laughed under her breath with Song. 'I like Big A too,' she whispered. 'Know what I like most?'

'What's that?' Song asked.

'I like that she knew you when you were still small and beginning to discover the world so big.'

'She did. She knew me from the start.'

'Boy from a backwater made good. Who can somehow see everything ahead of him with only one eye.'

'Who falls in love with the most perfect woman with mixed-up eyes.'

Song set up accounts at shops across Georgetown: Hardwood & Co Carpentry for new furniture; Happy Life Haberdashery & Upholstery; Stella's, known for her fine needlework; Hilton Ho's for a clock in every room; Gem's Florist for all the flowers Song had promised Hannah their first night.

'Make us a beautiful home,' Song said. 'I feel like I've been swinging in a hammock half my life.'

'Mother will come down hard on me if she sees me looking at anything with a bit of lace or an extra inch of material that hasn't got some use.'

'I'm in no doubt you'll be able to defy Mary Luck if you put your mind to the task.'

Hannah smiled. 'I'll do my best.'

Deliveries arrived every week. Tables built from greenheart. Mahogany chests. Cupboards of snakewood. An oak desk made in England arrived with a red leather top and secret drawers. Hannah put Father Holmes' typewriter on top. She ordered shelving along two walls in Song's study to carry all the books which she organised herself alphabetically by title. There was the yellowed globe and brass scales from Mr Leigh. She hung Father Holmes' oil painting of the Welsh hills on the wall behind the desk. Song loved and hated that picture. If Father Holmes hadn't gone back to Wales to look after his mother, maybe he would be here now. But he didn't like to ponder that. He also loved Wales because it was where Father Holmes was from. He could still whistle like the birds who lived in the hedgerows in the hills of north Wales.

For the dining room Hannah commissioned a finely carved table surrounded by a dozen chairs with bone china crockery and silver knives and forks. The parlour for entertaining was filled with sofas and chaises longues and kissing seats, with silk Chinese rugs underfoot. She had asked Jon Swire to draw illustrations of Song's favourite birds – including the whiskered white-headed song warbler – which were hung all over the room.

Upstairs there were new teak beds and deep mattresses with feather pillows and linen sheets hand-stitched with tiny rosebuds. Hannah bought porcelain jugs and bowls for the bathrooms and thick cotton towels.

Around the porch were rocking chairs, Berbice chairs and cane chairs. Hammocks were made of pink calico with white knotted fringing.

Mary Luck tutted at every new delivery but could not disguise her pleasure at all the pretty things around her. Of the three of them, she settled into Georgetown life the quickest. She joined St Saviour's church and a baking circle, and spent her hours at home teaching Little A new cooking skills. Her chickens were given a corner of the garden and she cared for them as if they were pets.

Song found it harder for him and Hannah to find their way. Georgetown did not welcome them warmly. There was suspicion of Song's swift success, and his past. A plantation boy made good; it couldn't be as simple as that, they'd say. Some crossed the street when they saw the couple walking towards them. Song and Hannah could silence a room when they arrived somewhere, not that they received many invitations.

'Of course it's like this,' Hannah said. 'We shouldn't have expected anything different. Mama was always going to be fine. Nobody's going to be afraid of an old lady with a couple of chickens and a barrowful of rocks. But a newcomer with a goldmine, that's another thing. And they'll be suspicious of his wife, too, by association, no matter how nice I am.' She winked at Song.

'I'm not a newcomer.'

'New enough.'

'It was easier arriving in Bartica.'

'Nobody's much afraid of a vicar either. Not one like Father Holmes. Nor a houseboy by his side.'

'You talk too much sense, Hannah. "Strangers don't like strangers," that's what my papa used to say.'

'A new family with money and without history. That's hard for a community to accept.'

When the house was ready they invited their old friends. Jon Swire came with his wife Rose, who was also expecting their first child. Hannah warmed to her. A Georgetown girl, Rose had a gentle disposition but was a good natterer and she could share with Hannah the ins and outs of the town's social life, its quirks and oddities.

'I don't know what it's like in Bartica,' Rose said, 'but I can tell you we do some things strangely here. At least I think so. Women don't go out much after mid-morning. If you're seen out, people talk. I don't care to listen. Then you can be seen to be going out again late afternoon – but always with a hat. Isn't that funny? Nobody wears much jewellery, unless there's a party. Your church is important. If you don't join a church, it will be difficult for you. Will you? If you do join a church, it will be just as difficult, depending which you choose. Georgetown's a funny place.'

Hannah listened to Rose's peculiar little tales, and was grateful. The two women drew close.

Meanwhile, Song and Jon had a chance to spend some proper time together.

'Your pictures are up, Jon. I love them,' Song said. 'I wish Father Holmes could have seen how good you have gotten.'

'Ah, the whiskered white-headed song warbler,' Jon replied. 'I loved drawing that one. Your bird.'

'It wouldn't have been if it wasn't for Father Holmes taking the books to England.'

'I still have the fourth volume. It's unfinished. We should revisit it some time. Pretend we're kids again.'

'I'd like that.'

Some new acquaintances came by, too. Mr House complimented Hannah on her home-making. Even Mr Hing, who was rarely known to leave his workshop, became a regular on Sunday evenings. There were the Ting-Lees, who owned the main perishables store, which never fully closed, day or night. Hannah first got to know Old Ting Lee, the blind mother of Mr Ting Lee, who made lime ices and sold them after dark through an open window next to the store. It had become Hannah's craving. She loved to watch the old woman make the lollies by feel – squeezing limes, mixing in brown sugar and cooling the mixture in moulded trays with finger sticks planted in each cup which in spite of her clouded eyes stood as straight as the trunks of greenheart trees. Hannah sometimes ordered three on the trot, walking in a circuit until she had finished one, returning for another, and another. There was also Edward Hoare, who was the household's most popular visitor; he stopped by whenever he was back in town. He shared Bartica gossip with Mary Luck, brought jars of forest honey for Hannah, and he and Song passed many evenings on the front porch together.

'I remember when I used to hide out in the hallway listening to you and Tom Jameson and Father Holmes talking. I was fascinated by your conversation. Although in truth I probably didn't understand very much.'

'How funny. And here we are now. You a grown man, me an old man. Why was it that I was the one of the three to survive? Should have been Father Holmes, of course. Tom Jameson and I? Well, there wasn't a lot to separate us.'

'I remember Tom used to moan about Bartica endlessly.'

'A lot to moan about when you're a PC in Bartica. I miss him. Never got to the bottom of that killing. Someone's walking free with blood on their hands.'

Song shivered. He thought of his own hands pressing deep into the throat of Jesus.

'Yet you love Bartica, don't you? I remember you saying that there's a kindness there that you can't find in many places in the world.'

'Kindness, yes, but a whole lot more, of course.'

'You choose to be there. We miss it sometimes, you know. Georgetown's a hard town to love. Or perhaps it's that the town finds us a hard couple to love.'

Later that evening, Song asked Hannah the same. 'Is Georgetown a hard town, or are we a hard couple?'

'Both, I'd say.'

'Do you think you will be happy here?'

'I'm already happy.'

'But you miss Bartica.'

'Not really. It just takes time.' Hannah's eyes softened. She ran her fingers through her husband's hair. 'I'm in no hurry. Not like you.'

'I can wait, but I don't want you to have to.'

'Georgetown won't be rushed. We'll find our place eventually.'

Song did not want to wait for the world to change. It had not changed in time for Jinda or Lady or Father Holmes. He felt the ache he always felt when he thought of Father Holmes. He missed their quiet conversations about the stuck stubborn world. He missed the way the pastor tried to hurry up change and Song vowed to do the same.

CHAPTER 24

Mary Luck had become a popular member of the congregation at St Saviour's, and had been encouraging Hannah and Song to accompany her.

'I'm not telling you which church to join but you need to join one,' Mary Luck said. 'Otherwise it'll be no wonder tongues wag.'

Song reluctantly attended. He would rather have bowed out of church-going society altogether but he knew that would raise more questions that he cared to answer. He had enough trouble as it was without courting more. He could imagine the whispering. 'What would the vicar say after everything he did for that boy?'; 'Thinks of himself above the church'; 'All that money and he won't share a penny with the church.'

'Let's go to St Andrew's this Sunday,' Song suggested. 'I'd like our firstborn to be christened there.'

Hannah frowned. 'I don't think we should, Song. It's not our church.'

'It was Father Holmes' church,' Song said. 'He'd have wanted us to go there. A church should welcome anyone and everyone, that's what he'd say.'

The next Sunday the couple walked to St Andrew's. It was over ten years since Song had walked the same route with Father Holmes. He knew the way so well, on foot or on his bicycle. He could ride there while reading a book at the same time.

The church looked no different to how Song remembered it. If anything it looked fresher now. The congregation was strong in numbers, and Song and Hannah sat near the back of the church. Song glanced around. Even after all these years he recognised the governor and his wife, the Burfords, Mr and Mrs Stewart. Beside Millie Stewart was a young man who was probably her husband. Song recalled the night at the sea wall and wondered about Scott. And there was Mr Carmichael and his family. Song had not seen him for many years but time had not mellowed how he felt.

The place was hauntingly familiar to Song. He recalled the days when he used to sit to the side of the apse, out of view of the congregation yet still able to watch Father Holmes deliver his sermon. Occasionally Father Holmes had caught his eye and they'd shared a half-smile.

Father Francis was preaching about infidelity, about idleness, about how losing one's way was a sure route to hell. Song allowed himself to daydream and could hear Father Holmes' voice instead of Father Francis'. Speaking about the power of kindness, the worth of compassion, the importance of love. The echo of his words carried in the unstirring air. Song remembered the way Father Holmes draped his arm across Song's shoulders as they walked back home to the vicarage and how he asked Song for his views on the sermon. Song felt a tear slip down his cheek.

After the service Song and Hannah were among the first to exit. At the door Father Francis didn't shake their hands. Song held a steady gaze but the vicar didn't look either of them in the eye. Song felt disgusted by his behaviour. How far he had veered from what was right and good.

Song steered Hannah quietly through the churchyard. As they were about to turn into the street, Edward Hoare caught up with them. He was breathless.

'Good morning to you both. I hope you don't mind me asking you, Song, when you're next heading back and if I can join?'

'Soon. Is anything wrong?'

'I'm tired of this town. Tired of the people here. It's that thing Tom Jameson used to say – that there are some things in life with no rhyme and no reason and I was one of them. He never understood why I preferred Bartica to so-called civilisation.'

'So-called. Exactly.'

While they talked, Hannah moved away to examine the headstones in the cemetery. Song noticed a woman approaching his wife. She was clearly agitated, gesticulating. He heard them both raise their voices. It was a heated exchange. Song excused himself from Edward's company.

'Hannah, are you all right?'

She turned to face her husband. She was pale. She took his arm. 'Yes. But let's go home.'

Song knew something was wrong. He looked at the woman opposite, who he did not recognise. 'Can I help you?'

'By staying away from here. You're not welcome here, and neither is that woman.'

'That woman is my wife. And this is a church, ma'am. Everybody's welcome in a church.'

'You stay with your own kind.'

Song had heard all this before. He knew her sort. He was only sad Hannah had to hear it, too. 'And tell me, ma'am, who are my own kind?'

'We are not.'

Hannah was pulling at Song's arm. 'Take me home, Song.'

'Take her home,' the woman echoed.

Song heard the anxiety in Hannah's voice. He turned to his wife and saw her lost eyes. He felt a pang of regret for having brought her here. Not just to St Andrew's but also to Georgetown. Was it really to give his family a better life? This was not a better life. Not yet. Song pulled Hannah close to his side and they walked into the street in the direction of home. He felt a new sense of resolve to rise up against this woman and her sort, not now, but in time.

A few days later Father Francis stopped by the house. 'I'm sure you know why I've come to see you,' he said to Song.

Song hadn't expected his call but he was prepared. He wanted Father Francis to think he was completely unaware of the vicar's prejudices. In fact, Song wanted him to think that he believed he was a very fair man.

'I'm glad you came by, Father,' Song said. 'I've been meaning to come and see you. We had a very unfortunate encounter outside St Andrew's on Sunday with a member of your congregation who believed it was their place to say we were not welcome in your church. I am sure you'd like to set the record straight. When the time comes, I'd like to christen my firstborn in St Andrew's. I know it would have been Father Holmes' wish and I hope you'll do us the honour.'

Father Francis stiffened. 'The individual you mention was expressing the feelings of my entire congregation. I have received lots of complaints. St Saviour's is your church and I know Father Collins will be happy to christen your child there.'

'Out of respect for . . .'

'I hear there is a wonderful choir at St Saviour's,' Father Francis interrupted. 'Isn't that so? I've been meaning to come myself and hear those beautiful voices. Wednesday evenings is when they practise.'

'I am asking you, Father Francis, to respect the wishes of one of your former fellow clergymen.'

Father Francis' tone changed. 'You used to clean St Andrew's. That was your only association.'

Song steadied his voice. 'Father Holmes believed a church should be open to anyone who had the courage to pass through its doors.'

'There is a respectable community at St Andrew's who have been attending services for many years. You have only recently arrived in this town and my congregation is not comfortable with newcomers. I know Father Holmes would have understood exactly what I am talking about.'

'He would not have understood at all. Father Holmes flung his doors open wide to anyone. Prostitutes, drunks, gamblers. We went out into the community looking for people who needed help.'

The vicar's face was flushed. 'Bartica is a different place altogether, thanks be the Lord. Whores and sinners. Father Holmes had to let such people into his church because that's all Bartica has to offer. It would have otherwise stood empty.'

'You have no idea if the church stood full or empty. Bartica might have benefited from the visit of a vicar after Father Holmes passed on. But you never came. Not once.'

Father Francis frowned. 'You are in no position to tell me what I should or should not be doing. Don't get ahead of yourself. Let's not forget where you came from. There are different churches for different kinds of people and my first duty is to look after my congregation. I will not be christening any child of yours in my church.'

This was not the language Song had expected to hear. Nothing this strong. Not now. Any leftover sentimentality he had for the church evaporated. He had observed Father Holmes' faith with respect and admiration but this man's ideology was something else entirely. He would not be silent in the face of these remarks.

'Trouble only comes to those who stand out.' Those were his papa's words. But he didn't want to hear them echoing about his head any more. He wanted to take on Georgetown. He wanted to write his own future.

When Song travelled back to Bartica, Edward Hoare joined him and it was in Song's own boat.

'I could get used to this,' Edward said. 'Look at you now, Song. A house in Georgetown. A boat of your own. A mine upriver. A family on the way. You've done good.'

'I haven't finished yet.'

'I don't doubt it. Edward looked at the name painted on the side of the boat. 'The *Dartmouth*, eh? What's that then?'

'That was the boat that brought me here from China. I lived a hundred lives on that boat. Everyone dying around me. I figured you can't forget where you came from.'

Back in Bartica, Song made his way to his room opposite Louis'. The space was breathless. Song noticed Jingy must have recently passed by to put orchids in the glass by his bed. He went to the window. Bronco feigned a salute. Song smiled back. The view, the street, it was all so familiar. Another home, in a way. Another life.

That night he went to Ruby Lou's to hear the B Boys. He missed their music. He missed them breaking their set to join him for a few words, and to take up his offer to buy them all a drink. He missed the way the girls nodded at him as they passed by, and the way Ruby Lou dragged up a chair to tell him how old she felt.

Jackson suddenly struck a top C and held his finger down hard. The girls stopped their chatter. For an instant it was the only sound. The echo of the note. Some closed their eyes like they were praying. Song lowered his head as if in mourning. Then Boney opened his mouth and used his smoky voice to churn up nostalgia

331

and longings for better times. It was a voice made of a thousand cigarettes and one big broken heart. Boney could make the hardest pork-knocker weep with his last set of the night.

The music stirred Song slowly. When he was listening to the B Boys it was the only time he was in no rush to go anywhere fast. The music carried him to a far-off place of muddled memories that he longed for and loathed, in equal measure. He saw in his mind San San lying next to him, restless, fidgeting, playing with the features of his own face. He imagined them floating on a field of water, holding hands, but there was a current pushing them apart. He was losing his grip on her tiny hand. He tried to hold on but her fingers were slipping out of his grasp. He called out her name but he lost her.

Boney's voice bounced him back into the room. Short John was strumming like a crazy man. The sweet melancholy rose up from Song's toes like the beginnings of a good orgasm. As Jackson tinkled the top notes Song could have whooped out loud. But instead tears streamed down his cheeks. Ruby Lou arrived at the table and slammed down her glass of rum. 'Take it easy, Song. Give yourself some time.'

'These boys are killing me tonight,' Song said.

'Gotta pause now and then,' Ruby said. 'Think what it is you want from life, what's important.'

'This place stops me in my tracks,' Song said.

'Door's always open for you.'

Song didn't plan on seeing Maia. Not ever again in that way. He was walking home from Ruby Lou's and she was walking home from Josie's when they came across each other in the street.

'Maia.' He didn't even want to say her name again.

'You look like you're fighting life again. Like the world's against you.'

How did Maia always get it so right? Song thought to himself. But he didn't want to want her.

'You have another home here you know,' she said. 'Come back with me. I need some company tonight.'

'I'll walk you home,' he said. But he found himself following her up the back stairs. Maia slipped down to the bar and came back with a drink. 'Not for me,' he said.

'I know.' But she took a gulp, and put her mouth upon Song's. He felt the liquor pour into his mouth.

This was Bartica, he said to himself. This wasn't his life. Maia. Bartica. It didn't feel real, at least that's what he told himself. After their lovemaking he lay there smelling the sweat on Maia's skin, hearing her light snoring, until he himself drifted.

When Song woke it was still dark. He left quietly without waking her. He promised himself he would never walk through Josie's door again.

The next day Song went to find Old Man Kuros. Bronco had been right about Wednesdays. Farad was out playing bridge and the shop was closed.

Song went to the back of the house. He was carrying something for the old man. 'Mr Ashkanzi,' he called out. 'It's Song.'

He heard a noise inside and waited. Sugar came to the door. 'Hello, Song.'

Song could not hide his surprise. 'Hello, Sugar. What are you doing here?'

'What are you doing here, more like? I live in Bartica, remember? Some of us remember where we come from. What's that under your arm. It's disgusting.'

'Is Mr Ashkanzi in?'

'Course he is. Do you think I'd just be hanging out here if he wasn't?'

'I really don't know, Sugar. You're full of surprises for me today.'

She nodded her head for him to enter.

Song followed Sugar into the house. It was as dark as the shop and even more untidy. It smelled of mould and candle wax.

Sugar pushed open the door. 'You ready?'

The old man was still buttoning up his shirt. 'Do you not wait for an answer? What's the point of asking if you don't wait for an answer? No, I'm not ready.'

'You so slow today,' Sugar said sleepily.

'You're slow, not me,' Mr Ashkanzi said. 'Let him in then.'

Song edged into the room. The air was heavy with sweat. 'Good afternoon, sir.'

'Took your time. I'll want interest on that payment I'm due. Did you bring back my eagle?'

'I've got it here.' Song approached the chair where Mr Ashkanzi was sitting. He gently held the bird in front of the old man. 'You can put your hands out.'

Mr Ashkanzi reached out and touched the harpy eagle. He moved his hands tenderly over the wings the same way he had when he let the bird go. 'Feels about the same,' he said.

'It's not,' Song said. 'It's all tidied up.' He called for Sugar. She approached and wrinkled her nose. 'Sugar,' Song said, 'describe the eyes to Mr Ashkanzi.'

'But it's dead,' she said.

'Doesn't matter,' Song repeated. 'Tell him about its eyes.'

'Dark,' Sugar said. 'Dark like Boney's voice. A bit frightening. It's like he's looking at me. Or looking through me. But he looks sad, too, like a mother mourning a child. Or like he wants to fly away but can't.'

Song looked into the bird's eyes and thought how perceptive Sugar had been. Wanting to fly away but unable to. He wished he could give the harpy eagle back its wings, too.

The night before Song left to go upriver he went to see Chi's family. There were the shadows of two figures on the porch. As he drew closer he saw it was Dorothy sitting with Yan. He was glad not to see Nina around.

Yan jumped to her feet when she saw Song. 'No bad news?'

'What's the matter?'

'Hurry up and tell me, Song. Is everything all right?'

'I haven't been yet, but everything's fine. I'm going up tomorrow. What's wrong?'

'Nothing,' Dorothy said drowsily. 'Woman's got a feeling there's been an accident.'

Song put his arm around Yan. 'We'd have heard. I only came by to see you before I left. To see if there were any messages.'

'Who in God's name would I have a message for?' Yan said. 'Some good-for-nothing pork-knocker who doesn't know his own children and don't remember to send a penny home.'

'You mad at me, too?'

Yan smiled. 'I will be if you don't want any dinner.'

'I'm starving.'

Yan went inside. Song turned towards Dorothy, slumped in the chair. She had one leg raised up on the swing-arm of the Berbice chair and was twitching her toes back and forth. 'Your sister's jumpy,' Song said.

'That's the only way they know, the women of pork-knockers,' she said. 'Glad to see the back of them. Worried senseless while they're away. Happy to see them back for five minutes. Sick of them after ten.'

'Yan's not like that.'

'All women like that. You men don't even notice. You don't think 'bout nobody 'cept yourselves.'

'What've I done so bad to have you two on me tonight?'

'There's a few of you is exceptions,' she said slowly.

'I'll take a seat then, if I'm welcome?'

Dorothy gestured beside her. 'You a rich man now, I hear. I remember when you was dirt poor. You're just as nice now as you was then.'

'I'm not so sure. Don't feel as nice.'

'You still nice.'

'Better not get richer then. Otherwise I might get mean. How's Berbice? How's Gloster?'

'Berbice is still being rocked to sleep by that sea breeze of hers. Only place in the world like it. You gotta see it one of these days, Song. You keep saying you're coming. And Gloster? He's another one of those men I been talking about. That damn man's too handsome for his own good. Ladies love him. Hell, I love him. That's why I come down here to Bartica. Can't bear to witness it. If I'm not there, it ain't happening as far as I'm concerned. I can live out my old lie, like the whole rest of the world lives out theirs—'

Song understood. Living two lives apart. Hoping they would never meet. Bartica, Georgetown, Georgetown, Bartica . . .

Yan came back with a tray.

'—and come see the best sister in the world,' Dorothy added. 'We all living our lies, ain't we, Yan?'

Yan nodded. 'Guess so,' she said, putting the tray in front of Song. 'Potato curry. No meat. You can tell Chi we're waiting on him for a bit of meat for our guests. There's a message for that old fool.'

'If it's wages you're waiting on, we can sort that out tonight,' Song said.

Dorothy whistled. 'This is one of the good ones.'

'Hannah's a lucky lady, let me tell you,' Yan said.

Song thought of Hannah. Was she lucky? He felt she deserved better.

'How's married life treating you?' Dorothy said, as if she was reading his mind.

'I'm the lucky one. I couldn't ask for a better wife. Hannah's made a nice home. We're expecting our first child. She says she likes Georgetown, although in truth we're both finding it hard.'

'Moving to a new town is always hard,' Yan said. 'Especially with the way you are now. If you were an empty-handed porkknocker who drank in the bars and used the whores, Georgetown would take you on as a son. Waltz in with a goldmine and that's something else entirely.'

'I know. Hannah said as much. You women are quicker than me.'

'Don't you worry about Hannah. She'll find her way. And if she don't make friends in Georgetown then that city's a meaner place than I imagined. She's a sweet woman.'

'Glad you got a sweet woman,' Dorothy said. 'You deserve it.'

'This man don't know how to treat a woman bad,' Yan said.

Song couldn't bear to hear them speak this way. 'I'm no saint. Don't make me one. I hope Hannah sticks with me.'

'That's what women do,' Dorothy sighed. 'Men walk. Women stick.'

'I'm sorry we do,' Song said.

Before Song left, he went to Yan's biscuit tin on the top shelf in her kitchen. He stuffed a handful of money into it. 'You can tell that man he can stay there as long as he wants,' Yan said, 'but his family needs more than rice and potatoes.'

Song walked home in the cool night. He turned earlier so as not to pass close to Josie's. He was done with living out two lives apart.

CHAPTER 25

By the time Song reached Omaia it was almost two months since his last visit. He was amazed by how quickly the camp had grown. They must have felled a hundred or more trees. Shacks had sprung up. The entire area was latticed by laundry hanging on ropes slung between posts and trees; the washed blue-grey shirts and trousers hung limply in the humid air. It was almost its own village.

Chi appeared out of a shack that he'd turned into a makeshift office. He had lost weight but he looked stronger, too. One of his front teeth was chipped. His cuticles were deep red from the earth.

'You're looking all right,' Song said.

'You're looking soft,' Chi said. 'Thought you'd given up on us.'

'I was in two minds but your wife insisted I bring you a message: "No meat. Send money." Does it slip your mind to leave her even a penny?'

'Women ain't never satisfied. You could leave them all the money in the world and it still wouldn't be enough.'

'Something's giving Yan the willies. Nearly jumped out of her skin when she saw me. Thought I was coming to break bad news.'

'No rhyme or reason to women,' Chi said. 'Now you want to hear the good news or the bad?'

'Only good news. I'm not interested in bad.'

'Good news is you didn't lose your eye for nothing. Bad news is you lost your eye.'

Song smiled. He had missed Chi's cheek. 'You're funny. But

that's not news. Give me something fresh. How much you got sewn in your shirt?'

'In my shirt? If I had it in my shirt I wouldn't be able to pull myself up in the morning. You ready for this? Seven pounds.'

'Seven,' Song repeated softly.

'Gold is pouring outta here faster than if it was molten. We've got rocks, too.'

'Rocks?'

'Diamonds. Sammy said they often come together.'

'Gold and diamonds,' Song said.

'They don't look nice as they are. But they'll polish up.'

'Where is it all? In the office?'

'Not a chance. It's up a tree.'

'What?' Song said, breaking into a laugh. 'Why?'

'Where the hell else am I going to put it? I'm not stowing it away where it's obvious. I swear I've never slept this bad. I'm going to get a knife in my back.'

'Everyone seems to be afraid of a knife in their back these days. So, how are the men?'

'They're good. Conditions here are better than anywhere. But I think that's exactly why I'm going to get a knife in my back. They're too good.'

'If the knife hasn't already gone in with you sitting on seven pounds I think you'll be all right. Sammy been around much?'

'In and out. Says he's ready whenever I need a break.'

'I'll need you to make a trip down to Bartica. If it really is seven pounds.'

'You better send word to him then. 'Cause if Sammy ain't here, I ain't going nowhere.'

'Anyone standing out? Good or bad?'

'The young 'uns are very keen. I'm only ever hiring young from now on. Haven't had any trouble yet. The camp's in good spirits. Honeymoon period though.'

'It's a nice set-up you've sorted here. Good job. Treat them well, and they'll treat us well. I want them all to get a bonus this month. Now take me to this tree of yours.'

After two weeks, Sammy arrived to take over managing the camp. He brought some young boys from the village, too.

Song greeted them in Arawak and they smiled.

'You sure about this?' Chi said to Song. 'I trust Sammy, but these other boys. Mixing them with the team and everything.'

'Nobody's going to step out of line with Sammy here. My only concern is that Sammy and his boys will want to get back before we return. We can't be too long. They're the restless sort. Like all of us, perhaps.'

Song made sure the men saw his bond with Sammy, so they would know he was part of the chain. What had Jingy said? Not breaking the chain, that's the thing.

Then Song and Chi headed downriver. They had over eight pounds of gold on them. Chi was carrying a pound, split and sewn into every seam of his clothes. Song carried the remainder in a bag at his feet. He didn't feel so calm either.

'I'm as jumpy as a rabbit,' Chi said. 'Like I say, too much gold can weigh a man down. Bring back too much and you're headed for trouble.'

'Bring back too little and you're headed for trouble. 'Specially with Yan at home.'

'Too true.'

*

When they were a day outside of Bartica, Song and Chi split into two boats. Chi travelled on to Bartica to declare the pound. Song went directly to Georgetown.

Song longed to find Hannah, yet couldn't face her. He headed first to see Ebenezer; he wanted to find some worth in himself before he went home. When he arrived, the old man's door was locked. Song yelled up to Nanny and was relieved to see her at the window. She shook her head when she saw Song but he heard her heavy footsteps on the stairs and then the lock slide. A key turned from the other side. Then another lock slid open. Finally Nanny lifted a latch.

'What's with all this?' Song said, gesturing to the keys in her hand.

'It ain't me,' Nanny said. 'It's you. People are talking. Know you're doing business with the old man. Say you're bringing him enough gold to fill a room. And what am I doing? I'm running up and down these stairs ten times a day, unlocking and locking and unlocking. Milk comes around, unlock. Meat comes around, unlock. Newspaper comes around, unlock. Unlock, lock, unlock. People used to waltz on up. That's the way to live a life. Freedom. Now he's got the willies someone's going to come and rob him or worse so we've got more bolts than Devil's Island, I swear.'

Freedom. Song had believed gold would bring him freedom. Not weigh him down, like Chi said, like Nanny was now intimating.

Upstairs Mr Ebenezer was standing in front of the painting of the goatherd with his back to the room.

'Took your time,' the old man said without turning around.

'Most people tell me I'm moving too fast.'

'How much?'

'Seven pounds on me.'

Mr Ebenezer slapped his hand on his chest. 'What do you expect me to do with all that?'

'Take it off me,' Song said. 'Right now.'

Mr Ebenezer looked out of the window. 'Let's have a look then.'

Song pulled an ingot out of the bag. 'There are fourteen like this.'

Mr Ebenezer took it in his palms, handling it like a newborn. 'Twenty-four carats?'

Song nodded.

Mr Ebenezer seemed lost for a minute. He let the weight of the metal rest heavy in his hands.

'I don't need any money yet,' Song said.

'Good thing, too,' Mr Ebenezer said. 'I'll need a wheelbarrow to pay for this in paper. You're going to be the death of me.'

'And me,' Nanny said, as she walked in the room with a tray of tea. 'What's the use of being rich if you're always worried about dying?'

Song smiled at her. 'I can't stay, Nanny. I've got a wife to see.'

'This is my kind of man,' Mr Ebenezer said. 'Sees his buyer before his wife.'

Nanny put the tray down hard, spilling tea from the spout of the teapot.

Mr Ebenezer continued to turn the ingot over in his hand. 'This is no goldmine. It's an El Dorado.'

Song left Ebenezer's to make his way home. It was a short but uneasy journey, with thoughts of his time with Maia playing about in his head. 'Every man's entitled to lose his way,' that's what Jingy had said after Father Holmes' death, when Song couldn't pull himself out of Josie's. Could Song fall back on that sentiment again?

As he approached the house he searched the windows for a movement but did not see anybody. There was a new sign on the gate reading 'Sugar House'. Hannah and all her thoughtfulness, Song reflected. Reminding him where he came from. That she didn't care about his past. He walked up the path, studying the changes he knew she would have overseen in the garden. There was every shade of hibiscus, just like there had been in her front yard in Bartica with tangles of bushes in red, apricot and flamingo pink.

At the end of the path, he pushed open the door. Hannah appeared in the shadows of the hall, dressed in sky-blue. Song saw how her body had changed in his absence. She looked ready to give birth soon. He stepped towards her and she came to him.

'I missed you,' she said.

Song buried his face in her neck. He thought of Maia because he was not able not to. Heavily, in the way Chi said gold could weigh a man down. And yet here was Hannah smelling so sweet – of soap and scent. Holding him, speaking to him as softly as ever.

'Every day,' she added. 'I missed you every day.'

'Did you? Say you did.'

'I did. Sometimes feeling afraid, as I do when you're gone. But also happy knowing you're doing what you love doing.'

He held her back to look into her face. 'I missed your morning smile, your heavy footsteps on the stairs, your mismatched eyes. I love you.'

Hannah smiled. 'Still?'

Song could see the innocence in her eyes. The trust. 'Always.'

She took his hand and rested it on her belly. 'I have news. The doctor thinks it might be twins.'

Song felt a fear rise up inside him for Hannah. 'Two?'

She raised two fingers and laughed her melodic laugh. 'He thinks he can feel two.'

Song looked at his wife's radiant face and tried a smile. But he was being carried away to a place where he could see his sister Xiao Mei's sad little face while his mother shouted at her about the lost brother.

'What is it?' Hannah asked.

'Nothing, my love. I just want you to be safe.'

Hannah's hand reached up and held Song's face in her hands. She spoke softly. 'Yes, of course.'

Song took one of her hands and pressed something into its palm. She turned it over in her hand. In the dull light it looked like a small black rock.

'What is it?' she asked.

'It's for you,' Song whispered back. 'It's our first diamond.'

Song stopped at the top of the stairs when he heard the voices in his and Hannah's bedroom.

'Do you know the name, child?' It was Mary Luck speaking. 'He named it after that girl.'

Song did not move.

He heard Hannah's reply. 'Yes, Mama, I heard the name.'

'Have you said something?' Mary Luck asked.

His wife's voice sounded tired. 'No, not yet.'

'Are you planning to?'

'Yes, Mama, of course.'

There was silence between the two women.

Mary Luck's voice was barely audible. 'Let it go.'

'You don't mean that, do you?'

'Listen to me on this one.'

'You're asking me *not* to ask him about it?'

Mary Luck's voice was steady. 'I am.'

'But – but it's so obvious.'

'He chose to marry you, not her. She was before your time.'

'I hope so. I don't know . . .'

Song wished he could undo what he had done with Maia on this last trip. Had Hannah guessed? Yet mixed amongst his guilt, his shame, he felt some relief, too. If she knew, she could forgive him.

'I'm warning you, child. Don't go there.'

'Mama, you scare me when you speak that way.'

'You can put a broken plate back together but you will always be able to see the cracks. It will never be the same again. You bring that up and your marriage will be cracked forever.'

There was another long pause between the two women. Hannah finally spoke. 'He could change the name of the mine.'

'He's a good husband, Hannah. And he'll be a good father too.'

'But everyone knows he's named it after her.'

'Is that what this is about? What everyone else thinks? Have I taught you nothing? If that's your worry then also remember that everyone also knows that he chose you to be his wife, not her.'

'But it's shattering.'

Hannah's words caught Song's breath. He was heartbroken to be hurting her. It had been so easy to be with Maia but how hard it was now.

'Don't be dramatic,' her mother said. 'Better you're shattered than the plate. Maintain the sanctity of what you have.'

'You've always taught me to stand up for what I believe in.'

'You believe in him. Stand up for what you two have together.'

'He says he still loves me.'

'Of course he does. Hold on to that. The mine is named already. He's not going to un-name it because you throw a tantrum.'

There was silence. Song held his breath. He remembered Mr Leigh telling him that women were the wiser ones.

'I just wish he—'

'Don't wish, Hannah. Forgive him his past without even mentioning it. You'll be stronger for it.'

Under his breath Song thanked Mary Luck, and swore to both

women he would never visit Maia again. This man, he promised, would stick.

Among Song's mail was a letter from Governor Johnson requesting a meeting. It was dated over a month earlier. He immediately sent over Little A with an apology stating that he was now at the governor's disposal. The governor replied requesting he come to his office at four o'clock that afternoon.

Song showered and dressed in a suit. The tone of the letter had been perfunctory. He could only guess at what Governor Johnson might want to see him about. There was more than one flashpoint for the pair of them. The church, the land upriver, tax.

On arrival, the maid showed him to Governor Johnson's office. Along the corridor were drawings: a scarlet ibis, glossy ibis and green ibis, and one of Song's favourites, the roseate spoonbill. Jon's work. Song could still hear Father Holmes telling Jon about the job; he and Jon had been so young then. It felt like another life.

'All grown up, I see,' Governor Johnson said, as Song walked through the door. He pointed at a chair.

'At some point we do that,' Song said.

The governor took a cigarette out of a box. He didn't offer one to Song. 'Life's changed a lot for you, hasn't it? The plantation. Shining shoes for a vicar. Why don't you tell me how you're making a living these days?'

'I bought some land, sir. I'm looking for gold, along with most of Bartica.'

'How much have you found?'

'I was doing all right at the start. Beginner's luck, perhaps. Now it's gone a bit quiet.'

'Quiet, eh? Should I ignore all these stories about a goldmine, then?'

'A man finds some gold. A town starts talking.'

'You've bought fifteen thousand acres.'

'I'm speculating,' Song said. 'I bought land because I can read a set of deeds. Most pork-knockers can't write their own name. If they could they'd be buying land, too.'

The governor lit his cigarette and took a first draw. 'Let's get some numbers down, shall we? How much gold is coming out each month?'

'Not enough to warrant the kind of stories that it sounds like you're hearing,' Song said.

'Let me be the judge of that.'

'A pound after the first three months.'

'Do you expect me to believe that? A pound?'

'Yes, sir.'

'There's a law against undeclared gold.'

'I'm declaring it. In Bartica. Ask Edward Hoare.'

Governor Johnson leaned forward in his seat. 'I need monthly reports on what's going on. I'll be sending a DC. We want to look at workers' conditions. There's a big push from London on that right now. We've seen it dozens of times. Out of sight, and you start treating people like animals.'

Song knew how much more he understood than Governor Johnson about workers being treated like animals. Inside he was simmering.

'Send a DC, sir. He'd be most welcome. Or I could take you myself.'

'I want this office to receive monthly reports. Accurate monthly reports.'

'Yes, sir.'

'Father Holmes might have taught you to read and write, but he was a man of the church and not a man of business. This kind of work goes way above your head.'

Song continued to keep his cool. 'Father Holmes taught me more than church matters. Please credit him with that.'

'What do you think he'd have thought about you choosing the life of a pork-knocker?'

'He was the one who introduced me to the interior.'

'Not looking for gold, though.'

'Pork-knocking isn't just about gold. It's about the river, the forest.' Song looked pointedly at the governor. 'The birds.'

The governor laughed mockingly. 'Ah, so that's it. You go upriver for the birds.'

'It's part of it.'

'And the rest? I know the rest.' The governor paused. 'I'll be leaving this all in someone else's capable hands. I'm heading back to England soon. A Mr Bolton replaces me. He has a formidable reputation.'

'I'll look forward to meeting him.'

Song was pleased to see Governor Johnson's exasperation with him. The man's tone was becoming increasingly irate. 'Tell me everyone you are in business with. I want a list.'

'It's a one-man list. A man called Chi. A pork-knocker from Bartica.'

'I mean here in Georgetown. Where are you selling your gold?'

'I'm still working on that.'

'I don't think you have any idea what you're up against.' The governor spat out the words.

Song held his gaze. 'Perhaps neither of us do.'

CHAPTER 26

Hannah was coming to the end of her pregnancy. She had taken to lying down in the afternoons.

'I'm so heavy now, I'm going to take a rest,' she said to Song and Mary Luck, slipping upstairs after lunch.

Song was in his study when he heard her call out for help. He met Little A in the hallway. 'What is it?'

Little A was out of breath. 'We need the doctor.'

Song could hardly remember leaving the house. The streets were empty as Song ran for a doctor. Only a stray dog wandered into his path. It felt as if he might be the only person left in the entire world. His head was a blur. There were thoughts of his mother and Xiao Song; the babies born down in the darkness of the ship; a mother's screams; the first yelps of newborns. Song was shaking as he arrived at the Patels' home. He found both Dr and Mrs Patel there, which momentarily calmed him. But while he waited for them to prepare to leave the house, his fears heightened. He thought about the ship doctor sent down to help the woman bearing twins. The lost twins. The lost mother. He tried to push the sound of her dying out of his mind.

By the time the three of them arrived at Sugar House, Hannah was in labour. Her groans rose and fell like the evening cicadas. Little A was running up and down the stairs with bowls of boiled water. Mary Luck was mopping the sweat on her daughter's forehead.

'Baby's already coming, Hannah,' Dr Patel said.

'Push with me,' his wife said.

Hannah's deep resonant groans had turned into waves of high-pitched screaming. Song left the room. His whole body had begun to shake. He leaned his head against the frame of the door and held his breath to listen hard while simultaneously trying to block out the sound. He couldn't bear to see the woman he loved more than anything in the world suffering this way.

Mrs Patel was speaking softly. 'Hannah. Listen to me. You know when you stop and say you cannot go on, that is when you must be strong.'

Song could hear the initial consonant of Mrs Patel's 'push, push, push.' Hannah's wailing had become unearthly.

Song could hear the woman on the ship in labour. He could hear the echo of her husband's howls. An image flashed into his head of Li Bai carrying up the three bodies of the mother and her two small still babies.

Mrs Patel's voice brought him back. 'The baby's getting tired,' she said. 'It has to be this time, Hannah. Once more.'

Song heard a baby cry and he flung open the door. He looked at Hannah's face. Her eyes were on the tiny baby in Mary Luck's arms. Mary Luck was wiping away strands of blood and milky film from its skin.

Song went to Hannah and grabbed her hand. 'Are you all right?'

'Yes.'

'Thank God.' He buried his face into her neck. Into the smell of her fresh sweat. Her skin was hot and alive. 'Are you sure? Tell me you're sure.'

'We lost one.'

Song looked again at the baby Hannah's mother was holding up.

'A boy,' Mary Luck smiled.

'There was a girl,' Hannah said. Her voice cracked.

Song pictured a little girl running through their garden. She twirled around and around letting her skirt float out. A daughter lost.

'It's hard for twins to survive on a first,' Dr Patel said.

Song reached out for Hannah's hand. 'We have one, Hannah,' he said, 'and we have you.'

They decided to have the christening only a few days later so they could hold the funeral of the baby girl on the same day. Song had been forced to give up on St Andrew's. They chose St Saviour's. Song would rather have chosen neither.

'We must christen him, Song,' Hannah said. 'Otherwise we will draw even more attention to ourselves.'

'Even if we were to do everything the way Georgetown would like us to, we will always be doing it wrong in some people's eyes. I can see that now.'

'Well, do it for Mary Luck then. Otherwise you'll never hear the end of it.'

Hannah had made him smile. 'That is a reason,' Song said.

They invited their closest friends. Jon and Rose Swire. Mr Ebenezer politely declined the church service but promised to come to the reception afterwards. The Ting-Lees with all their family could almost fill a church themselves. Dr Patel and his wife came, of course. Mr House arrived late and hot. Mr Hing filed quietly into the back. Father Collins conducted the service for both children. The baby was named Phillip Alwin. And then the baby girl, unnamed, was buried. Song closed his eyes as the tiny coffin was lowered into the ground. It was at that moment Phillip began to cry – as if for his sister. Song put his arm around Hannah.

Silently he promised her he would take care of their family forever.

Those first few months Song and Hannah stayed close to home. Sometimes Hannah chose to nurse Phillip in Song's study, and he read her long passages from her favourite book, *Wuthering Heights*, as well as the poems of Coleridge, Kipling, and the sonnets of John Donne. When Hannah slept or chose to feed Phillip in their bedroom, Song spent the time alone in his study, declining visitors.

One evening there was a knock on the frame of his open door.

'Sir, can I trouble you?'

Song heard the worry in Little A's voice. 'Yes. What is it?'

She hesitated at the door. 'It's my little brother. I was wondering – he was wondering – if he might come and work at Omaia for you? He's here now. Please could he have a word?'

'Sure. Send him in.'

She beckoned to the figure standing in the corridor.

'Sir, this is him. Tots.'

Song got up out of his chair. The little boy cowered as Song approached him.

'Hello, Tots,' Song said, putting out a hand. 'So you want to be a pork-knocker, do you?'

Little A nudged him. He shook Song's hand. 'Yes,' he mumbled. 'Sir.'

'And how old are you?'

'Nine, sir.'

'Nearly ten,' Little A said. 'He's stronger than he looks.'

'You're pretty young to be wanting to go upriver. You don't have to pretend you're tough at your age, you know.' Song had been pretending at Tots' age but he wished he hadn't had to.

'How about something else?' Song asked. 'I'm sure we can find you something to do here at Sugar House.'

'Can he not go upriver, sir?'

'I think you're too young, Tots. I was older than you the first time I went upriver and that wasn't even to work. Come back in a few years. If you want to do something else in the meantime, I can find you work here in Georgetown. You just let your sister know.'

Little A nudged him again. 'Yes, sir,' Tots said. 'Thank you, sir. I'd like to go upriver one day and work for you. Everyone wants to work for you. They say you're a good man. That you can get rich quick upriver. I'd like that.'

A good man. He didn't feel like one. Song tried to deflect some of Tots' praise. 'If only it were that easy. Although some say if you believe hard enough that you're lucky, you will be. I'm not sure I agree but it's a nice thing to hear. Take your time, Tots. There's no need to rush into life.'

Some weeks later, Song was in his study when Hannah came to him. She glided in with uncharacteristic lightness, and moved towards the back of his chair. As she put her arms around his neck, she glanced at the list on his desk.

'What's that?'

'Nothing important,' he said.

'But what is it?'

'It's a list of those who refused to come to Phillip's christening. The punishing of a baby for the father he happens to have.' He took her hands and pulled her around. 'What do you think, Hannah? Will we ever be accepted by this town?'

'In time. Rose herself says how odd Georgetown can be, and she's from here.'

He sighed.

'You're not happy here, are you?'

Song pulled Hannah closer. 'You make me happy. I love the home you've made for us. You, me, Mary Luck, baby Phillip. But Georgetown, I don't know. It's like two towns. One for us and one for them. I sometimes think I may as well be working on the plantation again. That's where they want to keep us.'

'But we have friends here now. Jon and Rose. Mr House pops in from time to time. Mr Hing.'

'But all of them are outsiders, too. We're on the very fringes.'

Hannah squeezed his hand. 'I have an idea. Let's go to the races on Saturday.'

'The races? Is that a way to be part of this town?'

'Everybody goes to the races. I think it would be fun. We haven't been out for ages.'

'You know I won't gamble or drink,' Song said. 'Isn't that what the races are all about?

'We'll just watch.'

Song pulled out the list. 'Will these people be there?'

'I expect so.'

'If you think we should go, let's go.'

Hannah clapped her hands together.

The following Saturday Hannah put on a modest yellow dress and sun hat. Song wore a three-piece suit with a tie the same colour as Hannah's dress. They walked slowly to the racecourse.

Hannah had asked the Ting-Lees if they could join their box. Mr Ting-Lee saw Song and Hannah from a distance and moved towards the couple. 'Finally,' he said. 'Georgetown's most talked about couple make it to the races.' He turned to Song. 'We've been asking Hannah to come for months. She said she wouldn't come without you but you're always upriver.'

'I'm to blame, that's for sure,' Song said. 'Thank you for not giving up on us.'

'I can't take the credit for that. The women do the invitations and all the social hullaballoo too. We men just bet.'

'You're going to be disappointed in my performance then,' Song said. 'I only watch.' Song still had no interest in gambling. He had already risked so much in life, he couldn't bear to lose lightly what he had earned at such a high price.

'Sounds like there's enough risk-taking in your real life,' Mr Ting-Lee said, winking at him. 'But what's a small bet on a horse from time to time? Have to sharpen your brain to work out the winnings. Bookies'll short-change a dull wit in a blink.'

'Race card? Race card?' A young boy called out as he passed.

Song gave him a coin and passed one to Hannah. It listed the afternoon's races with details of horses, jockeys and the odds at the time of print.

'The starting price is chalked up on the blackboard at the finish line,' Mr Ting-Lee said. He was studying his own race card and did not look up.

'Do you want to put a bet on the first race?' Song whispered to Hannah. He pressed some money into her hand. 'Just don't tell me which horse.'

Hannah walked off towards one of the bookmakers at the edge of the track. Song smiled as he watched her negotiate – her hands waving the bookie down – before returning with a chit. Her face was flushed.

'Ah, here's someone who likes to place a bet,' Mr Ting-Lee said. 'Women always do. What's your horse?'

Hannah caught Song's eye. 'It's a secret,' she said.

'Superstitious too, eh?' Mr Ting-Lee said, elbowing Song. 'Follow me. Let me introduce you to the others.'

Mrs Ting-Lee was as warm and welcoming as her husband. She put a rum punch in Hannah's hand and gave her a chit. 'We put a bet on for you since it's your first time,' she said. 'Duke of York is a super runner, especially with young Robin on his back. One of the exciting new jockeys.'

'Too late,' her husband said, nodding towards Hannah. 'This one's already given a bookie a very hard time.'

Mrs Ting-Lee caught sight of the chit in Hannah's hand and looked deflated. 'Oh, you already have one.'

'Two is twice as lucky,' Hannah said. 'I didn't choose the Duke of York so you've just doubled my chances.'

'What's your horse?' Mrs Ting-Lee asked.

Her husband cut in. 'It's a secret. Superstitious like you.'

Mrs Ting-Lee laughed. 'He's right. I never used to tell anybody my picks but I lost enough to realise it didn't matter a jot. You keep it to yourself though. We all have our oddities at the racetrack. I always wear blue.'

Song watched Hannah looked up and down Mrs Ting-Lee but didn't see anything of the colour blue.

Mrs Ting-Lee flashed her a smile. 'Somewhere.'

Mr Ting-Lee introduced Song to their other friends in the box. In addition to Dr Patel and his wife, who they were already close to, there were the Chungs, who owned a jewellery shop, and the de Waagens, who ran the hardware store on Fullers Street; Song felt a cool reception from both couples.

'Song is the man everyone is talking about,' Mr Ting-Lee said. 'And this is his lovely – and very lucky – wife, Hannah. She has the secret winning ticket.'

Mrs Chung pointed at Hannah's bracelet. 'Lovely thing. From Bartica?'

'I don't know. Song gave it to me before we were married.'

'*Before* you were married?'

'On our engagement.'

'Quite a different thing,' Mrs Chung said. 'Watch yourself with that kind of talk. There are women in Georgetown who can twist your words up until you no longer recognise them yourself.'

Hannah bit her lip.

'Don't worry.' Mrs Ting-Lee said. 'There are lots of lovely people here, too. And so many of them are in our box today. A toast! A toast to our box!'

Everybody raised their glasses.

'So tell us about this goldmine, Song?' Chung said. 'How much are you bringing out?'

'It's no goldmine,' Song said. 'We're just getting started.'

'I hear Ebenezer's buying from you,' Chung said. 'He doesn't like dealing in small amounts.'

Song didn't want to give anything away. 'We're only talking.'

'He's a funny fellow. Lives alone in a tiny rundown apartment. Never seems to spend a penny. He must sleep on a mattress stuffed with money.'

'And tell me about your jewellery shop,' Song said.

'Chung has the best gems in town,' Mr Ting-Lee said.

'We get stones cut in Europe and then set them here,' Chung said. 'Come by the shop and take a look. How much did you say you were bringing out?'

'We don't have average figures yet,' Song said.

'Last month?'

'Last month wasn't a good month.'

Chung pressed him. 'The month before?'

'It's early days.'

Mrs Chung interrupted their exchange. 'Stop harassing the

man,' she said to her husband. She turned to Hannah. 'You must come around for ladies' mahjong some afternoon. Do you play?'

Hannah shook her head.

'It's ever so easy. But hard to play well, of course. I'll teach you. Everyone will be dying to meet you.'

Song was glad to see Hannah making friends. At that instant there was a gunshot and the crowd moved towards the barrier. Hannah stretched up on her tiptoes but their group was too far back for her to see. The cantering came closer. The ground rumbled as the horses thundered by.

'Were you able to see?' Hannah said excitedly, turning to Song.

'Not a thing,' he replied. He was looking up at the second tier of boxes, a good fifteen feet above their heads, with panoramic views of the track. He could see the Stewarts from the tax office. There was the governor and Mrs Johnson, alongside a man he assumed might be Mr Bolton, the new governor that Johnson had described. He didn't look so stern. In fact, he was laughing at that moment. But Song knew the sort of man that the governor had hinted at. A man determined to keep wealth and power in the hands of the colonialists. Resentful at anyone else's success. Song knew they wanted a man like him to remain trapped by the station of his birth.

'Ting-Lee, do you mind me asking how much you pay for your box?' Song said.

'Six dollars a year. Best money I spend. Business expense, of course.'

Song pointed up to the second tier of boxes. 'How about those?'

'Same price,' Mr Ting-Lee said. 'But it's not about money up there.'

'What's it about?'

'Your last name, your friends, the colour of your skin.'

Song thought about himself, with an assumed last name, the wrong friends, certainly not the right skin colour.

Mrs Ting-Lee came squealing up to the group. 'You won, Hannah. The Duke of York won.'

'Really?' Hannah said. 'But it was your pick. The ticket's yours.'

Mrs Ting-Lee put her arm through Hannah's. 'I picked it for you. It's a sign.'

Hannah went to collect the winnings and with them bought a round of rum punches for the box. The group toasted her victory; as they raised their glasses, Song looked around, feeling heartened. The Ting-Lees were generous hosts and it was fun to be out with Hannah like this. Everyone warmed to her. And this wasn't gambling like he knew it from Bartica, the hard drinking, desperate kind, this was frippery.

'You were right, you know,' Song said, under his breath. 'Everybody's here.'

'And I won,' Hannah said.

Song pointed upwards. 'Next time I'll get a box so you can watch your horse come in.'

CHAPTER 27

Song felt the passage of time more slowly in Georgetown and he was glad to hear Edward Hoare had arrived on the ferry from Bartica. Edward sent word to Sugar House inviting Song that evening to the British Club for a drink. As the hour approached Song began to have doubts.

'But you already know most of these men,' Hannah said.

Song adjusted his tie. 'Not like this. It'll catch them off guard if Edward hasn't warned them. Which, knowing him, he probably hasn't.'

'You're his guest,' Hannah said, choosing some cufflinks. 'It's up to him who he brings. If you feel uncomfortable come home.'

'I'll see it through.'

Hannah took Song's chin in her grasp and turned it towards her. 'I think you *want* to catch them off guard.'

Song thought how well Hannah knew him.

Song reached the club a few minutes early and hung back.

'Loitering?' Edward said, as he approached.

'I thought I'd let you arrive first,' Song said. 'I didn't want a scene before the first drink.'

Edward chuckled. 'I'd quite like a scene.'

'I thought as much,' Song said.

The two men walked in together. The bellman glanced at Song and looked nervous. 'You'll have to sign in your guest, Mr Hoare,' he said.

'Damn paperwork,' Edward sighed. He wrote Song's name in the visitors' book.

Inside the club there was a large noisy room with smoke hanging low like river mist. Men sat in pairs upon red leather sofas speaking softly and drinking from glass tumblers. At the far end was the bar. Song and Edward headed across the room. There was whispering in their wake. Song envied Edward's natural ease, or his naïveté.

'A whisky,' Edward said to the barman.

'And a tonic,' Song said.

The noise level slowly picked up again. Song knew almost everyone in the room by face.

'Business crowd are in the pale suits,' Edward said. 'Civil servants in the dark suits. Latter think they're running the country. Former actually are.'

Song smiled at Edward's observations. He thought how Edward didn't belong here either.

'It's the same crowd, wherever you go,' Edward continued. 'That's the problem with the colonies. You can't get away. Except in Bartica, of course. No one here would want to be posted there.'

'Is that why you're in Bartica?' Song asked. 'To get away.'

'It's one of the reasons. Of course, there isn't a Mrs Hoare either. I guess that would keep me in a place like Georgetown. But I like my own company. I'd always preferred doing my own thing. I've never fitted into places like this. I mean, look around you.'

Edward was right. The men around them were noisy, the brash sort, nothing like Edward.

'There are the big drinkers; they're always good fun, of course,' Edward continued. 'Married men with good intentions. Married men with bad intentions. There are the good-looking single ones, bloody good at tennis, and sleeping with bored wives who insist to their husbands they want to improve their serve. The husbands are too proud or too ashamed to address it. Keeping it on an even keel. The problem with this place is that people have too much time. Boredom breeds mischief. Messages from London take so long to reach us – and besides they're so out of touch there with what's really going on here – that we just do what we can to keep everything on the same old heading, which honestly doesn't take more than five minutes' work a day. An even keel, a steady course. You don't want to show any initiative and stick your neck out. That could get you in trouble in the colonies.'

'My father used to say something like that.' Song thought how long it had been since he'd started rejecting that advice.

Edward continued talking about his other postings, in Colombo ('remarkably similar to Guiana') and Barbados ('much closer, geographically speaking, but wholly different'), and how he didn't regret not marrying but was sorry to have missed out on having children ('life centres around work and whisky for men like me').

Song let his eyes move around the room. He saw Mr Burford, the husband of the woman who had objected to Song living with Father Holmes. He was on the sofa talking intensely to Mr Stewart, Millie's father. In walked Governor Bolton and both men stood to greet him. Song also recognised Mr Boyle, who he thought would probably no longer remember the altercation between his wife and Father Holmes. How she had told Father Holmes that Song should have been 'out cutting cane, not reading books'. Song remembered hiding in the shadows before he disappeared into the night, angry but frightened, too. He could still hear the distant sound of Father Holmes calling his name, conscious that he might be sent back to the plantation. Song wasn't afraid any more; he would never run again.

One of the men tapped his glass and the room hushed.

Edward lowered his voice. 'Deputy secretary. Not sure of his name. New, I think.'

'Gentlemen,' the man said. 'I want to make you aware that we are still raising money for the swimming pool. Now I know you already know this, but I'm sorely disappointed by your shallow depths of generosity.' There was a ripple of laughter. 'Dig deep, gentlemen. This is a community project. It's also my personal mission to get the ladies wearing fewer clothes. What do you say to that?' There was a cheer. 'There'll be a box on the table.'

It was this hypocrisy Song found so distasteful about these men: they thought one thing, lived another, preached something else. They'd sit in the front pew at church, condemning the sinners, and pretending to be pious, to be perfect. Bartica was wholly different. There was no shamming, perhaps because there was little shame attached to sinning.

'They won't be getting anything from me,' Edward mumbled.

They had a second drink and then Song made his excuses.

'Thank you for inviting me, but I should get back. Besides, I don't want to get you thrown out.'

Edward scoffed. 'We're allowed guests. You could probably buy the club if you wanted to.'

'That's an idea,' Song winked. 'By the way, I'll be heading back to Bartica soon. Will that tie in with your plans?'

'Name the day,' Edward said.

Song exited the bar. At the door to the club there were two men on their way in. Song recognised their faces from somewhere, St Andrew's perhaps, but did not know who they were.

He tried to pass them, but one of them veered into his path. 'Who the devil are you?'

Song looked him straight in the eye. 'Song Holmes.' He did not offer his hand.

The second man nudged his friend. 'With the goldmine.'

'I don't give a damn,' said the first. 'What the devil are you doing here?'

'I'm a guest of Mr Edward Hoare and I came to have a drink,' Song said.

'Are you leaving?'

'By chance, I am.'

'A good thing too.'

Song tipped the bellman heavily.

'Money doesn't clean your skin, you know,' one called out from behind him.

When Song arrived home Hannah was waiting in the front room reading. She was so engrossed in her book that she did not notice him walk through the door. He put his arms around her from behind the chair.

'Scared me.' She smacked his hand. 'How was it?'

'You would have hated the smell of the carpet,' Song said. He squeezed his wife's shoulders.

'Did you have any trouble?'

'A couple of people seemed to take offence at me being there.'

Hannah turned to look up at Song. 'Who exactly?'

'I don't know their names.'

'Was there a scene?'

Song breathed heavily in Hannah's ear. 'You sound enthralled at the thought.'

She laughed. 'Not exactly,' she said. 'But I would like to hear something more than "we drank whisky", "we talked about cricket". Was the governor there?'

'He was.'

'The new one?'

'The very same.'

'Who else?'

'Everybody. At least everybody who thinks they're somebody.'

Hannah laughed again. 'And the scene?'

Song impersonated their accent. '*What the devil are you doing at our devilish club?*'

'Did they really say that to you?'

'We expected it.'

'Did we?'

Song slammed her book shut.

She gave him a half-smile. 'What?'

'Stop reading.'

'Little A has left you some dinner.'

'I don't want dinner. I just want you.'

Song wrote a letter to Mr Oakden, the secretary of the British Club, and applied for membership. He put down Edward Hoare as his reference. He also sent a cheque with the balance to build the swimming pool.

He never received a reply, but the cheque was cashed.

The next week Governor Bolton called Song to his office.

Song walked towards Governor's House, wondering if this would be different to his last visit with Governor Johnson. Governor Bolton hadn't been in his job long enough for much to be known about him. Rumours were that he was worse than the last, but that was almost always the assumption.

Song was made to wait nearly an hour before he was let into the study. Governor Bolton didn't look up for another ten minutes. He put down his pen deliberately before raising his eyes.

'You're here because I have deep concerns about working conditions at your mine,' the new governor said. 'I am hearing harrowing stories about long hours and low pay. Here at Governor House we take very seriously the welfare of labourers. If you are breaching any of our rules and regulations your mine will be shut down.'

Song felt his body stiffen. 'Any harrowing stories are gossip and lies.'

'Are you doubting my sources?'

'Absolutely. My team at Omaia take the greatest care of our employees. I have made that a top priority.'

'That is not what I am hearing.'

'I challenge you, sir, to find one man there who is not satisfied with either the conditions or the pay.'

'I don't think you are in any place to be doing the challenging. This is your first warning. I am watching your operation very closely.'

'I welcome the scrutiny. As I explained to your predecessor, I would be delighted to host a DC up at the mine to carry out an inspection. That is, if and when there is a DC finally appointed to Bartica.'

The governor's surprised expression was a giveaway; he probably had no idea there wasn't a DC in Bartica.

'Alternatively, or additionally, I can furnish you with information on any aspect of my business, including pay and lengths of shifts,' Song added.

'A man with your history does not lecture a man like me. I know your background. You're a plantation worker.'

'I was once a plantation worker, yes. And if you want to know about harrowing working conditions, I can tell you first hand. I could recount some stories about long hours and low pay, and

worse, on plantations run by co-operatives of the British government. I know of people still in charge of plantations who should be
in jail.'

The governor's eyes narrowed on Song. 'Watch your mouth. I'll
shut you down.'

Song looked back at the governor. 'If you find a legitimate
reason to shut me down, I will not object.' His voice was firm. 'That
is how confident I feel about the way I operate my business.'

'We will see who wins in the end.'

'It was a Welshman – a man of high ideals and strong values –
who taught me to speak out when I saw something wrong or
unfair. And I will.'

The governor laughed. 'Do you think anyone cares what you
think is wrong or unfair?'

Song got up to go. 'Is there anything else?'

'There is. I hear you're donating to the racecourse. New stables,
is it?'

'My donation is subject to receiving a second-tier box.'

'So I've heard. Well, I thought I'd explain something to you.
Donations are not a business deal. Not in the world I inhabit.'

'I see,' Song said. 'Then how would you suggest I go about secur-
ing a second-tier box?'

'Try as I might, I can't think of a way. It sounds like you'll have
to watch from ground level like everybody else.'

'Not like *everybody* else.' Song opened the door to leave. 'Do let
me know if you think of a way around this inconvenience. In the
meantime, I count your interest in my business as a small victory.'

The next morning Song raised an idea over breakfast. 'I had a
thought.'

'What thought might that be?' Hannah mused.

Mary Luck had picked up a sponge finger soaked it in hot milk and began feeding it to baby Phillip. 'Sounds like trouble,' she said.

'To build a new sports club,' Song said.

'Trouble,' Mary Luck repeated.

'What's wrong with the one here?' Hannah asked.

'What's wrong with the one here is that we can't join it. We can only visit as guests of a member.'

Hannah nodded. 'True.'

'So this would be a sports club for anyone who wants to join.'

'I like it,' Hannah said.

'I don't,' Mary Luck said.

Song smiled. 'One out of two is better than my average.'

'Older is wiser,' Mary Luck said.

'Where would it be?' Hannah asked.

'Land is cheaper to the north. There would be a running track, tennis courts, a cricket pitch and . . .'

'And?'

'And a racetrack!'

'But we can already go to the racetrack.'

'But you can't see anything.'

'Trouble.' Mary Luck said again. 'What do you want all that nonsense for? Wasting money on land. Encouraging gambling. A racetrack, you say? I fear it's going to become a habit with you two.'

'Mama, we've only been once and that was over a year ago.' Hannah looked thoughtful. 'I like the idea, Song, but Mama is right. They won't like it.'

'I did knock some sense into her after all,' Mary Luck said to baby Phillip, as if there was nobody else in the room listening. 'Song Holmes will get us all thrown out of this town and I'll be forced to move back to Bartica, this time carrying Georgetown rocks and two chickens more disoriented than I am.'

Song laughed. 'I'm not doing this to make trouble. I'm doing it because I want you to be able to see a race.'

Mary Luck snorted. 'That is the last thing I want to see right now. Just give me another grandchild and this old woman will be happy.'

Hannah held up a pine tart to Song. 'Want one?'

'A child, or a pine tart?'

Hannah blushed. 'Actually, I think I'm expecting.'

Tears unexpectedly came to Song's eyes. He moved over to Hannah's side of the table and held her close. 'I love you,' he whispered in her ear.

'Hallelujah,' Mary Luck cried out. 'I'll see another grandchild before my time's up.'

'Don't say that, Mama,' Hannah said.

'I'm not going to last forever.'

Hannah turned back to Song. 'Perhaps you should also build a church for the christening, if you really want to take on this town.'

Song nodded. 'There's a thought.' He knew what Father Holmes would have thought about that. He flung his doors open wide to anyone. Song could do the same.

CHAPTER 28

Song heard the news from Fowl Man, who was on the dock at Parika, before he even reached Bartica.

'I got news I think you ain't gonna know,' Fowl Man said.

'What's that?'

'You don't know, do you?'

'I don't know until you tell me what you know.'

'They found another seam. All of Bartica's talking about it.'

Song felt a tremor of excitement pass through him. But he also felt an unexpected trepidation; with each success would come greater scrutiny of his business. There were new risks associated with finding another seam. He was conscious of the resentment he was generating. There were those who wanted him to fail, or more extremely who wanted him gone.

He set off immediately, skipping Bartica and travelling through the night by a slender new moon. As he arrived he noticed some changes. There was another jetty. More boats than he remembered were tied up. Camp had swelled with more outbuildings and storage areas. The scar in the land had widened. Most of the workers were not in camp, but down the mine. Yet Song could still sense the rising fever at this latest find. Some came up to him to shake his hand. Others were too nervous to approach and watched from a distance as he moved about the camp.

He was told Chi was underground inspecting the new string, so Song took himself across to the office. He opened a ledger. As he turned the first page he heard the deep rumble beneath his feet. There were shouts outside. He flung open the door. Men were running towards the mine. A giant cloud of dust hung outside the opening.

Song didn't want to believe what he knew had happened. He caught a man by the wrist as he ran past him. He recognised him as Eldo, one of the first men they'd hired.

'What is it?' Song asked him. 'What happened?'

'A tunnel's collapsed,' Eldo replied.

Someone yelled. 'Do a count!'

'Get everyone out!'

'Do a count first,' Eldo cried.

'Everyone to the huts.'

There were men already scrambling out of the opening coughing. They looked like ghosts in the fine dust. Song could barely distinguish one from another. He shook one. 'Where's Chi?'

The man shook his head and pointed down the mine. Then his legs buckled under him.

'Fetch some water,' Song shouted to the others.

Another man came out choking. Song could see the fear and confusion in his wide eyes, but he shook him in desperation. 'Did you see Chi?' he pleaded.

The man shrugged.

'Which tunnel were you in?'

Another man answered for him. 'I think it was three. The new one.'

Everybody was shouting in the confusion.

'Start digging.'

'Which is it?'

'Tunnel two.'

'No, it's three.'

Song grabbed Eldo's shoulder and turned him around to face him. 'Do the damn count,' he said. His voice cracked as he spoke. 'Send me four teams of ten as soon as you get the first names. We need to work out which tunnel it is.'

'Yes, sir.'

Eldo raised his voice above the noise and confusion. 'Everyone by the new huts. We do the count first. Then we dig.'

Song's hands were shaking as he scrambled towards the mine opening. He was shouting at the men to get to the huts but there were brothers and fathers and friends down there and everybody wanted to start digging.

'When you're counted you can come back,' Song called out. 'We need to know which tunnel it is. And we need to know how many are missing.'

Missing. The word echoed around his head. His father missing. All the men from the village. Father Holmes missing. Mr Leigh missing. He went to the opening of the shaft. There was too much dust to see beyond an arm's length.

Eldo had been quick. The first team of ten were already back from the huts and at Song's side.

'Get your shovels,' Song said. 'Follow me.' He pointed at one man. 'You stay and lead the second group in. Bring barrows to take out the rocks. When I say I want carpenters, you send them in.'

Song led the dig. They worked as if they were fighting a war. The air was stagnant with dust. They wheezed and coughed. Their eyes watered. Every few minutes Song told everyone to shut up. They stopped their work and held their breath to listen. Nothing. Nothing yet. Song imagined Chi down there in the dark. Choking on the dust. Desperate for a drink. Running out of air. Dead Man's Bend, that's what he'd called this place. Was that an omen? He'd taken a life. Was a life being taken from him?

A message came from Eldo. 'It's tunnel three, sir.'

'How deep?' Song asked.

'Forty feet to the first level. Ten feet down to the second.'

'How many?'

'Nineteen, sir.'

The number was far higher than Song had imagined. 'Keep digging.'

Nobody flagged. Song also pushed his body hard, thrusting in his shovel, feeling the resistance shudder through him. It was like being back on the plantation again. The same movement after the same movement, like they'd been doing it all their lives.

'We must reach them before it gets dark,' Song said.

They worked in shifts, removing rocks, then letting the carpenters move in with supports. There was a heavy rain shower, which made it harder to work. They dug more frantically as the light began to fade.

'Get the lamps ready,' Eldo said.

Through the night progress was slower. A message came back from the head of the dig. They had found the first body. Dawn was slipping into the sky. A man was carried out. His arms hung down by his sides. Song knew it was Chi. His body was covered in thick grey dust and his face was battered. Song took him up in his arms like a broken lover. He felt his own chest crack. He remembered Chi's words. 'Too much gold can weigh a man down,' and Song wished he had listened.

There had never been a funeral like it in Bartica. The town was never short of untimely deaths but there wasn't always a body to put in the ground. A send-off was usually played out in a bar, a toast to a life cut short, rarely well lived, more likely wasted.

But this was different. All nineteen bodies were to be buried in

St Ethelbert's cemetery on the same day. The mourners travelled like rivers of black towards the church. Even the children realised they must be quiet and padded alongside their parents with worried looks on their faces. It was an unfamiliar silence for Bartica. Only the birds continued to sing.

There was not enough room in the churchyard for everyone. They gathered in the streets and strained to hear Father Lovett's service. He read out the names of the men and gave thanks for their lives. There was no burial. Their bodies had already been interred because of the heat. Song felt the grief rising up in him. He had lost his partner. He had lost nineteen men who called him their boss. He reached for Hannah's arm to steady himself. 'I'm here,' she said. 'Lean on me.'

After the funeral they stopped by the families of the dead men. During their visits some of the widows even offered comfort to Song and Hannah. Song passed to the widows brown envelopes thick with money. It didn't feel right, it felt cheap, but he knew they needed it. A body in the ground, and a brown envelope of money.

Chi's house was the hardest call. Hannah put her arms around Yan and she didn't pull away. 'I'm sorry,' Hannah said.

'I asked too much of him, Yan,' Song said, 'of everyone. I am deeply sorry for that. "Too much gold can weigh a man down", he once told me. I should have listened.'

Yan said nothing in return. The children hung back in the shadows, like the first time Song met them.

'You're family to us, Yan,' Hannah said. 'You know that.'

'Chi was a better partner than anyone could have wished for,' Song added.

Yan smeared tears from her face. 'There were better husbands, but he was the one I had.' She waved her hand around her. 'And the father of all these.'

The children were close by. Bibi ran to her. Yan caught her and lifted her up on her lap. The little girl touched the tears on her mother's cheeks.

The rest also moved in closer. Only Nina held back.

'We're all broken up,' Yan said. 'Nothing you can do about that.'

'If you need anything . . .' Song couldn't finish his sentence.

'I know.' Yan was perfunctory.

Song did not want to talk about food or money in front of the children but he wanted to tell Yan she'd want for nothing. He remembered too well how it was to be hungry. A burning hunger kicked him in the belly, even after all those years. He remembered sitting around the fire, poking at embers, with not enough rice to go around. While the women talked Song slipped into the kitchen. He pulled down the red biscuit tin and filled it with money. As he did he caught sight of Nina standing on the back step. She made him feel like a thief.

'Go ahead,' she said. 'Fill it up. That's what you know how to do.'

Song breathed out her name with a sigh. 'Nina.'

'Yes?'

'I want to say I'm sorry.'

'Sorry?' Nina repeated. She sounded disgusted.

'What do you want me to say?'

'What do *you* want to say?'

'I want to say I'm sorry I can't bring him back. Above everything, I wish I could bring him back.'

'Broken promises. Lies.'

'I know you don't want me here. But I'm here to make good on the duty he had as a father to look after his family.'

'Blood money.'

'No, Nina. It's given with love.'

'I don't want your money-given-with-love.'

Song looked at this bright, brazen, singular woman standing in the sunlight in front of him and wished she had been born in a different time and a different place. A time in the future when it would be easier to be the woman she was.

'I'm doing what Chi would have wanted me to do,' Song said.

'You have no idea what he would have wanted.'

'He'd have wanted you to have a good shot at life. You can do anything you want. I know you can.'

'Like what? Like find myself a pork-knocker, make a baby and wait around for him to come back so I can smile at his little trinkets and shout and yell and starve and make another baby until he comes back again to make another baby, and another, and another. Until he doesn't come back.'

'It doesn't have to be that way.'

'It doesn't have to be that way for you. You fill up the biscuit tin. You won't buy me.'

She was right, Song thought. Filling up a biscuit tin. Leaving a family without a father.

'I know what it's like to lose a father,' Song said. 'Believe that, at least.'

'I don't have to believe anything.'

Song heard footsteps. 'Are you both okay?' It was Hannah's voice.

'Yes,' Song said.

Nina snorted. 'Are you?'

'We'll come back another time,' Song said.

Nina called after them. 'You're not welcome back. You got my father's blood on your hands, Song Holmes. You'll carry that all your days.'

Song and Hannah withdrew. Outside, in the heat of the day,

they walked along familiar roads, but could take no comfort in them.

'She's grieving hard,' Hannah said.

'I once promised her I'd ask Chi if she could go upriver. I never did. Mostly because I forgot. But also because I knew he'd say no.'

'It's not your fault Chi died. Accidents happen. Even horrific ones like this one.'

'I'll carry it all my days, she said. I think she's right.'

'Time will soften how you feel now, Song. You gave those nineteen men opportunity, that's what you did. And I bet you none of the others'll quit because of this. They could have done small-time pork-knocking but they wanted to do something bigger, something greater. Commission on top of a wage, too. There'll still be a line of men wanting to work at the mine, in spite of this. Everyone wants to work for you.'

'I'm listening to you, Hannah,' Song said. 'And wanting to believe everything you tell me.' But he could not help remembering Nina's words the loudest.

As Hannah left in *Mimi* for Georgetown, Song went to the place he always sought in hard times. Ruby Lou's cast no judgement on the men who walked through its doors.

Ruby Lou was on the porch with some of the girls. She beckoned to him to sit down.

'Came here to pay some debts,' Song said.

'You got no debts here.'

'Half of the miners had no known next of kin. There are women here who deserve to share their last wage.'

'You're a good man, Song Holmes,' Dolly said.

'Not today I'm not.'

'Sure you are. You pay debts that aren't even yours.'

'They are mine now.'

'We miss you here in Bartica,' Sugar said. 'When you coming back? When you coming back to hear your beloved B Boys?'

Song felt himself breaking up inside. He knew why he had really come here. To cry.

'You all go inside,' Ruby said to the girls, ushering them away with a wave of the hand. She drew Song to one side of the porch. 'You don't go feeling bad about nothing, Song Holmes, if that's what you're doing. Those men died seeking a fortune. With or without you, they'd have gone out looking. You either die in a mine or die washed up on some greasy shore without two bits to rub together. It don't really matter. That's the life of a pork-knocker. Short, but punctured with sweetness. That's the life they choose. Upriver I know it ain't a picnic but it ain't that bad neither, or you wouldn't keep going up all the time, gold or no gold. No responsibilities. No women bugging. Nothing to do but a bit of digging in the sand and making a fire to cook up some fat labba. Then swinging back to town pretending to be rich for a day or two while talking about the hard times. Yeah, right. I'm smarter than that. You gotta end up dead doing something and they ended up dead doing something. Nobody to blame for that. Least of all you, Song Holmes. You're the best man this town saw.'

Song shook his head. 'Don't, Ruby.'

'Best man this town saw. I'll say it again. You come over every time you need reminding. Come and listen to some fine music and I'll make it my business to have you buy me a drink and remind you what's what.'

Song feigned a smile. 'What'd I do without you? Don't go dying on me now.'

'What in high heaven you saying things like that to a fine woman like me?'

'Everyone I love dies.'

'I ain't dying. Hannah ain't dying. Mary Luck sure ain't dying. Even Jingy ain't dying, though she's older than the trees.'

'Are you never short of an answer for me?'

'I'm short of many things but answers one thing I ain't short of.'

Song needed a thousand answers, but the most pressing was how to safeguard the mine. It would be under even closer watch after the accident. Song needed to find a way forward to protect his business, to protect his workers.

CHAPTER 29

Back in Georgetown Song had received a letter asking him to present himself at Governor's House. He knew what this meeting would be about.

'Could it really be nineteen dead?' The governor said. 'I made them repeat the number because I didn't believe it could be right?'

'It's a great tragedy.'

'I can't tell you how insincere that sounds when it comes from the mouth of the man benefiting from the toil of these poor men who gave their lives to line your pockets.'

Song was outraged by his remark, but wasn't about to show his real emotions. 'That is far from the truth. And those men would have agreed with me if they were here to speak for themselves. We all take our chances. They had a good wage. They knew the risks.'

'Is that what you want me to put in my report? Song Holmes says "they knew the risks". That's it. Until the next nineteen bodies get pulled out. Convenient, isn't it, that they're not here to speak for themselves?'

'They earned a good wage. Fifty per cent higher than the government wage for indentured labour, by the way, and with commission on top. They chose to work for me. They signed up to the job. I have a waiting list as long as my arm of other young men who want to work at Omaia.'

Governor Bolton bristled. 'You sound on the defensive.'

'Does this office always file a report after deaths in the work-place? Because if it does, there is a report I'd like to see. You probably don't know the name of a boy called Jinda. He was a friend of mine at Diamond. We worked alongside each other. One day he was sick. He didn't have the strength even to lift his machete.' Song's voice was calm and in control. 'For that, he was beaten and drowned in a canal.'

A heavy silence hung between the two men.

Song could recall a similar conversation between Father Holmes and Mr Carmichael when Father Holmes was trying to keep Song at the vicarage. 'I'm sure you keep a firm hand,' he'd said. 'I've had word that the children working at Diamond are being beaten.' Song was trying, like Father Holmes had, to give a voice to the powerless.

'Let's focus on the matter in hand, shall we? Not only do I have reports of terrible working conditions at Omaia, I now have hard evidence.'

'Launch an investigation. Speak to the families of the dead men. Come and see the mine. See for yourself how my wages compare to, say, the wages of the boys working at Diamond. Even today, it is a disgrace there.'

'You think you can buy loyalty with commission or compensation? British law does not tolerate inhumane working conditions. These nineteen men had rights. They don't die in a mine without a serious investigation. A mine that is helping to make its owner rich. A man who is not paying taxes. I know about rich men. What do rich men want? They want to be richer. They want to make more money, even if that means breaking the law. You break the law and I'll shut you down.'

Song waited until the governor caught his breath. 'Is that a threat?'

'That's probably the first bit of sense you've made today.'

'I'd like to get the details of these workers' rights, sir, so I can be sure I'm doing everything correctly.'

'I thought you were sure. Suddenly you're not so sure? Do I detect some anxiety in your voice?'

'I'd like to compare practices at Diamond and Omaia.'

'I'm afraid we don't have books on how to make a civil society civil. That is something which can't be taught. I know that might be hard for you people to understand.'

Song stood up to leave. 'Was there anything else?'

'You'll fall, mark my words. I've all the time in the world to wait and watch you fall.'

Song swore to himself he would never give the governor the pleasure of that.

Song knew he had a lot to do. He had to think up a clever way to protect the business, to protect his workers.

He sat in his study, deep in thought, surrounded by the influences of Father Holmes and wishing he was still around to give him counsel. There were all the books they had read together, stirring up memories of them studying alongside each other, turning the globe as they explored the countries of the world, questioning, debating.

Song looked across the room at the opposite wall and Father Holmes' painting of Wales. White smudges of sheep dotted a green hilly landscape. The black figure of a shepherd on the edge of a field. Song felt an empty ache. He wanted to watch over his workers the same way he had been cared for, looking out for the men risking their lives to better themselves.

He knew he must act quickly. He sent out messages inviting to Sugar House anyone who benefited from Omaia, including

Mr Ebenezer and Mr Hing. He also called on some of his most closely trusted friends: Jon Swire, Mr Ting-Lee, Dr Patel and Mr House.

'Gentlemen. As you will have guessed this is more than just a social gathering. Although I hope it is that, too.'

There was a murmur of pleasantries around the room.

'It is a more serious matter,' Song continued. 'For a long time now I've witnessed aspects of life in Georgetown which I haven't liked and haven't believed to be fair. Perhaps you have had similar sentiments at some time or another. What have we done about it? Nothing. It seems impossible to change things. So we let life continue the way it has for decades. Or, gentlemen, we reach a point when we say "enough". When we call a meeting of close trusted friends.'

The room was silent. There was an uneasiness in the air.

'I have a question for you. Is there anything wrong with the sports club?'

'Not enough domino tables?' Mr House volunteered.

'I don't know what it is but I'm sure I can smell trouble,' Mr Ebenezer said.

'I'll tell you what's wrong with it,' Song continued. 'We can't become members. I am going to build a new club – open to anyone.'

'Told you I could smell trouble.'

'Never were one to choose an easy life for yourself,' Jon said. 'You have my support, of course,' he added. 'But it won't go down well.'

'Take out the politics, everyone,' Song said. 'Think of it only as an issue of access.'

Mr House nodded. 'I like it.'

Mr Ting-Lee smiled. 'I'm in.'

'Trouble, trouble, trouble,' Mr Ebenezer mumbled.

'Exactly,' Song said. 'And that's why I'm enlisting your support ahead of time.'

'What kind of trouble?' Mr Hing asked.

'They'll try to stop me buying the land; try to disallow racing on certain days; try to refuse the bar a licence. They'll try any means to stop it happening or to close it down. But we must do this, gentlemen. And I need your support. This is bigger than just one person. The club will be owned by a foundation – and I want you to be on the board. A club supported by everyone and open to anyone. We all know there is absolutely nothing wrong with that.'

Mr Ebenezer made a strange noise.

'Mr Ebenezer?'

'It doesn't sound good.'

'They'll think you're trying to make a point,' Dr Patel said.

'I am,' he said. 'That in itself is a reason to go ahead. But the real reason we are doing this is because we want a place to relax, a place to play a game of tennis, a place to gather. Which we do not have at present.'

'I'm in.' It was Mr Hing.

'Thank you.'

'This is not as simple as putting up a building,' Mr Ebenezer said. 'You're taking on the town. That's what you're doing.'

'If that's how they want to see it, fine. But that's not how we see it.'

'How can we not support this?' Mr Ting-Lee asked the room.

Dr Patel nodded. 'How can we not?'

Mr Ebenezer frowned. 'I don't even play tennis.'

'Then it's not about tennis for you,' Song said. 'But you'd like a place to meet friends, to relax.'

Mr Ebenezer was agitated. 'Haven't relaxed since I met you.'

Song remembered Father Holmes teaching him how to argue a point. 'We've got to do this, gentlemen. It's the only way forward. And since we're in the mood for change, I want to propose we also establish a lodge. As leading members of the business community of this town, I invite you all to be partners. It will be called the Silent Temple, because what we say amongst ourselves will not go further. The idea is simple: when it comes to business, we will think of each other first. We will pull together when times are hard.' Song remembered how Jingy had put it. 'Not breaking the chain, that's the thing,' he said, echoing her words.

'That's more like it,' Mr Ebenezer said. 'Protection, that's what we need.'

'Protection may be part of it,' Song said. 'There will also be a social welfare fund to help families who fall on hard times and to provide education for children who need support. I'm sure we'll have other ideas, too. What we need now is a place to draw up plans. The club, the lodge, it's all part of the same vision.'

There was unanimous support.

'You bring business into it and you got me, too,' said Mr Ebenezer.

The seven men talked late into the night. Mr Hing was commissioned to design a seal for the new organisation. Song asked Mr House to start brokering the purchase of land to the north of Georgetown for the sports club. Mr Ting-Lee said his brother would be interested in tendering for the building contract. There was conviction and fear in the room in equal measure. It felt like a new beginning. Song remembered the other times he'd had this feeling: leaving his family to board the boat, moving to Bartica with Father Holmes, bringing Hannah and Mary Luck to Georgetown. Moments of change when he forced himself to look forwards, rather than reflecting on a more familiar past. He was going to build a new life for him and his family.

The idea of the club remained a secret until the land was purchased and construction began. Then the news swirled around town.

Father Francis stopped Song when he passed him in the street. 'I hear you're very busy on the north side of town.'

'I am.'

'You're building something?'

'That's right.'

'What?'

'When it's ready, you will be invited to come and see it for yourself. It will be open to anyone.'

Father Francis was growing exasperated. 'What will?'

Song had teased out their exchange, but was now glad to be blunt. 'It's a new church.'

Father Francis looked flustered. 'Whatever for?'

'I would think you of all people, Father, would know the answer to that.'

'You need permission for these kinds of things.'

'Find me a reason why I should not build a church.'

'Too many churches can cause divisions. We have plenty of churches in Georgetown already. There would need to be a very good reason why we need another.'

'I have a very good reason.'

Father Francis' tone was sharp. 'Churches aren't like shops. You can't just open one. You need to be able to show real commitment to the Christian faith. You need to show you can provide . . .'

Song interrupted. 'The reason I am building a church, Father, is because some of the churches in Georgetown are closed to me and – as I have been told – people like me. This church will be open to anyone who has the courage to walk through its doors.'

Song wondered what Father Holmes might have said. He suspected Father Holmes had known Song didn't believe in the ways of the church, but he hoped the vicar also knew that he shared many of his values.

Father Francis interrupted his thoughts. 'As I have said before, everyone can find themselves a church in Georgetown.'

'But you can take your pick. I cannot.'

Father Francis' voice was insistent. 'But there is a church – many churches, in fact – available to you. That is the point.'

'I cannot attend the church I want to attend. That is my point.'

'We cannot have everything we desire. This is the world we inhabit and we must be grateful to God for that.'

'You and I, Father, we inhabit very different worlds. And yes, indeed, I am grateful for that. Good day.'

When the Silent Temple held their next gathering, Song put forward his proposition to build a church. 'Not only a church. I want to provide a place of worship for anyone who wants one. Anyone who feels their spiritual needs are not already provided for in this community. A synagogue. A temple. Let's make sure everyone feels they have a place.'

'The way we're going we might as well build a second town,' Mr Ting-Lee said, chuckling.

'If we're not free to live in this one,' Mr Hing said, 'perhaps that's not such a bad idea.'

'Is this for our betterment?' Mr Ebenezer asked. 'In the long term?'

'It is the long term, I think, that we can be most confident about,' Song said. 'But it might be difficult in the short term.'

There was a knock at the door. It was Mr House. He was more out of breath than usual, with beads of sweat on his brow. 'Sorry

I'm late, but I've got good reason. Bad news. It's not public yet but it seems they're going to announce a new tax system.' He looked at Song. 'Sounds like they're targeting Omaia.'

'Any more details?' Mr Ting-Lee asked.

'There'll be a threshold,' Mr House said. 'If you're above it, tax payments will jump. Maybe double. Maybe more. It aims to hit the most profitable businesses.'

Song had to think hard and quickly.

'They can't get away with it,' Mr Hing said.

'Of course they can,' said Mr Ebenezer. 'They can get away with anything they want.'

'It should come as no surprise,' said Song.

'It's a reaction to the Silent Temple,' Mr Ebenezer said.

Song surveyed the room. 'I think we're going to need an account-ant in this group,' he said. 'And a lawyer.'

Song hired Tobias Shelf, a young accountant who was fresh out of school. He arrived at Sugar House breathless, apologetic, carrying an over-polished leather satchel and shoes that squeaked as he walked.

'I need your help, Tobias. I need a young pair of eyes that can see possibility.'

'Yes, sir.'

'Now, listen. This is in strict confidence.'

'Yes, sir.'

'A new tax system is being implemented. I don't know the details, but if Omaia isn't turning a profit, then there can be no tax bill, right?'

'Yes, sir.'

'Then I need you to ensure that we're not turning a profit. Here are the books.'

Tobias looked over the declarations. 'The company has made a lot of money. Every quarter.'

'And now it cannot.'

'Yes, sir. We have to find a reason why it would suddenly stop making money.'

'It's a goldmine. It could dry up overnight. That's a reality.' Song thought how innocent Tobias was.

'That sounds easy.'

'That is what I like to hear,' Song said.

'There are a lot of employees. It could even make a loss over the last quarter, if you like. I'll go ahead and prepare the books, and submit them to the colonial administration building.'

'By the end of the day, Tobias. No later.'

Within a few days, Song and other prominent businessmen of Georgetown received an invitation to Governor's House. Song was one of the first to arrive. He took a chair towards the back of the room. Men drifted in, mostly recognisable from church or Song's visit to the British Club. Members of the Silent Temple were also there, but they deliberately didn't associate with each other. When the room was filled, the governor rose to his feet.

'Gentlemen, thank you for coming. Why are you here, you may ask? I've brought you together because you are the highest earners in this colony. Yes, congratulate yourselves, gentlemen. Thanks to the fair rules and safe structures of Her Majesty's Government, you live and work in an environment which allows you to be productive and profitable. And in turn, it must be said, the colony is better off because of your contributions.'

There were murmurings in the room.

'London has always been generous. Tax adjustments have only

ever been slight and that hasn't given rise to enough regular income. We in Georgetown are addressing that, starting from the first of next month. Those at the top who can afford to pay higher taxes will be asked to pay more. Remember the colony's motto. *Damus Petimus Que Vicissim.* We give and expect in return.'

Song was passive on the outside but angered by the remark.

'Naturally,' the governor said, 'for those of you who earn a more moderate sum there may only be a slight increase. Not all of you will be affected.'

The governor held up an envelope. 'My secretary will be sending out letters to everyone with the estimated rise in your forthcoming tax bill. Any questions?'

Mr Winkworth, a successful sugar broker, sat a few places along from Song. 'When you say not all of you will be affected, who do you mean by that? Who specifically will *not* be affected?'

'I'm afraid you will be, Mr Winkworth. All brokers will be.'

'By how much?'

'As I said already, the rise will be in accordance with your income. Now, are there any other immediate questions?'

Song could see the resentment fizzing in some quarters of the room. He wondered if he could play the split in opinion to his advantage. There were lines being drawn.

'What about civil servants?' Mr Boyle said.

'Civil servants will not be affected,' the governor said. 'Your tax rate will remain the same. This change is primarily for commercial businessmen. Who have had a jolly good time the last few years. Wouldn't you agree, gentlemen? You know who you are.'

Song thought how laughable it all was. But he also knew how difficult it would be to fight this.

There was a rise in the noise level of the conversation. A few voices were expressing their disapproval. But there was a ripple of laughter in another corner of the room. Perhaps this time the governor had gone a step too far, Song thought. It could, in fact, be his undoing. This might be his chance to recruit more support for the Silent Temple.

There was a question from the front row. Song couldn't see who it was but he recognised his voice. 'And the plantations?'

'You'll be pleased to know, Mr Carmichael, that the plantations are also exempt from this change. They are co-operatives and will not be subject to the tax rise.'

Song was not surprised, but that did not make it any easier to swallow. Mr Carmichael. Forever unanswerable.

'So who exactly is affected, other than me?' Mr Winkworth asked again.

The governor ignored the question. 'As I have already said once, you can make an appointment with my secretary if you have any questions specific to your personal situation. Remember gentlemen, these changes will eventually come into effect for all the colonies, not only British Guiana.'

Mr Winkworth might be a candidate for the Silent Temple, Song thought. The man's anger was palpable.

Song raised his hand. 'Why are we doing this ahead of the other colonies? Does an early uptake of an elevated rate of tax benefit us in some way?'

'Good question,' Mr Winkworth said.

'Hear, hear.'

Song was quietly surprised. Here was the support of people who had long cast him as a foe.

'Here in British Guiana, at the governor's office, we have something called initiative,' the governor replied. 'That is why we are doing this now.'

'Initiative to pay more tax than any of the other colonies?' Mr Fereira asked. He traded spices at the port.

'As you well know, Mr Fereira, Her Majesty's Government has been extremely generous to men like you, and you should be grateful for that. What we are doing is coming into line.'

'No one else is in line. How can we come into line when there isn't a line?'

'Why penalise us early?'

'And why now?'

'There's no time like the present, gentlemen. Any other questions? No? Then I adjourn the meeting. I look forward to building a stronger British Guiana together.'

Mr Fereira tapped Song's arm as he made his way towards the door. 'What do you think?'

'Am I surprised?' Song shook his head in answer to his own question.

'What can we do?' Mr Fereira asked. 'I can't afford it.'

Song realised that he was turning to him for leadership.

'If you and the rest of us can't afford it, they won't be collecting any taxes at all.'

'True,' Mr Fereira nodded. 'If they put us out of business . . .'

'Come to Sugar House tomorrow night, Mr Fereira. I'd like to introduce you to some other people with views on this matter.'

The Silent Temple swelled over the next few weeks. Song looked around the room in satisfaction. There were more than twenty men coming from a broad representation of trade and business, as well as those in law, accountancy and even public service. He wondered if this latest legislation from Governor's House would turn out to be the making of his community. Together they drew up plans to protect their businesses and each other. Could it be that the outsiders were in such numbers that they were becoming the insiders?

Since the accident, Song had travelled up to Omaia as often as he could. They were usually short sharp trips; he discovered it was upriver where he wanted to be most, perhaps hoping that spending time supporting his workers might assuage his guilt.

He was rarely home and when he was, he retreated to his study. Hannah caught him at the door, as he was about to leave again.

'So soon?' she said.

'Not for long.'

Hannah sighed. 'We've lost you, Song. Do you know that? Not like the nineteen, but I'm losing you every day.'

Song was taken aback. 'But I'm here. I'm here now.'

'Then don't go again. Don't go so soon.'

'What's the matter?'

'You're never here. Even when you're here, you're not here. You've forgotten us. Phillip. Me. The baby coming soon. Mama. She's not well. But I don't think you've even noticed. '

'Mary Luck. Unwell. She's indestructible.'

'Maybe I'm wrong. I don't know for sure. But I know. If you know what I mean.'

'Can we ask Dr Patel to see her?'

'She won't agree. Too much fate in that woman's head. "When it's your time, it's your time," she'll say. I know her.'

'I can't imagine her even off-colour. But then you know she's always scared me.' Song had lightened the mood and Hannah laughed.

'Mama doesn't scare you.'

'Course she does. Ever since I placed an order for one of every-thing and she accused me of trying to steal her ideas. Terrifying.'

Hannah laughed again. 'You make me feel better.'

'You make me feel better, too.'

'You know the baby's coming very soon. It's not long now.'

'Yes, of course.' But Song had forgotten. Time had become indistinct since the collapse of the mine.

'Please don't go.'

'I won't,' Song replied. 'I'm afraid I don't know what I've been doing. Coming and going. Back and forth. Maybe you're right. I've been lost.'

'Remember the mine, Song. But don't forget your family.'

'I won't,' he whispered back.

Before the end of the week, there had been two important arrivals at Sugar House. The first was a baby girl, Florence, born swiftly one afternoon. Song watched Hannah cradling their newborn and felt a powerful wave of love for them both, and an even greater desire to look after his family.

The second was a letter from the governor's office. Song opened the envelope; his tax rate of 10 per cent had been raised to 33 per cent. Song leaned back in his chair, rocking on its two back legs. He had done what he could for now but he knew his work wasn't over. They wouldn't stop here. He wouldn't either. He had to come up with a way around the system.

CHAPTER 30

Construction of the Lucky Sports Club had begun and continued apace. The main pavilion was already standing. There were foundations for grass tennis courts, a swimming pool and a racetrack beyond that. Song had ordered that there be no boxes at the races, only open stands. Anybody could sit anywhere – with expansive views across the track.

Song was surprised at the speed of progress. His plan was becoming real. He was taking on this town and its injustices, like Father Holmes had intimated he should. The English sneered. The only ones who showed interest – like Edward Hoare – were already outside conventional colonial life. Song realised that the Silent Temple wasn't actually helping him integrate into Georgetown life, although perhaps he always knew that. He was in fact separating himself and his community even more. A parallel world. The difference was that he felt he was in control, even directing the tearing apart, the ever-growing rift, the deepening divisions.

One afternoon, several months after Florence's birth, Song found himself summoned again to Governor's House.

'This is becoming something of a habit,' the governor said. 'And not a good one. Do you have an idea what it might be about this time?'

'I can't imagine.'

The governor lit a cigarette. 'Are you sure about that?'

Song looked across the desk at the governor and nodded.

'The administration received your filed accounts. It seems this is the first ever quarter that Omaia failed to turn a profit. And there was negligible income too. A remarkable and sudden change in fortunes.'

'That's mining,' Song said. 'I always feared Omaia could dry up.'

'Do you expect me to believe the timing is a coincidence?'

'Coinciding with?'

Governor Bolton spat out the word. 'Tax.'

'The tax rate has risen in the past and Omaia continued to turn a profit.'

The governor fanned the smoke away from his face.

'If you check the dates,' Song continued, 'you'll see my accountant filed our numbers *before* we were notified of any rise in tax. The two are unrelated.'

'Explain to me how you're building a sports club without a shred of profit to your name?'

'*I'm* not building the sports club. It is the project of a charitable foundation. There are some extraordinarily generous members of this community coming together to make it happen.'

'And you're not one of them?'

'I'm a minority.'

'In every way,' the governor laughed. 'Want me to teach you something? There are rules and regulations in a civil society. That's what makes it civil. That's what makes it different to everything you have ever known.'

Song felt his anger rising, but he kept it in check.

'You won't get away with it,' the governor said. 'I'm making it my personal mission to ensure you don't.'

*

When the Lucky Sports Club was finished the following year, the Silent Temple planned a large celebration. There were no individual invitations. Instead they put a notice in the newspaper and posted bills across town:

'*The Lucky Sports Club inauguration party, on the third Saturday of the month, is open to everyone. Please come.*'

'Hundreds are coming, Song,' Hannah worried. 'The whole town's getting new dresses cut. Will there be enough food to go around?'

'We'll order more.'

'There's people journeying in from Berbice and Lethem and even New Amsterdam. You should hear the gossip: who's going with whom, the speculation as to the number of bottles of rum on ice, how many dishes are being prepared. Phillip is so excited. He thinks it's his birthday party.'

Song found Phillip in the kitchen with Little A. 'I hear you're having a party,' he said to his son. 'Can I come?'

'Yes. You can,' Phillip said emphatically.

'Do you know what we're celebrating?'

'My birthday.'

Song smiled. 'It's your birthday – and it's also the opening of a new sports club. It's a place to get together – open to all. That's how it should be. Remember that.'

'But there's already a sports club,' Phillip said.

'You're right. But not everybody can join it.'

'Why?'

'There's no good answer to that because there's no good answer to that. But this'll be different. And it's named after your mama. Lucky! And I'm lucky because I have her and because I have you.'

*

A few days later, Edward Hoare arrived in Georgetown. He and Song took a walk up to the sea wall. Nothing ever changed there. It looked no different to when he and Father Holmes had walked there all those years ago.

But Song thought how much older Edward seemed, his hair thinner, a stoop. He wondered if Edward thought the same about him.

'I want to ask you something, Edward,' Song said. 'Will you do me the honour of joining the Silent Temple? We need you.'

'Me? An Englishman. A civil servant. You don't need me.'

'That's exactly why we do need you.'

Edward sighed. 'You're a man of ideas, Song. Ideas and dreams and energy. I don't have your fight. That's why I live in Bartica. I'm not trying to beat the system. I'm trying to avoid it.'

'We need someone like you.'

'A white face?'

'It's true I want representation. Should it matter that you were born in England and I was born in China? It shouldn't. Join us, Edward. Just on paper. I don't know anyone who will cross the line other than you.'

'I know what you're trying to do. But this kind of change won't happen in my lifetime.'

'We'll be closer to it happening.'

'I'm a selfish old man living a selfish old life.'

'No man is an island. Father Holmes would have leaned on you to do this, too. I remember listening to your conversations with him and Tom Jameson in the evenings at the vicarage. Eating crab backs, rocking on the porch, me wishing I could join you. I want to create that kind of atmosphere – to talk freely, to share news, to look out for each other.'

Edward sighed. 'You're a dog with a bone, Song. Put me down

on your books then. It may not be for very long, though. In truth I'm thinking about returning to England. I'm getting tired of the heat and the work, and I have a little house in England that my mother left me. It's cold and dark and a good distance from the nearest village but it's somewhere to spend the rest of my selfish days with memories of the tropics to warm my bones.'

Song shook his head. 'I can't see you leaving Bartica.'

'Not for a damp dark cottage? Perhaps you're right.'

'You matter here, Edward. You matter to the Silent Temple, to the community here, to my family.'

'That's kind of you to say.'

They split up at the corner of Water Street. Song walked home slowly. Ahead he saw Mr Oakden with his wife. He remembered the letter he addressed to him applying to join the British Club.

Song tipped his hat. 'Good evening.'

In an exaggerated response Mr Oakden imitated Song tipping his hat. 'You'll never be one of us.' It was an unprovokedly vicious tone.

Song noticed Mrs Oakden squeeze her husband's arm.

'You are assuming I would like to be,' Song said.

'A sports club in a near mirror image of ours,' Mr Oakden said. 'Don't fool yourself that you're doing something unique.'

'This is not about tennis courts, Mr Oakden. It is about a membership system that's open to everyone.'

'Open to anyone who can afford it.'

'You can change your financial circumstances. You cannot change your circumstances of birth.'

'Exactly.'

'For your circumstances of birth to rule the rest of your life cannot be fair.'

Mrs Oakden caught Song's eye. He sensed her admiration, even as she stood beside her husband.

'You people don't understand,' Mr Oakden said. 'Civil society is not built on money. It's built on years of doing the right thing. Just because life has been good to you for a few years doesn't mean you can now buy your way into society. Your club won't be the new place for Georgetown society. It will be a place for second-raters with chips on their shoulders. Do you think any one of you would turn your nose up at the chance of joining the British Club?'

'There was a time when I wanted to join the British Club. Do you remember? I wanted to feel part of a community. Not the British community. Not the Chinese community. But Georgetown community. It is you who does not understand, Mr Oakden. I certainly would turn down the chance of joining the British Club now.'

'Let me teach you something: clubs are called clubs because of the shared interests of their members. Will plantation workers be joining your club? No. The homeless? The poor? The illiterate? No, no, no. That's called exclusion on the basis of money . . .'

'I was once a plantation worker,' Song interrupted. 'Today I am a pork-knocker. Neither fact matters. In our club it won't matter how people earn their money or where they come from. For those who can't afford it, there'll be open days and subsidies. Perhaps I'll waive all fees. At the church, the doors will be wide open. Nobody will be excluded. It was a man from your own country who taught me that a long time ago and I've never forgotten it.'

'I can see you're a very bitter man,' Mr Oakden said.

'Let's go home,' his wife said.

'Bitterness isn't driving this,' Song said. 'A call for fairness is.'

Mrs Oakden was pulling at her husband's arm.

'I hope you and Mrs Oakden will find the courage to come to the inauguration. Everyone is invited.'

Over a thousand people came to the opening party. Song surveyed the scene and wished Father Holmes could have been there. A place to come together for everyone, open to all. Song remembered what Father Holmes said: 'If we're demanding perfection before people walk through our doors we'll have very empty churches.' Song reflected on his own imperfect self, his transgressions. What a very unordinary vicar Father Holmes had been.

Lunch was spread on long tables with tall glasses of pink and orange rum punch. There were races all afternoon and as the last winner entered the enclosure the music started up. The party lasted long after the sun had gone down.

But as Song walked home, he thought about the limitations. The English who had shown interest in the organisation – like Edward Hoare – were already outside conventional colonial life. The Silent Temple was irrelevant to the people who wielded political power. For Song the fight wasn't over yet.

CHAPTER 31

Year on year Omaia continued to outperform any goals Song might have had for the mine. It continued, too, to be closely scrutinised by officials at Governor's House. They never found any evidence of malpractice, nor any inconsistencies in the financial records, but Song did not allow himself to become complacent, conscious that he needed to stay one step ahead. The pattern of his life shifted to accommodate his concern for both the business and the foundation, which he felt required his attention more than ever. He spent less and less time at home, throwing himself into work, and was often away for many months. He was conscious of Hannah's regular reminders about how quickly the children were growing up. Between his long trips he did notice how Phillip and Flo had started to develop their own personalities, to listen to the world around them more intently and to speak their mind. He knew he was missing out but he was also aware how much he needed to do to provide for his family and to protect their future.

Late one night, during one of Song's increasingly brief visits to Georgetown, Jon came to Sugar House. He probably hadn't seen his friend for over a year. Jon stood at the door of Song's study, his face pale and his hands shaking. When Song brought him into the light he saw a mix of fear and anger in his friend's face. This wasn't Jon's usual self. His typical steadiness, his quietude. Song led him into his study and shut the door.

'It's been a long time. How are you, my friend?'

Jon let his body sink into a large armchair. With one hand he half-covered his eyes. The other gripped the arm of the chair. 'What I'm about to tell you, Song, you must not repeat. Not to anyone. Swear it.'

'Of course.'

'Swear it.'

'I swear it.'

'She made me swear not to tell anyone.'

'Who?'

'Sonia.'

Song pictured Jon's sister. He remembered playing with her, swinging her around and around in the yard, hearing her carefree laughter. That was a long time ago. She would have been in her teens by now. 'Is she okay?'

'Kiddo. He . . .' Jon stumbled.

Kiddo had done some terrible things in his time but Song had never seen Jon like this. 'Tell me.'

'I'm going to kill him.'

Song was almost too afraid to ask. 'Where's Sonia?'

'At my place. She got in from Bartica earlier this evening. Rose is looking after her the best she can.'

'What happened?' Song asked again.

'Sometimes, when I was growing up, I used to wish to myself that I didn't have a family. Like you.'

'Kiddo was never your family.'

'She told me she'd rather be dead.' Jon's voice was fading away as if he was talking to himself. 'She still looks so young. Like a child. She's just a child. Why didn't I bring her here before? I didn't know. Why didn't I know?'

'What is it, Jon? You're not making sense.'

'She's pregnant.'

Song swallowed hard. 'By Kiddo?'

Jon's eyes were full of desperation. 'It's been going on for years, she says. He's been . . . for as long as she can remember. Since she was small. I never even knew. I never even noticed.' Jon broke down.

Song's head was spinning. He thought of the times he'd seen Kiddo make Sonia cry. And how he'd done nothing. He went over and crouched beside his friend. He put an arm around Jon's shoulder.

'I'm going to kill him, Song,' Jon said. 'I swear it.'

'Not tonight, Jon. Not now. You are needed in one place right now and that's here in Georgetown with Sonia. She needs you more than ever. Look after your sister. Let me look after the rest.'

Jon crumpled deeper into the chair as if he could no longer hold himself upright. 'I came here to tell you. But I also came here to ask you if I could borrow the *Dartmouth* tonight. To go to Bartica.'

'Jon, you listen to me now. Like I listened to you when you pulled me out of Josie's. If you go to Bartica now you'll wind up dead. And then you'll be no good to Sonia at all.' Song looked hard in his friend's eyes. 'Let me sort this out.'

'I don't want anyone knowing about this. She made me swear not to tell anyone.'

'Sonia's right. Nobody must know anything about this. Don't tell her you told me. Don't tell another soul.'

Back in Bartica, the jetty boys greeted him with the usual volley of gossip.

'You shoulda been here last week, man,' Joseph said. 'A few dozen boxes of rum came floating by the dock. Didn't belong to nobody. Like a gift. Happy Christmas, Bartica!'

Song threw them a rope. 'Do boxes of rum float then?'

'Ask any man here alive.'

'Whole town was high,' Dory said. 'Even if you weren't drinking it, you were high on the vapours. We were swimming in the stuff. The B Boys were on fire that night. Played till morning and then some.'

Song smiled. 'That is something I wish I'd been in town for.'

'Man, you'd have been up all night,' Joseph said. 'Streets were littered with bodies that next day. Like there'd been some kinda plague. People were too beat to make it home. They just fell right over on the street and slept there till the sun split their heads in two. Man, we couldn't have unloaded a basket of feathers the next day. We were out cold. Who knows what was in those bottles?'

'Good sweet rum, that's what,' Basil whistled. 'Got you between the eyes – and between the legs.'

'Glad I missed it,' Song said. 'You're all talking like a bunch of drunks. What else has been going on?'

'Usual,' Dory said. 'Still no DC. No PC. But the place is running itself, same as ever.'

'You hear Kiddo wound up dead?' Joseph asked.

'Finally,' Basil added.

Song didn't flinch. He pulled himself up on the dock. 'That so?'

'Knifed in his sleep.'

'Longest list of suspects in history,' Basil said. 'You know who's on the list? The whole population of Bartica.'

The jetty boys all laughed.

'I won't be shedding a tear,' Song said. It had been done quickly, he thought to himself. He'd asked Bronco to sort it out. He was the obvious choice. The big man who chose not to come to his wedding because he wanted to take care of Song's small worthless

406

room. 'The boy with promise,' Bronco called Song, and he'd do anything for him.

Bronco knew all the comings and goings of everyone, yet he wasn't a talker. And he knew people. 'Most everyone has a price,' he'd say, 'and the price in this town's pretty low.' He assured Song that he'd hire outsiders and that the murder wouldn't be able to be threaded back to Song.

'That man lived too long,' Dory said.

'Even his woman says she's glad he's gone,' Basil said. 'That man didn't have a good bone in his body. Course his old man was a dog, too. Bad breeds bad.'

'Not always.' Dory cut in. 'You seen Mad Dog's little 'un? Sweeter than honey. Eyes so wide, you think they might pop outta their sockets. Got everyone scratching their heads how that man can have such a nice kid. Please and thank yous. Always running and fetching and helping. Course with Sugar the mother he might not be Mad Dog's.'

'Man, I sure know where to come if I need any gossip,' Song said. 'Who can tell me how Jingy is?'

'Still moaning about last week's rum. Says the town stinks of liquor and piss. Does it?'

'Bartica always stinks, Dory,' Song said. 'You know that.'

'You been away too long,' Basil said. 'Stick around and you'll stop smelling it.'

As Song walked away from the dock, he thought how easy it had been to have Kiddo killed. Not a stain. Jon would have had to put the knife in himself. Putting the knife in yourself was something else. He remembered holding the blade against Jesus' throat, the hours trying to dig dried blood out from under his fingernails. Raped, before he became a killer. That experience had hardened

407

him. Jesus. Kiddo. They got what they deserved, Bartica style. But that wasn't always the way. Good lives cut short. Others, blood-stained, allowed to go on and on.

Song spent a month up at Omaia, glad to be away from the noise of Bartica, the kindness of home that he didn't want right now, that he didn't feel he deserved. When he eventually turned around to head back to Georgetown, it was with apprehension.

Even from a distance Sugar House looked as peacefully removed as ever. Stilled and glowing in the late afternoon light, far from unspeakable horrors.

Hannah was a shadow on the staircase. She said his name. 'Song?'

Song could hear a melancholy in her voice. 'What is it?'

'Mama passed on.' Her voice broke.

Song moved up the stairs and gently pulled his wife to him. He remembered what he'd once said to her, albeit many years earlier – that Mary Luck was indestructible – and felt terribly sad that he had been wrong.

'There was no pain, the doctor said.'

Song looked into his wife's face. 'And how are you, my love?'

'It was peaceful. We can't wish for more than that.'

Song nodded. 'A peaceful death. A life well lived. It's true. It's all we can wish for.'

'There's something else,' Hannah said softly. 'Amalia died the same night. We both lost . . .'

'They were two great women. The kind you think will never die.'

'Not two, but three. They both died on the same day the country lost Queen Victoria. Isn't that strange? All happening at the same time.'

'They all lived long and full lives.'

Hannah choked. 'I want us to live long and full lives. But I'm so afraid to lose you. I've been afraid since Chi and the accident. Every time you leave.'

'Every time I leave? Why haven't you told me?'

'I'm brave,' Hannah stammered.

'You are. I know.'

'But I can still be afraid. Your family needs you, not the mine.'

Song thought about the goatherd in Mr Ebenezer's painting. The lesson against greed. Against having too much. Was it time? Song was overcome with the realisation that everything he truly cared about was where he was now. He felt the sudden fragility of his own family, and how utterly unbearable a loss would be.

'I'm afraid, too,' Song said. 'Everyone I love dies.'

'Don't talk that way.'

Song held her closer to him. 'Everyone I love.'

'Not me, Song. I'm here forever.'

'Promise me that.' Song breathed in Hannah, his lips against her black hair. She smelled like she did their first night. 'Frangipani?'

'Jasmine.'

Song took another breath. 'Jasmine.'

'You promise me, too,' Hannah said.

'I promise,' Song said. They held each other in the dark.

CHAPTER 32

Song was in his study reading when Hannah came in.

'Something's wrong with Little A,' she said. 'She's too choked up even to talk. Will you see her? She's in her room. I think she'd be too afraid not to answer you.'

Song heard muffled sobbing as he approached her room. He knocked and pushed open the door. Little A was lying face down on the bed.

'Little A, it's Song.'

Little A stopped crying instantly and lifted herself up. 'Yes, sir.'

'What's the matter? Can we help you?'

'No, sir. I'm sorry, sir. It's my little brother, Tots. He passed on.'

'Why didn't you tell us? Was he sick? Was there nothing we could have done?'

'It's my fault, sir. I told him he had to find work. He got a job at Diamond but he didn't like it. I made him stay on.'

'At Diamond?'

'The sugar plantation, sir. He'd been there for nearly a month. He said he hated the work but I wouldn't listen.' Little A's voice had started to shake. 'He told me he wanted to leave but I told 'im he had to learn how it is. Every job's hard, he couldn't just walk out. But he was only twelve. Too young, too small. I know that now.'

Song thought of Jinda. So young. So small. He imagined him bent forward, resting on his cutlass as if it was the only thing holding him up in the world.

'What happened?' Song asked.

'They said it was a fever,' Little A said. 'But I think it was the hard work, too. The cane can get heavy, that's what Tots told me. He said he was frightened there.' Little A sobbed. 'I feel like I killed him.'

Hannah had joined Song. 'You were only trying to be a good sister.'

Song was blunt. 'Where's his body?'

Little A let out another sob. 'They buried him already. At the plantation. Told me it was too hot and what with the fever others might catch it.'

'Who told you all of this?' Song asked.

Little A took a letter out of her pocket, unfolded it and handed it to Song. 'Signed by Mr Carmichael. The boss. Doesn't say anything about the grave but the boy who delivered it told me it's a real cemetery. Course it would have been nicer to have him here in town but Mr Carmichael writes we can come by.'

Song scanned the page and handed the letter to Hannah. He felt the cover of the book of history lifting, and a decision being made inside. He left the room without another word and went to his study. His breathing had quickened. He thought of Jesus, of Kiddo. He pulled out his shirt and reached behind to run his fingers over the skin of his back. He felt the ridges of scars: smooth soft stripes and a puckering at the edges. There was little sensation now. His back could feel nothing of his hands.

Song was waiting in his study. The hours were passing slowly. There was a tap on the shutter. Song went to it and levered it open. A squeak of wood on wood.

'I'm Booker,' the man said.

That was the right name. Bronco had informed Song that

Booker could do whatever was needed. Song didn't know if this was the same man who had gotten rid of Kiddo, and he didn't want to.

'There's a grave at Diamond,' Song said to him. 'It's new. The soil will be fresh. A young boy's buried there. About twelve years old. I need you to dig it up. Do it tonight. I want to know how he was killed. Look for any marks on him. Rebury him at St Saviour's.'

Booker returned in the early hours, as it was getting light. Song was still up; he heard the same tap on the shutter.

Song opened it. 'Yes?'

'The body's rotting but I could see the marks. Smashed up bad. Battered to death.'

Song drew a long breath. It was by no means the first time he had wanted someone dead. He thought back again to his time on the *Dartmouth*. Willing two people to die every night so he could head up the ladder with Li Bai in the morning. He had been a boy then, and unknowing, forgivable. But then there was Jesus; dead, knowingly killed. Two wrongs. Was that unforgivable? And Kiddo, too. Now, Mr Carmichael.

A few days later Father Collins received a letter from Mr Carmichael, which he showed to Song. Mr Carmichael was furious about the removal of Tots' body and his reburial in St Saviour's cemetery. He said the dead boy had been buried on private property. The act was theft, he said, and whoever had removed the body was also guilty of trespassing. In the last line, Mr Carmichael said he would not take it further if the vicar agreed to draw a line under this very unfortunate affair. Nobody should mention it again, he said.

'Don't reply,' Song said. 'All I've done is right a wrong.'

The last time Song had seen Mr Carmichael was at the service at

St Andrew's. He was standing between his wife and grown-up daughters. Song pushed the image out of his mind.

News of the accident spread quickly across town. Mr Carmichael had been found by the side of a road near the plantation with a broken neck and a blow to the head. His horse was whinnying nearby. The planter who first came upon the scene said Mr Carmichael must have been thrown. His body lay twisted on the ground.

Rumours had already started circulating. After church the following Sunday, it was all anybody could speak about.

'Dangerous business riding in the dark,' Mr Ting-Lee said. 'Always prefer to walk myself. Especially after a drink or two.'

'I did hear that the coroner noticed a strong smell of whisky on his breath,' Mrs Ting-Lee said. 'Not that he wrote that on the certificate.'

Father Collins had joined them. 'Whisky on his breath? So it was an accident?'

'Ooh, what are you suggesting, Father?' Mrs Ting-Lee asked. 'Murder?'

'The man had enemies, that's for sure,' Mr Ting-Lee said.

'Did he?' Mrs Ting-Lee asked. 'Like who?'

'Anyone who had ever worked at Diamond. Isn't that right, Song?'

Hannah shot him a glance.

'Men in business always have enemies,' Song said.

'Did you hear the wife had the horse shot?' Mrs Ting-Lee said. 'She and the girls are returning to England with the next boat.'

'Probably the best thing,' Father Collins said. 'Too many memories here.'

'Too many memories,' Song repeated.

Hannah looked at Song. Song knew she knew.

Song withdrew to his study. He was tired. Hannah had told the children to be especially quiet and the house felt still and lonely.

He heard a soft knock on the door. Hannah came in with the front of her skirt gathered together as a bowl. Inside the cover of cloth were Brazil nuts. She let them fall on to his desk.

'Something's wrong,' Hannah said.

'I'm fine.'

She shook her head. 'Can we not talk?'

She picked up a Brazil nut and cracked it in a vice. It splintered open. She handed a piece to Song. 'We can't be as bad as them.'

'As bad as them? That, Hannah, we are not.'

'Don't let them change us. I don't want you to change.'

'I'm not changing. This has always been me. I fight back.'

'There are so many ways to fight. This is not the way Father Holmes taught you.'

'I know.' Song thought back to his years with Father Holmes. He did fight back. He did speak out. But he didn't kill.

'What would he have done?' Hannah asked.

'I'm no saint. I've never pretended to be.'

'If you choose this path, where will it take us?'

Song felt like he was on that path already, a path that had already taken him to some dark places. Yet oddly, he didn't feel like a murderer or a cheat or a sinner. 'Sometimes wrong and right can be the same thing,' he said.

'It won't bring Tots back,' she said.

'It won't bring Jinda back either. But now no one else is going to die at Diamond.'

Hannah cracked open another nut. 'I don't want you to go forgetting who you are.'

'This is who I am.'

'This is not the Song I know.'

Song could see the pain on Hannah's face. He bent down to pick up the stray nut on the floor. 'I need to head back up to Bartica and check on things.'

Hannah nodded. 'I know.'

'It's already been a couple months.'

'I know how long it's been.'

Hannah leaned on Song's desk and their eyes met at eye level. He wanted to say sorry, but he wasn't sorry, and he stopped himself from telling a lie like that.

He reached for her hand; she let him take it and Song brought it to his lips.

CHAPTER 33

The first thing Song did when he arrived in Bartica was to visit Josie's. It had been a long time since the day he promised himself never to walk through their door again. But he wanted to make this last visit to see Maia to explain, not just disappear.

'Maia. I came to tell you I can't see you any more.'

'You're seeing me now, ain't you?'

'From now.'

'You don't want me any more?'

'I can't. That's all.'

'Have a baby with me then. One more time to have a baby together.'

'Maia, I can't see you. Let alone have a baby. What are you thinking?'

'I'm saying ain't it time I had a chil'?'

'If you want a child you should find yourself a man and start a family the proper way. You deserve no less.'

'You been with me 'bout all my life. Making sweet love to me.'

'I've been coming to you and leaving you, Maia. That's what I've been doing. I'm not proud of that. I'm sorry.'

'Aw, Song, don't be so hard on me.'

'That's how it's been.'

'It wouldn't be no different. Just that there'd be a baby.'

'I can't have a baby with you, Maia. I have a wife and family.'

'That's all right. I don't want nothing but a baby.'

'There are a dozen men who'd scoop you up. Make you a decent husband. Give your baby a good father.'

Maia pouted. 'I hate it when you talk so hard.'

Song put his hand on hers. 'I know what it's like to grow up without a father. You do, too. We're both too smart to embark on something like that.'

'You sure that's the truth?' Maia asked. 'You ain't going off me because I'm getting older?'

'No, Maia.'

'Will you make love to me one more time?'

'No, Maia, I can't.' Song leaned over to put an envelope of money in her pocket. Blood money, or something like that, he thought. It didn't feel good.

'You wanna know something?' she said.

Song could feel the air thicken. It suddenly felt hotter in the room. 'I don't think so, no.'

'You do.'

Song stood at the door. He was filled with dread. 'I don't.'

'Vivi,' she said.

He had always liked Maia's little brother. Another good kid having to grow up in the surrounds of a drunken bar. He remembered what Vivi said to Maia on the day they finished school, that he believed her when she said she was going to see the world.

'What about Vivi?' Song asked.

'Do you know who his father was?'

Song shook his head. He knew something was coming that would take him by the throat, but he had not a shred of an idea what it could be. 'I think I don't want to know.'

'Father Holmes.'

Song could hardly breathe. He did not know if his face showed the shock he felt. He tried to picture the boy. He was probably about sixteen years old now. A mixed child, no doubt, but his father could have been any one of a hundred men.

Song's voice was trembling. 'Is that really true? I don't want you to lie to me to hurt me.'

'I ain't lying.'

'I don't want to hear about made-up nonsense Bartica gossip.'

'Ain't that neither. Mama says I was never to tell you but I think it's high time. Guess you and I both discovering not everyone is like they seem.'

'You are hurting me, Maia.'

'So? I'm hurting, too.'

'Your mama was right. There are some things we wish we never knew.'

Song turned and walked out of Josie's. The sun seemed sharper than usual. Everything was different. Father Holmes was not the person he thought he knew. A man first, a vicar second. But was that so terrible? Song had never cared about him being a vicar. A father, yes, but not a vicar. Had he let him down as a father because Song had a brother he didn't know about?

He was confused, devastated, obsessed. Bartica, the town where he grew up, that he thought he knew so well, had changed. Song lifted the palm of his hand against the sunlight, as if he was protecting himself from life falling around him. He remembered seeing Josie and Father Holmes outside the bar. Laughing together. Father Holmes not noticing him waving at him. It could be true. He remembered the strength of Josie's conviction that Father Holmes was coming back. And how she had looked after Song when he fell apart after Father Holmes' death. It was true; Maia hadn't lied.

He made his way to the river. It felt like the last time he would take this road. The river was high. It was good to be flanked by the folds of dark forest. The paddles dipped into the soft water. There was a swish of lapwings skimming the water. A bellbird's call rang out. Song felt consoled, more than he could be anywhere else. How far he had come, that little boy standing on the dockside of Guangzhou to the man who'd owned swathes of land on the banks of the great rivers of Guiana amid towering forests and the cries and screams of the world's most beautiful birds. He had found sugar, then gold and diamonds, just like he had hoped.

Inside, Song felt an ache for the memory that this journey would become. He knew in his heart that this was his last trip upriver.

He thought back to his first trip with Father Holmes, the man who he believed had given him everything. He had taken him in when he was a plantation boy. Standing up to everyone to do it. An unconventional man. Even more, an unconventional vicar – who had never wanted to enter the church. But he'd lived out its values of compassion, of generosity, more than anyone he'd known. Father Holmes had taken Song in. Song must now take in Vivi.

When Song reached the mine, the scar in the earth had doubled in size again. He picked up fifteen pounds of gold and two handfuls' worth of diamonds. It was heavy. Too much can weigh a man down, that's what Chi had taught him. He was beginning to believe that now.

He no longer felt the tussle: the desire to stay and give into the gold fever pitted against the compulsion to return. He only wanted to be home. He knew his responsibilities now more than ever. A growing family. Vivi, too. He couldn't take a risk that might leave any of them abandoned. Like Vivi had been at Josie's, not that Song could judge Father Holmes for that. After all, Song was coming to the realisation that he and Father Holmes had followed similar lines of behaviour. Josie. Maia. Father Holmes was a better man because he had probably loved Josie.

Song turned his boat around. There would be no further need for him to return to Omaia.

CHAPTER 34

'You're back so soon,' Hannah said, as Song came through the door.

'You're not disappointed, I hope?'

She came to him. 'I wish you always came back so soon.'

'How are you? How are the children?'

'The children? Well, happy, busy. They'll be home soon from school. You can ask them yourself.'

'Before they come back I want to ask you something. Hannah, can I bring Vivi here to live with us?'

'Josie's Vivi?'

'Yes.'

'For school?'

'For school,' he hesitated, 'but not only.'

Hannah was flustered. 'I think you need to explain.'

He understood Hannah would only know him as Josie's father-less son and the younger brother of Maia. He had to tell her the truth.

'I can barely say it out loud. I don't want to believe it, but it's true. Vivi is the son of Father Holmes.'

Hannah gasped. 'How do you know?'

Song didn't want to say. Even now, he couldn't be straight. 'I heard when I was in Bartica. I've been turning it over ever since. There are days it makes sense; I remember things and it all falls into place. Then there are times I shake my head; it cannot be true. But

421

I only have to picture him and I know. I see him and I see Father Holmes.'

'Father Holmes,' Hannah said wistfully. 'If it's true of him . . .' Her voice wandered off.

Song knew it was his chance to confess and he wanted to, but he didn't have the courage. He was too afraid of losing Hannah, of losing everything that mattered. 'I wish it wasn't so,' was all he could say.

'I wish you hadn't told me.'

'I'm sorry. I didn't want to, but I want Vivi to come here. Father Holmes gave me everything. He made me who I am today. I have to give Vivi the same.'

'If you need to do this . . .'

'You don't sound happy.'

Hannah's voice was quiet, almost a whisper. 'You need to know your own children.'

Her words cut. 'Don't I know them?'

'Perhaps you don't know how to know them. You didn't have a father for very long. Perhaps that's why. Give them time, Song. They are both so wonderful and they're growing up so fast. You're missing out. That's all I can say.'

Song felt churned up by Hannah's truths. 'You know I was just trying to make sure we had enough. So we were never short. That's what I wanted to do. That's why I've always gone away.'

'I know.'

'I know what it's like not to have enough. To feel the burning in your stomach.'

'I know, too.'

'I don't want my children ever to feel that.'

'They won't, Song. Not ever.'

'You never know what will happen tomorrow.'

'That's also why you need to get to know your children.' Hannah paused. 'And we're having a third.'

Song reached out to her. 'You always surprise me.' He held her face in between his hands. 'I love you, Hannah. I think I can't love you any more than I do and then you turn to face me and I love you even more.'

Song called Phillip and Florence into his study. They hung about the door.

'Aren't you coming in?' Song asked.

The pair moved into his room but stayed near the door. Song looked at them both and thought how he didn't fully recognise them. Phillip had grown; he had a faraway look in his eyes. Flo also looked taller, leaner, than he remembered. Hannah was right. They were growing up so fast.

'How are you both?' Song asked. 'How's school?'

'Are we in trouble?' Flo asked.

'What makes you say that?' Song asked.

'Why are we here?'

Song was choked. 'I want to see you.'

'So we haven't done anything wrong?'

'No.' Song was lost for words.

There was an awkward pause.

'How was upriver?' Flo asked.

Song was relieved at the question. 'Good. A shorter trip than I expected. It's good to be home. It's good to see you both.'

The children stared back at him.

'When I was a little boy, Father Holmes used to ask me to come to his study and we'd explore the room together.'

'How so?' Flo asked.

Song got up and went to a bookshelf. 'These are the same books

423

that were on his bookshelves,' he said, running their fingers up and down the leather spines like he used to with Father Holmes. 'We read hundreds of books together. I'd like to read more with you two, if you'd like that.'

'When?' Phillip asked.

'When?' Song repeated. 'I'll be in Georgetown more now. We'll have time. We'll find time.'

'We've been reading the books anyway,' Flo said. 'We've read lots of them already.'

'I'm glad,' Song said, but he wasn't. It made him feel all the more like he had been absent. That he had let them down.

'I like the world atlas,' Phillip said. 'Have you read it? It's an account of every country.' He pulled it out from the shelf and started flicking through the pages. 'The number of horses in Australia, the income from train tickets in India, the number of languages spoken in Sudan.'

'I love that book, and I loathe it,' Song said. 'It's all about how much each colony is worth.' Song walked over to the large yellowed globe. 'Come over here. This is how the world really looks. I travelled from this point to Guiana,' he said, pointing out China, then turning the globe on its axis, following the route with his finger. It looked far, even on a miniaturised sphere this size.

'It's a long way,' Flo said. 'Why did you leave?'

'If I hadn't, you wouldn't be here now.'

'You were so young.'

'Much younger than you are now, yes.'

Flo shook her head. 'You left your family, Papa.'

'It was a different, difficult time.'

'You're always leaving,' Flo said.

'Don't say that,' Phillip said to his sister.

How different they were, Song thought. Phillip, the diplomat, the daydreamer. He stared at the clouds, at the rain, at the birds: the dark silhouettes of macaws flapping overhead in an open sky; bright shimmering tanagers; hummingbirds hovering at the head of a stamen. The way Song himself used to. Phillip could be so quiet, you might not even notice him. He remembered that both Amalia and Father Holmes used to say the same thing about him.

Florence was impossible to overlook. Her voice rang out as she moved from one room of the house to another. She was whip-smart, like her grandmother. After Song taught her to play dominoes she could soon beat him. Song watched her eyes, planning every move, one step ahead, just like people accused him of being. There was something about the way she thought things through that reminded Song of himself.

Hannah had been right. There was so much he didn't know about these children, so much he wanted to understand about them, so much he wanted to share.

Bartica seemed older on his next trip. The houses seemed to have wilted in the heat. No one had bothered to buy a lick of paint to smarten up their street. In fact, nobody seemed to be around. Dogs moseyed up and down the streets. Perhaps the town did need a DC and a PC after all.

His friends had aged. Big Bronco seemed stooped. Yan looked tired. Even Jingy was moving more slowly.

'You making fewer and fewer visits to us in this old town,' Jingy said. 'But it's always good to see you. Father Holmes would have been so proud, you know that.'

'Maybe. I don't know what he'd have been proud of. I don't suppose Omaia would have much interested him except that it was upriver. Perhaps the Lucky Sports Club or the church, open to all. Or if I was a good father, maybe he'd like that most of all.'

'You've always been too hard on yourself. Don't suppose Father Holmes was proud of everything he did neither. You taking in Vivi, that's what he'd have been most touched by.'

Song looked up sharply. His and Jingy's eyes met knowingly.

Song went on to see Old Man Kuros, who was wracked with pain.

'Bones giving up,' he said. 'Eyes gave up and now bones giving up.'

'Can they not do anything to ease the pain?' Song asked. 'I have a good doctor in Georgetown.'

The old man grimaced as he shifted in his seat. 'I'm not going all the way to Georgetown to die there instead of here.'

'Long way to go to die, it's true. So, how's business?'

'Slow. No one trusts Farad, least of all me. That boy's more crooked than a mata-mata and lazier than a sloth. I sometimes wish I'd sold the shop instead of handing it over to him. That boy stole his mother from me and then been stealing from me ever since.'

'He's all you have.'

'Is that why you came? To lecture me about what's important and what's not?'

Song shook his head. 'I'm the last person to know that. Or perhaps I'm just finding out.'

'Are you?'

'Maybe. Sometimes I wonder what I'm doing all this for. I have more than I need. So is it greed? Promises to dead friends? To try to live a life that is a story worth telling.'

'Ah, the dead. We do more for the dead than the living.'

'True enough. I've spent more of my life upriver than I have with my family.'

'You giving yourself a hard time, boy.'

'Guess I'm learning late what's important.'

'Not too late.'

'True. I thank Hannah for telling me how it is.'

'You got away with it then. Just. Hannah saved you.'

Song looked at his blind crippled friend and thought how much this old man could see.

As he made his way to Josie's, someone called out his name from behind.

Song turned around. It was Edward Hoare. He was pointing towards his office and Song walked back to join him.

'Let's go inside,' Edward said. He locked the door behind them.

He looked at Song. 'You didn't hear this from me.'

Song nodded. 'Go on.'

'The governor is moving in on Omaia. It's not about tax loopholes or working conditions. He can't get you on that. He's claiming back your land.'

'The land? How do you know?'

'Says it was undersold by a DC who took backhanders.'

'William Wright?'

'He's willing to drag down a British civil servant to do this. He's got all the DC records in Georgetown already. Wouldn't be hard to add in something. He's bent on you going down.'

'We'll be all right.'

'Don't be so sure, Song. He's asked me for records of all your declarations. Right back to the beginning. Even to Jesus. He thinks he's finally found a way.'

'It's okay, Edward. I'm giving Omaia to the Silent Temple.'

'Well, I'll be blown,' Edward said. 'Am I the last to know?'

'You're probably the first.'

'Would I like to be there when he finds out? He is going to be

427

one angry man. And there I was thinking he's one step ahead of you.'

One step ahead. He now needed to be one step ahead again. Father Holmes. Josie. Vivi. He had to do the right thing.

Vivi was waiting for Song on the doorstep of the bar, clean and pressed, as if he was turned out for church. He clutched a new leather case in his hand.

'Mama's not here,' he said. 'She didn't want to say goodbye. She said she sends her regards.'

'It's not a goodbye,' Song said.

'I told her I'd be back often and regular. Told her I'd pull them all out of here as soon as I could.'

'That's a good plan.'

'I'm going to. I promised them.'

Song had heard those words before.

Maia's voice interrupted them. 'Hey, Song.'

He looked up to see her framed at the window. She was smoking a cigarette and her hair was draped about her face. Song could see her bare shoulders beneath her locks.

'You taking Vivi? All the best men are leaving town today.'

Song's voice was tender. 'Hello, Maia. How are you?'

'Better with both of you around. Not so good once you're gone.'

'Vivi'll be back and forth. You'll see him soon enough.'

'And you?'

Song hesitated. 'I'll be in and out.'

'Don't let the wind blow you around too much,' she said. 'You're your own man, Song Holmes, more than any other I know.'

Song could not help but be held by Maia's gaze longer than

he wished. He turned and started heading in the direction of the dock.

Vivi tried to keep up. He called back to his sister. 'See you, Maia. You send word if there's anything you need.'

Song could hear the smoke held in the back of Maia's mouth as she replied. 'You take care, baby. And you take care too, Song Holmes. Neither of you go forgettin' us here.'

Song raised his hand but did not look back. As Vivi caught up with him, Song felt a wave of relief that he was finally taking the boy away.

'You might miss home at first, Vivi, but you'll get to like Georgetown.'

'Yes, sir.'

Song recalled those were the first words Hai had taught him on the ship. 'You don't need to call me sir.'

Vivi nodded. 'What should I call you?'

'Call me Song.'

'I'll do that, sir, Song.'

'Tell me, Vivi, the things you like to do the most in this world? Fishing? Studying? Cricket? Being on the river? I want to know what makes you happiest.'

'Stories,' Vivi said. 'I like stories.'

Song thought about Jinda's stories, how he could taste them. And Hai's stories: how they gave him strength to travel right around the world.

'I like stories, too. From your head or from books?'

Vivi hesitated. 'I don't get to read much. I like telling stories. I listen to the customers at the bar and mix up their stories to make new ones. Like rum and lime mixed up and poured on sharp ice.'

Song smiled. 'We have a long journey ahead of us. How about a story on the way?'

Vivi looked flustered but pleased. 'About anything in particular?'

'You choose. It can be as blue as Josie's or as clean as a sermon.'

Song had not realised how quickly Vivi had grown up in the last year or two. He was tall and lanky, like Father Holmes. He even stooped in the same way to try to conceal his height. If Song only saw his silhouette out of the corner of his eye, he swore it could have been Father Holmes by his side.

Song recalled the journey – a reversal of the one he was doing now with Vivi – when he and Father Holmes left Georgetown together and struck out to take up the new posting in the interior. He felt a blow of sadness.

Vivi interrupted his thoughts. 'Do you know about the woman with red eyes?'

'I'd like to know more about her.'

'The patron of pork-knockers,' Vivi continued. 'She lives in the river. You will have seen her at night and thought, ah, a caiman. A flash of red eyes disappearing beneath the inky water. But you are wrong, my friend, for that is the woman with red eyes.

'You need not be afraid at night. She cannot do you harm in the darkness. But if you see her in the day,' Vivi paused and lowered his voice, 'then you are doomed. She will dazzle you with the golden jewellery draped about her naked body; chains looped around her waist; rings on every finger; strands of charms on her ankles; earrings so heavy they sit upon her shoulders.

'Blinded, a pork-knocker cannot resist. He will slip into the river and let her carry him downstream, cool water running over his skin. Enthralled, he gives in completely. She releases the gold from his pockets and pouches, snipping with golden scissors any nuggets sewn into the seams of a shirt.'

Song caught himself holding his breath. He thought about Jesus' body being carried down the river, his pockets empty.

'So I warn you. Remember this story on the day you strike gold.' Vivi was almost whispering now. 'Because the woman with red eyes will be already searching for you. If she finds you, your luck is over, my friend. You will give her everything you have found, the woman with red eyes.'

'Phew,' Song said. 'That's some storytelling.' He promised himself to put Father Holmes' books in Vivi's hands. Perhaps Vivi would read or tell his own stories to Phillip and Flo. He felt a deep inconsolable regret Father Holmes would never see that. Their children together. And as he pictured the three of them, he thought how unimaginable it was. Stirring too, knowing there was something of Father Holmes left in the world – in Vivi, and imprinted in himself.

'Did you like it?' Vivi asked.

'Like it?' Song asked, thrust back in the moment. 'Your story? I hated it. Won't want to go upriver again after that.'

Vivi laughed.

He thought how much Vivi brimmed with the traits of his parents. The easy laugh of Father Holmes. His optimism. His warmth. Here was a part of Father Holmes right here, and Song felt choked. But there was also Vivi's mother in the mix, he could see that strongly too. Her forthrightness. And a vulnerability beneath the grit. Yet Vivi was also very much his own character. Shaped in the confines of Josie's lightless bar, overhearing the stories of customers drunk and desperate. A mixed-up kid caught in limbo between boy and man. Song wanted life to be better for him now. A delayed childhood. A delayed education. When he was Vivi's age, he had read all the books in Father Holmes' study. Now it was Vivi's turn to have a chance at life, and Song would make sure he helped him.

*

As they approached Georgetown, Vivi confided in Song. 'I've never been anywhere but Bartica, you know. Never been to George-town.

'I guessed,' Song said. 'You'll discover it for yourself. Nothing to be afraid of. Jingy would say "folks is folks".'

'I'm not afraid. I've been dreaming of leaving Bartica all my life.'

'I'm glad I could bring you here, Vivi. I wish I could have earlier.'

Song watched Vivi taking it all in as they rolled into town.

'We're going to make a stop before we head home.' Song had pulled up in front of Ebenezer's.

Vivi got up as if to join him.

'Wait here; I won't be long,' Song said. Vivi looked disap-pointed. Song wondered why he didn't invite him in, as if he was ashamed of what he was doing. He headed up to Ebenezer's room and handed over the weight of the satchel. The old man howled. 'You're going to kill me.'

'Enjoy it,' Song said. 'This is the end for me, Ebenezer. It's time.'

'Time for?'

'I've passed on the mine.'

Ebenezer looked horrified. 'Passed it on? What in heavens does that mean?'

'To the foundation. It doesn't cut you out. But it cuts me out.'

Ebenezer suddenly looked older. 'This keeps me going, remem-ber that. You're killing me in other ways now.'

'Nothing's going to change. You'll just be dealing with the foun-dation, not me.'

Ebenezer pulled himself out of his chair and he walked over to the painting of the goatherd on his wall. 'You know this paint-ing?'

'I do. A lesson against greed.'

432

'Is that what this is all about? You better than the rest of us, Song Holmes?'

'My partner once told me how too much gold can weigh a man down. I need to be home now. I need to be free of it.'

Vivi was waiting outside. He smiled when he saw Song reappear.

'I'm all done,' Song said, with greater meaning than Vivi would have understood. 'We're going home. You ready?'

Vivi nodded.

'It's not far. We're just down here.' Song pointed ahead of them.

Vivi looked at the big house. 'Why do you ever come to Bartica when you have this? Why do you ever go upriver?'

'I have this *because* I go upriver.'

'I've only seen such a house in my head, in my stories.' Vivi read the sign on the gate. 'Sugar House.'

'Hannah named it. That's how I started, more or less. I worked on a sugar cane plantation when I first came to Guiana. That's a long time ago.'

Speaking of Hannah made Song long for her even more. He felt anew, freed. He moved swiftly towards the front door, wanting urgently to tell Hannah about his decision. To tell her everything – like when he first met her. But she was out.

Instead Flo was standing in the hallway. He went to her and cupped her cheek in his hand. 'You're looking beautiful and determined. How are you, Flo?'

'Who's this?'

'This is Vivi. He's the son . . . of a friend of mine,' Song stumbled as he spoke. 'He's going to be staying with us. I'm hoping to get him into Queen's College.'

'Hello,' Flo said. 'How old are you?'

'Nineteen.'

'I'm thirteen. And Phillip's nearly fifteen. But I'm smarter than him.'

Song thought how much older Flo came across.

'Let's be nice, Flo. Vivi's new to town. I remember when I was new to Georgetown, it was terrifying.'

'I'll look after him,' she said.

'Thank you. Now where's Mama?'

'Out.'

'Where's Phillip?'

'Out.'

'Where are they?'

'I don't know where Mama is. Phillip's out looking at birds.' She turned to Vivi. 'Phillip spends a lot of his time looking at birds. That's his thing. What's your thing?'

'Stories.'

'That's good.'

'How about you?' Vivi asked her back,

'I don't have one thing. I'm interested in masses of things.'

'Tell Little A that Vivi is here, Flo,' Song said. 'Then, Vivi, you can tell Flo some of your stories.'

Song was just heading to his study when the front door opened and Hannah walked in.

'You're back,' he said. He fell into her arms and buried himself in her smell. 'I missed you. Over and over.'

Hannah held him, then whispered softly. 'Song, my love. Is everything all right?'

'I missed you, that's all.'

'That's all?'

'Yes. It felt longer.'

'It wasn't. It was shorter.'

'Time feels more marked. Perhaps that's what happens as we get older.'

'How was the trip?'

'I've brought back a lot of gold. More than we need. Diamonds, too. For you. I'll have Mr Hing make you something.'

'More than we need?'

'I never thought I'd say that either.'

'How are the men?'

'As loyal as an old dog.'

'And Bartica?'

'No different. Are you resting? Is it madness to ask?'

'This baby's taking it out of me but I'm tired of resting. Tell me what's going on out there. Tell me everything.'

'I'll tell you this, Hannah. I've told you already. I think we have more than we need. I'm ready to pass on Omaia.'

Song saw a glimmer of a smile in Hannah's face. 'Are you pleased?' he asked.

'If you are.'

'We have enough. Enough for us. Enough for the children. Enough for the children's children. It's the right time.' Song paused. 'Or maybe I'm late. I should have done it years ago. Should I?'

'Maybe.'

Song stroked away the strands of loose hair from his wife's face. 'I've been away a lot. If not in body, in my head. I miss you. I'm missing the children. I know that now.'

Song saw Hannah was holding back the tears. Her eyes were wet. She looked more beautiful than ever.

'I'm sorry.'

'Don't be sorry, Song. You were providing for your family, I know that.'

'It was getting all muddled up though. I wonder why I was still doing what I've been doing. Can I blame gold fever?'

Hannah shook her head. 'Ambition, I think.'

'You're kind to me, Hannah. Kinder than I deserve. I fear I've disappointed you over the years.'

Hannah shook her head. A tear rolled down her cheek. 'You haven't.'

'I haven't always been a good husband, a good father, a good man.'

'There are always struggles. I knew what I was taking on, Song.'

She had forgiven him. He had needed that. More than he realised. He pulled her close. 'Who would I be without you, Hannah?'

CHAPTER 35

The next day Song called Tobias Shelf into his office.

'I want to bequeath Omaia to the Silent Temple Foundation,' he told the young accountant. 'I need you to do whatever you need to do to make it happen. The foundation can manage the company and the profits but I want there to be a direct feed from the mine to the sports club. And I want the structure there to be unchangeable. That anyone can join the club. Anyone. For always.'

'You're giving up the mine?'

'We need all the numbers and paperwork in perfect order. Not a flaw.'

Life at Sugar House slowed down. Dr Patel had requested bed rest for Hannah. Jon and Rose stopped by from time to time; Rose was pleasant company for Hannah, always ready to regale her with funny little life sketches of Georgetown. There was Mr House, who sometimes showed up unannounced. Mr Hing regularly came for dinner on Sundays, although Hannah didn't always stay up. 'The world gets smaller as you get older,' Edward Hoare used to say. It was true.

Vivi had settled in, although Song noticed how he still behaved like a guest sometimes, asking permission to enter a room or to choose a book to read. He had brought something to their home that had been diminishing, a greater sense of appreciation, of gratitude. Phillip and Flo had taken to him, begging Vivi to tell them stories from his head or to read passages from their favourite books with all the drama of a bawdy tale told in a dark bar.

Beyond family and their close group of friends, Song shunned Georgetown life, preferring to spend his days at home. He was no longer interested in receiving or accepting invitations. He was done with those battles.

One afternoon Song watched Phillip and Vivi lying on the lawn from the bedroom window. Hannah was resting. The boys weren't aware he was there and Song was reminded of the many times he'd sit in the hallway listening into Father Holmes' conversations on the terrace with Edward Hoare and Tom Jameson.

His thoughts were interrupted as he saw Flo walking down the path.

'Where've you been?' Phillip said to his sister.

'Is that all anyone asks me?' Flo let herself go limp and fall to the ground. She lay back, staring up at the sky. 'Where've you been? Where've you been? Can I not do a thing without being asked where I've been?'

Song smiled to himself. He hoped always to remember this scene. It looked like a painting, the three of them on the grass as they were. A pure uncomplicated existence. Lives yet unsullied. Fresh, full of hope and wonder.

'Stop hassling your sister,' Vivi said to Phillip. 'She can come and go as she likes.'

Phillip pressed her. 'Were you with Ash?'

Ash? Song hadn't heard that name. He wanted to know more.

'And what if I was?'

'You think we don't know? We know, don't we Viv?'

'What do you know?'

'He's sweet on you. You're sweet on him.'

Song was startled. Was his daughter already old enough for this? And who was this boy?

'What makes you think that?' Flo asked.

'Phillip's right. You two aren't so subtle,' Vivi added.

'Mrs Burford says you're sinning,' Phillip said.

Flo sat up straight. 'Mrs goddamn Burford. Like she knows anything about sinning.'

Song watched on. He could hear how his children were challenging the world now, eager to be part of it, to explore beyond the range of their home. He remembered that eagerness, that curiosity, but was also glad they'd had more years than he had sheltered from the hardship and the horrors, with only books to speak to them about the realities of life.

He watched Flo let herself lie back on the grass again. 'It's my life,' she said. 'I can do what I like with it.'

'And if Papa finds out?' Phillip asked.

'Finds out what?'

'Finds out you're seeing him.'

'Papa always tells us that we shouldn't pay attention to gossip. He doesn't care what others say. And nor should we.'

She knew something, Flo did. Song was touched that his daughter had suggested she was learning lessons from him. It was Jingy who used to say a town's no good if it's built on gossip and half-truths.

Vivi whistled. 'But he'd 'bout have a heart attack if he knew you were sweet on the governor's son.'

Song was taken aback. Ashford Bolton. The son of the governor. Could he be so different from his father? Perhaps this was Song's test. It sounded more like literature than real life. The children of sworn enemies finding each other.

'I am not sweet on him,' Flo said.

'Imagine if you married him . . .'

'Married? Suddenly I'm getting married, am I? Never. You watch me. I'm going to cut my hair, smoke cigarettes and play tennis.'

Vivi laughed again. 'Marrying Ashford Bolton might still be the more shocking option.'

'Ash is nothing like his father. He's like us. He hates everything we hate. He wants to change Guiana, too. Jeff Jeston and their lot.'

Phillip's attention had been caught by a yellow-breasted bird but he repeated their schoolmate's name. 'Jeff Jeston?'

'Don't you know anything? They control the sugar, the rice, the logging. And they're taking us back to the days of slavery. People have to work for them but they are treated no better than animals.' Flo saw she had lost her brother's attention. 'Are you listening to me?'

Song looked at this fierce young woman. His daughter.

'I'm listening,' Vivi said. 'Sounds like someone needs to take them on.'

'I think I've seen a Guianan trogon,' Phillip said.

He could see Flo was exasperated with her brother. 'There is abuse going on all around us and what do you have to say? That you've seen a bird.'

And here was his son, in wonder at birds.

Phillip was crouching down looking up at the bird in the branches. It let out a few small whoops in close succession. 'It is. It's a Guianan trogon.'

Flo rolled her eyes. 'And so the world keeps turning. What are you going to do? Look at birds all your life?'

'Worse things that that,' Vivi interrupted.

Flo picked up a book on the ground. 'What is this?'

'Phillip found it in Song's study,' Vivi said.

'Birds of the Coastal Regions, British Guiana, Volume I, Part I,' Flo read out loud. She opened the first page.

'Whose book is it?'

'Papa's, of course,' Phillip said.

'It isn't his handwriting.'

'I think it must be Father Holmes'. Later in the book I think it's Papa's. I think they're Uncle Jon's drawings.'

Flo flicked through to the end of the book. 'You're right. The writing looks like father's, I think, but also that of a child.'

'And it's only part one of volume one,' Phillip said. 'Why did he never show us?'

Song was struck by their interest. Had he never shown them? He hadn't even realised he hadn't shown them.

'Look at the letter about halfway through,' Phillip added.

Flo leafed through the pages swiftly. She slid out a loose leaf of paper, picking out some of the written words. 'Master Song Holmes, Esquire. Parish of Bartica. How funny that sounds. A whiskered white-headed song warbler. That's one of Uncle Jon's pictures, isn't it?'

'The one in the dining-room.'

'A song warbler,' Flo continued. 'It's named after him.'

'I want to go there,' Phillip said.

'Where?'

'To London. To the Royal Ornithological Society. But it would break Papa's heart.'

'No, it wouldn't,' Vivi said. 'You must. You have to continue what Song started. It's important.'

'It's true, Phillip,' Flo added. 'I'll put Papa's heart back together again after you leave. You have to go to The Royal Ornithological Society. It's at the heart of everything that you love. And everything Papa loved.'

Song looked at the three of them supporting each other and wondered about his own sisters and brothers. Is that how it would have been? In another life.

'And the journey?' Phillip asked. 'What about the boat?'

'Papa is unreasonable about boats. After all he goes on a riverboat all the time. You can't allow a boat ride to halt your dreams.'

Song felt a welling of pride; he was close to tears.

'I guess I could set up a chapter of the Society here.'

'The Society is in London, not in Georgetown,' Vivi said.

'It's halfway around the world.'

'It doesn't matter how far it is,' Flo said. 'Now that we know about it, you have to go.'

Phillip smiled. 'Are you sure you're not looking for me to take the heat off you?'

'I'm serious. You have to do this. We have to live out our lives.'

The following week, Vivi had gone to see his family in Bartica. He'd become a treasured member of the Holmes household, and after a few weeks without him around, and all his sharp observations and seductive stories, everyone was missing him.

'We've grown used to him,' Hannah said. 'He's a special young man. He brings humility to this house of ours.'

'Humility?' Flo scoffed. 'It's stories that he brings, Mama. Stories that make the hairs on my neck stand on end. Stories that make me weep. Stories that make me whoop with joy.'

Hannah smiled at her daughter. 'Sometimes it's hard to remember life before a child arrives in a home.'

'When do you think he will be back, Papa?' Phillip asked.

'He'll be back soon. But remember there are people in Bartica who miss him very much when he's here.' Song hated to think of him at Josie's. Among the smoke. Among the fumes of liquor. He

442

imagined the strained conversations with his mother, with his sisters. Vivi full of hope; them depleted.

It was another week before Vivi finally returned. Song could smell Josie's on him as he walked through the door. Vivi looked crushed.

'They wouldn't come back with me,' he said, 'I promised I'd make them a home in Georgetown, the loveliest thing they could ever imagine.'

Song had known they would never have come. Not Josie. Not Maia. None of them. 'Bartica is all they know, Vivi. Don't take it personally.'

'It was all I knew, too. But I left.'

'There is much more for you here than for them. It's easier for a young man, you know that.'

'But what are they going to do? Stay there all their lives?'

Song sighed. 'I know. I know how you feel.'

'It was so hard to see them there. I didn't know myself what a place it was when I lived there. It's terrible. The darkness. The stale liquor.'

As Vivi described it, Song could smell the bar. 'I know. I wish they would leave, too.'

'I could never go back. I wish I could say I'll go back and be there for them and make something of a life in Bartica. But I can't.'

'I didn't go back either.'

Vivi was unconsoled. 'It's much further to China.'

'I wouldn't have gone back if it had been close.' Perhaps for the first time, Song realised that was true. 'Maybe the distance gave me an excuse. Looking back now, I know I would never have wanted that life.'

Vivi sighed. 'I'm grateful for you bringing me here. But I feel like I've abandoned my family.'

Song thought how abandoned Vivi had been for so many years.

'A mother once told me, "mothers want what's best for their children, not what's best for them,"' Song said. 'It's cruel but it's true. Let me tell you this. Your mother is about to be very proud. While you've been away, you were awarded a place at Queen's College.' Song picked up the fountain pen on his desk, the gift of Father Holmes. 'I want you to have this.'

Vivi's expression was how Song had imagined his might have been all those years ago when he received the same pen.

'It's all down to your fiery imagination and your storytelling skills,' Song said. 'It's time you wrote down some of those stories.'

It was late when Flo came home that night. Song was still waiting up when he heard her padding through the hallway. He called her into his study.

Flo saw he was reading. 'What's the book?'

Song looked at his daughter's bright eyes, even more dazzling in the sweat of the night with her skin shining like molasses.

'You're asking me what's the book?' Song echoed quietly. 'I was going to ask you, Flo, what's the time?'

Flo glanced up at the wall clock. 'Sorry. I'm late. What are you reading?'

'*Robinson Crusoe*. It captivated me when I was a boy. But it reads differently now. A desert island seems like a welcome uncomplicated life. With a friend, too.'

Song was aware how Flo had cleverly distracted him. 'So tell me about your evening?'

Flo was studying one of Jon's framed drawings. It was a hoatzin. 'Have you really seen this one?'

'Many times. Come and sit down, Flo. Do you want to tell me something?'

'I'm tired, Papa.'

'Too tired to sit with your papa?'

Flo threw herself into the armchair. 'No, not too tired. I'm glad you sold the mine.'

She had startled Song. 'Are you?'

Flo nodded. 'But don't you miss the river? Mama says the Essequibo runs in your blood.'

Song shook his head. 'I don't miss it at all.' That was a lie.

'Tell me more about *Robinson Crusoe*,' she said. 'And I'll tell you about Phillip. He found your bird book. Why didn't you show it to us?'

'I don't know. Maybe it makes me too sad.'

'Phillip loves his birds. That's all he does. Looks at birds. Records birds. Draws birds. Badly. Not like Uncle Jon.'

'We can't all be good at everything. Except you, perhaps.'

'Phillip's going to ask you if he can go to London. Will you try to stop him?'

'I don't think you should be telling me this.'

'I won't then.' Flo was unravelling her tied-up hair and then picking off tiny strands to plait. Song looked at the fixed countenance of his daughter. She was captivatingly frank, like her mother. Bold, too, he hoped, like him.

'What is it *you* want to do?' Song asked.

'You know what I'm going to do? I'm going to put the Jestons out of business.' She looked up at her father with her strong dark eyes. 'After that, I'll buy racehorses and play tennis every day.'

Song wondered how the personalities of his children could be so mismatched with the roles society would try to foist upon them. He wanted Florence to live an unhindered life but knew in his heart how hard that would be. 'I'll look forward to watching that, Flo.'

She got up to leave. As she walked out of the door, she turned around and said: 'I love you, Papa.'

Flo's words started Song. His heart was full of love. But he also realised his daughter had completely outsmarted him to avoid the subject he had wanted to address. It seemed there was nothing she couldn't do.

The following night, Song was writing in his study. When he looked up, Phillip was standing in front of his desk. 'You moved so quietly, I didn't even hear you.'

Phillip looked lonely there in the big space of Song's study. 'I know this will be hard for you, Father,' he said, 'but after I graduate I want to go to England.'

Song sighed. 'Will you sit down, Phillip?'

His son shook his head. 'I don't want to talk about this too long. I can't ask you, Father. I can only tell you. It was your other dream. The one you didn't live. A life of birds.'

Phillip wasn't to know, after seeing the books and illustrations around his study, that it had never been a dream of Song's. Song could never have indulged himself in that life. But he realised how hard that might be to understand if you'd always had a full belly. His son had never been hungry and Song was glad of that.

'Choose something you enjoy, that is what you told us,' Phillip continued. 'Birds is what I enjoy. What else did you say? If you work for someone else choose a profession where you are rewarded on the basis of seniority so you leave nothing open to the prejudices of individuals. But my rewards will come every day I look up into the trees. You of all people must be able to understand that. Let me go to London, Father. Let me secure the qualifications I need to earn the respect of my peers. Then I will come home.'

Song caught himself gripping the edge of his desk. He looked down and saw his knuckles white. He shut out any noise in his head urging him to deny his son this. But he was too choked to look Phillip in the eye.

Song nodded. 'Go and find some life,' he said. That was the line Song's own mother had said to him. Fragments of words floated about his head like dust-motes. 'We'll be here when you come back.'

CHAPTER 36

Song thought how pale Hannah looked. 'Are you sure you're all right?'

'I'm fine, Song. Just heavy. Don't worry.'

'I do.'

'Don't.'

'When the baby comes, I want you to rest.'

'I expect the baby will have other things in mind.'

'Lean on me,' Song said. 'I will be a better husband this time. A better father.'

'You already are. You're here with us every day.'

'There's nowhere else I want to be. I feel like I know my children now. Phillip and all his faraway dreams. Flo and all her fight. Vivi with his incomparable imagination. I could be in Bartica, or upriver, and missing all this. Thanks to you, I'm here.'

'I didn't do anything,' Hannah said.

'You told me.'

'You listened.'

Song rested his hand on Hannah's belly. 'A new life, Hannah. A new beginning. So what do you think? A boy or girl?'

'A girl. We already have Phillip and Vivi. We lost a baby girl. I want another girl.'

'If she's anything like Flo, I'm not sure I'll be able to cope,' Song said. 'Girl or boy, I promise to do better this time, Hannah. I'll be by your side always.'

The following day, Hannah collapsed on the landing. Song heard the fall from his study. He found her slumped on the floor. He crouched down and held his wife close. 'Tell me you're all right, Hannah.'

'I think the baby's coming.'

'The baby?' It was too soon.

Song rushed to fetch Dr Patel, who arrived quickly at the house.

By then Hannah was moaning, almost unconscious, and losing a lot of blood. Song looked at the bedclothes, stained red. 'Help her, Doctor. Help us.'

Dr Patel was too busy to reply. He was trying to deliver the baby. Song moved towards Hannah's side. He rested his head against hers, held her hand gently; with his other he stroked her clammy forehead, sweeping her tangled hair back from her face, whispering to her, as if the room was empty. 'Your mismatched eyes, Hannah, that's what got me all those years ago. Do you know that? The way you kissed my stitched-up eye. The way you kissed my scars. You saved me, Hannah. You saved me all those years ago. You save me every day.

'Stay with me, Hannah. Stay with me here in Sugar House with our beautiful children. We have so much yet to do. I have so much yet to show you. Let me have the chance to show you.'

The baby came too early, lifeless. Dr Patel passed her to Little A. Song stepped in and took her in his arms. A little girl, like Hannah had wanted. So small. So unready. He held her to his chest, awash with pain and guilt.

'She's lost a lot of blood,' Dr Patel said.

'Please help her, doctor. Do everything you can.'

'I'm trying,' Dr Patel said. 'I'll do my best.'

Song moved back to Hannah's side, eventually giving up the

baby to Little A. His eyes were full of tears. He had hoped their little girl might yet open her eyes and breathe.

'Hannah needs to rest,' Dr Patel said. 'Watch over her.'

'I will.'

Song stayed by Hannah's side, clutching her hand, feeling her warmth.

'Song,' she said faintly.

'I'm here, Hannah.'

'The baby?'

'We lost the baby, my love.'

'We lost the baby.'

'She was too little to be born so soon.'

Hannah slipped back into the folds of sleep. Drowsy. Sometimes making no sense.

'I'm here, Hannah. I'm never leaving.'

He stayed by Hannah's side watching her. Seeing her summon up a fight. He knew she didn't want to let go. Desperate to stay, to watch her children grow up, to be together. She said as much, albeit weakly. She reached out to hold Song's hand when she found some strength. When she was tired out Song could still see her eyes moving under her eyelids. He imagined the shine of her mismatched eyes.

Days blurred into each other. It was a heartbreaking routine. Trying to coax Hannah to eat something. To sip some water. Watching her sleep. Waiting for her to wake. The children were a distraction. They brought in books, trays of food, vases of fresh flowers, messages from outside. Flo spent hours sat beside her father, discussing her lessons at school, what she had read in the newspaper that day, imploring him to tell her more about his life upriver. She'd rearrange Hannah's pillows and sit at the end of the bed, peeling back the sheets to squeeze and gently rub the soles of her feet. Song could hardly bear to watch the tenderness unfold between mother and daughter. He longed for their old life instead of this one full of dread, of fear.

When Song dressed in the morning, he imagined what clothes Hannah would have chosen. When he ate a new pineapple cake Little A had baked, he told her about it, even if she was sleeping. When he heard the call of a bird, he identified it for her, knowing she would have asked him what it was. Every instant he felt the rawness of his shredding heart.

CHAPTER 37

Night had not yet ended but Song could see the sky lightening at the window. It was the hour Hannah liked to wake, before the children, before the house. Song felt the room still. Something was missing. He listened for Hannah's breath. He could hear the trill of a nightjar. Song reached for her hand to pull her towards him. In the milky light, she looked too beautiful not to be alive.

He let his fingers slip between hers, as if they were holding hands like they did so often. The slants of early sun fell on them both, passing sharply between the slats of the jalousie shutters. He felt warmth, believing he could almost hold these golden beams in his hand. He remembered the same on the ship, the hope that came with the light splitting open the darkness. Like the hope he had seeing a seam of gold in exposed rock. Like the hope he held now to be with Hannah again. How hard he had lived. He closed his eyes to shut out the light.

Acknowledgements

Thank you to my family and friends who stood by *Song*, even as I wondered if. Thank you also to my dream team at Unbound (John, Liz, Miranda, Imo, Anna, Philip, Tim). With immense gratitude to you all.

Supporters

Unbound is a new kind of publishing house. Our books are funded directly by readers. This was a very popular idea during the late eighteenth and early nineteenth centuries. Now we have revived it for the internet age. It allows authors to write the books they really want to write and readers to support the books they would most like to see published.

The names listed below are of readers who have pledged their support and made this book happen. If you'd like to join them, visit www.unbound.com.

Ruthie Abel
Andrew Adamovich
Ann-Marie Allen
Ben Allen
Darren Allen
Marco Ammannati
Martin Angelov
Elena Angelova
William Armstrong
James Astor
Greg Barbour
Matthew Barley
James Bedding
Howard Bennett
Jane Black
Henry Blake
Anne-Sophie Bolon

Andrew Booth
Leander Borg
Julie Brace
Kathleen Bradley
James Braham
Stephanie Briggs
Amy Brittain
Finbarr Brogan
Matthew Buck
George Butler
Ianthe Butt
Hannah Cadwallader
Chris Cameron
Roderick Cameron
Louise Cartledge
Andrew Catlin
Geoff Chan

Heather Chan
Manta Chan
Michael Chan-Choong
Mimi Chan-Choong
Yi-Hsin Chang
Paul Charles
Josephine Chen
Camelia Ciobanu
Galahad Clark
Benedicte Clarkson
David Clasen
P Clasen
James Claydon
Bill Colegrave
Evelina Conti
Christopher Conybeare
Gabi Conybeare

Oliver Conybeare

Steven Conybeare

Anna Conza

Jean Cornet

Katie Cosstick

Paul Custerson

Rachel Darby

Elizabeth Davies

Dominic de Vere

James Dean

Caitlin Decker

James Delaney

Claire Delattre

Giulio Di Sturco

Torbjorn Dimblad

Ginny Dougary

Roger Dugmore

Robert Eardley

Tim Earl

Alan Eisner

Julian Ellis

Joyce Emons

Alex Evan-Wong

Amanda Evans

Fleur Evans

Bernardine Evaristo

Laura Eynon

Chris Eyre

Annabel Falcon

Natalie Faulkner
Robertson

Crystal Feimster

Fiona Firth

Nicky Fitzgerald

AD Flint

Frangelica Flook

Melissa Foo

Beverly Forzley

Lysbeth Fox

Stuart Freedman

Gil Garnier

Frances Geoghegan

Juliet Getzel

Moshe Gilad

Lisa Gill

Tara Goldsmith

Lisa Grainger

Ashley Green

Christopher Gregory

Andrea Gromme
Baxter

James Guy

James and Kate Guyton

George Hackett

Barbara Healy Smith

Jemma Hewlett

Françoise Higson

Emma Hill

Logan Hill

Vivienne Ho

Phillip Hofmeyr

Susan Holmes-Siedle

Kate Innes

Dean Irvine

Adrian Isaac

Andrew Isaac

Derek Isaac

Hamish Jacobs

Geetika Jain

Robert Joseph

Noel Josephides

Tabitha Joyce

Annabel Kalmar

Robert Kaplan

Eszter Karvazy

Saleem Kassum

Francisca Kellett

Deirdre Kelly

Michael Kerr

Dan Kieran

Atticus and Willow
Kilpatrick

Jonathan Kirkwood

George Klat

Moritz Kleine-Brockhoff

Nico Kos Earle

Li-Da Kruger

Charlotte Lambkin

Grace Lee

Grace & Connie Lee

Victor Lee-Own

Isabelle Legeron

Vicky Legg

Nick Leith-Smith

John Leonida

Shia Levitt

Paul Levrier

Karoki Lewis

Winnie Li

Karen Lichtin

Noel Anne Lichtin

Shiamin Lim

Linus Liu

Renée Lotenero

Henrietta Loyd

Maria Machera

Evelyn Marr

Gary Martin

William McCormack

John A C McGowan

Alex McMillan

Ben McNutt

Charlotte Methven

Robert Miller

Simon Miller
Sam Mills
John Mitchinson
George Morgan-
   Grenville
Leila Moseley
Parker Moss
Natural World Safaris
Carlo Navato
Carel Nell
SJ Nelson
Chris Nicolson
Sandy Nielsen
Cara Nora
Martin Nowell
Timothy O'Grady
Sue Ockwell
Bee Osborn
Carole Parr
Sylvia Penn
Hugo Perks
Julia Perowne
Adriaane Pielou
Justin Pollard
Simon Ponsford
Carla Power
Jessica Pyman
Adlan Wan Abdul
   Rahman
Paco Rangel
Linnie Rawlinson
David Rearick
Fiona Reece

Vicki Reeve
Mara Reeves
Mike Reeves
Miro Reeves
Stella Reeves
Michiel Remers
Dawn Riley
Thomas Robinson
Jodisue Rosen
Caroline Rowland
Kate Rowswell
Amy Royce
David Royle
Isabelle Santoire
Rupert Scott
Emma Semple
Sonashah Shivdasani
Valerie Shrimplin
Tom Silk
Tracy Sjogreen
McGregor Smyth
Tim Soar
Janine La Croix
   Sorenson
Richard Soundy
Kate Stancliffe
Oliver Steeds
Henry Stevens
Melinda Stevens
Stanley Stewart
Lee-Ann Strelzow
Shehnaz Suterwalla
Jonathan Taylor

Liviu Tipurita
Nigel Tisdall
Paul Tompsett
Margaret Tongue
Brooks Turner
Jules Ugo
William Underhill
Francesca Evers
   Venning
Jo Vickers
Carsten von Nahmen
James Walsh
Davin Wang
Alexandra Warr
Steven Wassenaarf
Kate Watt
Sally Whitford
Jamie Whittle
Andy Wiles
Martin Williams
David Wong
Evan Wong
Gordon Wong
Adam Woods
Claire Wrathall
Andrew Wright
Song Yang
Ken Yeadon
Colin Ying
Lijia Zhang
Yan Zhou
Jun Zhu